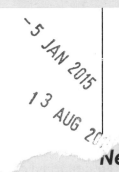
...bling Guide to
New York City

"Now THIS is the urban fantasy heroine we want"   *i09.com*

"If Buffy grew up, got therapy for her violent tendencies, moved to New York and got a real job, it would look a lot like this"
New York Times bestselling author Scott Sigler

"Zombies and vampires and golems, oh my! This is a comic tour de force by a writer who lives and breathes popular culture. Mur Lafferty is throwing a monster party and you're invited"
James Patrick Kelly, Hugo and Nebula Award winner

"*The Shambling Guide* sets the wonderful world of the supernatural— and the slightly more esoteric world of travel guide publishing—on its ear, and the result is nothing short of delightful"
New York Times bestselling author Seanan McGuire

"Mur Lafferty's debut novel is a must-read book for those who like their urban fantasy fast, furious, and funny. Terrific stuff!"
National bestselling author Kat Richardson

"An engagingly funny, and fun, romp through NYC. You'll love Zoë...to bits"
New York Times bestselling author Tobias S. Buckell

GHOST TRAIN TO
NEW ORLEANS

"I am heading away tonight. New Orleans. I've got a new book to work on. I'm nervous." She felt awkward talking to the open air, but she always had a sense that someone was listening. "I didn't feel New York talking to me when I was a kid, and I never felt Raleigh at all when I lived there. I'm just wondering what's going to happen when I get to a new city. And how can I find another citytalker to train me? How many of us are there?"

It was a circular discussion that Zoë often had with herself. She had no one else to talk to about it. The only people who knew of her talent were her sort-of boyfriend, Arthur from Public Works, and the zoëtist, Benjamin Rosenberg. Arthur had found out about citytalkers when Zoë had, and Benjamin knew about them but never wanted to talk about them, even when Zoë begged for answers.

Zoë preferred being a plain old human to her coterie coworkers. Resilient, and strangely able to adapt quickly to frequent strange incidents, but human all the same. She liked her coworkers, mostly, but was always acutely aware that many saw her as a meal they weren't allowed to touch.

By Mur Lafferty

The Shambling Guide to New York City

Ghost Train to New Orleans

GHOST TRAIN TO NEW ORLEANS

MUR LAFFERTY

www.orbitbooks.net

ORBIT

First published in Great Britain in 2014 by Orbit

A CIP catalogue record for this book
is available from the British Library.

ISBN 978-0-356-50191-8

Printed and bound by CPI Group (UK) Ltd, Croydon, CR0 4YY

Papers used by Orbit are from well-managed forests
and other responsible sources.

MIX
Paper from
responsible sources
FSC
www.fsc.org   FSC® C104740

Orbit
An imprint of
Little, Brown Book Group
100 Victoria Embankment
London EC4Y 0DY

An Hachette UK Company
www.hachette.co.uk

www.orbitbooks.net

To my parents, Donna Smith and Will Lafferty, who provided to a young writer the Time-Life fantasy books, the Brother word processor, and the love and encouragement she needed to thrive. I love you both so much.

And to Ursula Vernon, who provided to an older writer a last-minute road trip, a beignet-stealing adventure, and a swamp tour in which a misinformed guide learned about ivory-billed woodpeckers.

CHAPTER ONE

Zoë Norris would have rather had a root canal than conduct this interview for a new writer. Her stomach rolled forward at a slow, constant pace, nearly pulling her along toward her fate: an interview with an angry Norse goddess.

Zoë reminded herself that it was *her* turf, *her* job to give out, and that she was only doing this interview as a favor for Gwen, her head writer, who had recommended the Norse goddess. Zoë could easily tell this woman no, she couldn't have the travel writing job.

The problem was, she needed to fill the position, and fast.

The offices of Underground Publishing were in a condemned off-Broadway theater, mainly to accommodate the vampires who worked with Zoë in publishing travel guides for nonhumans. Being human, Zoë wished her office at least had a window, but was simply grateful she had a door that locked.

She conducted her interviews on the stage, where the office kept its break room. In fact, the break room looked an awful lot like a set—it held a refrigerator, a counter with a microwave, a bookshelf filled with travel guides, easy chairs, and a lunch table.

The audience was full of dusty red velvet seats that had seen better days many decades before. Zoë was fairly good by now at ignoring the expanse of emptiness beyond the break room, and she no longer felt that getting a cup of coffee was paired with handling stage fright, but right now all she wanted to do was flee into the audience.

The goddess, Eir, sat at one end of the lunch table, her spine ramrod-straight, her hair in one thick golden braid across her shoulder that brushed her hip. She wore a gray Yankees sweatshirt that did nothing to hide her very obvious divine nature. The woman practically glowed. Gwen had once told Zoë that Eir was a relatively minor goddess, a Valkyrie, but even a minor goddess was more divine than Zoë, and Eir knew it.

It didn't help that Zoë had interviewed Eir once before, and that had ended with Zoë's completely offending her.

But that was a while ago, Zoë firmly reminded herself. Since then she had become much more comfortable with the world in which she worked: a world where vampires, zombies, and the occasional demon or deity were tourists just like humans and, therefore, needed travel guides. She had successfully edited one book about New York, and was building a writing team for a travel guide to New Orleans.

Zoë weighed the subtle power dynamics of the situation: the goddess had already taken the head of the table, which was the interviewer's seat, but she decided that she would let Eir have this one. Zoë was the one with the real power here, despite Eir's impressive ability to intimidate.

And heal, apparently. Morgen would have laughed at her being afraid of a healing goddess. But Morgen wasn't here; the water sprite had been missing for over a month (since the rather destructive events last December), and no one was around to make Zoë laugh at herself. Everyone was so damn serious here.

Eir was much taller than Zoë, even seated her height was impressive, and her stony features depicted a perfect picture of a pissed-off Norse goddess. If, as a child, Zoë had been instructed to draw a pissed-off Norse goddess, she would have drawn Eir. Long golden braid, crossed arms, furrowed brow.

She probably would have put wings on her, too, because Zoë as a child thought everything was made better with angel wings, even bugs, which already had wings. Also, she wouldn't have included the Yankees sweatshirt. But besides that, Eir still impressed Zoë with her palpable divine presence.

Zoë fought the urge to cringe, but instead smiled at Eir and sat down at the table.

Before she could speak, Eir asked, "Why have you called me back here?" Her voice boomed, echoing through the auditorium. She had great stage presence, Zoë thought, wondering if she should encourage the goddess to go into acting instead of publishing.

"It's good to see you, Eir," Zoë said, ignoring the imperative question. "All right, so our first encounter was handled poorly, and the fault was entirely mine." (*And your crazy temper's*, she didn't add.) "We've had an opening in the writing team, and I've had a chance to look over your résumé again, so I wanted to see if you were still interested in a job at Underground Publishing."

Eir's face softened, but she just segued into a skeptical frown instead of a look of relaxed ease. "Why me?"

Because Gwen made me, Zoë didn't say. Instead she said, "Gwen tells me you have spent some time in New Orleans, yes?"

Eir eased her huge form back into the chair, relaxing at last. "Yes. A couple of decades selling music. It is a beautiful city."

Zoë smiled. "That's why we need you. My team is talented but having someone we know who knows the city is quite useful. Gwen, ah, mentioned you still didn't have a steady job?"

Eir nodded her regal head, her braid bobbing. "Employers respond poorly to my passion. They make me angry too often."

"Here you would be working with coterie, and I'm sure they can handle your . . . passion," Zoë said carefully.

"What about you? Are you not a human?"

"I am," she conceded. "But I think I've had enough experience now to not be surprised by the actions of one of your kind. Or if I am surprised, I can at least keep my head. When you met me, I was new to this whole world. I've had some experience since then." She stopped, realizing she sounded as if she were interviewing for the job, not Eir. She bit her tongue inside her mouth.

Eir smiled, a touch of malice on her broad face. "Oh? And where were you on December eighth? Hiding in your apartment from the scary coterie?"

Zoë's smile froze on her face. On December 8 she had been fighting a crazy woman who was raising golems to attack the city of New York. Many had died, and the authorities had explained it away as an earthquake. Zoë had been injured in the battle, and had lost friends. She didn't like talking about December 8.

"Someday we'll have a drink together and Gwen and I can tell you what happened the night of December eighth." She looked down at the table and shuffled Eir's résumé papers around, surprised at the tears that sprang to her eyes when she thought of that night, and her friends Morgen and Granny Good Mae, both of whom were gone. "But no," she finished. "I didn't hide."

She took a deep breath to steady herself. "Your employment has been interesting through the centuries," she said, looking at the résumé. "What can you tell me about your service to, um, sorry, I can't pronounce it. Menglod?"

Eir nodded. "Menglöð, or Freyja, was my mistress, and I served her as a Valkyrie, choosing who lived and who died in war. After the wars died down, she had no more need of my service, so I spent time as a mead-server to heroes in Valhalla."

"From Valkyrie to food service, got it," Zoë said, making a note. She would give Eir the job—Zoë had no other choice—but she had to go through the motions. "It seems you had a spot of unemployment here, some twelve centuries of it?"

"Times were tough all over," Eir said.

"And you applied to med school in 1975 but left because you didn't need medical training since you already had divine healing power at your hand. I'm trying to find your New Orleans experience...ah, here!" She found the line she wanted on the résumé. "The store Mama Peat's Records in New Orleans, you were assistant manager for ten years. Did you stay in the city long after that?"

"Some. I mostly traveled around, visited a war here and there, but choosing the living and dying has lost its sparkle for me. I haven't found my true calling yet."

"And do you think writing travel books is your calling?" Zoë asked.

"It could be. I will not know until I answer the call, will I?" Eir's stony face had begun to flush, and Zoë broke eye contact, hoping not to rile her further.

She sighed and turned over the paper. "I will be honest with you, Eir. We need a writer now, and you know the city we're working on, and Gwen has vouched for you." Zoë's eyes flicked backstage, where she knew her head writer was eavesdropping. "But I'm not crazy about your temper. If you took this job, I would need you to respect the word of the head writer and the editor."

Eir sat, impassive. She said nothing.

"That would be Gwen and myself, respectively," Zoë said. "The death goddess and the human will be your bosses. And the vampire above them," she added, since Phil was the publisher and boss of them all. "If I can trust you to rein in your temper, I can offer you the job."

"I will take your job," Eir announced, as if she were doing Zoë a favor. "I will start tomorrow. Where is my desk?"

Her abrupt acceptance shocked Zoë. Did Eir accept the conditions? She shrugged mentally and continued. "Actually, we aren't going to assign you a desk yet; we are heading out of town tonight to go to New Orleans, and we need you to come help us with our research. We're going on the new high-speed train that runs the East Coast."

Eir showed real interest for the first time. "Really? The ghost train? I have been wanting to ride that!"

"So have we all. It's good to have you on board," Zoë said, and shook the goddess's hand. She was testing Eir, putting a lot of faith in the hope the goddess wouldn't crush her hand, but then she remembered that Eir was a healing goddess, and her grip was firm and warm.

Zoë gave Eir the information she needed to meet them at Grand Central and told her to go meet Phil and Aneris, Phil's new office assistant and acting coterie resources (the monster equivalent of human resources) representative, for the welcome-to-the-company speech.

"Phil and Aneris will discuss salary and benefits with you," she said. "After that, you'll need to go pack and then meet us tonight at midnight."

The goddess nodded imperially and walked off the stage. Zoë flopped back into her chair and forced her shoulders to relax.

She stared at the acoustic tile on the ceiling and then called into the wings, "I know you're there, can you come chat?"

Gwen, Underground Publishing's head writer, peeked out from behind the curtain. "How did it go?" Her black eyes— completely black, with hints of stars within—were shining.

Zoë closed her eyes and rubbed her forehead. "You know how it went because you eavesdropped on us."

"I did, I admit it," she said. Zoë opened her eyes and mock-glared at her friend.

Gwen came onto the stage, a flowing image of 1985-era goth—night-black skin, black gown, long black hair. Zoë had no idea how she passed for human—her skin would place her as African in origin, but her hair was thin and straight, and her eyes were just plain freaky.

"If you had wanted privacy you should have gone into your office," she said primly, and sat across from Zoë at the table.

Gwen was a Welsh psychopomp death goddess, once responsible for chaperoning the dead to the underworld, but with Christianity having taken over the British Isles, she didn't have much to do anymore. She looked up with her glittering black eyes in her inky black face, and smiled slightly. "Thank you for giving her a chance."

Zoë liked Gwen. The death goddess and Morgen the water sprite had been Zoë's first friends in the office. But the death goddess was the polar opposite of the bubbly water sprite. Talking to Gwen was often, well, grave. It also wasn't comforting that Gwen could sense at any time how close Zoë's death was, and sometimes seemed comfortable telling Zoë when her odds of dying changed. This made conversation tense.

"You're welcome. If she screws up, you're responsible," Zoë said. Gwen nodded. Zoë began gathering her papers back into her interview folder. "How are you doing? Trip prep going all right?"

"It takes very little for me to prepare for a trip," Gwen said.

"Well, sure, you're always wearing the same flowy dress that apparently doesn't need dry cleaning," Zoë said, "but don't forget you'll need to back up your laptop before you pack it up. And remember to pack power cords and all that."

Gwen frowned, then said, "Wait one moment, please." Zoë snickered and got up to get some coffee as Gwen headed offstage to, Zoë assumed, go ask the IT staff—two tiny gremlins—for help, as she always did when dealing with her computer.

She came back a moment later. "I'm not entirely sure what

you said to me, but I repeated your words verbatim to Cassandra and she assured me she would take care of it. *Now* I am ready," she said, and sat back down.

"So how did you meet Eir, anyway?" Zoë asked.

Gwen looked at her hands, which were calmly folded. "We'd seen each other on various battlefields through the centuries and became friends. Last night I was at the hospital and encountered her there, volunteering. We had a cup of coffee together."

Zoë knew this meant that Eir had drunk coffee while Gwen fed silently on the desperate sense of fear of the dying, but she didn't pick nits. She tried to imagine Eir's bedside manner in a hospital, and shuddered.

"We talked about work, and it seemed she was still looking for a job. She tried faith healing, but that has largely gone out of style in favor of people who claim to talk to the dead."

"That's more your style," Zoë said, and looked at Eir's résumé again, having missed the hospital volunteer job at the end. "You know, we should talk to Phil about a book on business planning for coterie, including a chapter on how to write a résumé."

"It has only come up as a necessity in the past few decades. Acquiring new knowledge requires overcoming centuries of habits for most of us," Gwen said mildly. "But a book is a good idea."

Zoë took a sip of her coffee and smiled. "That's why they pay me the big bucks."

Gwen stood. "Thank you for giving her another chance, Zoë. You will not regret this." She swept from the stage.

"I regret nearly every decision I make around here," Zoë muttered. Her phone beeped and she checked it—it was nearly time for her meeting with Phil. She put Eir's information back into her file and got that and her coffee and left the stage. She stopped by her office to grab her notebook and look mournfully at the still-untouched croissant she'd grabbed for breakfast, and headed to the big dressing room turned office to meet her boss.

Phil had never looked threatening to Zoë. He was white, thirtyish-looking, and comfortably plump, with glasses. When she was getting to know him, she had known that her coworkers were scared of him for some reason but she could never quite figure it out. But during that night in December, she'd seen him attack her former lover in a rage, and then kill a powerful zoëtist. His pleasant face transformed into monstrous rage was something Zoë wouldn't forget.

You didn't fuck with Phil.

After the incident, Zoë had taken some time off work to "heal," ostensibly, working from home. She'd also needed to get her confidence back. Before, Phil was a nerdy puppy. Now he reminded her of a fat, dozing cat that could awaken and draw blood anytime if he needed to. A fat cat could still pounce, could still eviscerate.

"Morning, Phil. We need to make it quick, I still need to do a million and one things before the train leaves tonight."

The fat cat smiled. He hadn't done much to change his office from the dressing room it had been; he worked in front of a mirror that did not reflect him, which always disoriented her.

She took her customary seat on the couch and he swiveled his chair away from the computer to face her.

"Right. I spoke to your new writer, I was surprised you went with the Valkyrie."

Zoë nodded. "Yeah, so am I, frankly. But she was the best of everyone we talked to, is familiar with the city, and Gwen wants me to give her a chance. Really, I only hesitated because she's got a wicked temper."

Phil laughed. "Like half the people in the office."

Undaunted, Zoë said, "And that's why I was hesitant about adding yet another volatile personality. We need more people like Morgen to diffuse the tension, not angsty people like Kevin to ratchet it up."

Kevin was a young vampire, a writer who chafed at having a human for a boss. Zoë wasn't happy about having to take him with her, but the fact was he was a damn good writer. When he wasn't smelling her like a creepy guy in an elevator.

"I'm sure she'll be fine," Phil said. "Gwen has had thousands of years to work on her judgment of character."

"Too bad you can't have her in coterie resources," Zoë said. "Sometimes I think we're writing the wrong books. It seems there are several books we could write to help coterie in more ways than travel. I mean, you should have seen Eir's résumé, it was a mess. Someone needs to run a course or write a book on how to write a résumé that covers thousands of years. How to do business in the twenty-first century when you've lived for twenty of them. Or something like that."

"Put it in an idea folder," Phil said. "I'm open to growth, but only after we get our footing. Now tell me what you have planned for New Orleans."

Zoë looked at her notepad. "We arrive early tomorrow before sunup on the new ghost bullet train, check into Freddie's Ready B and B—"

"Excuse me?" Phil interrupted. " 'Freddie's Ready B and B?' "

"Yeah, it's run by a minor New Orleans deity, Freddie Who's Always Ready. He's got that name because he can accommodate any guest—vampire, sprite, fire demon, what have you. I like to think of him as some sort of hospitality god. Anyway, tomorrow we start exploring the city, I will check in with the local Public Works to let them know we're in town and not going to cause trouble. After that I need to get to know Eir and her strengths, figure out where to put her, and then just get everyone to get to work." She shrugged. "We're on new ground here, with a New York–based writing group researching a new city. We're going to have to make friends with the natives pretty fast."

"Or your writers will have to, anyway," reminded Phil.

Zoë rolled her eyes. "Yes, we'll keep your pet editor safe, boss man. I won't go meeting any scary vampires or zombies without an escort."

"Good." Phil walked to a hook on the wall where his jacket hung. "I nearly forgot. I got you something." He pulled something rectangular out of the pocket and tossed it at her.

She caught it and examined it. It was a black phone, but she didn't recognize the brand name, Talkankhamun. "I have a phone," she said, raising her eyebrows at him.

Phil held his own phone out to her, showing her the leather case he'd placed it in. "This is new, it's from a coterie company. It makes us less easy to track by Public Works, for one thing, and it makes it easier for some among us to communicate. Undead find it difficult to get phones, for example, especially if their families canceled their plans after they died."

"Sounds like a great idea," Zoë said, turning it on. "But you remember that I don't have a problem getting a cell phone, right?"

"We don't want our calls to you traced, necessarily," Phil said.

"I thought you guys worked in cooperation with Public Works?" Zoë asked, smiling slightly.

Public Works, along with keeping the city running with sewer lines and trash pickup, was the front line of human monster fighters/police. It had an uneasy truce with coterie who wished to live peacefully in the city, but still protected humans from coterie who broke the law.

"We like them tracking us as much as you like your government tracking you," Phil said. "Wasn't there some mess in the news about your NSA spying on you?"

Zoë enjoyed baiting Phil with Public Works comments, as she knew he got along with New York City Public Works better than most coterie in the city. It didn't hurt that both she and Phil knew someone who worked for it, someone who owed his life to Phil. Someone Zoë had an early dinner date with before she caught the train.

Zoë slipped the new phone into her pocket. "All right, fine, I'll juggle two phones, anything else?"

"Just one." Phil turned back to his desk and fiddled with his laptop mouse. "John got back this morning. We're calling off the hunt for Morgen."

Zoë felt as if she'd been kicked in the belly. She'd actually started feeling somewhat warm toward the incubus who had taken a sabbatical to look for Morgen. But now he was back empty-handed, and she closed her eyes against the white-hot rage that rose in her. She took a deep breath and let it out slowly.

"That's too bad. Thanks for letting him try."

"He wants to see you. I told him only if you agreed to it." Phil was referring to her request not to have anything to do with John, whose power made her dizzy with lust. He had attempted to seduce her last fall, and had nearly succeeded. She avoided him when she could.

"No. I don't need the distraction. Tell him to e-mail me." She rose from the couch and raised her eyebrows. "If we're done here?"

Phil nodded. "And for what it's worth, I'm sorry. She gave her life to protect us that night. She's a hero."

That's a lot of comfort to her. Zoë bit back the comment and silently left Phil's office.

*　　*　　*

The city was quieter in the winter.

Not the part of the city with the traffic, or the obnoxious old lady who yelled out the window at the children who played on the sidewalk, or the jackhammers—that stayed loud as ever.

It was the city's soul that was quiet. After work, Zoë went daily to the park for a contemplative wander around the Reservoir to see if she could get a sense of the city under the water. In December, a rogue zoëtist—a human who manipulates life forces—had built a giant golem from buses and taxis and a small building and had captured the soul of the city within. Only Zoë's friend and mentor, Granny Good Mae, was able to calm the rampaging golem, and she and the city had sought refuge under the waters of the Reservoir in Central Park.

Granny Good Mae was a very strong citytalker, one who could hear and communicate with the soul of a city. She had a very close relationship with New York.

Zoë had discovered she also was a citytalker. Granny Good Mae had been teaching her how to live among coterie (and more important, how to stay alive amid them) but had never taught her much about citytalking. Now that Zoë knew what she was, Granny was gone, and no one could teach her how to interpret the strange sensations and thoughts she sometimes got.

Since the night Granny Good Mae disappeared, life had been enough of a distraction that Zoë hadn't had a lot of chances to explore her newly discovered skill.

She had hidden that skill from the coterie she worked with. She yearned for answers, but instinct told her not to share this information with people who might want to eat her, or use her power. Vampires can gain zoëtism powers if they drain a zoëtist, it's possible they could get the same effect if they drained a citytalker, and Zoë wasn't going to take that chance.

So no mentor, no teacher, no Obi-Wan. Zoë found herself going over the events of the previous fall, trying to figure out what had been going on when she had thought Granny Good Mae was merely a poor homeless schizophrenic.

Homeless, yes. Schizophrenic, not so much. A quite powerful coterie? Definitely. Zoë had been struggling with the idea of human coterie. She had been looking at coterie as a black-and-white thing, monsters on one side, humans on the other. But it seemed that some humans had powers. First there were the zoëtists, manipulators of life. People like Dr. Frankenstein and Jewish mystics who raised mud golems. Then she had learned of citytalkers.

It was ironic how Zoë, whose name meant "life," had ended up being a citytalker and not a zoëtist, but she had stopped looking for clever meanings to things a long time ago.

Then there was the matter of Granny Good Mae being "poor."

"I got the call from your lawyer today," Zoë said aloud, her breath puffing in the dying afternoon light. The ice coating the Reservoir glittered in the sunset, and she focused on it, knowing Granny Good Mae likely still lived below the waters in her city golem, like Voltron.

"I'm not sure why you left me all that money, I'm not even sure why you stayed homeless if you were that rich." She paused and continued her wandering around the frozen lake. "Why did you sit on that much? Anyway, thanks, I guess. I don't really feel worthy, but thanks. I'm not sure what else to say."

Zoë still couldn't wrap her mind around the number the lawyer had quoted. The first thing she had done after the call was go online and purchase new work boots. Solid, steel-toed, wool-lined boots. She had bought a second, lighter pair for summer.

One of the first things she had learned about Granny Good Mae was that the old woman was homeless and dressed in layers of old clothing, but she never scrimped on boots.

At lunch Zoë bought some cashmere gloves, but immediately felt extravagant and embarrassed when she paid the surprisingly high bill. She wiggled her fingers in the luxury and dared the winter's bite to go through them.

Then she stopped spending.

"I am heading away tonight. New Orleans. I've got a new book to work on. I'm nervous." She felt awkward talking to the open air, but she always had a sense that someone was listening. "I didn't feel New York talking to me when I was a kid, and I never felt Raleigh at all when I lived there. I'm just wondering what's going to happen when I get to a new city. And how can I find another citytalker to train me? How many of us are there?"

It was a circular discussion that Zoë often had with herself. She had no one else to talk to about it. The only people who knew of her talent were her sort-of boyfriend Arthur from Public Works, and the zoëtist Benjamin Rosenberg. Arthur had found out about citytalkers when Zoë had, and Benjamin knew about them but never wanted to talk about them, even when Zoë begged for answers.

Zoë preferred being a plain old human to her coterie coworkers. Resilient, and strangely able to adapt quickly to frequent strange incidents, but human all the same. She liked her coworkers, mostly, but was always acutely aware that many saw her as a meal they weren't allowed to touch.

Zoë checked her watch. She had two hours before her date with Arthur. She peeled off her gloves and stuffed them into her coat pocket, then quickly took off her coat, hat, and sweatshirt. The arm she had broken last month ached in the subfreezing temperatures, but she calmly piled her discarded clothing on the grass and began going through a slow, tai chi–like form that Granny Good Mae had drilled her on.

"If you do it right, then you don't feel the cold," Granny had scolded in November when Zoë had complained. Now Zoë patiently did her forms daily to keep her wits about her. She worked out for an hour, going through forms and various attacks for the different coterie she would likely encounter. From the smooth and unpredictable bob and weave to avoid a zombie's shambling to a jumping drill to work her fast-twitch muscles to avoid vampires, and even down to the ever-elegant straight punch to the mouth while avoiding eye contact for when an incubus tried to hit on her, and the fast search through her bag for a wrench to open a fire hydrant to battle a fire demon, she went through them all. When she was done, she had worked up a sweat and even her fingers and ears were pleasantly warm. She dressed, hefted her satchel (which held, among other things, her wrench, a knife, a complicated string puzzle that Granny had told her would help foil animal spirits, and a small bag of gold coins Granny had given her to distract dragons), gave a furtive look toward the silent, icy Reservoir, and turned to walk to the train station.

Two words floated into her mind as she left, the clearest words she'd heard since Granny Good Mae and the spirit of the city had gone under the waters.

Avoid citytalkers.

Zoë was still pondering the words when she opened the door to her apartment. She dumped her bag next to the weapons rack that stood by the door and stretched. She chewed on her lip, wondering if she should visit Arthur before getting ready for the date, but when she heard swearing coming from his apartment next door, she left hers and knocked on his door.

Arthur was panting when he answered the door. He was tall, bald, thin, and had a way of moving that suggested a wiry strength. His dark skin shone with sweat and his eyes were wide behind his wire-rimmed glasses. He wore a simple blue T-shirt and jeans. She had been feeling self-conscious coming over directly after a workout, but it was clear her appearance was the last thing on his mind.

(Not to mention that Arthur had seen her covered in blood, sewer water, and demon goo, so sweat was nothing.)

Arthur rubbed the back of his head. "Zoë, hey. I thought we weren't meeting for another half hour?"

She smiled. "You sounded like you were fighting a band of pixies or something, I wanted to check on you. Is everything OK?" She peeked around Arthur and gasped at the disheveled state of his always-neat apartment.

"Come in," Arthur said, stepping aside. "I have to cancel our date. Shit is going down."

"What's going on?" Zoë said in alarm. "Public Works business?"

He shook his head absently and started rummaging around in the cushions of his brown leather couch.

"It's Ben. He's on vacation and I can't reach him. I think he and Orson took a cruise."

Zoë nodded. Their zoëtist friend was married to a man who hated the coterie, and had insisted on a vacation far away from cell towers. "You knew this. He set you up with enough medicine, right?"

"It would have been enough if I could fucking find it," Arthur said, throwing a small cushion back on the couch.

Zoë went cold. Last November she and Arthur had discovered that Ben was a uniquely powerful zoëtist in that he had access to obscure medicinal herbs that could keep the zombie curse at bay if someone had been bitten. And Arthur had gotten a bite from an enraged zombie when he tried to help out Zoë and her boss during a fight that had gotten nasty fast.

The last Zoë had heard, Arthur was healing nicely and the zombie curse was completely stable, but he would need to take Ben's herbal drinks for the rest of his life.

Zoë and Arthur had asked Ben to make the remedy available to Public Works to protect the other people likely to be bitten by zombies, but Ben had refused.

"It's not just a matter of a pinch of sage and a cup of basil. It requires zoëtist magic, and frankly our magic is dying out. We are getting fewer and fewer students, and the older masters are dying. Lucy had mortally wounded my master, the Doyenne, before she left the bayou. I get my herb shipment from her last student, whose name I don't even know."

Lucy was the crazed zoëtist who had tried to take over the city in December. Phil had eaten her.

Ben had said that the recipe was a sacred text and refused to give it to Public Works. Arthur had grudgingly accepted it as long as Ben promised a lifetime supply of the herbs.

Zoë tried to avoid all the obvious questions as she slowly cast her eyes around the apartment. "When did you take your last dose?"

"A week ago," he said absently, glaring at his coffee table, which held one magazine, a *Guns & Ammo* issue, as if the table were somehow hiding the herbs.

"OK. You made the tea in the kitchen, right?" She walked to the kitchen without waiting for him to answer.

The kitchen was in an even worse state of chaos. Cupboards were open, drawers had dish towels and utensils sticking out of them, and globs of dust sat on the floor around the fridge. Zoë realized Arthur had been looking for his herbs on the rarely cleaned fridge top.

She went to the cupboard where he kept his tea and coffee, which stood ajar, and opened it wider. The tin Arthur kept his herbs in wasn't there.

"And you haven't had a break-in or anything, right?"

"Of course not," he snapped. "Besides, nothing else is missing."

Arthur did have a large collection of antique weaponry that any thief would be attracted to.

Zoë grabbed a kitchen chair, dragged it over to the counter, and stood on it to get a different view of the cupboard. At the very back of the top shelf, only visible if you looked at it directly, was an envelope. Zoë snagged it.

ARTHUR was written on it in neat, feminine handwriting. Zoë handed it to him.

"Oh shit," he said, his voice weak and empty.

Zoë hopped off the chair. "I guess you know who left that?"

He nodded slowly as he opened the envelope. He was silent as he read the letter inside, and his long fingers tightened until the paper was creased and quivering.

"I take it that it's not good news," Zoë said lightly, trying to siphon off some of his obvious rage.

Arthur abruptly collapsed into the chair Zoë had used to retrieve the envelope and he leaned over, cradling his head in his hands. "My sister Katy. She dropped by this weekend. She had to have found them."

"Why? Did she steal them? Why would she need zoëtist herbs?"

"Because she doesn't know what they are," he said, his voice devoid of emotion. "Our sister Kimberly OD'd when we were teens. When we grew up, I went into Public Works, but Katy went to work for a drug rehab facility to help others. She found my herbs and thought they were pot."

Zoë winced. She had smelled his herbs and they did smell like marijuana, among other things.

"So she took them, and I'm supposed to call her when I find this letter so she can do an intervention."

"An intervention isn't going to stop you from becoming a zombie," Zoë said in alarm. "And you can't reach Ben."

He shook his head.

"This is bad," she said.

They had to come up with a credible lie as to what the herbs were, and Arthur called his sister to try to get them back. They hadn't hoped for much, and when Katy archly informed Arthur that she had washed the herbs down the garbage disposal, Arthur hung up on her.

They sat at his kitchen table, sipping coffee; the only power it had was stopping metaphorical zombification.

"Do you want me to stay?" she asked, holding his hand.

He shook his head as if to clear it. "Shit, that's right, you're on your way out of town. I can't think of anything you could do if you were here, so I guess not."

It stung that he didn't want her there for simple moral support, but Zoë was distracted from her hurt feelings by a dawning recognition on Arthur's face. "Wait, you're going to New Orleans, right?" he asked.

"Yeah."

"That's where Ben studied with his mentor, in the swamps down there! There might be someone down there who can get me more herbs!"

Zoë wanted to kick herself for not thinking of it. "Of course! You want me to try to find any master zoëtists down there for you?"

He shook his head. "Sorry, but I gotta do this myself. I'm going with you."

As pleased as she was that they had a plan, Zoë couldn't help but feel her spirits drop. *Now I'm traveling with vampires and a member of Public Works. This has no chance of going very, very badly.*

They had a quick dinner together, Arthur bright-eyed and invigorated with his new plan. He served steak and baked potatoes and red wine.

"Something weird happened today," she said.

"Weird shit always happens to you," Arthur replied, smiling for the first time that day.

Zoë shrugged. "OK, weird in the citytalker way, then. I was working out in the park, and when I'm there, I usually talk to the Reservoir. I know they're in there, but they never talk back. I mentioned I was going to New Orleans tonight, and complaining about not knowing any other citytalkers, and as I was leaving I got a clear impression that I should avoid other citytalkers. What does that mean?"

Arthur frowned. "I don't know. Most everyone wants to find their own people, don't they?"

Zoë nodded slowly. "I just wish I could learn how to connect with the city as well as Granny could."

"I hope that won't make you a schizo homeless woman," he said, giving her a peck on the cheek as he poured more wine.

"I don't think it will," she said, but she wasn't sure. Something had definitely snapped within Granny Good Mae at some point. Was she willing to go through that to talk to a city?

INTRO
Welcome to New Orleans!

SIDEBAR:

Welcome to the Big Easy! Before we get started letting you know about the wonders of this city—the unofficial coterie capital of the US—we need to do a public service announcement.

New Orleans is under sea level. This means no one digs in the city, not even rats. All graves are above ground, and while this means there are lovely mausoleums to rent out, using sewers or subway tunnels to move around is completely out. As of this writing, there are few to no safe daytime travel options for photophobic coterie. Several housing options are light-tight, though, and are safe places to stay and rest while the sun is in the sky. (See chapter 11, "Lodging," for more information.)

That said, for those of you who do not fear the sun, the city has walking and driving tours, and charming (yet limited) streetcars. (Desire has been decommissioned, but Despair, Death, Destruction, Dream, Delirium, and Destiny still run for coterie passengers.) You can always get a coterie taxi as well. ■

CHAPTER TWO

"Granny left you *how* much?" Arthur asked over their second bottle of wine.

"I'm not sure how much after inheritance tax," Zoë said. "But it's upward of a million."

"But she was homeless," Arthur said. "It doesn't make sense."

"Don't tell me how weird it is, I know it already. I saw the shithole she lived in. But you know, she did always insist on good footwear. I remember thinking how weird that was."

Arthur drained his wineglass. "So when are you handing in your notice? After the NOLA book?"

Zoë blinked at him, surprise clearing her inebriated head.

"My notice?" she managed to say.

"Sure," Arthur said, sniffing the wine in his glass awkwardly as if he knew he was supposed to, but not entirely sure why. "You're rich. You don't have to work. You can quit and live the life of luxury. Learn what we're supposed to smell for when we smell wine. Or take a sabbatical and study whatever. Or just take your time finding a job that doesn't constantly put your life in danger."

She bristled. "Are you objecting to women fighting monsters?"

Arthur gave her a patient look. "Of course not. You know there are plenty of women at Public Works that I would trust with my life. But you are a book editor, not a plumber-slash-monster-hunter. Last month you got seriously beat up. You got swallowed by a snake demon, for God's sake. Do many book editors encounter those kinds of workplace injuries? I thought all you had to worry about was carpal tunnel syndrome."

Zoë ignored his mocking tone. She swirled her wine around the glass and took a sip, not tasting it. "I hadn't considered quitting. It didn't occur to me. Saving, sure. Maybe a new computer. Book a trip. But quitting?" Arthur waited, and she appreciated that he could tell she wasn't done. "Yeah, my job is dangerous. But I've never felt more alive in my life. I'm seeing cities from a different point of view." Her voice dropped to a whisper. "And that doesn't even count the fact that I can *talk to cities*. How fucking cool is that? If I didn't discover that, I probably would have eventually ended up on antipsychotic drugs to fight the voice in my head. And God, Arthur, if I didn't have this job, we probably wouldn't be dating. If I didn't have this job, I'm sure I wouldn't understand what you did, or appreciate the danger *you* place yourself in."

"If you have such a passion for working with monsters, you should work with me," he said flatly.

"Are we going to do this again?" Zoë asked, rubbing her face. "I don't want to work for Public Works for several reasons." She counted them off on her fingers. "I actually like my job. Aside from all the in-the-field danger, I'm actually using my skills as an editor. I couldn't get a job with a human publisher, I tried. I don't know one thing about the sewer, or the water, or whatever else Public Works does. And come on, Arthur. We already live next to each other. Let's say this relationship goes south, and you see me at work and here in the hall. I have a firm belief that people in healthy relationships need their own space."

Arthur looked at her, not saying anything. She finally grew uncomfortable under his gaze and blurted out, "Well, say something. Are you going to storm out? Argue with me? Tell me I'm crazy?"

" 'Relationship'?" he asked.

Zoë burst out laughing, startling him. She had to admit to herself that it was nervous laughter, but it broke the tension and Arthur grinned sheepishly.

"I think the real reason is I'm trying to figure out what it means to be who, and what, I am. And the best way to do that is to research cities from within. And it also seems the best way to find people who can help me learn about what I am."

"You could do that on your own. You could afford to travel."

Zoë gritted her teeth. "Listen. I don't *want* to quit. That should be a good enough reason for you, if you respect my decisions." She took a deep breath and relaxed her shoulders, which had been creeping up to her ears. "Let's drop work talk, and relationship talk, and just have a good dinner. We'll head to New Orleans, you'll do your zoëtist-hunting thing, I'll do my book writing, we'll spend some time together, and when we get back we can see if I'm still interested in this job, and we'll see where this relationship—yes, relationship—takes us. How's that?"

He agreed, and they spent the rest of the dinner talking about their childhoods, and books, and even touched a bit on dating history. He admitted that he had once fallen for a succubus, and Zoë told him the whole story of the affair with her married boss that had eventually driven her to New York.

After dinner they watched *Doctor Who*, and got into a friendly argument about who the best Doctor was. Zoë had watched the show as a child, and had a soft spot in her heart for Tom Baker, but Arthur was only familiar with the new show, and had decided David Tennant was the only Doctor worth his salt. They split the difference and watched an episode of the ninth Doctor, whom Zoë quite liked though she was pissed he had lasted only a season.

Later, in her bed, Arthur dozed and Zoë gently touched the

zombie bite scar on his shoulder, puffy and shiny on his dark skin, and thought about the other unspoken thing between them, the other big "what if" that could affect their relationship.

Could she date a zombie?

Could she kill him if he begged her to, to keep him from turning?

She woke him up at ten and he left for his apartment to pack for the trip. Zoë was mostly packed already, just had to add some weapons and make sure her laptop and phone—phones, she reminded herself—were charged.

She sent a text to her friends from Raleigh, with whom she played a weekly Dungeons & Dragons (version 3.5) game via Skype, and told them to have her paladin doing penance in some temple or another while she was away from the campaign. She would try to get online in New Orleans, but she couldn't promise anything.

Her goldfish, Lister and Kochanski, drifted lazily in their tank, showing no concern when she dropped in a seven-day feeding tab. The house-sitting service would check her mail and her fish every three days, but she might as well give them as little work to do as possible.

She met Arthur in the hallway at eleven. He had slung a duffel over his shoulder. She blinked at him.

"Is that all you're taking?" she asked.

He shrugged. "I don't have to write. I don't have to work. I've got some clothes, toothbrush, iPod, and wallet in here."

"No books? No other toiletries?" Zoë managed to squeak. "No *books*?"

"I've got e-books. I don't feel the need to carry five fantasy doorstops with me at all times. No wonder you're so strong." He grinned at her.

"The George R. R. Martin fitness plan, that's me," she said. "Besides, I might finish one. And then where would I be?"

They walked down the stairs together, Zoë still glancing at his duffel in astonishment. The streets were quiet in the late night.

"Did you call for a car?" he asked.

Zoë snorted. "Please." She pulled off the necklace she wore all the time—a circle with a small claw etched in the center, a talisman that told coterie, "Hands off, I'm an ally, not lunch"—and held it in the air. As always, this summoned a coterie cab driven by her favorite demon, Max.

He pulled up seemingly from out of nowhere, smoke wafting from the cracked windows. Inside he hulked under a heavy jacket and hat, but he smiled up at Zoë. "What's the plan, kiddo?"

"Grand Central, please, Max. For me and my friend."

He heaved himself out of the car and looked Arthur up and down. "I remember you. Public Works, ain't you?" Arthur nodded stiffly. Max laughed, a "har har" sound, and grabbed their luggage with his massive red hands. He tossed the bags into the trunk, then held the door open for Zoë, grinning past his massive tusks. She settled into the back seat, Arthur got in after her.

"Hey, Max," she said as he got back behind the wheel. "What do you know about the new ghost train?"

Max grunted. "It's the first high-speed rail in da country and it shares the same track as the new human bullet train. It's called the Slaughtered Kid and it goes from Boston to N'Awlins in a night."

Zoë nodded. "Yeah, that's about what I hear."

Max jerked the wheel and they careened toward the stone wall that surrounded Prospect Park. Zoë tried not to wince, but she always did, even as the cab slipped through the concealed hole and down into the tunnel system the coterie used to get around quickly.

"What's the matter? Scared or something?"

Zoë started to bristle at the insult but realized he was grinning at Arthur's tense face in the rearview mirror.

"No," she answered, trying to save Arthur some more needling, "I'm just wondering if a human can ride on a ghost train. I can just see myself trying to board and just walking right through it. And I'm not afraid of ghosts, but I'm not sure what to expect. I found surprisingly little in my reading. There are a lot of conflicting reports."

"Eh, ghosts are nothing, don't worry about them," Max said. "They can't affect much in the world around them, so they're largely bitter, lonely people. You'll fit on the train, I'm sure. They gotta accommodate meals and thralls, after all. And if not, you call me. I'll get you to the Big Easy."

"Tell me there's not a Rat's Nest all the way down the East Coast," Zoë said, eyes going wide. The Rat's Nest was a coterie system of roads underneath the New York subway system. Zoë had only ever driven through it but wanted to spend more time there.

"Nah, but there's a whole lot more than you think. Even you, Ms. 'Human among the Scary Monsters.'"

"Noted," she said.

Outside Grand Central Station, near the taxi line, a man sold necklaces off an overturned cardboard box. As Zoë was now accustomed to doing, she looked a little closer at the man. He moved with slow purposefulness, and the chilly January air didn't seem to affect him at all. He was a zombie, with a wide-brimmed hat shading his graying skin and milky eyes. This was the guy Max had told him to buy tickets from.

Zoë showed him her talisman and asked to buy seven first-class tickets (uncomfortably aware that the first-class tickets would look like a bribe to the members of her team who chafed under the leadership of a human). The zombie looked stonily at Zoë's talisman and shook his head. "No."

Zoë blinked. "I have the hell notes, I have cash if you need it, what's the problem? Sold out?"

"Humans are not allowed in first class," the zombie said. He looked from her to Arthur, then back, and smiled slowly, showing rotten teeth. "For your own protection."

Instead of railing at the bigotry, Zoë wanted to compliment him on how clearly he spoke but figured that would be an insult instead of the ass-kissing compliment she intended. She might as well compliment him on his cleanliness. She still wasn't sure how to kiss up to the undead, aside from tempting them with her bodily treats, which she wasn't going to do.

She felt a presence at her side and saw that Gwen had appeared silently, waiting for Zoë to notice her. The rest of her team—the vampires Opal and Kevin, the baby dragon Bertie, and the goddess Eir—stood behind Gwen. Kevin smirked at her, and she realized they had heard the problems she was having.

"Won't let you in the first-class car? That must be embarrassing for the boss to be in coach," Kevin said. His sire, Opal, elbowed him in the ribs, and he subsided.

"I'm traveling with a bunch of coterie to vouch for me, what's the problem?" The zombie shook his head. Zoë finally slipped a hell note out of her pocket and slid it to him. "Can I convince you otherwise?"

His slow eyes never hit the money, but his hand reached out and snagged it. "Five first-class. Two coach." He reached under the box and counted out five green tickets and two yellow. Kevin snickered behind Zoë, and she gritted her teeth.

"Bigot," she muttered as she took the tickets.

The zombie sighed in a way that implied it was done out of habit instead of an actual need for air. "It's nothing personal. It's for your own safety. We don't even allow vampires' thralls to travel with them. The humans are just too vulnerable and we can't be responsible."

"He's got a point," said Arthur. "I'd rather sit with my own kind, anyway."

Zoë glared at him. "You're not helping," she muttered.

"We don't need to go first-class, Zoë," Gwen said, putting her hand on her arm. She looked at the others pointedly. "Do we?"

Bertie, the baby dragon, or "wyrm" (who looked more like an Italian linebacker than a lizard), shrugged. "I usually fly."

Eir folded her formidable arms. "I was planning on purchasing an upgrade to experience the full trip, so I will take the offered ticket. Thank you, editor."

Gwen sighed at Eir, exasperated. Kevin reached out and grabbed his and Opal's tickets. He glanced at Arthur, who took his and Zoë's tickets from her.

"Did you bring your own meal, Zoë?" Kevin asked, pointing to Arthur.

"My friend Arthur is also coming to town, for a different reason. You will not harass him," Zoë said.

"Maybe," Kevin said. "Maybe not."

Arthur folded his arms and stared at Kevin. "Zoë's mentioned you. The weakest writer on the team, I understand. I'd recommend focusing on doing a good job rather than bothering humans for no reason." He showed his own talisman, a medium-size medallion he pulled from his jeans pocket. "Besides, I'm Public Works."

Instead of engaging further, Kevin just winked. "See you in

New Orleans, Zoë. Have fun in coach." The vampires walked away, Opal chiding him for his behavior, sounding like a mother with a son whom she chastised out of habit and not because he listened to anything she said.

Zoë winced. She wasn't sure traveling with a team like this would work very well. "Kevin, we'll talk about this in New Orleans."

He waved over his shoulder. "OK, boss."

It's like they're just waiting for me to fail. If she had thought that they would respect her more for saving the *whole fucking city* from a crazy zoëtist, she had apparently been wrong. It would take more to impress them.

"Right," she said. "Gwen, you're in charge while we're apart. Make sure they don't screw anything up. I'll see you after we get off the train in New Orleans."

She didn't wait for an answer, but turned and strode away, pulling her luggage behind her.

Arthur followed her. "That's your team? Seriously? I'd fire half of them."

"Kevin's a prick, but the others are OK. Opal is really good, and I'd hate to lose her. And if I fire Kevin, I'll probably lose her, too. She's his sire. I hear that makes them tight."

Arthur nodded, understanding.

"What's with the talisman? I didn't know you had one," Zoë said, nodding toward his pocket.

"Higher-ranking members of Public Works have them," he said. "Got a promotion last week."

"You didn't tell me; that's fantastic!" Zoë said. "What are you doing now?"

"Head of Sewage Maintenance," he said. "Comes with a pay raise, a talisman, and more authority when it comes to sewer coterie."

"Awesome," she said. Arthur was very good at his job, both keeping the city's water flowing and dealing with demons in the sewer. Although, admittedly, he was more likely to enter into a fight with a demon than ask it questions, but she hoped that time with her had given him reason to ask questions before he shot.

She heard a laugh float down the empty train station, and recognized Kevin's voice. She cringed. She hated being laughed at.

She knew that was like saying she hated being sick, or hated being late, because she didn't know anyone who actively enjoyed being laughed at, vomiting, or having all their friends resent them. But she was pretty sure she hated being laughed at more than most people, and she knew Kevin was laughing at her.

She didn't feel threatened by any of the other people on her staff. While the vampires and zombies (one zombie, anyway; the other two had died because of zoëtist meddling last December) could eat her, none had threatened her beyond Kevin—besides Rodrigo, but that poor zombie had been messed with. Someone had put brain-freezing formaldehyde in his brain supply and he had gone feral. But he hadn't threatened Zoë before that. The other coterie in the office ranged from friendly to neutral.

A week before, Zoë had gone to Gwen's desk and said, "I want to do an experiment. If I intend very strongly to do something that is dangerous, like, say, think really hard about jumping in front of a bus, will you see my chances for death grow?"

Gwen sat back and studied Zoë with her glittering eyes. "Yes, intent can change your fate, if you're honest about following through."

"Right. I'm going to change my mind about something right now. You don't even know what it is. I just want to know if it will be a dangerous thing to do."

"Zoë, I'm not your carnival game—" Gwen started, but then

her eyes grew wide as Zoë concentrated. "You could be dead within the day. What in the world are you planning on?"

Zoë sighed, thinking that she should be proud of her little "hacking the future" trick, but just feeling depressed. "I was thinking about firing Kevin."

Gwen nodded. "If you fired him, he'd kill you."

Phil had placed strict orders on all of the employees at Underground Publishing: do not harm the human. If she fired Kevin, he would have nothing to lose, no reason to fear Phil.

She did know how to fight vampires, but why fight them if you didn't have to?

Now, trudging with her luggage behind her, leaving the smirking vampire, she wondered if she could handle herself if he attacked her.

She and Arthur followed the crew to the platform, the only busy spot in the terminal. Homeless people dozed against the wall here and there, but some of them had their eyes open—occasional homeless were spies for Public Works, making money here and there by reporting on coterie shenanigans. A dim whistle sounded in the distance, and she shivered as the air—already a frigid New York January brittle—grew humid. The air seeped in through her layers of clothing and pulled at her skin, making it break out in goose bumps. She craned her neck to look for the incoming train. It was only her keen awareness that Kevin was watching her, gauging her reaction for human weakness, that kept her jaw from dropping when she spotted it.

"Holy shit," Arthur said behind her.

"No kidding," Zoë replied.

She wasn't sure what she had been expecting. A white bullet train? She was used to only subway trains, all modern and practical. This train was wispy white, insubstantial, and not like the modern human bullet trains at all. Instead it was an old-fashioned steam train. The locomotive engine's smokestack belched smoke, which sounded like the memory of a hiss of steam. It looked like a luxury train, Orient Express–style, with what might once have been chrome lining the engine, and heavy curtains covering the windows.

The words SLAUGHTERED KID were etched along the side of the engine, and Zoë shivered again.

Coterie faces looked out of some of the windows, each of them looking ghost-like itself, but she could clearly identify some demons and zombies among them. One of the cars was completely dark, with covered windows, a first-class vampire car, Zoë guessed. As the coterie started boarding, they stepped up on perfectly solid steps but then became transparent themselves, becoming ghosts as they entered the ghost train.

Zoë bit her lip, hoping she and Arthur could board this amazing train, knowing it would be supremely embarrassing if they just walked right through it. She watched with envy as her coworkers boarded the first-class cars, Kevin turning to flash her a pointy grin and wave. She looked away.

Something caught her eye. Several obviously human women were among the coterie lining up to take the ghost train. Zoë had spent a good amount of time studying people in the past few weeks, trying to discern who was coterie and who wasn't—and it was harder than you'd think. With vampires and some fae looking fully human, gods and goddesses tuning down their divine presence, and shapeshifters such as dragons looking like humans did, Zoë found it tough to peg the coterie. But there was often a way of moving, of standing, and for some creatures of regarding others, that spoke of who, or what, they were. To her, the group of humans stuck out like a sore thumb, and she went to join them.

"Pariah car, ahoy," she muttered.

Some humans, male and female, filed toward the train, some looking as if they knew what was going on, others simply following like sheep.

The zoëtists were obvious: most of them were women, each of them served by a small, three-foot-tall golem that carried her bags. A couple of thralls stood dazed, getting instructions from their master vampires, many of whom left their humans, concern looking odd on their vampiric faces.

One of the women had a boy of about ten with her, and he held his mother's hand and poked little holes in the mud back of their service golem.

One man stood apart, clearly traveling alone.

He was white, thin, in his forties, with the easy way of standing that spoke of years away from sedentary office work. He wore Doc Martens as if they were still in style, laced tight, with jeans, a sweatshirt, and a heavy red trench coat. His hair was short and spiky, black with green tips. His face was slightly lined, and he looked around him without the defiant expression found so often on the younger men who dressed as he did.

He knows exactly what he's *doing,* Zoë thought. *And he's getting on that train.*

Arthur, too, approached the train with little trepidation, and Zoë cursed her hesitancy, stepping quickly to fall in behind him. She remembered that confidence was like the value of money— it was there as long as you had faith in it. She gripped her ticket and followed Arthur to board the ghost train.

Zoë noticed with a start that while it had seemed insubstantial while she was outside it, once she was on board it was as real as any train she had been on, and the rest of the terminal seemed to go gray and far away.

And oh, what a train. She had trouble thinking of it as a modern bullet train. The walls were mahogany and brass trim shone in the gaslights—seriously—*gaslights*—as the soft fires illumi-nated the interior. And this was just the coach car.

The seats were deep-blue leather and shone as if just polished. She ran her finger over one and was unable to identify what ani-mal it came from, and realized with a start that it might not have been an animal at all. She swallowed, and spied a window seat that hadn't been claimed by the dreamy thralls or chatting zoëtists.

She peeked out the window at the station and gasped. While she and the train were as real as anything she had ever encoun-tered, the world outside the train had gone shimmery and trans-parent. The people and coterie outside the train seemed unreal, drifting along, and she could see nearly through the walls.

The zoëtists were talking loudly among themselves about their trip to Atlanta, Georgia, and how they were looking for-ward to touring Olympic Stadium. Apparently it had been built by the mentor of one of the women, an architect who com-manded metal golems. They were all staying at a swanky coterie hotel and were greatly looking forward to the vacation. Luckily their chaos, with their golems and their luggage, was at the other end of the car, letting Zoë and Arthur stow their luggage above their seats. They settled in, and the man Zoë had noticed sat in the seat facing them over a table.

Zoë still hadn't figured out how to ask someone else, "So what kind of monster are you?" so she busied herself with her laptop bag, stowing her heavy coat, red hat, and gloves, and getting her ticket ready for the conductor. She placed it on the table and then traced the grain of the dark wood with her fingertip.

The man across from her smiled. "First time on a ghost train?" His accent had that kind of lilt that was clearly not American but difficult to place; he was quite good at masking whatever it was.

"Oh, yeah," said Zoë. "Is it that obvious? I guess even

36

when you know what to expect it's kind of a shock to start out with."

The man nodded, his spiky hair bobbing a little. "Here's a bit of advice. When the conductor comes through, leave your ticket and a hell note on the table and go to the bathroom. Best to do that rather than answer questions."

Zoë frowned. "Is that what they're going to do?" she asked, pointing to the women and the thralls. "The bathroom will be kinda crowded if we all do that."

"Nah," he said. "But they might ask questions to make sure you belong here. Don't want just any human on the train, you see."

She nodded slowly. Arthur looked at the man with suspicion, wriggled in his seat to get his hand into his front jeans pocket, and pulled out his talisman. "What do you think we have to hide?" he asked.

The man held up his hands, non-threatening. "I'm just saying it's the path of least resistance. And if you deal with coterie a lot, you deal with a lot of resistance."

Arthur grudgingly allowed that, but mumbled something about not liking bribes.

Zoë looked around the car at the zoëtists again, who didn't seem uptight or offended in the least. They were perfectly happy to be in the human car, and were settling in for their trip.

Some had instructed their golems to climb inside duffel bags and then removed the magic command word from their foreheads, causing the creatures to crumble into the dust from which they had been formed.

The man thought, as if trying to pick his words. "Let's just say," he said slowly, "that the zoëtists are commonplace."

Zoë noticed he wasn't carrying the same bag of dirt as the women. "You're not a zoëtist?"

The man grinned at her over his glasses. "No. And neither are you, are you?"

"Uh," Zoë said. She didn't want to reveal her status to a stranger, but clearly this man knew more about her than she had offered.

"We don't have to tell you anything," Arthur said. "Zoë, are there any other seats?"

Zoë looked around the car, but the seats were either full, or occupied by people stretching out for a nap during the trip.

The man was completely unoffended as they looked for escape. He leaned back in his seat and watched them.

"Looks like we're here for the night," she said.

"I don't know about you, but I'm going to get some sleep," Arthur said. "It's been a hell of a day, and I need it. It won't take long to get there."

"Yeah, you'll need your rest for the next few days," she said. "I'm not terribly comfortable sleeping on a coterie train. I'll stay up."

"We don't need someone to keep watch like that D&D game you made me play," he said. "Kobolds aren't going to attack in the night. There's a reason we're in the human car. Get some rest."

"I will, when I'm tired," she said pointedly.

Arthur shrugged, balled up his down jacket and put it under his head, crossed his arms, and leaned against the window.

The train started to hiss and move, lurching forward slowly. Zoë felt the red wine begin to make insistent pokes at her bladder, and she wondered about the bathrooms, and how her human waste and the ghostly plumbing would work.

She decided not to think too much about it. Half of dealing with coterie was just nodding and accepting what was in front of you. Ghost train toilet? Better than wetting herself.

Zoë placed her laptop bag on the floor below her seat and rose, swaying slightly with the movement of the train. Bullet train or no, ghost train or no, the feeling was familiar to Zoë, who had gone on Amtrak trains with her mother when she was a kid.

Worried she wouldn't have enough books, she had filled a black garbage bag with half her bookcase and her mother hadn't noticed until the train station. She had tried to explain that she didn't know what she'd be in the mood to read. Perhaps she wouldn't be in the mood for Aerin the Dragon Slayer or Mad Harry who held the Blue Sword, maybe she'd want to read about Ramona Quimby or Harriet the Spy, or maybe Bilbo Baggins.

Her mother hadn't been happy.

Zoë smiled when she realized Arthur had had the same reaction when it came to her packing heavy paperbacks for this trip.

As she made her swaying way to the bathroom, Zoë realized she was in a very fast, enclosed space with a lot of coterie. The humans wouldn't be a huge threat, but the cars on either side of her would have creatures happy to hunt her and Arthur.

Attitude. That's what she needed.

I totally belong to this club, she thought to herself as she walked down the aisle. *I'm the biggest, baddest monster*—She stepped on the foot of a mud golem standing guard beside its mistress's seat as she dozed. The foot squashed beneath her, and she tripped forward, stumbling against the door to the bathroom, which fell inward. One hand went into the tiny toilet, and the other went onto the floor to break her fall. Her recently broken arm protested at this new stress, and she groaned in disgust as she pulled her soaking hand out of the toilet.

At least, she told herself, it was a modern toilet with only an inch of blue water within. She hadn't soaked her sleeve.

It was a new train, right? And they would have to clean the bathrooms before a big trip, right? Sure, she told herself, but this trip had originated in Boston, not New York, so many of these people had been on the train for half an hour or so.

"Are you all right?" asked an amused male voice. The non-zoëtist man stood at the door, arms crossed and smiling.

"Oh goody, an audience, that makes this even better," she said aloud, and pulled herself up, using the toilet, no longer the dirtiest thing in the room, for leverage.

"Ta-da! Totally planned that," Zoë said, wondering if the train had any pure lye soap to wash her hand with. She didn't meet the man's eyes as she furiously washed her hands, impatiently hitting the faucet to engage the automatic water release.

He leaned against the doorframe, clearly not ready to leave. He stuck out his hand. "I'm Reynard, by the way."

Zoë looked at his hand, and then at her own, which was growing red and cold from all the washing in the icy ghost water. "Really?" she asked.

He raised an eyebrow. "It's the polite thing to do, isn't it?"

She took his hand and shook it, trying not to react to the realization that Reynard was missing the ring and pinky fingers of his right hand. The grip was solid and skeletal at the same time.

"Zoë," she said.

Reynard didn't say anything more, and Zoë looked pointedly at the toilet. "So...I came in here for more than acrobatics, and I'd kinda like some privacy. Is there something you need?"

"Just conversation," he said. "Where are you and Mr. Cranky headed?"

"Why?" she asked.

"Making conversation," he repeated.

"I have to pee," she said.

"So you're not doing what I suggested about the conductor?"

he asked, mock sadness causing a frown as his eyes still looked amused.

"Why should I? I have every right to be here," Zoë said.

Reynard nodded. "Sure, I just thought you might want to avoid zombies."

Zoë forgot her bladder and narrowed her eyes. "Do you think I don't know where I am, or who I'm riding with? Do you think I'm afraid of zombies? Why do you want to hide from the conductor, anyway?

"Human coterie aren't always tolerated. And if you don't have a golem by your side, they're going to think that either you're easy prey, or you're not where you're supposed to be. Or"—he dropped his voice—"you're not *who* you're supposed to be."

He left her then, and Zoë gratefully shut the door and took care of her business. When her mind was clearer and not occupied with avoiding a six-year-old's potty dance, she wondered what he'd meant. Then decided he had been baiting her.

Lord, I'm tired, she thought. She furiously washed her hands again, examined the bags under her eyes in the mirror, and took a deep breath to face the smarmy dude with hair he really should have left behind him in college.

The gaslights in the car had been dimmed, and many of the zoëtists were dozing or reading tablets. Zoë realized with distracted interest that zoëtists seemed to be an Android-loving bunch, not iPad.

She returned to her seat, where Reynard faced her with wide-awake interest. Arthur was out, and Zoë envied him the ability to sleep anywhere.

She decided to go on the offensive and introduce herself again. "OK, now that I'm thinking past more immediate needs, and my hand isn't in a toilet, I'm Zoë," she said quietly. She pointed at the sleeping Arthur. "That's Arthur. I'm the editor of a book about travel for coterie. We're researching New Orleans."

His eyebrows shot up. "Really. That's fascinating. Do you have humans writing for you?"

She shook her head. "Just me, and a bunch of coterie. I'm there because of my editorial experience. We've put out a New York book, now we're branching out.

"So," she continued. "Your turn. You're clearly not a zoëtist either, so why are you heading south on a coterie train?"

"My employer is sending me to New Orleans, too," he said, stretching his long legs across the unoccupied seat next to him. "I guess you can say I also work for coterie. I'm doing some research."

"Who do you work for?" Zoë asked.

He shrugged as if it didn't matter. "Vampires too lazy to travel. They don't want to deal with the risk of sunlight, understand."

He nodded his head toward Arthur, who was breathing softly as he slept. "If you have no humans on the team, what is his story?"

Zoë shook her head. "His story is his to tell. But he's traveling with me, so he's seen a lot of what I've seen."

They sat in silence for a while. Zoë pulled out a fantasy book and was trying to remember who was betraying whom in the current chapter, when Reynard spoke again.

"How long have you worked among coterie? How long have you known of them?"

Zoë put a finger in her book to mark her page. She grinned ruefully. "Is it that obvious?" Reynard nodded. "About three months now."

"But you're a talker, yes?"

Zoë squinted at him. A talker? She was a *city*talker but she had never heard the term "talker."

Then again, the only people she'd heard reference it were a reticent male zoëtist and a schizophrenic wealthy homeless woman. She hadn't had the most reliable mentors.

Still, a coterie train was not the place to reveal a secret, even to a human.

"Talker? I'm not sure what you mean," she lied.

"There aren't a lot left," he said. "They were more numerous generations ago. They're humans who have like a sixth sense when they're in cities. They have intuition as to what alleys not to go down, that kind of thing. They have insane luck to avoid trouble in cities. But they're useless in rural areas."

Zoë blinked. "That's amazing. I've not heard of that. How do they get the power? I know zoëtism is largely genetic but needs to be studied, right?"

"It's genetic, cultivated in families. There are some very old families that were all citytalkers. It used to be that only magical humans would breed with magical humans, thereby keeping the magic strong."

Zoë looked at her hands. "What about orphans?"

Reynard winced. "That's not a good situation, it's one of the reasons the skill is dying. While the magic is genetic, it has to be practiced, studied like any other skill. Someone with raw power won't be able to do much but sense odd things and intuit the future. They probably won't even notice this feeling only happens in urban areas."

Zoë worked hard to keep her features even and interested, not alarmed. "Wouldn't too much inbreeding make human coterie have weak hips, or idiot children, or English princes?"

Reynard smiled and brushed his spiky black hair back. "You'd think, but there were enough of them, once upon a time, to thin out the inbreeding problems. And the gene is recessive, so sometimes parents would have a child who wasn't a talker, but that kid could go on to be a parent to a talker. If he or she married right, anyway."

Zoë looked out the window at the countryside whizzing by at amazing speed. "So how do these huge families let orphans happen? How is that possible if they treasure the gift so much?"

"Well, in the sixties, there was a bit of a genetic purge," Reynard said.

"A...bit of one? Just a little bit of genocide?" Zoë asked, eyes wide.

Reynard watched her briefly, looking uncertain, then lowered his voice further. "You really don't know anything about human coterie history? Nothing at all?"

Zoë shook her head. "Like I said, I'm new."

Reynard kept his voice low. "The coterie decided they didn't like the humans that had magic. If you weren't an actual magical being like a vampire or a fairy, then you were shit in their eyes. They began hunting us. Some of the humans panicked and did a very stupid thing. They all hid in the same place. It took the coterie years to find them, but once they did, the slaughter was monumental."

Zoë nodded slowly. "Like Battleship?" Reynard blinked at her. "When I play Battleship, I clump all my ships together so that the opponent's bombs are falling everywhere in the ocean. But once they hit, they can find all my ships together and kill me instantly.

"Oh, and now that you know my strategy, remind me never to play Battleship with you," she continued. Reynard stared at her, and Zoë realized the proper response to the revelation of a massacre was probably not board game strategy discussion.

"Sorry. I talk a lot when I'm nervous. That's pretty horrific."

"Right, Battleship," Reynard said. "That's an...interesting strategy. But yes, that's similar to what I'm talking about."

"Where did they hide?" Zoë asked, her voice in a whisper.

Reynard acted as if he hadn't heard Zoë. "Anyway, a lot of the magical humans died. I mean a *lot* of them. Some had plans to put their kids in orphanages so they would never be discovered, and then the parents got slaughtered. So that's how come there are orphans with a coveted talent."

Zoë sat back, feeling the color go out of her face. She hadn't searched much for her birth parents; her adoptive parents had been the only ones she had known, so she hadn't worried about the unknown "sperm and egg donors," as her dad had called them.

"It takes five seconds to father a child, but a lifetime to raise it," he was fond of saying.

But if that five seconds helped create another, altogether stranger genetic brand than most humans got, then what did that mean?

"How many are left?" she asked, her voice barely audible.

He heard her, had been watching her closely. "They don't know. The genocide fervor calmed down in the eighties, same as the civil rights fervor stopped boiling over among the other humans. But no one has done a census. Coterie know some have to be out there, but we don't know where they are."

Zoë's mind was a whirl. Her birth parents probably had the same skill she had, and they could be alive. This was too much. She searched for another topic—any more questions and she would reveal herself, if she hadn't already. "So who are the human coterie? There's talkers, and the zoëtists, I guess, right?"

Reynard nodded. "Keep going."

Zoë thought. "I don't know. Werewolves? Superheroes? Ninjas?"

"One out of three is not bad," Reynard said, laughing. "Nearly all the weres are gone now. I don't know where they are hiding, but I'm fairly sure they haven't been eradicated. Got any more guesses?"

Zoë chewed her lip. "Can humans do magic, I mean beyond what the zoëtists can do? Wizards, witches, those types? Is Hogwarts real?"

Reynard snorted. "I wouldn't say that. Well. Actually, I don't know, honestly, but wizards are like weres—they may still exist but I haven't seen any. At best they've been hunted to near-extinction and likely do not want to be found."

Zoë rubbed her face so she could focus. "But wait, why are zoëtists not hiding? They seem to be out in the open."

Reynard chanced a peek at the still-talking women down the aisle. "Zoëtists are powerful, crazy powerful. They're the only ones who could stand up to an army of coterie since they could build an army themselves."

"Wizards aren't powerful, then? Do they just throw cantrips around?"

Reynard looked at her.

"You know. Cantrips? Lame-ass D&D first-level mage spell? Am I the only well-read person of my generation?" She sighed. "Cantrips are like making a noise sound in the next room, distracting people, make lights dance, you know. Parlor tricks. Obi-Wan distracting Stormtroopers when turning off the tractor beam. That kind of thing."

Reynard blinked. "Oh! Yes! Actually, I think the writers of D&D consulted with a wizard at the time of that writing. They didn't know he was a wizard, but he was so intrigued by their project that he was happy to weigh in."

Zoë laughed, covering her mouth so that Arthur wouldn't wake up. "You're shitting me. D&D is based on real magic? Even the really stupid spells? Bigby's Crushing Hand? Portable Hole?"

Reynard shifted, and Zoë realized she suddenly knew more

than her companion did. "I don't know the details. If you ever meet a mage, maybe you can ask him. Anyway, you've got a sense of the human coterie genocide. And these people were doubly fucked because Public Works didn't think they needed protection since they were coterie, even though it was the coterie attacking them. The humans either went underground or fought to the death. Except for the zoëtists, who managed to carve out a position for themselves. Then a truce was formed in 1978."

The late hour was starting to catch up to Zoë. "Why did no one tell me about this? It feels like something somewhat important to tell the new girl who is learning about coterie relations."

"Well, you already know they likely want to eat you. Why give you another reason to fear them?"

They had to have known she would find out about it, right? Especially as she had befriended a zoëtist. But Ben was oddly reluctant to discuss human coterie issues, and Zoë could see why, now.

Reynard glanced at the door leading toward the front of the train. "So your whole team is in first class while you, the boss, are back here in coach?"

"That's about it, yeah," Zoë said.

Reynard sighed. "That blows."

"I've had to deal with much worse," Zoë said. She yawned, despite her growing anxiety.

"So what happens if my coworkers find out I—know about this?" She had nearly slipped up and said, "I'm a talker" but had caught herself. "Are they going to kill me? Besides the ones who already want to kill me, I mean."

Reynard waved his hand, as if brutal murder was a minor threat. "No, it was only a small, zealous faction of coterie who hunted the humans. I'm sure they're not actively hunting anymore."

"Then why do they keep themselves hidden? If it's safe for talkers, weres, and wizards, then why not come out?"

Reynard stared out the window. "Habit, I suppose. No one has heard from active human coterie—beyond zoëtists—in decades. Some younger coterie are thinking it's a myth. The zoëtists don't like to talk about the other humans. They try to distance themselves."

Zoë's brain buzzed with troubling thoughts and more questions. But every answer brought more questions, and she was getting very tired. The adrenaline rush from what she had found out was wearing off. She stretched and yawned.

She pulled a neck pillow from her laptop bag and leaned her seat back the scant inches the train allowed her. Only as she was dozing off did she realize that Reynard was just like her, a hidden human coterie.

Zoë stirred awake when the train pulled into Baltimore, the slowing of the rocking having disturbed her. Reynard was awake, staring out the window at the ghostly train station. Only a few coterie boarded.

Zoë yawned. "Did you sleep at all?" she asked.

Reynard shook his head and kept looking out the window. "I really don't like to sleep with vampires around. Even if they're not hungry, they may remember the Great Hunt and want to take it up again. Not a lot of places to hide on a train."

Zoë blinked several times to try to wake her tired eyes up. "Do you know how many talkers are left in the world?"

"I think each city has at least one," he said. "New York was notoriously without one for years, or so we thought. Some witnesses on December eighth thought there may have been one in the city, but there was so much chaos we don't know. Many could have gone underground, literally or figuratively. If you don't talk to the city, it's hard for other talkers to notice you."

This guy was talking as if he was a citytalker and had already confided in her. Zoë tried to squash her excitement.

"I still find it hard to believe none of my friends have mentioned talkers to me," Zoë said. "I mean, I work with zombies and vampires, yeah, who could be only a little older than me, but there's also a couple of goddesses, a nine-tailed kitsune, and others. Do you think if I asked them about the genocide, they'd tell me?"

Reynard shook his head. "I wouldn't. If nothing else, they will be interested in where you heard about it, and ask questions. I can't afford that. Because you've already figured it out about me, haven't you?"

Zoë smiled. "You didn't make it difficult to figure out. I'm surprised you were so forthcoming with a stranger."

Reynard took his eyes away from the Baltimore station as the train began to move. "I think I see a kindred spirit in you," he said. Before Zoë could start to panic, he added, "You like to court danger, don't you?"

Zoë sat up straighter. "What do you mean?"

Reynard ticked the points off on his hand. "You've got a job with people who will eat you if they get a chance, including a fucking incubus, and it sounds like you were in the middle of the action on 12/8 when surrounded by vastly better-qualified people."

Zoë sputtered. "OK, that's not fair. If you hadn't noticed, the economy is shit, and I needed a job. And the other stuff…" She sat up straighter, her back feeling as if an ice spike had been inserted where her spinal cord should have been. "How do you know all of those things?"

He slouched comfortably in his seat, his head in a shadow. "There's only one way I could have found out. *She* told me."

49

Was this why the city had said she was supposed to avoid citytalkers? She had communicated with this dude? Zoë paused then laughed.

"As for why, well, it seemed like a good idea at the time. As for now, I just really am going to need some caffeine if I am going to stay alert to watch for killer vampires tonight. Want anything from the café car?"

Reynard smiled and got up. "I'll go with you. I doubt the train will have much for human consumption, but we can go check. They probably have something for the zoëtists. Do you have your talisman?" Zoë nodded and brought her necklace out of her shirt. Reynard nodded. "Just let me do the talking, OK?"

"If you say so."

Reynard removed his trench coat, carefully folded it, and left it on his seat. He and Zoë walked down the aisle past the dozing zoëtists. Zoë watched with amusement as a little dirt golem about six inches tall stood watch at one table, seeming to glare at her as she walked by.

The train thrummed beneath them, smooth and powerful. They had left the city by now and Zoë marveled at their speed. They really would reach New Orleans before the morning, amazingly enough.

She realized she was unlike Reynard, who firmly demanded his place among coterie. Zoë herself wanted to spend some time on a human bullet train, no matter what "club" she belonged to. She held her breath as they passed into the adjoining car, not sure what they would find, but they encountered a bunch of dozing sprites.

The car was dark, but the slightly glowing air sprites drifted along the top of the car. Zoë would have freaked out and assumed they were ghosts a couple of months ago, but now she knew they were dozing elementals.

She thought about Morgen, her friend the water sprite, and her heart rose in her throat. "Let's keep moving," she whispered to Reynard.

"You know they're not ghosts, right?" Reynard asked.

"Yes, but sprites remind me of someone, that's all," Zoë said. "Can we just keep moving?"

The next car was also dark, and completely full of sleeping zombies. One woman sat in front of an untouched Tupperware container of brains, all gray and shiny, and Zoë averted her gaze. Some zombies' elbows stuck out into the aisle and Reynard and Zoë had to inch around them. The train lurched a bit as it went around a curve, and Zoë flailed, catching the luggage rack over their heads to avoid tumbling into a zombie's lap.

Reynard snickered and offered Zoë his hand. Zoë pulled herself up on her own, glared at him, and they went on their way.

She wondered how she was going to make it back through with a drink in her hand.

The third car was finally what they were waiting for. A vampire stood, bored, at the snack stand, flipping through a magazine. He was a tall and lithe Indian, who sneered at them as if they were rodents on his pristine train.

"Zoëtists," he said, blowing his bangs out of his face. "What can I get for you?"

"What do you have that's caffeinated?" Reynard asked.

The vampire reached under the counter and pulled out a can of Diet Coke and a can of Coke. "Not much call for it around here."

"Thanks," Reynard said, and took them both, handing the vampire a hell note. He presented both cans to Zoë, who took the Coke. She was dismayed that the can was warm. She thanked the vampire but he ignored her.

"Pleasant," muttered Zoë to Reynard.

Reynard shrugged. "Told you it wouldn't be very human-friendly."

Underneath their feet the train's hum changed timbre very slightly, and both the vampire and Reynard raised their heads, alert.

Zoë looked from one to the other. "What's going on? Is something wrong?"

"This train has reached its maximum safe speed. It just sped up. That's not supposed to happen, is it?" Reynard said this last sentence to the vampire, who ignored him.

The vampire exited from behind his little café counter and peered out the window. He said something in Hindi and fumbled for a walkie-talkie on his belt.

"Engineering. This is Deepu in the café car. If you're trying to outrun an old-fashioned train robbery, you're going to need to go faster."

CHAPTER 1
Getting There

The Ghost Train Slaughtered Kid

The human creation of high-speed rails has made it possible for the coterie to piggyback on human railroads and create the first-ever ghost bullet train. The ghost train Slaughtered Kid is the first high-speed coterie-only train to go from Boston, MA, to New Orleans, LA (with stops in New York City, Baltimore, DC, Richmond, Raleigh, Columbia, Atlanta, and Pensacola, for some reason), in about ten hours. It serves all coterie, human and nonhuman, and you can buy your ticket at most train stations if you know where to book with a coterie agent. While it is open to all, it does segregate by cars, so vampires, gremlins, and deities will be seated with like folk, as well as all humans, including thralls.

Being that it is a ghost train, it is staffed mainly by ghosts, as they can find themselves in a corporeal existence on the train, while stepping off makes them go insubstantial again.

Accommodations include single seats, booth-type seats, and sleeper cars. The train has compartments for all sizes of coterie, and encourages little people, leprechauns, and gremlins to take advantage of their quality interiors.

The train allows the carry-on of weapons, claws, symbiotic relationships, and other ways of protecting yourself. The train is affordable—for those who can afford such things—and fast, and may very well revolutionize travel in American coterie circles.

Everyone must experience the ghost train at least once in their lives. Or deaths. ■

CHAPTER THREE

Zoë and Reynard looked out the window. Snow covered the fields, and the moon shone brightly over them. The train was going far too fast for anything to pace it, but something was. It was hard to tell through the ghostly windows, not to mention the darkness and the snow, but something white and insubstantial seemed to be keeping up with the train.

"Ghosts," Reynard said grimly.

Once he spoke, Zoë's eyes finally made sense of what she was seeing. Two men and one woman rode horses that thundered beside the bullet train. Their mounts were clearly straining, but managed to keep up. The men had pistols in their hands, while the woman was prepping a lasso. They were all hazy and white, like the train itself.

"This is a bullet train!" Zoë said. "How in the world are they robbing a bullet train? And train robberies went out with the century before last!"

"Which is why only ghosts attempt train robberies," Reynard said. "We need to head back to our car, now."

They left Deepu the vampire arguing with engineering, he trying to give them information, and they being irate about it considering that they *knew* they were being robbed thank you very much and that's why they were taking measures against it.

"I know this is a stupid question," Zoë asked as they slipped between the cars. "But why are we afraid of ghosts, beyond the normal reasons for fearing vampires, zombies, and the other coterie?"

"Ghosts don't want to consume us, or feed off us. They want to *be* us," Reynard said. "They want to inhabit us for our warmth, go joyriding by eating everything they can get our hands on, or fucking everything in sight. I knew one woman who was possessed who woke up nude in Macy's fur department, lying in a pile of sable coats, totally unaware of how she got there.

"Ghosts aren't official coterie, since they don't really form societies like the rest of us," he said, "and they can't be killed. To the nonhumans they're irritations, like memories that won't go away. To humans they can mean anything from embarrassment, to framing for crimes, to violent death."

"Death?" Zoë choked. They were hurrying through the zombie car, taking less care not to wake the undead. The train had begun to shudder with speed, but Zoë could see outside that the robbers were keeping perfect pace.

"Sure. Thrill-seekers, you know. They can take your body, go skydiving, rock-climbing. You've got to still have the adrenal glands to have an adrenaline rush. And if they slip or something goes wrong, they just casually exit your body as you go plummeting."

Zoë shuddered. They maneuvered around a zombie whose elbow stuck out in the aisle, who grunted at them, and hurried back to their car.

When they reached their seats, Reynard stopped and looked at Zoë. "But the real threat is when the other coterie find out ghosts are stopping us, they're going to want to throw us off to placate the ghosts."

"Oh, right. But wait—if the ghosts are insubstantial and all they do is hurt humans, why can't the engineer just keep driving? If all it's going to hurt is us, why do they care?"

Reynard sighed. "We are on a ghost train, Zoë," he said. "The ghosts are as substantial as the train. If they want to derail us, they can. If they want to get on board and start killing coterie, they can."

"So ghosts are insubstantial, and therefore untouchable, when they're off the train," Zoë mused. "And they can only act when they're on it."

Reynard ignored her and went to each of the sleeping zoëtists and gently shook her awake. "Ladies, I'm sorry to bother you but it looks like the train is being robbed."

An older, plump woman that Zoë had identified as the leader stirred in her sleep and grunted, "'Sa bullet train. Can't be robbed." She waved Reynard away and settled back into her seat. Reynard's mouth twisted in annoyance.

"They're no help," he said, sitting down in his seat.

Zoë shook Arthur's arm. His eyelids fluttered but he remained asleep. Something worked loose in his hand, though. A squat white-and-pink bottle fell from it and rolled down his thigh. Zoë caught it.

"Benadryl? Are you kidding me?" she asked in a loud voice. Arthur didn't stir.

"OK. He's no help. The zoëtists are no help. What can we do?" Zoë asked. She couldn't remember anything Granny Good Mae had said about ghosts. She had given advice on how to fight many of the coterie, but every time Zoë thought she had them all covered, she was introduced to a new one to worry about.

"Hang on a second," she said. "If a ghost's main threat is its ability to possess us, they can only do that when they're off the train, right? What's the threat when they're on?"

Reynard thought for a moment. "They're as solid as we are, which means they can attack, use weapons, and worse," he said. "Right now they're a threat on or off the train."

"So we stay on the train. And if we have to fight, we do so." She glanced at the dozing zoëtists. "It would be nice if they made something that could help us fight."

"Come on," Reynard said. "I've got another idea."

"Where are we going?" Zoë asked. "We need to fight those guys. From what you said, none of the coterie here are going to fight for us."

Reynard grabbed her hand and pulled her to her feet. "There you go again, demanding to be in the middle of things," he said. "Let someone else fight the fight for once. It's not our train, not our problem."

Zoë glared at him and wrenched her hand free. "It's my problem if they attack me. And I'm not leaving Arthur." She reached into her computer bag on the seat and pulled out a short Filipino fighting stick. Granny Good Mae had just begun teaching her the finer points of Arnis, and Zoë loved it, the stick being a lighter weapon than a sword, but quite effective. Also easier to carry without getting too much attention.

She slid the rattan stick, about two feet long, into her belt, then crossed her arms. "Go if you have to. I'm staying here."

"So how am I going to fight ghosts?" Zoë muttered to herself.

It would be me that gets on a ghost train that somehow gets robbed, she thought after Reynard left to save his own ass. This shit doesn't happen to people like Stacy Bellingham. No, Stacy just goes to work, comes home, drinks beer, and watches reality cooking shows. I'm the one who met the weird dude who tells me about genocide and then expects me to leave my boyfriend behind.

She hadn't thought of Stacy Bellingham in years. Her friend from high school had had simple goals in life. Physical therapist, marriage, bunch of kids. Zoë was fairly sure that working for a vampire was not something Stacy would even consider. She would probably be insulted by the concept. Stacy had no vision. No sense of adventure.

Zoë was pretty sure Stacy was also not aboard a ghost train getting robbed.

Zoë hated Stacy right then. A small logical part of her mind wondered why she was wasting time hating Stacy instead of, say, the mysterious Reynard or the drugged-out Arthur or even the ghosts robbing the train. Or Kevin, who delighted in torment-ing her so much. Or the bigots who hadn't let her sit with her coworkers. She'd have been safe there.

She realized with disgust that she was longing for the safety of vampires and gods instead of standing on her own, which was something Granny had hammered into her. *No matter how nice they are to you, they are still coterie and they are always dangerous. Work with them, but don't count on them.*

She didn't have to count on them, but she could use them.

Zoë got out her special coterie phone and looked up Kevin's number.

The train had not put out an alarm that it was being robbed. Only Zoë, Reynard, and the train personnel knew about the threat, as far as Zoë could tell. They and whoever was in the car Reynard was running to, she guessed.

COME TO THE HUMAN CAR. NEED TO TALK ABOUT YOUR ATTITUDE she typed out, and hit send.

While she waited for Kevin to receive the text and respond, she again poked Arthur, who made a face and turned away from her as best he could, considering he was hunched up against a window and a train seat. But it was pretty clear he was out of commission.

Zoë put her face right up to his. "We are going to talk about the wisdom of drugging yourself into a stupor when you are on a train with people who would eat you. Pencil me into your schedule when you fucking wake up."

Checking out entirely was unlike him, but she didn't have time to wonder about it.

She had expected a sardonic text from Kevin, or a flat-out refusal to come to the car, but as Zoë stood guard in the aisle, with the blank faces of mud golems facing her in an interested, alert manner, she heard a low voice behind her.

"This ought to be good," Kevin said.

"Wow, you really fell for it," Zoë said, and felt the train shake slightly again under her feet. She caught a flash of something out the window, a wispy white. "I didn't think you'd actually obey."

Kevin sneered at her. " 'Obey,' nice word there. What do you want to do, fire me?" He leaned in close, and Zoë could smell blood on his breath. "Please fire me."

She smiled at him, a sweet smile. "Fire one of my best writers? I'd never do that. Besides, you're a big, strong vampire, and I'm only a little human. Phil would kill you deader than you already are if you laid a hand on me. Or allowed me to get hurt."

At that point the ghosts boarded. Being insubstantial, they just jumped from their horses and phased through the doors, where they landed physically on the steps leading to the human car. A couple of the zoëtists stirred, but everyone but Arthur and the thralls jumped when the lead ghost, a white man looking to be about forty-five, fired a shot in the air.

"This here's a robbery, everyone put your hands up!" he shouted.

Kevin's eyes went wide with alarm and he stared first at the ghosts and then at Zoë. "You knew about this."

"You know, if you liked me just a little more, you might actually respect the manipulation here," she said. "But yeah, I knew."

"You could have called anyone to your little-distressed-princess side, they would have jumped at the chance. Why did you fucking bother me?" he hissed in her ear as their hands went up.

"Because I wanted to reinforce that you have to do what I say, I'm your goddamned boss," she whispered back, keeping her eyes on the ghosts. "I have a plan but I need someone who can move faster than me."

"Yeah, the moving-faster-than-you is going to be me leaving this fucking car and going back to the first-class car. If they boarded here, they must want something that the humans have. It's not my problem."

The zoëtist women were awake and in various states of panic. The thralls, of course, simply sat in their seats and stared blankly at the new events. The younger women fumbled with their bags of dirt and mud, and one was concentrating on forming a small golem out of Zoë's half-full soda can. It twisted and stretched and little fissures opened, forcing Coke to dribble out onto the table. Four mud golems stood guarding the aisles. The woman Zoë had mentally named the Matriarch, the oldest, who looked to be in her sixties, was awake now, and glaring at the new people in the car.

The ghosts stood at the far end, grinning at them. Now that they were substantial, Zoë could see their clothing much better: the men's cowboy outfits fit poorly over khakis and tailored button-down shirts. Their chaps were stiff and light brown, and their hats clearly cheap fabric. The woman wore a smart business suit with a modest knee-length skirt that had been bunched up to allow the chaps to fit over them. The guns at their hips, however, were real.

"Who the hell are these guys?" Zoë asked out loud.

"Good evening," the head cowboy said, his accent much

closer to New England than the American Southwest. "I'm sure you ladies know what an old-fashioned train robbery is." He smiled with very white teeth. "Now hand over your valuables. Hell notes, talismans, any magical items you may have. And when you're done with that, you can tell me which one of you is Reynard Arseneaux?"

"What are you going to do with our valuables?" the oldest zoëtist asked, smiling. "The moment you leave the train, they will be worthless to you. Are you going to go shop in the snack car with the money?"

"Hey, we have employers!" the woman said, sticking her chin out. She was maybe twenty-five, Hispanic, and very short.

"Shut up," the leader growled. "It's no matter to you what happens to us. We just want your stuff. And these bullets are plenty real on this train, so you'd best do what we say, y'hear?" The word sounded odd coming out of his mouth, as if he had a script.

Zoë stepped forward and was stopped by a golem. It held a goopy arm out to block her, and she held up her hands, trying to show she was not threatening. It refused to let her pass.

She raised her voice then. "What do you want with Reynard?"

"That ain't your bidness," said the third cowboy, a fat white man about the size of a refrigerator. He would have looked intimidating except that his Western garb was stretched tight over him, and he looked like a grown man who had raided his children's costume trunk. His hat was pulled over his face, and she could see only his mouth.

"I'll get the leader, you get the fat one," Zoë whispered to Kevin.

"You think I'm going to take fighting directions from a little editor?" he asked. "I'd rather drink holy water."

"Prove it. There's some holy water in my bag there," Zoë said, pointing at the bag on the floor.

Kevin whipped his head around to her. "You're not serious."

"No, the word you're looking for is 'stupid,' I'm not stupid. Can we please focus on the ghosts with the real guns?"

"Fuck this," he said, and turned and ran out the door.

"Why is every guy I encounter on this train a complete coward?" she asked out loud.

Zoë tried to climb over the seat to her left, but the golem hit her with its suddenly very solid mud arm, smacking her into the wall. She grunted and fell, and the golem flowed around her feet, trapping her.

"Dammit, I'm not the threat, it's them! Go get the fake cowboys! I'm on your side!" she said, struggling to free herself from the insidious mud that trapped her. She stood, but the mud was still gluing her to the floor.

"We're not fake! We'll put a bullet in you!" shouted the woman, and Zoë snorted.

"What happened to you guys, anyway? Did you get killed while on some corporate dude ranch visit? Did something interrupt your team building?"

They looked at each other, uncertain. Zoë laughed. "I was kind of kidding. Are you serious? That's utterly tragic. So you're doomed for eternity to wear fake cowboy outfits? You must be in hell."

She actually pitied the cowboys for a moment. The zoëtists had noticed her at this point, and the Matriarch flicked a hand, and the mud fell away from Zoë's jeans and shoes, although she was still filthy. The golem stepped back and let her get up.

"No matter what we were in life, we're here in death, and we're robbing you," the woman said, stepping in front of the man. "And the costumes we died in may not be real, but the guns are."

Zoë nodded. "You said that. I'm sure they're very scary. Now what I'm interested in is who is your employer? And what do ghosts get out of employment? What could you need?"

The woman shook the gun as if worsening her aim would make her more threatening. "Hold it right there! And it's none of your damn business. Give me that talisman, and whatever hell notes you have, now!"

Zoë had been slowly inching forward, but still had two golems between her and the ghosts. She held up her hands to show she wasn't armed. "Hang on, Calamity Jane, I'm just curious. Can't I be curious?"

"You can be dead!" shouted Calamity Jane. Zoë stopped and waited for the inevitable violence. She didn't think the woman could hit her; her hand was shaking too much. But she didn't want to go hand to hand with the big guy.

When the woman didn't pull the trigger, someone snickered off to the side.

"You're really not very good at this," Zoë said, not unkindly. "Why don't you just step off the train in Charlotte and go watch some NASCAR, or something?"

The fat ghost, the one who hadn't spoken yet, lifted his head. He'd had his head down, the hat obscuring him, and he looked dreadful. While the other ghosts looked somewhat human, this one looked chewed on, as if by a zombie. Half his cheek and one eye were missing. Zoë winced.

"She's not good at it, but I am," he said, and took aim.

Granny Good Mae had taught Zoë an awful lot about intent, and how you could judge what someone would do based on the intent behind their movements. This was why she was confident the woman wouldn't shoot. But when she got a look at old rotting one-eye, she knew she was in trouble.

She dove behind a seat as the cowboy pulled the trigger, and heard a wet squelch as the shot hit the golem that had jumped in front of her.

"OK, real bullets. We're done with the mocking, I guess," she muttered.

She peeked over the seat back. The golems rushed forward to engage the ghosts, and the ghosts fired again, followed by the cry of one of the zoëtists. "Shit," Zoë said.

The ghosts now struggled under a torrent of mud. The door opened behind them and a zombie porter came through, along with the snack car vampire, Deepu, and a hulking demon with green skin and far too many teeth.

"There, Raoul," the vampire Deepu said, pointing to the ghosts. The demon grunted and picked two of the ghosts—the leader and the woman—up by the necks. He slammed them together as if he were clapping his hands, their heads clashing together. He dropped them and they crumpled. The porter opened the door and the wind roared into the car, picking up paper and trash and putting out the gaslights. In the darkness Zoë heard a grunt as the demon tossed the ghosts into the night, and the bodies faded as the ghosts went from corporeal to insubstantial again.

There was still one ghost left. Zoë crawled over another seat, able to see very little, but knowing the golems, the demon, the zombie, and the vampire could probably take the one remaining ghost.

But then something slammed into her shoulder and she flew forward, sprawled on a thrall's lap, thinking vaguely that it was a shame to bleed on the new ghost train. She heard another scuffle, another scream, and then her name being called.

"Oh. Hey, Kevin, what are you doing here?" she asked, and fainted.

*   *   *

When she came to, her head was pillowed on Eir's lap. The lights were back on, and Zoë could see mud and blood spattering the walls and windows. The zoëtists were crowded around one of their own. The train was still.

Zoë blinked and tried to sit up. Eir held her down gently. "I think one of the zoëtists got shot," Zoë said. "Did you help her?"

"Shhh, Zoë," Eir said. Zoë stared at her. A smile crossed the severe goddess's face. "Everyone is all right."

"I don't know about that. For one thing, you never call me Zoë; what the hell is wrong with you?" She pushed Eir's arm off her and sat up. Gwen and Reynard sat in the seats opposite them. Arthur still dozed in his seat.

"What happened?" Zoë asked.

"Kevin came to get us. When we got here, the ghosts were gone. You and one of the zoëtists had been shot. Eir healed you both, and now we're close to Charlotte." She glanced at Zoë's filthy feet. "What happened here?"

Zoë ran her hand over her shoulder. Her sweater was still ripped and sticky with blood, but she seemed just fine underneath. "Stepped in a golem," she said absently. "So you're saying Kevin came back for me?"

"Not exactly," Reynard said. "A vampire I sometimes deal with was on the train and I had time to work out a business deal." The "business deal" on his neck still leaked blood, but it didn't look serious. "He met up with your Kevin and, well, vampires don't like to look cowardly, so Kevin turned back around right away and came back here with us. Together they helped stop the third ghost. Unfortunately, they're both quite ill right now."

"Ill?"

"Ghosts aren't real people. So what they drank wasn't real blood," Gwen said.

"Oh," Zoë said, and heard retching coming from the bathroom.

"So what happened after I left?" Reynard asked.

"Lame-ass ghosts from some sort of corporate team building stunt gone bad decided to be cowboys. Then they asked for you, then I got shot. I think some other things happened, but it was dark."

She glanced at Eir. "Uh, sorry I was rude before. Thanks for healing me. I just, well, you weren't acting like yourself."

Eir just smiled at her.

"And you still aren't," Zoë said.

"Eir gets a hit of euphoria when she saves a life," Gwen said softly. "It's a lot like being high or drunk. She will come down soon. But she will remember how you treat her."

"Got it," Zoë said. She smiled widely at Eir. "Thanks again, so much. I love you, man."

Eir smothered her in a giant hug, and Zoë tried not to wince at the crushing embrace. "And I you, Zoë my editor. I am so glad you are not dead. We are truly heading on a great adventure!"

The train began to slow, and a zombie entered the car, shuffling through and moaning that the next stop was Charlotte.

"You said they were looking for me?" Reynard asked quietly, after Zoë had carefully removed herself from Eir's huge arms. His face grew a bit pale.

"If your last name is Arseneaux, then yeah, they asked for our valuables, but really wanted you."

"Then I think Charlotte is where I get off," he said. He stood abruptly and said, "I'd recommend the same to you, Zoë. If they find you're here, too, you will have nowhere to run."

"Wait, who's 'they'? Why me?" Zoë asked. But the train had stopped, and Reynard had already left them after a short bow to

66

the goddesses. He didn't even grab the trench coat he had left on the seat opposite Arthur.

"What is he talking about?" she asked Gwen, but her friend shrugged.

Zoë frowned. "Hey, why didn't you notice I was in trouble?" she asked. "You usually check in when shit goes down."

A flicker of irritation crossed Gwen's face. "I was concentrating on something else," she said. "I can't focus on your well-being all the time, Zoë. Kevin saw you got shot and came to find me and Eir. You're fine now."

Zoë frowned. Gwen's voice had a "the lady doth protest too much" tone to it, but it wasn't Zoë's style to argue with a death goddess.

"Yeah, totally, I'm great," Zoë said. "I'm going to go check on the zoëtists, OK?"

Gwen walked with her, leaving Eir leaning back in the seat, eyes half-lidded. "I'm not even going to pretend I know what's going on with her," Zoë said.

"That man. Reynard. Who is that?" Gwen asked.

"I really have no idea. I met him on the train. He's not a zoëtist but clearly knows a lot about coterie. Says he's doing work in New Orleans for his employer, but he ran when he found out the ghosts knew his name. He didn't tell me much else about himself. He apparently sells himself to vampires for protection." She shuddered. She didn't tell Gwen what she had found out about the genocide, or that Reynard was a citytalker. It would be something to worry about later.

The zoëtists fussed over their own, a young girl who was pale and confused, but healed fully. Her eyes met Zoë's and she tried to smile. "Thanks for fighting with us," she said.

"I'm not sure I did anything, truly, except piss them off," Zoë said. "They could have shot me in the head. Glad you're OK."

The train began to start up, and she and Gwen headed back to their seats.

A voice pushed at the edge of Zoë's consciousness.

Fuck, girl, what were you doin' cowering like that in your little chair? You gotta fight if you wanna get anywhere in this world! The voice was loud and bossy and more strident than New York had ever been.

"Charlotte?" she whispered. "Are you speaking to me?"

The voice was gone.

Gwen was looking at her curiously. Zoë said, "Uh, hey, about those ghosts. From what Reynard said, they're pretty scary, and you guys have never mentioned them. Especially since they seem to be on the train, too."

Gwen joined Eir at the table and motioned for Zoë to sit. "Now why do you think ghosts are scary?" Gwen asked.

"Reynard said—well." Zoë began to feel uncertain. "One of them shot me, for one thing!"

"Anything with a gun is scary, then. Give a gun to a harmless creature like a rabbit and it can be scary," Gwen said. "Why are *ghosts* frightening?"

"Rabbits don't have thumbs," Zoë said, but relented. "Reynard said that ghosts possess humans and then take them for a joyride, like stolen cars. That they want to live again." She didn't want to meet Gwen's fathomless eyes; she suddenly felt like a kid trying to explain why she was shaving a cat when her best friend had suggested it would be a fun idea.

Gwen shook her head. "I think your friend was embellishing to you, Zoë. Ghosts can possess you, but they can't take complete control over you unless you're unconscious. And there aren't a lot of ghosts; they're made when a vampire or zombie has tried to turn someone, but they messed up the job somehow."

"Why would he lie?" Zoë asked, face burning, this time from anger.

"I don't know," Gwen said. "Maybe he was trying to scare you, get you into the vampire car with him? But clearly he was going there for protection, and was planning on coming back. It doesn't make sense. But it does seem he purposefully tried to frighten you for no reason."

"He certainly was terrified when he jumped out at Charlotte. So there's something to be afraid of," Zoë said grimly. "That dude is way too mysterious, and he likes it that way."

She wished she knew who the "cowboys" were.

Someone was sitting in Reynard's abandoned seat when Zoë and Gwen got back to where Arthur was sleeping. A small woman, a girl, really, wearing a black maid's outfit and with her hair in a style that harkened back to the 1940s. She was black and short, a demure girl who shyly looked up at Zoë's face.

Zoë took a step back. She had been burned before by coterie who didn't look dangerous.

"Are you a ghost?" she asked, feeling rather stupid for saying it. "I mean, you look like one, but..."

The woman smiled and fixed her eyes on the ground at Zoë's feet. "Pardon, miss, but I'm a porter for this area of the train and I'm coming to check on your well-being. After the excitement, I mean." Her voice had a slight Irish lilt to it.

"So you're not going to attack me to get me off the train and then go joyriding in my body?" Zoë asked.

"I told you, that's very difficult to do," Gwen said.

The porter's eyes widened as she looked up at Zoë. "No, ma'am, of course not. I'd lose my job if I abused a passenger like that!"

Gwen gestured for Zoë to sit next to the ghost. She sat beside Arthur, who still dozed against the window. "Zoë, this is Anna. I convinced her to take her break with us so that she could teach you a bit about ghosts."

This was starting to feel like an after-school special. But Zoë realized the ghost train must be the best place in the world for ghosts to work, since they would have a corporeal body here. Step off the train and they're a wisp again.

"I'm—OK, we can talk. I mean, I believe Gwen over some stranger who told me a bunch of lies, but, I guess—" She stopped, realizing she was babbling.

"What do I need to know?" she asked simply.

"That man lied to you," Anna said.

CHAPTER 11
Lodging

HAUNTED HOTELS

Human tourists in New Orleans delight in the so-called "haunted hotels," but truly those hotels are merely fronts for good places for coterie to stay.* The rooms available to humans are few and separated, the rest of the hotel is always "booked for a convention"—and open to coterie. These hotels include the Hotel Provincial, the Omni Royal Orleans, and the Andrew Jackson Hotel—which is actually staffed by Andrew Jackson, a vampire who is much happier owning a hotel than he was being president. The hotel is often picketed by Native American ghosts, so be aware you may need to cross a picket line. ■

---

* Incidentally, the same goes for haunted restaurants, including Muriel's, which has a full banquet ballroom open for coterie purposes.

CHAPTER FOUR

Anna the ghost spread her hands on the table as if she enjoyed just feeling it. "If it pleases you, I don't have a lot of information beyond my own experiences, but it takes a lot of work to enter a human who isn't willing, or welcoming, or unconscious. It's painful for me and them, and it's not a perfect match. I mean, if we're not welcome, we have little to no control over the body."

"So what if I am willing. How do I let you know?" Zoë asked. "I mean if I can't see you."

She smiled. "That is why there aren't a lot of possessions."

Gwen leaned forward and fixed her eyes on Anna. "Ghost, tell me why the passenger known as Reynard would want to lie to Zoë about what ghosts are, and what they can do?"

The girl looked frightened. "I—I don't know. I didn't see Reynard. I don't know who he is. He's a citytalker like you, yes?"

Gwen slowly turned to focus on Zoë. "Citytalker? Does this mean you have the same particular gift as your addled elderly friend?"

She forced herself to look Gwen in the eye, which was like looking into a demanding starry sky. "I can trust you, right, Gwen? I mean, you feed off me and everything, but you don't actively hunt me. You don't view me as a sentient sandwich."

"I thought we had well established that."

Zoë shrugged. "I'm sorry. It's just my one secret I'd like to keep from Phil and many of the others."

"I knew that you're a magical human." Gwen's voice was steady as always, but Zoë stared at her. A small smile crossed Gwen's face. "I can tell by your life force. I've known it for a while."

Zoë leaned back and sighed. "Can I keep nothing from you people?"

Gwen waved her hand dismissively. "Only people who have fed on you would know. As far as I understand, that includes myself and John. You haven't let a vampire feed, and a zombie would have killed or turned you by now. So it's only us."

"John isn't necessarily someone I trust," Zoë said, remembering with discomfort the time the incubus had nearly seduced her to feed on her sexual energy.

"He has told no one about you thus far," Gwen replied calmly.

Zoë glared at Anna. "Thanks for outing me," she said, and the girl's eyes went wide when she realized she'd offended. "I hadn't planned on talking about it yet."

"Because the more coterie know about citytalkers, the more dangerous it is for us," Anna said quietly, looking down. She touched her neck where a vampire had savaged it—something Zoë hadn't noticed since Anna kept that side away from people when speaking. "I was killed during a purge, Dublin didn't tell me the assassin was coming. I don't know why."

"Were you killed by a vampire?" Zoë asked, and then felt stupid because it was an obvious question, but the girl shook her head.

"I don't know what took me down, but once I was down, they were on me, tried to turn me. It was part of the second wave of attacks, if you will. The city didn't warn us, and by the time it realized what the vampires had planned, we were too incapacitated to prepare."

"I remember," Gwen said. "I witnessed some. Zoë, you were right, it's not something you want people like Kevin knowing.

And if Phil knows you have this power, he will figure out a way to use you to his advantage."

Zoë frowned. She realized she had been hoping that Gwen would deny all her fears instead of validating that she was correct to hide her secret. This made it even worse if it came out.

"OK, so you're not mad and you're not going to give me up. Good to know," Zoë said. "But how come no one told me about this genocide thing? It's a pretty big freaking deal to humans, I figured you guys would know that little bit of history ought to make a difference to me. I know lots of coterie eat people, but this is so much worse."

Gwen sat back and closed her eyes, then licked her lips, and Zoë got an uncomfortable feeling of her remembering a specific taste. The taste of people like her, and their proximity to death. Her dark eyes opened then, and she leaned forward.

"We didn't think you needed to know. They don't know you're magical, so they figured you wouldn't be threatened, and if you'd found out, you might not have taken the job."

"No kidding," Zoë mumbled. "What can you tell me about any citytalkers left? Granny is the only one I've ever met. I barely understand what this power is, and now people exist that want to hunt me for it?"

Gwen inclined her head. "I came into being astride a black mare, galloping across a moor in pursuit of a wayward soul. Coming to terms with your sudden existence is a shock."

"You'll have to tell me that story sometime." Zoë wanted to take a drink of her soda, and then remembered it had walked off to fight a bunch of fake cowboys. "So no, I don't know where my people come from. I don't know how I became a citytalker, and I don't know how to control it, even. Riding on this train is bizarre as I'm getting a taste of personality from the occasional city, but we're moving too fast for anything to solidify."

"I don't know if I should be the one to tell you this—" Gwen began, but Zoë interrupted her.

"I trust you, Gwen," she said. She started to count down on her fingers. "You are not interested in eating me. You have kept my secret from Phil even though you didn't know exactly what it was, and you have shown yourself to be concerned about my well-being despite what you say about being an impassive death goddess."

Gwen waited for a moment, then said, "Are you going to finish counting your fingers?"

Zoë lowered her hands, feeling her face flush. "I had only three."

"I see. And all of those things are true. I simply fear that you finding out the details will make you less interested in working with us."

"I've been attacked by zombies, zoëtists, golems, and demons. One of them even swallowed me," she reminded Gwen, shuddering at the memory. "What can you tell me that will turn me off more than those have?"

"I can tell you what we have lost."

"What we lost?"

"What everyone lost when we lost the citytalkers. The cities."

"But the cities are right there!" Zoë waved her hand, although only South Carolina farmland was beyond the train's windows.

"The spirits of the cities are fractured and confused. The citytalkers not only talked to the cities, but they supported the cities, too. Obviously the buildings and bridges and infrastructure are still there, but the city itself is weakened. If no one can talk to the city, no one knows if a disaster is imminent, or if a bridge is weakened. And frankly, healthy cities are happy, and happy cities have happy people. Some cities are near death now that the talkers are all but gone. And those who are here"—she gestured to Zoë—"are not taught what they need to know."

Zoë sat in stunned silence. Gwen patiently signaled to Anna, who rose, left the car, and hurried back, carrying a red can. She gave a soda—cold, this time—to Zoë.

"Drink something. It will ground you," Gwen said, gently pushing the fresh drink toward Zoë.

"Dying cities? You are kidding me, right?"

Gwen frowned. "I'm very bad at kidding. Jokes were Morgen's job."

"Why would the coterie want the cities to die?" she asked.

"It wasn't logic that made them hunt, it was bigotry. They didn't want humans to have any access to magic. They saw it as offensive, heresy, what have you."

Beside Zoë, Arthur stirred. His eyes opened briefly, and he caught sight of Gwen and, across the aisle, the dozing Eir. He spied the blood on Zoë's shirt, and frowned in concern.

"What the hell did I miss?" he asked.

CHAPTER 18
Coterie NOLA

This city is called the unofficial coterie capital of the world, for good reason. Carnival and Mardi Gras make it easy for coterie to walk freely in the public eye no matter what their physical appearance. This city accepts, even embraces, the "weird"—aka any nonhuman.

Vampires are the dominant coterie, and have influenced much of the mythology in the city. Many of the myths are true, some are false. Visitors are encouraged to determine what is fact and what is fiction.

But don't go searching out the more prominent celebrity vampires. They are not fond of visitors who do not bleed.

The city is famous for its food, and naturally the hedonistic partying makes it good for any deity or demon that feeds off human energy, especially the succubi and incubi. Its port status leaves it open for water-loving demons and sprites; however, the events after Hurricane Katrina have left the city in less of a welcoming mood with regard to water sprites. So keep in mind that visiting water sprites may face intolerance.

Zoëtists are encouraged to check in at Public Works, as New Orleans is the voodoo capital of the US, and zoëtism and voodoo are sister specialities. ▪

CHAPTER FIVE

"Ghosts. Guns. Heroics. I'm fine, by the way," Zoë said stiffly. "Why the fuck are you taking Benadryl on a coterie train?"

"I just wanted to sleep. Public Works had to inspect this train before it started its service, and Fanny assured me the human car was safe." He blinked, clearly still under the influence.

Fanny was his boss at Public Works, a huge woman who intimidated all who met her, except Zoë, who had seen that she was a goddess nearly immediately. Even Arthur didn't know. (A fact Zoë felt vaguely guilty about keeping from him, but he wasn't as open to working directly with coterie as she was.)

"It clearly wasn't safe against wannabe cowboys boarding the train with guns, trying to kidnap a human," Zoë said. "They shot me and another woman, and would have kidnapped Reynard if he had been in here. But he ran away to his daddy vampire."

Arthur passed a hand over his face. "I'm pretty sure this is a dream."

"No, Arthur. But go back to sleep. I'll yell at you in the morning," Zoë said, sighing. "I need to talk to Gwen."

But they didn't talk. Arthur dozed off, Gwen looked out the window, and Zoë found a new sweater in her bag to replace the torn and bloody one she was wearing and headed to the bathroom to wash up.

She paused in the bathroom to study the gunshot wound.

There was a puckered scar on her shoulder blade, but nothing else. "Is this even really happening?" she asked the mirror.

Zoë was strangely comforted by the utter lack of response from the mirror. Bathroom mirror normality: achieved.

They were in Georgia before the subject of Reynard came up again.

"Why did he lie to me, Gwen? If he's a citytalker, he's likely to want to find more of us, right? Wouldn't he want to recruit me or something?"

Gwen looked up from the window.

"That guy had me fearing ghosts more than I've been afraid of any coterie," Zoë continued. "I thought I'd be possessed the minute I stepped off the train. And what was with those fake cowboys? Does that happen a lot on ghost trains?"

"It happens, especially to ghost trains," Gwen said. "This is one of the few places ghosts can have corporeal bodies, after all. If they can't get jobs, or tickets, or if they just have a desire to sow some chaos, they will."

"But they weren't even real bandits! They were corporate assholes that wanted to play at cowboys and Indians! Or cowboys and vampires."

"They keep the clothes they wore in life, so they are forever dressed as cowboys," Gwen said.

Zoë was tired of all of this. Or perhaps she was just tired. She checked her watch. "Sheesh, it's three a.m. I have to get a nap or I'll be useless tomorrow. Today. Whatever."

"Feel free to nap, I'll wake you if we're attacked," Gwen said. Zoë smiled at her, but realized the goddess wasn't joking.

"You really don't joke, do you?" she asked.

"I'm quite bad at it," Gwen agreed. "Morgen once said I was

so bad at humor that I had looped around to unintentionally hysterical."

Zoë nodded. "I can see that. Think Anna can get me some coffee when I wake up? I don't like the idea of heading to the snack car again."

"I will arrange it," Gwen said. "That first-class ticket should be worth a cup of coffee, after all. We'll be in New Orleans in about two hours, go to sleep."

"Thanks, Gwen. Really."

Zoë leaned back again. She couldn't keep her eyes open. The bullet train moved in a dreamlike motion, more like a ship on a gentle ocean than a swaying and rackety corporeal train.

Are you an idiot? Wake up!

Her eyelids snapped open, but felt as if weights were attached to them. The train had stopped, but it was still dark outside. "What? Where—Oh. Atlanta." She knew it instinctively, the city's personality was all around her, she could nearly taste the flavor of Atlanta, metal and heat and activity, a soft peach with a sharp aftertaste. "What's wrong?"

There were no more words, just a strong taste of fear. Zoë shook her head to separate her own feelings from those of the city.

"Atlanta is really worried for me," she told Gwen, who watched her with interest.

"The final purge was in Atlanta," Gwen said. "I wouldn't be surprised if the city was perpetually paranoid for citytalkers. We're probably safe here."

Zoë sat with her back to most of the car, and heard the zoëtists come aboard. The emotions and warnings of Atlanta were nearly overwhelming, and the people behind her, handling bulky luggage and snapping at each other, were secondary.

"I get it, I get it, please stop," she muttered, holding her head in her hands. The city gave her the tangy taste of anxiety and the secure warmth of secrets, none of which Zoë could differentiate from the others.

When the train started up again, she breathed a sigh of relief as they left the heart of the city.

"That's her," came a whispered voice, high and girlish. Zoë closed her eyes, dreading the next encounter. She opened her eyes when she felt a small touch on her shoulder.

She opened her eyes and nearly leaped out of her seat when she saw a little humanoid about six inches tall and made of dirt perched on the back of her seat. It held a daisy out to her with one chubby hand, and moved its other arm to its head, where it made an attempt to pull off a hat, but the hat was made of the same material as its head, so it just feebly tugged at it.

Zoë laughed at its attempts at politeness and took the flower. She looked behind her and was startled to see a young boy smiling uncertainly at her. He had sandy-blond hair and freckles and looked to be about eleven. She glanced at the little golem, which was shimmying down the edge of her seat to the floor, and then back up at the boy. "Do I thank it, or you?"

"Uh, me, I guess," he said, coloring. "Mom told me to give it to you. I mean, I wanted to, too, just that she told me what you did for our friends. You fought for them. Without golems." His eyes were shiny, and Zoë realized he thought she was a zoëtist.

"Oh, well, yeah. You're welcome. It was nothing, really," she said, realizing that she had been shot trying to defend these people, and it actually was a pretty freaking big deal.

He leaned forward over his seat, his eyes wide. "Mom said there were *ghost cowboys*, is that true?"

Zoë winced. "Sort of. They were the ghosts of people who wanted to be cowboys. But the guns were real enough. They were really kind of sad, but dangerous anyway."

"Was it exciting? How much did you fight?" he asked.

"Galen!" The call was sharp, and brought him up short. He bowed once—he *bowed*—and turned back to the group of women he traveled with, his little golem jumping off the back of Zoë's seat and lumbering up the aisle to him.

Zoëtists were almost exclusively female; the fact that there was a young boy learning the art was interesting. Zoë made a note in her book to ask Ben about how genetic the gift was, and if most boys went without it. She had come to believe it was a learned magic, but from what Gwen had said, it had a hereditary aspect.

She thought of her birth parents, and how she wanted now to know them even more than ever. She had been adopted as a baby, and her parents had told her that they adopted her from a young teen mother who had signed away all rights, including the right to contact Zoë in the future. The documents were sealed, and her parents had told her enough about the girl that Zoë hadn't wanted to know her. They let her know that she had escaped an existence of drugs and poverty, of prostitution and disease. They'd never said her mother was a prostitute, but had implied as much. She had never much liked the idea of being born to a teen prostitute, and on bad days she hated her birth mother, but on more generous days pitied the girl her mother had once been.

Never had she questioned the truth of the story. But now that she realized one or both of her birth parents were likely talkers, and very possibly had been in hiding after the final purge, it seemed a more insistent reason for putting her up for adoption than not being able to afford a baby. She wondered if her adoptive parents knew. Probably not; few regular, non-coterie humans knew of the coterie and their skills. And the coterie world liked it that way.

"Ma'am, I'm Beverly," came a shy voice, breaking her from her reverie. "I'm Galen's sister, and I wanted to thank you as well for caring for our aunt."

The girl was clearly related to Galen, tall and blonde, lanky but starting to look like a woman. A little person made of newspaper sat on her shoulder and held on to her ear, waving at Zoë with its arm.

"You're welcome. It really happened so fast, I'm just glad no one was hurt badly. And thank Eir." Zoe pointed across the aisle at the goddess, who had collapsed on the table in front of her. "Well, thank her when she wakes up, I guess. Where are you heading?" Zoë asked.

The girl smiled shyly. "New Orleans. Are you attending the festival?"

They thought she was a zoëtist, Zoë remembered. "I thought I might," she lied, smiling. "I have relatives in the area, so it seemed a good excuse for a visit."

The girl nodded. "I hope you visit Café Soulé in the French Quarter," she said. "My other aunt owns that, and she's the most powerful in my family." She dropped her voice and leaned in. "But don't tell my mom I said that."

Zoë grinned and promised to check out the restaurant, and made a note of it in her notebook. "Any night I should visit?"

"Wednesday nights are best, actually. The human crowd is always told there's a private party, and the coterie come out." She glanced back at her traveling companions. "We should be there tonight. Well, if my mom lets us out. She won't let us hang with the real coterie until we're twenty-one."

Zoë thought back to her own youth, and nodded. "Can't blame her, at that. I didn't have any coterie to hang out with and I was wild enough back then." Then she winced.

Beverly caught her mistake. "No coterie at all? Where did you grow up, a cleansed city?"

I am such a terrible liar. And I'm not even sure where the cleansed cities are, so I can't go down that route. Shit shit shit shit shit—"No, my parents just kept me super sheltered. Never trained me. I didn't even know I was coterie for some time. They were paranoid, you know. Grew up in the sixties." She tried to give Beverly a knowing look, and to her great relief the girl nodded.

"My mom was too young to remember the biggest battles, but her mom was on the front lines when the tide turned for the zoëtists. Where did you train, if not with your parents?"

Zoë did not like being the topic of conversation anymore. She was running out of lies to keep straight. So she went for a slight truth. "New York. A man named Ben. Mom told me not to train with a man, but he had some pretty cool stuff to teach me."

Beverly's eyes went wide. *Uh oh.* "Benjamin Rosenberg? He's legendary! He's the last living mentee of *the Doyenne*. Did he teach you his secret spells? Are you looking for a mentee? I don't eat much, and I can handle mud, paper, air, and plant golems."

The girl's newspaper golem on her shoulder was jumping up and down, reflecting her excitement, and the girl tried to sit in the seat across the aisle from Zoë, beside Eir, but her mother called her back sharply. Beverly's face fell. "I'll be right there, Mom," she said. Then, lower, "Still, I want to talk to you and learn what I can, OK? No one knows what Ben Rosenberg knows, and they say that centuries of knowledge will die with him."

Zoë waved at her as she left, and then leaned over to poke Arthur. He grunted and opened an eye.

"We being attacked?" he mumbled.

"No, but—"

"Then it'll wait. Can't think straight anyway," he said, and went back to sleep.

Zoë sighed in frustration. She felt he might want to know that the loss of Ben would mean the loss of centuries of knowledge, like, possibly, how to keep a zombie bite from festering.

Atlanta to Pensacola was, unbelievably, nothing to write home about. The bullet train stopped for a lengthy break because several people were going to catch the other ghost train, the Kasumi, which provided service up and down the state of Florida.

Zoë didn't get a good sense of Pensacola's personality. She got several images of basketball for some bizarre reason—to her knowledge, Pensacola didn't have an NBA team, but basketball seemed to be the only thing it thought about. She didn't even know if the city registered her arrival.

Not every city was easy to figure out, she guessed. Well, none of them had been thus far.

Zoë managed to doze for an hour between Pensacola and New Orleans. She woke up, startled, around five a.m., when Gwen said her name.

"What?" she asked, rubbing her face and reaching for the cup of coffee that sat in front of her on the table. She was beginning to enjoy being waited on by a ghost who had taken a liking to her.

Damn that lying snake Reynard, anyway.

"We will be there soon. We will need your leadership when we get off the train. It would be prudent to have a plan, as I anticipate Kevin will want to challenge your leadership now that we are far away from Phil. He is still angry that you summoned him during the robbery."

"You think?" Zoë grumbled. "I hate that guy."

"So do you have a plan?" Gwen asked.

Instead of answering, Zoë looked around the car.

The thralls had not changed at all from the beginning of the trip to now. Even during the ghost attack they had sat passively. The one Zoë had landed on after she was shot sat, blood all over his jeans, his blue eyes staring blissfully out the window. She wondered if she ought to tuck a hell note into his shirt pocket to cover the dry cleaning bill.

The zoëtists had fallen asleep, leaning against each other. Zoë thought for a moment they looked like a pile of puppies, and envied their familial bond.

Her adoptive parents hadn't been terribly physically affectionate. They'd hugged and kissed her, but Zoë had almost sensed a mental clock hanging above them, marking the proper time that a hug should go, or a cuddle. And anything longer would get stiff and uncomfortable.

The ghost porter, Anna, was walking through the car, alerting people that they were nearing the end of the line. She paused and smiled at Zoë, and Zoë smiled back.

"Thanks for the coffee," Zoë said.

Anna smiled. "My pleasure, ma'am."

"Zoë, please. Call me Zoë."

Anna nodded and continued through the train car.

Zoë turned back to Gwen. "My plan is what it's always been. My priority is to make a good book." She frowned, and reconsidered. "OK, my priority is to stay alive. But after that, it's to make a good book. If Kevin is against either of those plans, then I will have to deal with him."

"And you're prepared to do that?" Gwen asked.

Zoë nodded. "If I have to be. I'm pretty sure knowing that he's a coward will be in my favor."

The zoëtist children were now awake and packing up their tablets and game systems, and Zoë caught the young zoëtist

Beverly's eye as the girl made sure she had all her things. *Café Soulé*, the girl mouthed, reminding Zoë, and Zoë the Liar, Zoë the Not-Zoëtist-Despite-Her-Clever-Name, nodded and smiled.
I really need to come up with a better lie.

She wished she could see outside as the train shot into New Orleans, but it was still well before dawn when they came to New Orleans Union Passenger Terminal. Zoë stretched and got up, shouldering her satchel and removing her luggage from the overhead rack.

Arthur had finished her coffee and was grumbling something about a shower. She ignored him.

Anna walked by again, and smiled shyly at Zoë. "I would really love to talk to you more, can we arrange that? I'll be in the city for four days on vacation."

"That sounds great," Zoë said. "I'm meeting that girl Beverly at Café Soulé, maybe you can meet us there? Tonight?"

Anna looked delighted. "I'd like that. There is one way I can enjoy food, and tell you everything I know about being a"—she glanced around at the chattering zoëtist family, and lowered her voice—"talker. But you might think it's a bad idea."

"Hey, try me, you never know."

"Well, in order for me to eat again, and to share everything I know with you, I'd have to, you know." She looked to the side and didn't meet Zoë's eyes. "Possess you."

Zoë felt her face freeze. "Let's talk about that when the time comes, OK?" she said.

Anna nodded and went back to work, but Zoë didn't miss the disappointment on her face.

*　　*　　*

Even though she had politely turned down the young ghost's offer, and even though she trusted Gwen and Anna's assurances that ghosts wouldn't just leap into her and kidnap her the moment she stepped off the train, and even though Gwen and the very groggy pair of Arthur and Eir were right behind her, Zoë still stepped from the bullet train with trepidation. She felt her wits remain with her, and took a deep breath.

That's when New Orleans discovered her.

She was immediately assailed by sensations: heat and humidity, even though it was January, hurricane-force wind, the sound of jazz, and an immense sense of stability and comfort. She stumbled slightly and grabbed onto Eir's arm.

"Editor, excuse me, I do not need to be assaulted on our first working day together," the goddess said, setting her back on her feet as if she weighed nothing.

"Glad to see you're back, Eir," Zoë mumbled, trying to clear her head. Slaves and riverboats and madams and charlatans and a deep undercurrent of magic. The ground practically vibrated. One clear thought came through, and then was gone.

Hello? Ida like to bid y'all welcome.

CHAPTER 11
Lodging

Freddie's Ready Bed-and-Breakfast

Freddie is always ready. In fact, that's his name, Freddie Who's Always Ready. He runs Freddie's Ready B and B and will have your every need catered to, even before you get there. Vampires will have light-tight rooms, zombies will have dehumidifiers, elemental spirits will have the proper living arrangements (he even has a room that is nothing but tubs for various water-loving coterie). His breakfasts suit everyone, and he even has a deal going with some citizens of the town for fresh blood donation and brain delivery. Each sleeping arrangement we encountered was superb, and Freddie was always ready with anything our team needed, from a first aid kit to a spare phone.

Freddie has had a fascinating past, and if you can get him to slow down for a moment, he'll tell you about his grandfather, or his poetry, or the time he fought Muhammad Ali (and won).

Just don't ask him about his great-great-grandfather. ∎

CHAPTER SIX

They met up with the rest of the writing team, Kevin steadfastly ignoring Zoë. She had intended to thank him for deciding that saving face and therefore her own life was more important than running like a coward, but she thought he might not appreciate attentions right now.

New Orleans in the early morning was quiet, even the last partiers finally sleeping, or passed out, by five a.m. The train station filled with coterie, and some black-windowed taxis waited at the curb.

Some coterie waited in the lobby to welcome friends or relatives, and it struck Zoë as odd to see zombies shuffling forward, arms outstretched for a hug. Zombies as a rule didn't like touching humans—you never shake hands with a zombie—but apparently that didn't apply to other zombies.

(The exception to the rule was if they planned on eating someone, but that was pretty obvious.)

"So we should get two cabs," Zoë said, pointing at the vampires and Bertie the dragon for one, and herself, Arthur, Gwen, and Eir for the other. "Daytime walkers, let's meet at noon, nighttime folks, we'll meet after sundown." The two groups headed for two different cabs, but Arthur didn't move.

"I'll get my own," Arthur said.

Zoë stopped walking. She nodded to Eir and Gwen and told them to go on without her.

She turned. "OK, why? We've sat six in a cab before and you were even angrier at me then than you are now. Not that I'm real clear on what you're mad about."

Arthur had said few words since he woke up, but that was probably due to the Benadryl effects. So she had told herself.

"You are here to write a book. I'm here to find someone who can save my life. If I go with you to your hotel, we'd just get in each other's way." His eyes flicked to Opal and Kevin, giving their baggage to a tall wood sprite to put in the back of his cab. "And besides, I try not to sleep in the same building as vampires. I don't have the same death wish as you do."

"Death wish? *My* death wish?" Zoë took a deep breath. "Listen, we need to talk about this. I need to know why you drugged yourself to the gills last night. And I'm pretty sure I won't be in your way if I am helping you find the Doyenne or whoever took over her research. If you go, it's just going to make things tougher for both of us."

"I respected you when you said you wanted to keep working with monsters," he said, his voice tight. "You need to respect me when I say I want to sleep in a monster-free building. I need to get some sleep, and so do you. Call me if you're free for coffee or something this afternoon."

He turned and went walking past the coterie cabs, clearly looking for a human-driven cab.

"You still haven't answered the Benadryl question!" Zoë called after him. "Damn."

Her team was gone, and Zoë halfheartedly waved at a cab driven by a group of green-and-gold-wearing leprechauns. Four waited outside the cab to grab her suitcase, two held on to the steering wheel, two hopped from the driver's seat to work the pedals, and all of them waved cheerfully at her.

"Uh, how do you guys not crash?" Zoë asked as she took the back seat.

"We rely on luck, and Darby's our veteran up there," said one of the little women who had helped carry her suitcase, now perched on the headrest of the driver's seat. A little man with a white beard, presumably Darby, waved at her from the steering wheel. "Darby's been driving for five whole weeks!"

Zoë's cab pulled up to the bed-and-breakfast, a brownstone one block outside the French Quarter. She frowned: each window she could see was covered only by white curtains. She wouldn't cry if Kevin caught fire, but she didn't want to be down one writer because of the wrong hotel booking.

She paid the leprechauns one hell note apiece and gathered her luggage. She steadfastly did not think about Arthur as she climbed the three steps to the stoop, and then her not thinking about Arthur was interrupted when the door was swung open by a tall, grinning man with light-brown skin and a golden front tooth. He opened his arms and said, "Hello there, I'm Freddie Who's Always Ready, and this is Freddie's Ready B and B. You must be the last of the writing team, and you're a human, but that's OK by me, I got a real nice human room set up for you. The rest of your team are already in their bedrooms, the vampires down for the day, the others just getting the train off of them, I don't care how new the fancy bullet train is, if you travel, you got travel stink on you, am I right? My daddy always told me you got fresh stink on you when you go to a new city, boy! He could scare away the white man, and he once cast a spell that got the police off our porch and they never come back. He gave me, a skinny little boy, enough strength to fight Muhammad Ali. I'll tell you that story later. Now where y'all from?"

Zoë watched this man with wide eyes. As he chattered he had gotten her bags and ushered her inside the foyer. It was ornately wallpapered in red and gold and had dark wood paneling. He led her up the stairs, and by the time they had gotten to her room, he had stopped talking and was looking at her as if expecting an answer.

"Oh, uh. Born in New York City, moved to North Carolina when I was a kid, and recently returned to the city."

"No'Calana, huh?" he asked, unlocking a white door. "Then you got a taste of the South in you. I mean, you can't make a true Southerner out of a Yankee, I beg your pardon, but as my mama said, you can put a kitten in an oven but that don't make it a biscuit."

"I'm not a biscuit," she agreed.

He led her into the room. It was decorated with antiques: a comfortable-looking hand-carved chair with blue upholstery sat next to a fireplace, a bookshelf of worn, well-loved books stood on the opposite wall. The bed was a king-size four-poster with old-timey curtains blocking the whole thing.

She had a fort! She had devolved to being seven again.

"Is this room to your liking?" Freddie asked, suddenly professional and deferential.

"Oh, yes, sure, it's great," she said.

"Now, you're gonna hear about haunted hotels," he said, pouring her a glass of water from a metal pitcher that sat on a table next to the chair, "but I assure you, the ghosts here are paying customers and I don't double-book rooms."

"Ghosts? What do ghosts pay with? I thought they couldn't have physical items," Zoë asked.

"Some barter, some make deals with humans, some have built bank accounts with the ravens, they make do. They gotta.

"Now, you get yourself some sleep and then come on down for some Freddie's ready breakfast, it'll set you right."

Zoë tried to tip him a hell note, but he ignored it and left.

She collapsed onto the chair. The fire erupted into life beside her, and she just accepted it as a result of Freddie's special skills. The chair was soft and conformed to her body, and she leaned her head back and dozed off without realizing it.

An angry voice. "What the hell is wrong with her, Gwen? I told Phil we can't have a fragile human as our leader! She can't handle ghosts, can't even handle her own boyfriend, how is she going to be able to handle anything?"

A calm voice. "Last December she was fighting to protect the city. Where were you?"

A soft, no-nonsense voice. "He was looting the Upper West Side."

The angry voice. "Fuck you, Opal. That doesn't mean anything. We need her now, and we can't count on her!"

The calm voice. "She will be fine."

The angry voice. "I'm calling Phil."

Zoë didn't want to open her eyes. She felt she was lying on something soft, a bed, and the room was dark.

How did I get here?

Her door opened. She cracked her eyes and was less than pleased to find Kevin standing there, drawing the curtains back, fangs extended, looming over her. His phone was in his hand, and Zoë was sure he was trying to look threatening with it, but he just looked like an angry banker.

"What is wrong with you?" he asked.

"Hi, Kevin," she said, leaning on her elbow to struggle to a sitting position. Her head felt very heavy. "How's your room? I guess hoping you'd opt for a sun-room was too much to ask, huh?"

"Don't give me that," he said. "I want to know if you can handle yourself when we fucking need you. You're in charge here, in case you forgot."

"Stop, your concern is unwarranted and might make me think you like me or something."

He hissed at her.

"We are just concerned, Zoë," said Opal, standing behind him, looking almost demure even though she was the dominant in the relationship as Kevin's sire.

Gwen stood, silent in the doorway, with Eir looking over her shoulder.

"So you think I can't handle myself if ghosts rob us. You think I'm going to die if I get shot." Zoë rubbed her shoulder, wondering if the ache would always be there. Then she decided to be honest, as far as she dared, anyway. "Yeah, if I get shot, I'll likely die. If something big is going on and I can't handle it, yeah, I'll call for help. Show me someone who doesn't do that, and I'll show you someone who doesn't have long to live."

"That's not what a leader would say," Kevin said.

She sat up and crossed her legs under her. "OK, you win, Kevin. Go ahead and call Phil for me and tell him that after intense discussion with you, I've decided to quit."

Doubt flickered in his eyes. Zoë was under Phil's protection, and verbal bullying was about as far as Kevin was allowed to go. If Kevin harmed her, Phil would react rather violently. Zoë didn't know what Phil would do if he found out Kevin had bullied her into quitting, and by the look on his face, neither did Kevin.

Bluff called, Kevin whirled on his heel and left the room, shouldering past the others and almost knocking down Opal, who followed him.

"So glad our trip is starting out well," Zoë grumbled.

She sat up straighter and attempted to clear her head. She had a dim sense of the city's presence, indignant and demanding that that vampire respect her or else.

No, I'm not killing my coworker, even if he is a prick.

The door opened again and Gwen came in, followed by Eir. "What time is it?" Zoë asked, looking at her phone to answer her own question. It was ten in the morning.

"I came in, fell asleep in the chair, and then woke up here." She squinted at the window, which had light curtains allowing the daylight to filter in. "How could Kevin come in here anyway? It's daytime."

"This is a most remarkable bed-and-breakfast," Eir stated, settling her huge frame into the antique chair that suddenly seemed much bigger to accommodate her. "It suits each guest. If a vampire walks into the room, the windows go black. If you need sleep, it will get you sleep."

"Never mind that I didn't really want to sleep right away," Zoë said, shrugging out of her jacket. "What bee crawled in Kevin's scrotum?"

Eir looked alarmed. Zoë sighed. "Figure of speech. Why is he so angry?"

"Kevin's mostly mad that we insisted on giving you the big room because you're the boss. The fuss about the train was just his way of trying to show you weren't fit to be the boss."

"I'm the boss till Phil says otherwise," Zoë said. "Someday I'll make him realize that. Or die trying."

She had meant it to be a flippant remark, but it sounded too likely for comfort.

"We will hope it doesn't come to that," Gwen said. "The vampires have retired, and Bertie is napping. Eir and I were biding our time until you contacted us. She wanted to show me some of her favored places. Should we explore the city?"

Zoë felt like an odd third wheel, the one without godlike powers, but she nodded. "I'll do my own exploring and we can catch up with each other later."

*   *   *

Zoë walked with her head down, thinking she was like Ariadne from the Greek myth. Then she realized Ariadne had very likely existed, and it sounded as if she had been a citytalker. Zoë had exited the house without speaking to anyone else, glad to go out into the morning sunlight where she knew Kevin couldn't follow—also glad to avoid Freddie and his machine-gun chatter. She imagined she could feel the vampire's eyes on her back, but knew—or at least was pretty sure—he would fry if he looked out the window at her. Unless the house somehow let him.

She walked with her head down because instead of using her eyes, she wanted to use her fledgling citytalker abilities to tell her where to go.

"Please understand I'm new at this," she muttered. After a few blocks into the French Quarter, Zoë had no idea where she was, but noted that the streets were cobblestone and the sidewalk cracked. She picked a direction at random and started walking.

"Can you communicate with me?"

The sensation was of an affirmative flavor, but Zoë got a distinct sense of a grandmother sitting on her porch, rocking and waiting.

The city wasn't going to work too hard to connect with Zoë. She had to do the work.

"I'm not clear about what I'm doing, you know. I know of two other talkers, and one isn't so much dead as . . ." She thought of a good way to describe Granny Good Mae. "I guess she merged with the city. It was a whole thing."

Silence and patience again.

"The other one, well, he's a dude I can't trust at all. So I'm not going to be asking for his advice."

She turned down another street at random, seeing people in

her periphery. Trucks and cars lumbered carefully down the narrow streets, and a zombie snoozed in an alley.

She felt a sudden burst of inspiration. "But I came here specifically to meet you, and write about you. Not enough people know how wonderful you are, and I'm here to talk to you and tell them all about you."

Interest sparked.

"But I need your help; can you help me? Can you tell me the best places to go for blood and brains and where to sleep and the best Carnival parties?"

A bleary-eyed white guy wearing a Dartmouth sweat shirt obscured by ropes of plastic beads passed her on the sidewalk and looked at her with alarm, but then shook his head and went on walking.

Cats.

"Cats?" Zoë asked, doubt creeping into her voice. "Which cats?"

Zoë looked up and saw the street had widened into a courtyard that contained a small park surrounded by a wrought iron fence. A statue was in the center, a man on a rearing horse. Zoë had a dim memory of a rearing horse meaning that he had died in battle or something, but she wasn't sure. Circular paths wound around the statue, and flowers and decorative bushes bordered the paths. The street she had walked on had emptied into the courtyard that surrounded the fence on three sides, Decatur Street and the river bordering the fourth. In the courtyard, artists and fortune-tellers were setting up their tables. Zoë jumped when the tall white church behind her with a bell tower began to bong out the half hour. Ten thirty, she realized, and then noticed how hungry she was. She had forgotten Freddie's promise of breakfast.

"I don't see any cats," she said, and was startled when an audible voice answered her.

"You won't, not during the day. The cats only come out at night." The speaker was a tall African American man in a gray suit. He leaned on the cane in his left hand and held a briefcase in his right. Black leather gloves covered his hands and a gray wide-brimmed hat shaded his face from the weak winter sun.

"Oh, thanks," Zoë said, blushing. "I'd just heard there were cats here."

"Cat person, are you?" the man asked, shifting his attention to an empty table at the corner of the courtyard by the fence.

"Not really," she said. "Was just interested, I guess."

"Come back to Jackson Square tonight. You'll see them." He opened his briefcase and began unpacking things, an old tarot deck, a pair of black dice, and a small statue of a dancing old man. "And they will see you."

"Thanks. I'm Zoë Norris, I'm writing a book about New Orleans. Can I ask what you're doing out here?"

She saw a flash of white teeth as he grinned. "Isn't it obvious? I'm making coffee."

"Uh-huh," she said, smiling back. "I like mine Empress-flavored."

He drew the top card from the tarot deck and slapped it down. An African queen stared up at Zoë, and at the bottom the words THE EMPRESS stared up at her.

"OK, that's impressive," she admitted.

"Wasn't me," the man said. "Was the cards. Looks like I gotta do a reading for you."

"I'm game," she said. "What did you say your name was?"

"I didn't," he said, and made a show of carefully sitting down in his chair, favoring his left foot. He reminded Zoë of a spider carefully settling itself in the corner of a web to wait patiently. A shiver ran through her.

He looked down, staring at the Empress card long enough to make Zoë fidget. He looked up at her, tilting his head back far enough for her to see his eyes. She wasn't surprised to see they were glowing golden under his hat. "I don't need to read for you," he said. "She already waiting to tell you all you need to know. Ain't she?"

Why did everyone seem to know about Zoë and her secret? Her stomach tightened. "I'm not sure what you mean."

He smiled at her, a touch of sympathy in his eyes. "Careful with our little girl. She been hurt bad with the storm, ain't been the same since. But you not the one I sent for, is you?"

Zoë frowned. "Sent for? OK, I was evasive before, but now I really don't know what you mean."

"Never you mind. Although there are some interesting things going on now that you're here. Interesting as all get-out. I'm keeping an eye on you, Zoë Norris."

"OK," she said, completely lost. "Thanks, I guess."

He turned over another card. "The World," he said. "You got a real sense of journey and place. Here's a bit of free advice, Zoë Norris. When your power is tied to a place, you stay in that place to be safe. Don't leave your power behind, then you have nothing."

"Who are you?" she asked.

"You don't want to know my name, child. I'm just a man who lost something, just like everyone else. We all lost something, ain't we?" He gestured down the row of tables, then at two men, one carrying a trumpet and the other a tuba, and finally to a street statue, clad in black paint and gold glitter, who stood perfectly still, a silver trumpet held close to his lips and his eyes closed.

"Thanks for the reading," Zoë said. "What do I owe you?" She reached into her pocket and pulled some hell notes out.

"Not a thing, true readings is free. Otherwise they tainted. If you want to do me a favor, then ask her where I can find what I'm looking for."

"Her?"

"You know who I mean."

"Right." Zoë stood awkwardly for a moment, then nodded. "OK then, thanks again. If I find out anything about what you're looking for, I will tell you. I guess I'll find you here?"

"I'll see you again, Zoë Norris," he said, not really answering her question.

"Maybe then you'll tell me your name," she said, turning to walk away.

Great. Another coterie with a secret, that's what she needed. She'd figure it out later. She would look him up, or ask Gwen.

Zoë walked around the garden, noticing the gate was open. She made a mental note to check it out later, but she wanted to see the human street statue. An older white couple walked by wearing thick, garish New Orleans sweat shirts, fanny packs, and white sneakers. Tourists, clearly, marked even more by the travel guide the woman frequently checked before squinting at street signs. The statue changed, dropping the trumpet and picking up a shopping bag with one hand and a handful of plastic beads in the other, a look of determined stress on his face. The couple walked by without noticing him, staring into their guidebook and arguing about whether to breakfast at Café Du Monde or McDonald's.

A pair of women walked by, also clearly tourists but enjoying themselves much more. One stopped to photograph the statue, and he moved lightning-fast again, picking up an old plastic camera and aiming it back at her. She laughed and took a couple of pictures. He moved again, gesturing to her. She frowned momentarily, but then grinned and they exchanged cameras, her real for his fake, and they began to strike photographer poses for the friend, who took pictures with her phone. The women tipped him and walked on toward a large green awning covering many small tables.

The street statue was so covered in paint and glitter Zoë could barely tell that he was African American, and she couldn't identify if he was human or not.

How important was identifying as one of the supernatural beings? Could you just deny it? Zoë chewed on these questions as she walked to the green awning of Café Du Monde. The statue blurred, changing again as she neared. She stopped to look at him. He'd put plastic fangs in his mouth and his face was twisted into a mask of hatred, fangs bared, eyes blazing. He had his hands up in exaggerated threatening manner, and loomed over her.

She sighed. "You're too intuitive," she said, and walked on past. She was pretty sure she wasn't wearing an "A vampire hates me" sweat shirt. But he seemed pretty aware of how Kevin felt about her.

Zoë stopped before crossing the cobblestone street. The smell of Café Du Monde's only menu items, café au lait and beignets, drifted into her nose, and her stomach complained loudly. But she hadn't done any work yet, and had some questions to ask about the city before she got complacent.

She had meant to call Public Works that afternoon, but dropping in was better. It couldn't prepare for her that way.

She made a silent promise to her stomach that she would give it what it needed soon, and pulled out her human smartphone to look up the location of Public Works and double-check the hours of its main office.

Zoë turned to walk toward Canal Street to catch a taxi.

As she passed him, the statue changed again. He wore glasses now, and posed writing furiously in a notebook. His lower lip was trapped in his teeth exactly the way Zoë's was when she thought.

She laughed and dropped a five-dollar bill into his tip hat. She thought for a moment and then dropped in a hell note as well.

CHAPTER 3
City Infrastructure

Public Works

Public Works is uptown, south of Tulane University. You needn't check in with it as in some cities, but New Orleans is unique in that it has a coterie ambassador to Public Works. If you can't get in touch with any of the leading coterie in the city and you need help, you can call Public Works and ask to speak to the coterie ambassador. At the time of this writing, that person is Trey Frumbleton, a vampire made in 1931. He is under a geas to keep your secrets, and unless you are breaking the law, you can get help from the city without having the whole of Public Works involved in your business.

But abide by the rules. After Katrina, the head of Public Works was fired and a new crew took over management, and they are no-nonsense. They are dedicated to keeping the city safe from coterie, and take their job seriously. ■

CHAPTER SEVEN

Public Works didn't screw around.

Its home office was a mansion south of Tulane University in the Garden District, painted a criminal gray so it didn't stand out like the gleaming white Wedding Cake House or the deep-red Hotel St. Helene. It still had pillars holding a balcony over the front door, sharp spires lining the roof, and beautiful stone workmanship. Unlike the rest of the mansions Zoë had seen, it was flanked by small, neat, nonflowering bushes, and no tourists even glanced its way as they walked by.

Zoë walked through the rusted iron gate and saw the front door held a modestly small sign with the New Orleans city seal on it. The building stank of fresh paint despite the run-down look of it.

She opened the door and saw a woman sitting behind a desk, a veritable jungle of houseplants covering nearly every inch of her desk. Philodendrons draped the front of the desk, while a crown of thorns flowered on the bookshelf behind her. Orchids, begonias, and other flowers Zoë couldn't identify nearly obscured the woman, who looked pleasantly out from behind her wall of green. Lamps with bright bulbs shone down from several places on the walls. Behind her, ivy wound its way up a curving staircase with red carpeting. The floors were a brilliant white marble. Antique chairs lined the walls, and a cherrywood end table held an issue of *Newsweek* bearing the image of George W. Bush.

The windows that flanked the front door were covered by heavy black curtains; those were also thick with climbing flowers, morning glories, Zoë guessed.

Her skin broke out in a sweat, and she realized that the humidity was not what one usually associated with January. New Orleans in summer, sure, she knew it was worse than in North Carolina or New York, and it was pretty bad in both of those places. But January wasn't usually the muggy part of the year.

A honeyed voice drifted down the staircase. "Penny, can you check on the paving efforts of Willow Street? We need to make sure they follow code so that the lair of—" The man stopped talking when he saw Zoë, and smiled widely. He descended the stairs as if he were the king of a manor, and she swallowed nervously.

He was over a foot taller than Zoë, with extremely broad shoulders. His hair was white-blond and his eyes a glacial blue. When he smiled at her, Zoë felt her stomach lurch.

"Well, shit," she said without thinking. "An incubus runs Public Works?"

Christian the incubus led Zoë to his office, up the glorious staircase and down the hall past countless antiques to what clearly was a master bedroom turned office. While she was grateful to leave the greenhouse that was reception, she had a clear feeling of being led into a lair by a predator.

The incubus's office held an antique desk on which sat a slim black laptop. Pictures of politicians lined the wall next to the desk, and it was flanked by a small American flag and a small Louisiana flag. The window behind the desk was covered in more heavy drapery. This was all in the sitting room area of the bedroom; the other side of the room still held a king-size bed with four posts and bed-curtains, and the smell of lavender on the sheets made its way over to Zoë's nose. She took the offered high-backed antique chair as Christian sat behind his desk.

"What can Public Works do for you?" he asked, smiling.

"Well, for starters you could go off and have your lunch and I could come back in the afternoon," she said, looking at his chiseled chin instead of in his eyes. "You're a little distracting."

"If I had known a zoëtist was coming to visit, I would have eaten last night," he said. "Most people make appointments."

Zoë took a deep breath and, with one last look at his blue eyes and his full lips, she looked at his desk, fixing on the closed laptop. She was dying of curiosity: two cities, two divisions of Public Works with coterie at the head. That made no sense, but she didn't want to show her hand and threaten the incubus. "You're right, that was my fault. I came to visit on a whim. You have to admit that finding coterie running Public Works is a surprise, though."

"In New York, humans police coterie. Doesn't that seem counterintuitive?" He shifted in his chair and she refused to look at his broad chest in his powder-blue shirt. He must have had to get his shirts tailored specially; he was simply too big to shop at a normal store.

She remembered when the incubus John had nearly succeeded at seducing her, and snapped out of her distraction.

"Well, in one way, it seems odd to have humans handle people who are much stronger than them in several ways. In another way, how can we be sure you'll look after the humans' best interest? Do you hunt the stray vampire or zombie that goes rogue? Do you hunt your own kind?"

The paneling on the wall looked very interesting, and Zoë stared at it as Christian answered her. "We have humans on staff, but because Penny, Trey, and myself are uniquely equipped to understand coterie, misunderstandings like that rarely happen."

"Trey would be the vampire?" Zoë asked, thinking of the heavily curtained windows.

Christian raised his eyebrow. "Yes, he is. So misunderstandings do unfortunately happen, and when they do, we do what needs to be done. This city has suffered too much in the past decade to have our balance disrupted." Only then did she realize his voice was strong and velvety, and she imagined him reading erotica to her.

She took a deep breath. *Never. Again.*

"Why have your human employees not noticed the coterie that are running Public Works?" she asked. "You're not very subtle, to be honest."

The beautiful face of the incubus creased for a moment. "I've been here for nearly a decade now. Nearly."

Zoë nodded, understanding. "So, Katrina."

"Yes. The city was in chaos, and the humans were in a panic. They—they think Public Works turned off the water because of a desire to push the poor—those who stayed—out of town. But it was something more sinister. With the storm came the water sprites, and they dominated the city."

Zoë snorted. "Water sprites aren't malevolent!"

He cocked a silky eyebrow. "How many have you met?"

She thought of the perky, pink-haired Morgen, and dropped her eyes. "One."

He nodded. "Right. Some of the more wild ones like to travel with storms. When they make landfall, they like to raise hell. Most need freshwater though, so when it stops raining, if they're raising hell, the last resort to deal with them is to stop the water supply. The city was under brackish water. Sprites hate that. So Public Works cut off the water."

"But the people still here..." Zoë said, her voice trailing off.

"It did more harm than good," Christian said, nodding. "Police with agendas, poor humans with nowhere to go, rampaging coterie taking advantage. The Superdome was a perfect place for coterie who hate the sun. Vampires had a field day there.

"So, once things settled down at last, the establishment fired the humans in charge of Public Works. A bit of politicking happened, and I got put in as the new head. I kept on a lot of the humans still employed, but brought in a few coterie that I trust."

"The establishment," Zoë said. "Who would that be?"

"Ain't you a sweet thing," Christian said. "I don't know who taught you your coterie facts, but your education is really lacking, and it's not my job to fill in the holes. Well," he paused, looking her up and down, "not those holes, anyway."

Zoë glared at him. "Back off, man. I've got more sense than you think I do."

He spread his hands and looked down, taking his defeat gracefully. "I'm only saying if you have any needs you need attending to, please call me."

"I need nothing so bad that I'm willing to get an incubus hangover from it, thanks," she said.

"The offer remains," he said.

She cleared her throat. "Anyway, I came here to let you know that I am here with a group of five others to research the city. We're going to be writing a travel book about the city, similar to this." She reached down and got *The Shambling Guide to New York City* out of her satchel and slid it across the desk. That she removed her hand from the book before he could touch her felt ridiculously like a triumph.

The room was silent as Christian flipped through the book. "This is a brilliant idea. Who created it? Underground Publishing...haven't heard of them."

"We're new," Zoë said. "That's our first book. We want *The Shambling Guide to New Orleans* to be the second."

"I'm honored," Christian said. "Of course, I can't allow you to print that coterie run Public Works."

"What? Why? It's really important for visiting coterie to know!" Zoë was so startled she looked him in the eye and immediately regretted it. "And besides, if they see you, they'll know immediately. You don't hide that this is a good place for coterie to work."

"You make it sound like coterie make visiting Public Works part of their vacation plans in a city. I can assure you, the majority of resident coterie don't know."

"But why?"

"If coterie knew that we controlled Public Works, they would use it to their advantage. At least, some of them would. It's safer for us to remain as hidden as possible. Just like normal coterie."

So not every coterie knew that Public Works had a coterie boss, she thought. Interesting. "If your secret is important, you can trust me with it," Zoë said. "I wouldn't want to undermine the structure of the coterie police force."

The incubus smiled, and Zoë got the feeling that honey was smeared on his lips, and all she had to do was taste it. "I'm so glad you see it that way. Thank you for letting me know about our visitors. I hope you enjoy your time in the city."

She dropped her eyes and took a deep breath. Damn incubi. She couldn't trust them as far as she could spit a dead cat. "Thanks. Is there anything I should know, or anything you can suggest for us to see, or avoid, for visiting coterie in the city?"

Christian tapped the dimple on his chin in thought. "It's Carnival season. Obviously it's not as crazy as Mardi Gras, but there are balls and parades from now until Lent. You should of course start there. But all of the masquerades are invite-only, so it would be a trick to see them from the inside. However." He winked at her. "The average tourist is unlikely to get an invitation, so I suppose you don't need to cover that for your book. Be sure to catch the parades, at least half of them are put on by coterie. Carnival is the best time of the year for coterie to visit, half of us can walk out in the open without fear."

"Would you say New Orleans is the best place for coterie to visit in terms of being out in the open?"

He laughed, and Zoë nearly swooned. She had to get out of there. "I'm obviously quite biased, but yes, I'd say this is the best city to visit if you like walking out in the open. It's also the best to work magic, so we're a major destination for zoëtists. I've been calling this the unofficial coterie capital of the US. Possibly the world."

Zoë weighed the pull of his sexual magnetism versus her need to delve into further questions. She sighed and decided on just one more. "Coterie capital, that's good. And where do most zoëtists go for their magic?"

"Most work within the swamps. No one destination, just… the swamps. They know where to go." He looked at her curiously, and she realized she had made a misstep. A zoëtist would have known that.

I'll be investigating the swamps anyway, she thought. "OK, thank you, Christian. You've been most helpful."

He smiled again and stuck out his hand to shake hers.

Zoë looked at his hand, which was distressingly large and strong, with fingertips that looked as if they were ready to slide along the palm of her hand, and then looked at him. "Did you know that humans have a finite amount of willpower? Yeah, so I'm going to respectfully decline your handshake for reasons

I hope are incredibly obvious, and that will be the end of my willpower for the day, so I'm going to Café du Monde to eat all the beignets I can. If you have any more information for me, and you've had a large meal beforehand, feel free to call me. I'm staying at Freddie's Ready B and B."

Christian removed his hand and smiled at her, and she stifled a groan and turned and left the office/bedroom, steadfastly not looking at the bed. She waved a weak good-bye to the receptionist, who was cooing sweet nothings to a particular purple orchid that seemed to reach for her with its flower, and left the office.

By the time Zoë got back to Decatur Street, the crowd at Café du Monde had gotten thick, and she had to wait for a table. She spent the time looking across the street at the living statue, whom she had decided to call Sammy Statue. He continued to pose as passersby, attempting to mirror their lives. Some poses were obvious—frowning at an empty bottle when a drunk staggered by, still ripe from last night's drinking—but some were not so obvious, like hiding his face when a woman in a long black dress walked by.

Zoë blinked. That wasn't any woman, it was Gwen. Her black dress was made of a lighter fabric than she usually wore, and she looked more African than completely ink-black, which made her fit in a little more. She was still barefoot, and her eyes were still like looking into space. No one looked into the eyes of a death goddess, however. She walked unerringly toward Zoë, stepping into traffic without checking right or left. The cars stopped for her without honking.

"Morning," Zoë said, as Gwen joined her in line.

"You look well," the death goddess said.

"I'm doing much better. Had a walk, talked to the city, met a mysterious dude," Zoë said. "Dropped by Public Works. And we need to schedule a trip to the swamps."

"Swamps," Gwen said, frowning. This death goddess fed off dying humans: urban areas and wars were her buffets. Swamps not so much.

"Yeah. Let's sit down, and I'll fill you in," Zoë said.

"Kevin was not happy that you left," Gwen said.

Zoë made an exasperated noise. "What now? I'm not even there to pee in his morning cereal-and-blood breakfast!"

Gwen paused and took a deep breath as an old man wandered by. He was hunched over, but immaculately dressed in a gray suit and bowler hat. His skin was a deep tan and his hair, peeking out from under his hat, was white. Zoë couldn't see his eyes, squinted against the morning light. Gwen focused on him, and Zoë realized she was feeding off him, off the desperation of a dying body. She shuddered. She still had a little trouble with the death goddess's way of eating, even though Gwen assured her that she wasn't actually feeding on the life force, and didn't hurt the person.

When the old man shambled by Sammy Statue, he closed his eyes and solemnly crossed his arms over his chest. Zoë frowned and turned back to Gwen.

"Kevin?" she prompted.

"Ah yes," Gwen said, nodding to the short young white hostess who motioned for them to follow her. "He thinks you're secretly a zoëtist. He's also unhappy about you leaving, mainly because he couldn't follow you and interrogate you further. He thinks you're here for Life Day."

Zoë laughed out loud. "Life Day? Seriously? Is that the zoëtist festival the kid on the train was going to?"

Gwen blinked at her, confused at her mirth. "Yes, it's a zoëtist festival where they celebrate life. Life Day."

Zoë snickered again. "Life Day is the Christmas of the Wookiees in *The Star Wars Holiday Special*, a piece of *Star Wars* history so bad that George Lucas himself has stopped its distribution. I've seen it once, that was enough. Just, well, Life Day. It's funny."

Gwen didn't smile. "You do realize that zoëtists have been celebrating Life Day since the Dark Ages."

"Oh. Well, no. I didn't realize that. I guess there was a zoëtist on Lucas's writing team. Or it's a coincidence. Anyway, I didn't even know the festival existed," Zoë said.

The hostess had stopped at a dirty table, and stacked the dishes and wiped the powdered sugar away with an efficient swipe. Her hair was coming out of her ponytail and she barely met their eyes. "Pedro will be by to get your order. We have café au lait and beignets. You can also have juice."

"People really like places that give them nearly no choice," Zoë remarked, looking at the menu, which allowed for water, café au lait, and two or four beignets.

Pedro, a thin, angular man, came by and raised an eyebrow.

"Café au lait and beignets, two please," Zoë said.

Pedro nodded and walked away.

"Oops. I think I just ordered for both of us, sorry," she said, glancing at Gwen.

"People seem to like rude servants, these days," Gwen said. "I don't understand the appeal."

"Adds to the ambience," Zoë offered, looking around at the green awning that covered them, and into the sunny New Orleans day beyond. They had a clear view of Sammy Statue.

"Why does Kevin have such an issue with me?" Zoë asked.

"You're his boss, but lower on the food chain. You offend him, but Phil respects you and he idolizes Phil. This does not work within his world. In his opinion, why would you respect food?"

Zoë grimaced. "Thanks."

Pedro came by and shoved two plates of powdery squares at them, and two cups of light-brown coffee. He walked away.

"Would you respect that item you're about to eat?" Gwen said, pointing at the hot beignet Zoë was gingerly handling.

"Well, no, but it doesn't really have sentience, does it?" Zoë said, looking at the pastry. "I can at least talk to Kevin and argue with him, telling him he's a dumbass. This little guy isn't going to call me anything." To prove her point, she took a bite, and smiled as the deep-fried glory spread in her mouth, crispy and powdery and light.

Gwen frowned. "You have detritus all over your face now."

"Hush," Zoë mumbled. "I'm having a moment." She chewed slowly and swallowed. "So, the swamps. Arthur is here because if you remember he got bit by a zombie some time ago, and he's lost the herbs Ben gave him." Zoë took another bite while Gwen took in the information.

"That seems more irresponsible than he has appeared," she said.

Zoë shook her head. "Wasn't his fault. His sister tossed them, thinking they were drugs. And Ben is on vacation. We can't reach him. Ben trained here; his mentor was local, so Arthur is going to search for her. Or, since there's a good chance she's dead, we're going to try to find another one of her students."

"This could distract from the book," Gwen said, frowning.

Zoë stared at her for a moment. "This may be hard to understand, but I'll choose Arthur's life over the book. He's important to me. And heck, I'd choose any human's life over my job. It's just a job."

Gwen inclined her head, allowing Zoë her human idiosyncrasies. As Zoë polished off the second beignet, Gwen pushed her untouched breakfast over the table, and Zoë's eyes lit up in appreciation.

"I had a brush with an incubus this morning. I need something to indulge in." She took a bite of the third pastry and felt the powdery snow drift down her chin and onto her jacket.

"An incubus?" Gwen sat up straighter. "Did he attack you?"

"Not as such," Zoë said, taking several napkins from the dispenser on the table and attempting to wipe her face. "Not any more than incubi usually do. Well, that's not true. He wasn't as forward as John was. He just stood there, being offensively gorgeous at me. He didn't try anything."

Gwen relaxed. "Good. I don't like you being around them. You're weak."

The warm feeling Zoë had just barely begun to associate with Gwen—the one where her haughty goddess friend might actually care about her—fled with the end of her statement.

"Gee. Thanks a lot. I am stronger than I was, you know." She hated how petulant she sounded, and stuffed another bite into her mouth, showering herself with powdered sugar again.

"I do not assuage egos, Zoë," Gwen said slowly, as if Zoë were very young. "I speak the truth. You are stronger than you were. But you are still weak in some areas. It is not a bad thing. You have nothing to prove; if you are aware of your weaknesses, you will focus on them and improve on them. If you deny them, then your enemies will use them against you."

Zoë wished Gwen weren't making so much sense. She wanted to feel hurt and wounded, but instead she just felt annoyed. She didn't want to admit that Gwen was right, but it was true that the incubus had affected her more than she had anticipated.

"I didn't expect to find an incubus." She paused, remembering she had promised not to divulge the Public Works secret.

"I didn't expect to find an incubus this morning. That's all. If I had, I'd have been prepared."

"Always be prepared," the goddess said, picking up the café au lait and sniffing it.

"Were you a Boy Scout?" Zoë asked.

Gwen put the coffee down and gave her a blank stare.

"Never mind. Let's just enjoy breakfast and not talk about how incompetent I am for once."

"Agreed," Gwen said.

"I'll want you to do write-ups about the graveyards. I can't think of many other places in the US that are as welcoming to undead as the New Orleans graveyards," Zoë said as they left Café du Monde. She felt a bit slow and thick due to her belly being full of four beignets, but knew that she had to get started on work soon.

"Are you trying to put me on a diet?" Gwen asked.

"What?" Zoë asked.

Gwen frowned. "Because I feed off dying people, not dead people. It's a sort of joke."

"A joke."

"I tried a job change after several thousand years, proving I could grow. So I thought I might try to see if I could gather a sense of humor, like you and Morgen have. I can see it went about as well as I expected it to."

"Oh, no," Zoë said, backpedaling. "It *was* funny, don't get me wrong. I just completely didn't expect it coming from you. You kind of blindsided me."

Gwen thought for a moment, looking down at her feet as they walked. "I thought part of humor was the unexpectedness of it."

"Well, yes," Zoë said helplessly.

"I have much more to learn," Gwen said.

Zoë didn't want to discourage Gwen from growing, but she would have liked a warning about her new experiment with humor.

"So . . . the cemeteries. Can you do that?"

"Of course," Gwen said. Her voice never changed timbre, but she exuded a definite sense of defeat.

"I'm going to set Kevin and Opal on the restaurants tonight, but I'll be checking out Café Soulé on my own. Would you like to come with me? Apparently coterie hang out there on Wednesdays."

"That sounds good. Along with humor, I'm trying to understand why humans consider eating such a social experience," Gwen said. "Speaking with your mouth full is a repulsive habit, and I don't understand how copulation could happen after seeing half-digested food being masticated."

Zoë held her breath for a moment. "Was that . . . another joke?"

". . . Yes. In the way that I do in fact understand that humans find food before copulation a desired thing. But it is not what I myself prefer."

Zoë laughed, mostly in relief. "You're very subtle." She realized she had no idea if the goddess fell in love, or dated, or had sex. It was not really something she wanted to think about. "But yes, we consider eating as a passionate thing, and most of us like to share our passions with people we like. Also we don't like experiencing passion alone."

Gwen inhaled and opened her mouth, as if to speak, but Zoë cut her off. "Please, no attempts at passion-alone/masturbation jokes yet. Start with poop jokes and work your way up."

Gwen closed her mouth. Then she said, "Should I start with how gods excrete?"

Zoë stopped walking. They were back in Jackson Square in front of St. Louis Cathedral, near the now-bustling business at the tables of tarot readers and caricature creators. "God excretion. God shit. You're going to tell me a joke about god shit."

"I was not thinking of a joke. I didn't know if you knew how our physiology works."

Zoë squinted at the morning sun instead of looking at Gwen. "Do I want to know?"

Gwen waved her hand flippantly. "Oh, no, I was just kidding." She walked on, and Zoë sputtered in exasperation and ran to catch up.

"Your attempts at humor are kind of misplaced," she said. But Gwen didn't pay attention to her. She had caught sight of the old tarot reader, who was doing an animated reading for the old tourist couple Zoë had seen earlier. The old woman giggled, her gray New Orleans sweat shirt shaking with her laughter. Gwen stood stock-still about twenty feet away from the reader, waiting patiently.

Death goddesses can wait forever, Zoë thought, as she stood beside her friend. Finally the old man looked up, and his stars-filled black eyes met Gwen's, and he froze. He nodded his head once. She nodded hers. She moved on past him and toward a brass band.

Before Zoë followed her, the old man caught her eyes in his, and she felt lost as if she were falling. She wrenched her eyes away, swallowed the vertigo, and ran to catch up.

"What was that all about? And don't say anything about god shit," she said to Gwen, who was stopping to smell a flower in a storefront box.

"An old friend," she said. "I didn't know he had ended up here. It was good to catch up."

"Catch up? You nodded to him. Was it good to remember how he held his head?"

"Zoë, gods communicate in ways that you can't comprehend. He thinks very highly of you, by the way."

"Who? Who was that guy? He wouldn't tell me."

"A god, a very old god. That's all you need to know," Gwen said.

"I don't know a lot of African gods," Zoë complained. "Most of my knowledge is of Greek and Norse and Egyptian mythology."

"Egypt is not in Africa?" Gwen asked.

"Well, yes, but..." Zoë felt heat rising to her face. "Oh, never mind. No, I don't know the world's pantheon. Also I'm a stupid white American douchebag. How's that?"

"Acknowledging one's own limitations is admirable," Gwen said. "However, I do wonder what he's doing in the city. He's a long way from home."

"He said something about losing something. I have no idea what. He wants me to ask the city, but it's not like New Orleans is very chatty. It's said one clear thing to me so far. And what's so secret about this god anyway?"

Gwen finally turned to face her, and Zoë felt a rare feeling that her friend was entirely alien, a different species altogether. Her eyes were black and starry, glowing like the old god's had, and held the power to grab her and not let her go. "He is a god of both life and death. His name can conjure either. It's safest not to say it at all."

They were interrupted by a shout from an alley. "And there is no God but the one God!"

"That's oddly on topic," Zoë said. "What's going on?"

They looked down the alley, shady in the morning sunlight, and saw a tall white man, a street preacher, a man in a three-piece white suit and a wild white beard who shook the Bible over his head. He looked to be about sixty-five or seventy, with white hair and bright blue eyes. Crazy eyes, Zoë thought.

Noticing that he had an audience, he increased his volume. "JESUS is the real cure!" he said. "New Orleans is rife with sin and evil and the worship of false prophets, give your life to the LORD and he will give you his only begotten son!"

"Didn't he already give his son, like two thousand years ago?" Zoë asked Gwen, whispering. "That kind of gift doesn't get returned."

Gwen sniffed. "That boy was doomed anyway. The crucifixion was a convenience at best. He was determined to be martyred, he wanted to go back to Heaven. He was pretty resentful at being an earthly being." She glanced at Zoë sidelong in a very human way. "More so than most of you."

"Really?" Zoë blinked in surprise. "He wanted to die?"

Gwen nodded, ignoring the man, who began waving his arms as he shouted, trying to get their attention back. "Of course. Dying in defense of what you believe in is the same as dying to save another—you die so something or someone can live on. Those are the noble reasons to die. If he hadn't been martyred, Christianity might not have formed. Judas would have only been the first to lose faith in him."

"This is fascinating. So Christ had a death wish."

The man overheard her and his eyes nearly bugged from his head. "Christ was the one and only messiah!" he screamed. "Christ will come again and lift up the belieeeeevers into the sky and leave the infidels behind! It will come any day now, repent now!"

"Come on," Gwen said. "No one needs to write about this fool. We are wasting our time. The god he's praying to went into retirement years ago."

"Come again?" Zoë said, following her.

"Often when humans suddenly become wealthy, they quit their occupations, yes?"

Zoë nodded. "Sure."

"The god of Abraham is wealthy with belief; he quit his job, left it to his son. He's in retirement. He's not healing the sick or sending hurricanes after the homosexuals the way some of your people believe. If you want weather issues, you need to take it up with the weather gods."

"God's on permanent voice mail." Zoë had never been terribly religious, she more identified with agnostics, with a vague feeling that something was out there, but she didn't know what.

The fact that she now could count gods and goddesses as coworkers and friends seemed to be separate from this agnosticism, and something she didn't spend sleepless nights over, although she knew she could if she tried. Maybe when she found the time.

Still, she celebrated Christmas and the other Christian holidays, and had gone to several Passover seders, and she had a vague feeling of letdown now that she knew that god wasn't even bothering to give a shit.

"That's pretty sad," she said at last.

Gwen patted her arm and they crossed a street, moving away from the cathedral. "There are plenty of other gods who would be glad for your attention. Don't worry about it."

"Don't worry about it. Sure," Zoë said. She felt very odd. Then her eyes got wide. "Um. What about Santa, the tooth fairy, all those supernatural people?"

Gwen laughed then, and Zoë stared at her. It was a sound of deep resonating glee, something she hadn't heard from Gwen before.

"That's funny, I guess," she said, face burning. "But hey, remember where I'm coming from here."

"St. Nicholas existed once, but like all mortals, died a while ago. That's why parents buy presents for their kids and claim it was him. Parents in the US, anyway. Other cultures don't focus so much on him."

God's quit. Santa's dead. "I need a drink."

"It's eleven thirty," Gwen said.

"We're in New Orleans. And I was up most of the night. It's like still yesterday for me. Or something."

"What you need is to walk the city, get to know it, and plan out the book. Then you need a nap. Tonight we can get you some wine and I can tell you the truth about the Easter Bunny."

CHAPTER 13
Dining

Café du Monde ****

Some people say that tourists tried to circulate the joke, "Do you serve beignets here?" "Yeah, we serve anybody," about Café du Monde, but the hostess, a Cajun swamp spirit by the name of Marie, had those tourists boiled in the holy blessed oil that cooks the classic New Orleans breakfast.

Famous for its 24-hour, 364-day-a-year schedule, its limited menu of juice, café au lait, and beignets, and its pushy waitstaff who get paid in pastry whether you stay there or not, Café du Monde is a must-visit. Located in Jackson Square, it's a lovely place for breakfast, but also good for a late-night snack if you wish to watch the cats conduct their business in the locked citadel that is the park across Decatur Street.

Don't tease the hostess. Tip your waiter. And don't use a napkin—wiping away the powdered sugar is considered an insult to the chef, the demon Annie Derveaux. ■

CHAPTER EIGHT

Zoë's phone woke her. She had fallen asleep on her desk back at Freddie's Ready B and B, sketching out the book outline and jotting down writing assignments. The room had, in its inexplicable way, transported her to the bed again. The phone was back on her desk, and it buzzed, making an angry staccato noise on the hardwood.

She tried to leap off the bed but wasn't fully awake, and got tangled in the bed-curtains. Swearing, she reached her phone as it stopped ringing, the fleeting image of Arthur's face disappearing from the screen. He was in his sunglasses and Public Works coveralls, holding his hard hat in his hand and looking slightly annoyed at her. She had insisted on the picture when she got the phone, since she didn't have any of him.

She called him back.

"Hey, Arthur," she said, trying to force the cobwebs from her mind.

"I was leaving voice mail," he said.

"I will remember that when I get a truncated message from you. Sorry I missed your call, I was asleep, and this hotel has crazy bed-curtains and shit. I got tangled."

"I can't find anything out about the Doyenne. Public Works down here was no help at all, even when I asked Fanny to vouch for me."

"You'd think your promotion would have helped that," Zoë

said, thinking about Christian and his evasive comment about the swamp. "What can I do to help?"

"Nothing."

"Listen, let me help, it's going to be OK."

"What if it's not?" His voice was flat and cold.

She paused, and then was honest with him. "Then I guess you have a decision to make."

He snorted, and Zoë couldn't tell if it was from fear or bitter amusement. "Whatever, I just wanted to tell you I'm off to the swamps now, and to not expect me for coffee or dinner. I'll call you when I get back."

"Wait a second, Arthur! You're acting really fucking weird. You're pushing me away, why?"

He had hung up.

Zoë glared at the phone. "I don't get that guy," she muttered. "It's like...shit."

If there was one thing she knew about Arthur, it was that he had a strong desire for control over his own destiny. Spiraling out under the grip of a zombie curse was not a way to die. Dying in an attempt to thwart the curse, that would be preferable.

She tried to call him back, but got his voice mail.

"Dammit, Arthur, you're acting like you've got a death wish, and if you go get yourself killed doing some sort of heroics, just to avoid becoming some horrific undead thing, I'll, well." She tried to think of a good threat to match death, and she couldn't. "I'll tell your family that you were secretly a teen pop fan, and I will go out and buy a bunch of One Direction posters and hang them in your damn apartment. I'm not afraid to fight dirty. Just call me, OK? I'll help you."

Zoë put the phone down and put her head in her hands. "Well, shit. That went well."

She was hunched over the desk, despairing, and didn't see the door open. She did, however, see the light in the room dim as the windows darkened to accommodate a vampire visitor.

It was Kevin. "'A horrific undead thing'? Good to know what you think of your coworkers."

Zoë picked her head up and glared at him. "I wasn't talking about you. And if you eavesdrop on my personal phone calls, you get what you deserve. What do you want?"

The vampire sidled into the room, a sneer on his face. "How was your day?"

"You don't care about my day. What do you want?" she said again.

"Who was on the phone?"

She considered saying, "My boyfriend," or "A dude who's using his misplaced anger on me," or "A future zombie," but settled on "No one."

"Didn't sound like no one."

She spun around in her desk chair, and the vampire actually stepped back. "Look, Kevin, what do you really want? You want me gone, right. Not going to happen. I'm sure my death would please you, but if that happens because of you, you will have to deal with Phil. And you're too much of a wimp to stand up to him. You don't really care who I was talking to, you're just trying to find something else that will get under my skin. But we're here to do a job, and if you're not prepared to do that, then say the word and I'll personally foot the hell notes to get you back on that goddamn train going north. Because I can't deal with your shit for this whole trip. So choose. You can be a scary-ass vampire in New Orleans, embracing all the cliché that you can, or get to fucking work. Now what's it going to be?"

Kevin's fangs elongated. His eyes glowed slightly red in the dusk light.

"Oh please," Zoë said, hiding the cold feeling in her belly with indignation. "I've seen it before. As the folks in the South say, don't pull out your weapon if you don't intend on using it. Are you going to use it, Kevin?"

Kevin snarled at her, but he backed out of the room.

Zoë wanted to collapse into a puddle of nerves, but Gwen swooped into the room. "What did you do to enrage Kevin? He just left the house in a most agitated state."

"I told him he could either be a vampire or a writer."

"He needs to be both. You can't ask him to choose."

Zoë turned her back to Gwen. "Yeah, well, the vampire part of him was focused solely on fucking up my life. So I told him he could be a broody killer who didn't actually have the balls to kill me, or he could do his damn job."

Gwen was silent for a moment. "So you stood up to him."

"It was that or let an employee know he could walk all over me. So yeah, damn right I did." She looked at the book outline on the desk and tried to concentrate on it, but the words were just random markings at this point.

"Good. Now let's go see the cats at Jackson Square. I think you might enjoy meeting them."

"I should go with Arthur," she said faintly. "Follow him or something."

"Do you know where he is?" Gwen asked.

"No."

"Do you know where he is going?"

"No. Swamps, that's all I know."

"Does he want your help?"

"Dammit, no."

"Are you aware that the southern Louisiana swamps span miles, and are not likely to have an information desk?"

Zoë glared at her friend. "I liked your attempts at humor

better when they weren't used to batter me about the head with reality." She put down her pencil. "Fine. Arthur is on his own. Could we get some food, after the cats? I need something soon."

"I keep forgetting that. Yes, all right, cats, then food."

Zoë reached down and got her satchel, checking for her recording devices and notebook. She got her leather jacket and slung her bag over her shoulder while Gwen waited patiently.

"We need to go to the swamps tomorrow," Zoë said.

"I thought you had already planned on it," Gwen said.

"Yeah, well, it's more important now," Zoë said. "If he can't find anything tonight, tomorrow we look. Regardless of whether he wants my help, we have to go out there."

"Right. I can help you find this mentor, if you want the help." Zoë relaxed a bit, grateful for the support. "Thanks."

When they exited Zoë's room, Eir was in the hallway. Zoë felt a sudden pang of guilt—she had been concerned with her own issues all day, the city, then wandering, then napping, then Arthur's issues. She hadn't bothered to meet with her team, or even the new employee.

The goddess had changed to a fresh sweat shirt with NEW ORLEANS on the front, her braid hanging thick over her shoulder down to her right hip. Her arms were crossed, and she looked as if she had been waiting for some time.

"Editor," she said, nodding briefly to Gwen but focusing on Zoë. "Where do we dine tonight?"

"I—uh—hadn't even thought of a group dinner plan. Gwen and I are going to see the cats at Jackson Square, and then to dinner if you'd like to join us. There's a place, Café Soulé."

She nodded once. "I will join you." Like everything with her, it was said with an air of bestowing a great gift.

"Great!" Zoë said, forcing a grin. She realized she had to get to know this goddess, even if she wanted to wallow with her friend tonight. She was at work, after all. "Did you get a chance to get out today? I'm sorry I wasn't around much."

Eir looked straight ahead, her face stony. "I spent the day looking for the old record store where I once worked. It is no longer there. This upset me, so I raged."

Zoë pictured a new crater in the middle of a block where Eir's anger had manifested. "Did you, uh, well, did you hurt anyone? Or anything?"

Eir looked at her as if she had suggested Eir invite Hitler to a barbequed kitten dinner. "I don't *hurt*. I went to the hospital and healed everyone I came in contact with until security found me and escorted me from the building."

"That's an interesting way to rage," Zoë said. Then she realized that healing that many people would likely have affected Eir like a bottle of whiskey. "Are you all right now?"

The goddess nodded once.

"OK, then, I guess we're on our way," Zoë said. "I'll gather everyone in the house when we get back after dinner. We'll go over assignments and schedules. But for tonight, we just enjoy ourselves."

"After the cats," reminded Gwen.

Zoë nodded. "After the cats."

Jackson Square was about as busy at night as it was during the day, with performers contorting and breathing fire, tour groups meeting, and bar hoppers staggering around. The park's gate was closed, however, and though the park itself was lit along the fence, few lights penetrated the middle aside from the lights illuminating the statue.

They walked past a group of people wearing large stickers indicating they were with a tour group (the "vampire tour"—

Zoë wondered if they were going to visit any real vampires), following a tall man in a top hat, black coat, and fishnet gloves.

They approached the park and peeked in through the bars.

"I don't see any cats—" Zoë began, but she saw something move under a bush. And, as if a spell had been broken, she could see dozens of shadows or silhouettes of ears, tails, and legs. The streetlamp glinted off an eye, and one cat leaped to the statue in the center, its body sleek and strong against the sky.

"Wow. How many are there?" she whispered.

"I don't know. I focus on humans," Gwen said, her eyes on the tour group.

"Currently there are eighty-three feline life forces in the park," Eir said, a bit too loudly for Zoë's taste. "More are coming. Many more."

Zoë lowered her voice even more to compensate for Eir's loud voice. "And what do they do there? Do any coterie get involved?"

"Only the cat gods," said a voice next to them. It was said with a heavy Cajun accent, *Ohnlee da cat gads*, and spoken by a stout young African American woman who had sidled up next to them. "You got business with the cats?"

"No, I'm just here to see them," Zoë said. She pulled out her notebook. "Cat gods, you say. Bast, I assume. Who else?"

"Most of the gods is from Egypt, yah?" the girl said. "All of them, I suppose. There aren't as many who visit as before, but the cats still come here. They still call their names." The woman's voice grew sad.

"And you are?" Zoë asked, raising her eyebrows.

"I'm no one," she said.

The woman wore a denim jacket and baggy work pants, with muddy work boots. Her face was round and young, and her hair was a bushy Afro contained under a wide headband. Zoë wouldn't have assumed she was older than twenty.

In Zoë's experience, "no one" could certainly describe a lot of people in coterie circles. She could be a lost god, an ancient vampire who had forgotten her name, or someone under a geas to keep anonymous.

"But you know about the cats," Zoë said.

The lost god waved her hand. "Sure. Everybody knows the cats."

"But most people don't know that they are calling to their gods," Zoë pointed out.

"Well, no, not that. But you can hear them sing."

Zoë's companions were ignoring them, Gwen still fixated on the tour group and Eir watching the cats. Her brow was furrowed as if she was trying to remember something.

Zoë put away her notebook and stuck out her hand to the young woman. "Well, I'm Zoë Norris, I'm working on a travel book for coterie visiting the city. Any information you can give me about the cats would be great."

The woman grinned and slapped Zoë on the arm. "Nah, you got everything you need right here. You got your eyes and your ears. You watch the cats and learn." She turned and ambled away. Zoë noticed that no one in the square looked at her as she walked past.

"The city keeps its secrets," Eir whispered.

The goddess turned back to the park. The cats were assembled on the fountain now, one large, fluffy black-and-white cat moving among them, touching noses.

"It's like…like that one cat is giving out blessings, or greetings, or something," Zoë said.

Gwen finally took her eyes off the group, and her eyes shone black and sparkly. She'd been feeding from the humans. "Or the cat is like you, Zoë. Giving out assignments."

"Huh. Assignments. Maybe," Zoë said. Each cat, after being

touched, would melt away into the darkness of the park. "What assignments would a cat give?"

Eir shook her head. "Not just a cat. Bygul."

"Bye-gul," Zoë repeated. "You know that cat?"

"I surely do. His name in English is Honey. And he is here, like he is every night, because he is looking for his mate, and his god."

"His mate? There are plenty of cats here. Cats don't mate for life, do they?"

Eir turned to look at Zoë, her eyes gold-blue and slightly glowing in the dark. Zoë fought the urge to step back. "These cats do. He and his mate belonged to Freya, my queen, and they pulled her chariot."

Eir spoke with such reverence that Zoë fought the urge to giggle. A cat-drawn chariot. Zoë pictured the chariot staying still, with one cat pulling to the right, and the other one curling up for a nap, with the goddess swearing mightily and cracking a whip.

"I didn't know Freya was a cat goddess. Is she here?" Zoë asked.

Eir shook her head. "I was not entirely honest with you, and I regret this. When I came to New Orleans, Freya came with me. She was hiding from a vengeful rival. She brought her belongings—her necklace and her cats, and nothing else. We tried to start a new life, but Freya couldn't adapt to the area. She didn't like the zoëtist magic or the vampires. There was...an incident. Freya and Trjegul went missing. Bygul had no love for me, so he came to Jackson Square and became leader of the cats here, and works nightly to patrol the city and search for signs of the missing goddess. But I knew she was gone. Perhaps not dead, but definitely not in this area of the country."

Zoë looked at the black-and-white tomcat, who still moved

among the others, touching noses, rubbing faces, hissing on occasion. "Do you think she left, or was she taken?"

Eir didn't answer, and moved away from them and ambled along the fence surrounding the park. Zoë exchanged a glance with Gwen, who had remained stoic through all this. Zoë tried to reach out for the city's consciousness, and was rewarded with a sense of melancholy and an empty room.

"Whatever it is, she's gone now," Zoë murmured. "I wonder if the cat knows Eir is here."

With their missions, whatever they were, the cats faded into the darkness again, leaving nothing but the huge tom sitting at the edge of the statue. He leaped from the base to the boot of the man on the horse, and then to the horse's head, and sat primly, watching the sky.

"Watch this," Gwen whispered with none of her usual gravitas. Zoë glanced at her and then followed her gaze back to the cat and saw that Bygul had grown visibly. Whereas before he had been nothing more than an overly large alley cat, now he resembled something closer to a bobcat or lynx in size. Zoë looked over her shoulder: no one else was watching this bizarre spectacle of the growing cat in the park, but that was par for the course with coterie goings-on.

When she looked back he was even larger, the size of a small panther.

"Jesus," Zoë said, and when Bygul leaped from the horse's head and landed on the ground, he was the size of a lion, and Zoë imagined she could feel the ground shake. The fluffy great cat padded through the park lazily, until it was keeping pace with Eir as she skirted the edge of the park.

"He knows she's here," Gwen whispered. "He wants to know if she's heard anything, and she wants to know if he has. They will both be disappointed."

"Do you know where Freya is?" Zoë whispered.

Gwen shook her head.

"What do you do if you are a goddess and don't want to be found?" Zoë asked. "Or, alternatively, if you do want to be found?"

Gwen pursed her lips and took a deep breath. "Follow me."

Zoë took a look over her shoulder at Eir turning the corner of the park to head toward the lights of Café du Monde. "Will she be able to catch up?"

"Of course."

"Do you goddesses have some sort of magical connection?"

Gwen cocked an eyebrow and pulled something out of her pocket. It was a phone identical to the one Phil had given Zoë. "No, I'm going to text her."

They noticed barricades being erected down the street, and crowds growing. "And the chaos of Carnival begins. Let's watch the parade to give her some time," Gwen said.

Music began floating down the street, and Zoë and Gwen walked to the front of the crowd, people stepping back for Gwen without realizing they were doing so.

The parade began to lumber closer, shouts and music drifting ahead of it.

Zoë leaned over and saw beautiful, tall black women dressed in purple and gold, tossing strings of gold beads into the crowd. They grinned, and Zoë realized they were all vampires. Once she got through that mask, she realized the whole parade was made of coterie.

A strand of beads landed around Gwen's head, and she looked startled.

After them came the band, lanky dancing horn players with

purple top hats. They played marching tunes and danced, and the crowd screamed around Zoë and Gwen. Gwen remained stoic, searching the parade for something in particular, and then she pointed.

"Him," Gwen said, pointing to a grinning man atop a throne on the only float in the parade. Young women and men, fae, according to their frightening, alien beauty, clustered at his feet wearing jester costumes. His face was painted with black paint and gold glitter, like Sammy Statue's, and he nodded and tossed a strand of black, glittering beads here and there.

Zoë felt his eyes lock onto hers, and he grinned even more widely, if possible. She recognized him as the unnamed man from Jackson Square. He poked the back of a male fae at his feet. The subordinate turned and accepted two golden envelopes.

The man jumped off the float and came up to Zoë.

"Ms. Norris. I have a message for you."

"For me?" Zoë felt dumb, staring at the envelope with her name written on the front, in a very beautiful handwritten script.

"Oh yes. And you." He looked at Gwen, handing her an envelope similar to Zoë's.

"A message?" Zoë repeated.

He laughed, booming and louder than the departing parade. A drunken group of frat boys stumbled by, and screamed at Zoë to show her tits, but Gwen fixed them with a stare, and they fell backward, scrambling away as if they had looked death in the face.

"Ms. Norris, this is an invitation. There is a masque tomorrow night. We'd be most honored if you both would join us."

"We would be delighted," Gwen said, taking both envelopes. "Thank you. And please thank the host."

"What was that all about?" Zoë asked.

The float was past Zoë and Gwen now, and more dancers made up the end of the parade. Gwen pointed to a woman dressed entirely in feathers. She was under five feet tall and had skin the color of milk. "Look. A Valkyrie, a sister of Eir."

"Does every city have so many gods, or is New Orleans special?"

"I believe New Orleans is special, but New York has our share. Many gods stay in their home city, but many travel to America, too. That's why we are doing what we're doing."

Zoë winced as a string of green beads hit her in the face. She bent and picked them up, amazed that people went so crazy for these cheap baubles.

She slipped the beads over her head and took the envelope from Gwen. She broke the seal with her finger and pulled out the engraved—*engraved*!—invite inside.

Ms. Zoë Norris and one (1) Guest:

The pleasure of your company is required for January 24, the Year of Our Lord 2016.

In this, our 237th Annual Masque.

Come masqued. Bring an offering. Unmasquing at midnight, then revelries begin.

"I thought these parties were invite-only," Zoë said.

"There *is* your invitation," Gwen said. "Did you need something else alongside it?"

Zoë's face flushed. "Well, I'm not used to men coming up to me on the street and knowing my name and handing me invitations to parties. Everything I'd read said these older parties were invite-only, and tourists should plan for the public parties. Hell, I wasn't even going to mention them in the book, except to say that you shouldn't expect an invite."

Gwen shrugged and headed down the street, lifting her skirts and sidestepping a vomiting woman. "I got one."

"Yes, but you clearly know the host—I guess that's what we're calling him since you don't want to tell me who he is—and I don't. You need to find out why we both got invited. We need to tell our readers what they can expect during Carnival."

"Surely," Gwen said. Her phone dinged, and she glanced at it. "Eir will be joining us. Her meeting with Bygul was less than satisfactory, it seems."

"Like you said it would be."

"Indeed."

CHAPTER 5
The French Quarter

JACKSON SQUARE AT NIGHT

Once the sun goes down, New Orleans transforms. A couple streets up, Bourbon Street is wild with booze and strip joints, but in Jackson Square, things are slightly more sedate. The fortune-tellers go home, Café du Monde stays open for the night owls, the ghost and vampire comic tours meet, and the cats come out.

Led by the Norse cat Bygul, who once pulled Freya's chariot, the cats serve as the eyes and ears of the city. Being cats, they sometimes report to Public Works, sometimes report to the coterie leaders, and sometimes merely share secrets among themselves. They ultimately call to their gods, but Bast hasn't been seen in the city for several hundred years.

You can't trust a cat to give you information, but you can always trust it when it decides to tell you a secret.

Listen to the cats if they decide to tell you something. They know more of what is going on in the city than anyone. ■

CHAPTER NINE

Café Soulé was across the street from Antoine's Restaurant, the oldest restaurant in the city. Two criers stood at Antoine's door and called out to them, waving menus. Zoë squinted at one of them. He was tall and thin, with olive skin and a big smile. His black hair was gathered at the nape of his neck in a neat ponytail, and he wore white gloves.

"Is that a zombie?" she whispered as she waved apologetically at them.

Gwen nodded without looking. "Only one life force coming from that area, definitely. How did you tell? He's very well preserved and fresh enough to be working in public with humans."

Zoë shrugged. "Something about the skin under his ear. Looks a little rotten. So I figured could be eczema, could be something else."

"You are developing a good eye," Gwen said. They walked across the street to Café Soulé, which was in a four-story street block with the street-side wall able to open like a garage door, opening the restaurant to the street. Only it was closed tonight, and a thick, short black man stood at the door.

"Are you sure it's open?" Gwen asked.

"The kid said it would be, to coterie," Zoë said.

When the bouncer caught sight of Gwen, he smiled, showing a gold tooth, and opened the door without comment. He didn't even glance at Zoë.

"Oh. That was easy. I guess," Zoë said, irritated at being treated like the token human again.

The restaurant was small, with one main dining room on the left and a few tables in the bar area on the right. It was empty aside from two women looking bored behind the bar and a third with a full mask over her face. One, a tall woman with red hair, waved at the empty tables. "Sit anywhere you like. Cheryl will be with you in a moment."

Zoë and Gwen took a seat next to the roaring fireplace. Zoë appreciated the heat that drove the clammy New Orleans humidity from her bones.

"I've actually heard about this place, I've been eager to try it out," Gwen said.

"You have been *eager*?" Zoë asked, trying to imagine her friend "eager." Then she paused. "*You* have been eager? How is that possible? You don't eat food."

"And on Wednesdays, they don't serve food," Gwen said. "You should have eaten something before we came."

Zoë opened her menu, dreading what she was about to encounter. The menu read like an obituary column.

1893, William D. Campbell, 37. Died of infection from minor gunshot wound. Catholic.
1964, Mabel R. Greer, 12. Died of smallpox. Southern Baptist.
2011, Hiroko Honda, 72. Died of heart attack. Agnostic.

The list went on. At the very bottom, where human restaurants would have the children's menu, written in a very small print, was FOR ZOËTISTS: CHEESEBURGER. TOFU SANDWICH. COKE PRODUCTS.

Zoë turned the menu over and looked at the back, but saw

only a list of drink options, from seawater to blood types. She groaned.

"I can see your point about how well the human coterie have been respected," she said. "My choices are limited. Remind me to commiserate with my vegan friends more."

"They do have a bar," Eir said, making Zoë jump. The powerful woman had joined them without a sound, pulling out her chair with a smooth, silent motion. She was rigid, more so than usual, which was saying something.

"I don't plan on eating just cocktail onions and olives all night," Zoë said.

The waiter slouched up to the table. Zoë did a double take and then asked, "Uh, are you Cheryl?"

The thick mud golem stood about four feet tall and shook its expressionless head. It pointed its stump of an arm behind the bar, where a dark-haired woman in a white feathered mask shook a cocktail shaker. The golem turned back and gestured with the pad it held in its stump. It turned first to Gwen.

She frowned at the menu. "I've never had souls before, not prepared," she said. "I'll take whatever the chef recommends. You can tell her I'm a psychopomp."

The golem inclined its head a bit, and took its other stump and thumped the pad it held. Its hand left a smear of black mud behind, and it turned its face to Eir.

"Rainwater, preferably pre–industrial revolution."

Zoë stared at them, her stomach making that uncomfortable forward roll it did when a particularly uncomfortable aspect of coterie life revealed itself. But she tried to ignore it.

"Living it up here in the Big Easy, huh?" she asked Eir. She knew from hanging out with Morgen that water bottled from before humanity made machines to mess up the environment was the equivalent of wine that cost hundreds of dollars a bottle.

Eir glared at her. "I don't need sustenance often. When I do, I only get the best."

Zoë spread her hands, fending off her hostility. "Just curious what the occasion was." The golem's head was pointed her way, and she could see small indentations of eyes and a mouth, like those on a child's snowman, on its head. These attempts at making the golem look more human had the opposite effect on Zoë. She shuddered and looked at the menu again. "I guess I'll have the cheeseburger. And something from the bar with gin, I guess. I'll leave it in the bartender's hands."

Another smear on the paper, another nod, and the golem wandered away. It left muddy footprints behind.

"I wonder how the health inspector views this kind of place," she wondered aloud.

"The health inspectors are paid handsomely," Eir said. "They turn the other way during the nights that coterie restaurants hold 'private parties.'"

"Do they know what they're being bribed to ignore?"

"Most don't, no, unless they are coterie working for the health department. It's a good job for the fastidious, like air sprites," Gwen said.

The restaurant was starting to fill up. A family of demons, two zombies on a date, a succubus and her meal, and two drunk vampires.

Cheryl, the masked bartending zoëtist, sent other golems to wait the tables, most of them made from thick Louisiana swamp mud, according to Eir, but one paper golem danced around the dining room, and one that appeared to be made from menus alone presented itself as the menu and waiter to the zombie couple.

Their golem returned with their drinks, the bottoms of each glass pressed into its arm so it carried them as if they were missiles it had blocked during battle. Zoë took her lowball glass, trying to hide her distaste at the mud, but smiled when she sipped the drink. She didn't know what was in it, but it was unlike anything she'd had before. Salty, red, and very cold, served over ice.

Her companions took their drinks, Eir downing half of hers in a gulp. She nodded at the golem for another.

"Did you speak with Bygul?" Gwen asked.

Eir looked at her wineglass that held water so pure, it was nearly light blue. Her cheeks had flushed. It would be a book in itself to figure out what substances intoxicated the different coterie, Zoë realized. Her friend Morgen the water sprite could get drunk off seawater, as she was a freshwater sprite. Vampires got drunk off people with high blood alcohol levels. Zombies could go insane if they ate formaldehyde—something about the preservative would mess with their higher brain power—but she didn't think that counted as drunk.

Regardless, this very old water was having an effect on the healing goddess. Maybe because water equaled life? The goddess was so prickly that Zoë wasn't sure how to ask without offending her.

Eir finally spoke. "I found him, we spoke. He doesn't know where Freya is either. He calls the cats to the square every night, to search for her. He's worried that she is stuck wherever she is, since he isn't there to pull his half of the chariot's weight."

Gwen put her hand out and placed it on top of Eir's. "I'm so sorry," she said.

Eir turned her hand over and took it, squeezing.

Zoë narrowed her eyes. She began to wonder if Gwen had given every single reason she had wanted Zoë to hire Eir. She was surprised to think Gwen might have made a move that was more selfish than professional, but she guessed everyone had their weak spots.

Despite her prickliness, Eir hadn't disappointed Zoë yet. And there was that bit about saving Zoë's life. So she wasn't going to quibble.

At least one of us has found love, she thought morosely.

Zoë's own drink had gone distressingly low. She picked it up, trying to hold it by the clean parts of the glass, and walked to the bar.

She greeted Cheryl the bartender, who turned out to be the woman with her face obscured. How did she see out of that solid white mask? Zoë wondered if she saw through the eyes of her golems.

"Yes, is there something wrong with your drink, ma'am?" the bartender asked, her voice sounding irritated as if she had been talking for some time while Zoë was off in her own little world.

"Yes. Um, no. I mean, what's in this, and may I have another one please?" She quickly downed the rest of the drink and put the empty lowball glass on the table.

"It's a Captain Spaulding, my own concoction. Some gin, a little brine from the Red Sea—pre–industrial revolution—and a little demon blood."

"Demon…" Zoë caught herself. *They'd drink my blood in an instant. One nearly did, if you count swallowing me whole as drinking my blood.* "So what kind of demon?"

The mask shook as the woman laughed. "I'm just fucking with you. Sadly you can't see my wink. It's just the specific kind of gin, that's all. It's a distinctive taste. I'll get you another one."

As she started making the drink, Zoë watched her. "So what causes the red coloring, then, if it's not demon blood?"

The blank face rose to focus on her. "Grenadine," she said after a pause, then returned to the drink. "Tell yourself it's grenadine."

She put the drink on the bar and Zoë looked at it briefly, then took the dare she imagined was coming from the bartender's blank face, and picked it up and returned to her table.

She needed the gin. At this point it was medicinal.

Eir had finished her water and looked a bit more cheered up. More people were coming into the restaurant now, and Zoë recognized Beverly and Galen, the kids from the train, coming in with their family.

Beverly caught sight of Zoë immediately and grinned and waved. She made an apologetic sound to her family and left the table to see Zoë.

"Oh wow, I'm so glad you made it! Isn't this place utterly amazing?" she said.

Zoë took a drink of her Captain Spaulding. "Yeah, great, thanks very much for suggesting it. Eir, Gwen, this is Beverly."

The girl stared at the goddesses, eyes wide, and blushed. Zoë wondered if she saw many goddesses during her day-to-day life. Beverly then leaned into Zoë. "Can, uh, I talk to you for a minute?"

Zoë frowned at her friends, and then at the girl. Her friends were eating souls and she was probably drinking demon blood and gin. The thought of getting up was very tiring right now. The girl's eyes were very wide and she fidgeted from foot to foot. Zoë considered telling her where the bathroom was, and then realized she wasn't that much of an asshole, and besides, she didn't know. Also, she had to go, too, so she figured they could kill two birds with one stone.

She got up, a little uncertain. Those drinks had hit her empty stomach hard. "I'm going to find the ladies' room," she said to her friends. She had to hold back giggling about asking whether they would need to go, too. Then she felt rather stupid.

The girl led Zoë to the bathroom, looking over her shoulder a couple of times. Zoë was struck by how tall she was. There was something about the way she moved: she walked as though she was trying to look much shorter. Zoë had known a woman in college who was six feet tall and who walked with a slump to look smaller, and this girl walked like that.

Beverly pushed the bathroom door open and then checked under the stalls. Zoë put a steadying hand on the wall in what she hoped was a casual way. She could blame the demon blood, but that would mean she was lacking faith in her old friend gin, and she decided to believe the gin could carry her through anything.

"You know, you're really quite striking, you shouldn't be ashamed of how tall you are," she said without thinking. The girl straightened from her peek under the stall door to stare blankly at her. "I mean, I know that's a really rude thing to say, but it's true."

"I—" the girl shut her mouth and then laughed, relaxing against the sink. "No, it's not that at all. You see—" The young zoëtist's form shimmered, then blurred, and solidified again. Nothing had changed in front of Zoë, but she glanced in the mirror and yelled.

Beside Beverly stood Anna, the ghost from the train.

Beverly straightened, her body language taking on a sudden confidence that hadn't been there before. "She was just hitching a ride. She wanted to talk to you, but it's harder now that we're all off the train. No ghost train, you know."

I may be too drunk to deal with this. Let's see. I am still aware of my surroundings, I am capable of rational thought, and I'm not done with my drink yet. Let's go, Zoë did not say to the teen girl in front of her. *Don't drink, girls, it'll mess you up. It'll be the evil pillow to fall on after a bad day. It tastes great. And sometimes you can avoid a hangover. But don't drink. Yeah. That's what I'll say.*

Zoë backed up, looking at the mirror and back at Beverly

again. Now she could see it, a slight break in reality, like a heat shimmer, next to her.

Beverly frowned. "What's the matter?"

"G-ghosts. Someone said. Never mind." *Use nouns AND verbs together, moron.* She took a deep breath, hoping it could clear her mind. "Someone told me possession was a bad thing, and I'm still trying to get used to the reality of it. That it's not. Apparently. Is it?"

Beverly laughed. "If I say she can do it, then what's the harm? She wanted to see New Orleans, I wanted to know what it was like to have a ghost inside me."

She leaned over and narrowed her eyes. "We deal in life, we imbue the earth, the plants, whatever we have the power to, with life itself. She is a spark of life that stuck around after death. I had to see what it was like. Haven't you ever?"

Zoë's eyes didn't leave the shimmering haze. "Haven't I ever what?"

"Wanted to know what it was like to taste that tiny bit of life left over. We draw life from all around but there's real life here, we don't have to draw from it, it's right here. So if we can use it, then it should have a chance to use us, right? I scratch your back, you know?"

Oh yeah. The girl thought she was a zoëtist, and Anna hadn't told her the truth. Zoë's gratitude toward the ghost helped ease some of her fright.

"Oh sure, it makes sense on paper. But giving someone complete control, that's..." Zoë trailed off.

"But God, Zoë, what I get in return..." Beverly trailed off as well, cocking her head and looking at Zoë as if she had never seen her before.

Zoë's booze-addled brain struggled to catch up. She

swallowed. "Of course. I've just heard stories, that's all. I—well, what's it like?"

The girl grinned. "It's awesome. I think my mom once called it euphoria. That means all floaty and happy, right?"

Zoë nodded. The ghost shimmered and then edged closer to Beverly. The girl stepped into the shimmer, and they merged. She lost her posture, stooped over, and refused to meet Zoë's eyes.

"I didn't mean to startle you, miss," she said. The voice was softer, with a slight Irish lilt. "I just wanted to talk to you again. You did mention you were coming here."

Zoë smacked her forehead with a little too much gusto. It hurt. "Right, of course, I'm an idiot. I'm sorry. Yes, I did say that. Look, I'm sorry. I've had a rough twenty-four hours." She paused to count on her fingers. Twenty-four was about right, since Arthur had discovered his herbs had been destroyed by his sister wishing to scare him straight. "The train ride, and the getting shot, and then my, uh, boyfriend or something wandered off when we got here. Demon blood in my drink. Maybe. It's a whole thing."

"Sure, I get it. I slept most of the day myself, we're all fucked up," Beverly said, then clapped her hand over her mouth.

Zoë blinked dumbly at her. *Sure, kid, your nap-grogginess equals my boyfriend's impending zombiedom.* But she had to remember what it was like to be fifteen and have your biggest fear be your parents catching you swearing.

"We shouldn't hang out in here too long," Zoë said. "Your mom is going to start looking for you."

"Yeah," Beverly said. "And I want to see Reynard when he gets here."

Zoë's head swam. "Reynard? You have a friend named Reynard?"

"Sure, he's a zoëtist who is studying with my mom," Beverly said. "He was supposed to be on the train last night but didn't make it, so he flew down. He got in this afternoon and is staying with us in our suite. He's cute for an old guy." She screwed up her face and studied Zoë. "He might be your type."

Zoë ignored the unintended insult. The sink. That was a good place. Water was there. She started washing her hands. "Cool, well, I hope you have fun with your mom's friend. I'll see you around." Her tongue felt thick and awkward as she spoke, and she cursed herself. She had wanted to be sober and angry if she ever met Reynard again, not drunk and scared of a ghost—which was Reynard's fault.

"But we haven't talked," Beverly protested.

"Oh, right. What did you want to talk about?" Zoë asked, drying her hands on her jeans. She hated electric dryers.

Beverly's body language had taken on Anna's. Her stance was less confident, more submissive, *fragile*. "I just wanted to talk to another citytalker. It's been so long." The body straightened up, switching control back, the eyes going wide. "You're a *citytalker*?"

"Shit," Zoë said.

The ghost girl looked immediately crestfallen. "Oh dear, oh dear. I'd promised to keep that a secret, didn't I?"

"You did, and until now I'd figured you were doing a really good job," Zoë said without inflection. She sighed. "Well, I guess that saying 'Three can keep a secret if two of them are dead' doesn't apply here."

"I'm so sorry!" Anna wailed. "I just wanted to talk to you again!"

Zoë held up her hand. "Listen. Let me talk to Beverly?"

The girl stood taller, still managing to look abashed. "I won't tell. I promise."

Zoë nodded. "Right, I'm sure you'll keep the secret as well as Anna did." The girl flinched, and Zoë wasn't sure if it was Anna or Beverly making the movement. Zoë sighed. "Listen, I am sorry I lied, Beverly. I'm not a zoëtist. But from what I'm learning, there aren't a lot of my kind left, and there are still plenty of people that don't want us around. I had to lie. Defense mechanism."

The girl nodded, her head bobbing up and down as if she were being shaken. "I got it. Mom told me about the war, it was nearly over when she was a kid. The zoëtists won, but barely. You guys and the weres got wiped out, or enough of you did to ensure the death of the talents in a few generations."

"And since nonhuman coterie are long-lived, then the people who wanted my kind dead are likely still around?"

Beverly looked uncertain. "I don't know, honestly. No one knows what happened to them. They kind of just blended back into society."

"So it's the KKK of coterie. Take off the hoods and make nice nice at the corner grocery. Great," Zoë mumbled. "Anyway, I'm kind of tired of bathroom confessions. Anna, if you want to talk to me later, I guess we can. If you can find me. Can you still talk to the city?"

The girl took on the aspect of the ghost. "I can hear echoes, like she's calling me, but I can't understand her most of the time. I think New Orleans is hurting, I've never seen a city so... fractured." She spread her hands out, and looked as if she were viewing a shattered piece of glass.

"OK. Well, I don't know how to put this delicately, but Reynard was on the train last night; he just got off in Charlotte instead of New Orleans. We spent some time together on the train, and I'm not real keen on meeting Reynard again, so if you could tell him nothing about seeing me, I'd be obliged. Anna, let me know when you want to talk again. Uh, I guess you can use Beverly." She fished a card out of her pocket and handed it over, aware that she had just referred to a young woman as she might a phone. "Text me if you need to. And remember. The one rule?" Both girls looked at her out of one set of eyes, the expression so blank that she didn't know which one was in control. "Citytalker? Remember? I'm not one? As far as you know, they're all wiped out?"

"OH! Right! That. Totally will keep your secret. And Anna will keep it from now on, right, dude?"

The voice turned on the Irish lilt. "Right-o!"

Beverly paused with her hand on the bathroom door. She frowned. "I guess this means we won't see you at the Life Day celebrations tomorrow?" she asked.

Zoë thought of Princess Leia singing the Life Day song. "No, afraid not. Sorry."

As they walked out of the bathroom, Zoë mentally counted how many people knew her secret, and how many of them were dead. And how that didn't seem to matter anyway.

She mentally asked the city if she knew something about Reynard, but the city was conspicuously silent.

Zoë swore, and then stumbled out of the bathroom.

Reynard sat at a table across the restaurant with the zoëtists Zoë had seen on the train. He sipped a glass of cold pink wine—for which Zoë decided to judge him—and told an animated story to Beverly's mother. A small movement on the table caught Zoë's eye: the woman had constructed a tiny golem made of sugar cubes and was using it to act out Reynard's story. It raised a fork in its fist and brandished it, and Reynard and Beverly's mother laughed.

She tore her eyes back to her friends, and saw a fresh drink waiting for her. Demon blood and gin. *Hooray for Captain Spaulding.* That was all she needed.

Their food arrived when she sat down, and she congratulated herself on excellent timing.

Zoë nearly dove into her burger, but she stopped, the food halfway to her mouth, when she saw what Gwen had been served.

The goddess held a glass flask full of some sort of gas, pearly opaque with lines of purple threading through it. She held it up to the light and squinted at it.

"What—what did you order?" Zoë asked.

"I ordered the soul of a French girl, seventeen, who died after falling off a horse in 1946." Gwen put the flask to her lips and took a sip. Her starry eyes grew wide and she smiled. "I've never tasted anything so good since the Black Death."

"That's...good?" Zoë ventured. Gwen closed her eyes and nodded slowly. "I thought you only ate human desperation or whatever?"

"That is what I survive on, same as how you can eat food that doesn't sustain you but you enjoy," she said, pointing at Zoë's fresh drink.

Zoë tossed back her second drink and started in on the third, taking in this information.

Eir was guzzling her beer stein full of water, some dribbling down her cheeks and into the braid that lay on her shoulder. She put the empty stein down with unexpected delicateness, and dabbed at her face with her napkin.

"So is it...ethical, I guess? to devour another's soul? I always thought that was the mark of someone evil." She finally took a bite of her own hamburger to avoid their looks in case they wanted to incinerate her.

Gwen swallowed and licked her lips. "Not every soul goes to heaven. Not every one goes to hell. Some wander. Think of it like picking up dropped fruit from the ground."

"Fruit. Great. But what happens after you devour it? Is it... aware of what's happening to it?"

"Probably not," Gwen said.

"'Probably'? Doesn't that bother you? A little?" Zoë asked.

Gwen shook her head and took another drink. She finished her flask and put it on the table. She watched Zoë eat, eyes sparkling. "And that cow that died for your meal. Was it aware of what was happening to it? Does it bother you?"

"You did not just compare my soul to a cow," Zoë said without looking at her.

"No, she did," Eir said helpfully.

Zoë felt something pull at her awareness and realized Reynard was trying to get her attention.

"Editor. You often go to the toilet with girls?" Eir asked. Was she trying to change the subject?

"God, you make me sound like a pervert," Zoë protested. "It's better than eating human souls."

Eir sniffed and gulped at her water.

Gwen slowly swiveled her head to look at Zoë. "You sound angry."

"I thought you were just a benign death goddess, and now you're here devouring souls like Cthulhu!"

Gwen opened her mouth, but Zoë held up a finger. "No. Do not tell me if Cthulhu is real. I can't handle that right now."

"You do not object to the zombies eating brains or the vampires eating blood," Gwen said.

"Drinking blood," Eir corrected, studying her empty stein.

"That's different somehow. The body is finite, the soul is infinite. If I die, I can hope my soul continues, while the body rots. But if I'm eaten by some partying god in New Orleans, then that's it for existence. Boom. I'm done. *'Probably.'*"

Gwen placed her palms on the table, and Zoë felt as if reality were shuddering.

I've done it. I've pissed off a death goddess. I'm really rolling crits tonight, aren't I?

"The restaurant is called Café Soulé. What were you expecting?" Gwen's voice was cold.

"I don't know what I expect, ever, when I'm hanging out with you people," Zoë said. She picked up her glass and drained it, and with three drinks on an empty stomach, she stood up and fished in her satchel for her wallet. "Here, just get a receipt so I can expense your meal." She tossed several hell notes at Eir and staggered away from the table. "I seriously need some human companionship tonight. You know, Gwen, I thought you would be the one person I could count on not to eat me. You were my safe place. I don't even know why I work with you guys. Maybe Arthur is right. Maybe I do have a death wish."

She caught sight of Beverly's table, complete with Reynard, staring at her as she lurched from the restaurant, and wondered how loudly she had been talking.

"Sorry, folks, no room for embarrassment tonight, I'm full up on shitty emotions, see," she announced to the restaurant, and pushed the squat man by the door out of the way.

She wished she knew a human in town, someone who lived in the blissfully ignorant world of no monsters. An atheist skeptic, even better. No gods, no souls, no monsters, just cold science. Where did they hang out in New Orleans? Holiday Inn?

Problem was, she was far from home, and she didn't know anyone even in New York who wasn't associated with coterie.

"Christ, I need new friends," she said out loud, and no one on the sidewalk paid any attention to her.

Part of her wondered why Reynard was in the city, was he following her? She should have talked to him. She should have stayed sober and watched him. She should have let her friends know her objections in a less sloppily drunk way.

While she was kicking herself, she shouldn't have moved back to New York in shame. She shouldn't have slept with her boss in Raleigh. She should have studied actuarial science. She could keep going back in her past and figured if she tried hard enough, she could send some self-loathing back to her five-year-old self for her destructive choices.

Zoë felt a strange sense of belonging, realizing she was a stumbling drunk on a sidewalk in the French Quarter. She was clearly underdressed, completely without masks or finery, but at least she matched the inebriation of the crowd.

"Hey, Zoë," came a voice behind her. It was male, and she whirled in fury, prepared to fire Kevin on the spot if he even looked at her funny.

It was Reynard, looking at her with eyebrows raised. "What the hell went on back there?"

Zoë weighed many responses, but just decided to walk away.

He followed. "I guess you figured out that I lied to you about the ghosts. Listen, can I please explain, and then you can decide if you hate me or not?"

"I'm really not wanting to hang out with anyone involved with that world right now," Zoë said, waving her arms vaguely and nearly knocking a tall woman's mask from her head.

"Let's get a cup of coffee. I'll explain. Then you can continue with your rampage through the streets and find some interesting shoes to vomit on," Reynard said, pointing at a restaurant on the corner.

"Like we can get a table," Zoë grumbled, but followed him. Food might help sober her up.

Reynard walked past the line—all human to the best of Zoë's perception—and approached the host, a Japanese fae man with haunting eyes and shaggy black hair. Reynard showed something in the palm of his hand and the host nodded and smiled, and beckoned to them to follow him.

Zoë felt the glares of the line. She turned to a couple and said, "He's got dirt on the host. It's not preferential treatment, it's blackmail." She thought she pulled it off except she had trouble saying "preferential" with her alcohol-soaked tongue. She jogged a bit to catch up.

They took a seat in an intimate corner of Loup, and Zoë frowned at the water glasses on the table. She missed Captain Spaulding. He had been her only friend this evening.

"OK. So you met me on a train and immediately began lying to me. What gives?" Zoë asked.

He sat back in his seat and regarded her. "Let me make a guess. You're a citytalker who knows very little of your own skills. You probably only recently discovered this skill, and you have no one to show you how to use it. How am I doing?"

Zoë smiled widely, as if she were on a roller coaster and had to decide whether to scream or enjoy it, because she was moving along with the ride whether she liked it or not.

"Pretty good. Now my turn. You're an asshole who enjoys putting other people off their game, whether it's by lying to them outright or showing that you know too much about them. You really love it when they ask you desperate questions like 'How did you know that?' Then you get to show your incredible intelligence and abilities and prove yourself their superior in all ways. How am I doing?"

His eyes widened when she called him an asshole, but then he grinned, clearly enjoying her diatribe.

"You got me. I do like feeling superior," he said, inclining his head. "Now was I right about you?"

"You still haven't answered my question about why you lied to me."

"I wanted to see how you'd react to something new that could be seen as a threat. You already knew how to deal with vamps and zombies."

Zoë unrolled her silverware and placed her napkin in her lap. The waiter, a harried human woman with light-brown skin and East Asian eyes, came up to them and pulled out her pad. "Hey there, I'm Heather, what can I get you to drink?"

"I'll have a black coffee, a water, and can your bartender make a drink called a Captain Spaulding?" Zoë asked.

The woman frowned. "I'll have to ask her, but I've never heard of that."

Zoë nodded. "Shame. I'll take a gin and tonic then. Just line up all three drinks in front of me."

Reynard smiled at her, then looked at Heather. "I'll have the same."

"Be right back," she said.

"I figured you'd had enough," he said.

"Oh, I haven't even begun to drink," Zoë said, placing her hand over her heart as if she were making a grand proclamation. "My life is fucked up right now and if I don't drink to cushion everything, I might go mad." She squinted at him, as if trying to see through him. "Hey, did you organize the train robbery?"

"What?" He dropped the fork he was fiddling with. "No, of

course not. Why would I have hired ghosts to come aboard to capture me?"

Zoë shrugged. "You lied once, I have no idea your motives for anything now. Now you're pretending to know all about me, tell me something about you. Earn my trust. Go."

She crossed her arms in front of her chest and leaned back, hoping that her numb face conveyed a sense of skepticism.

Reynard nodded once. "I'm a citytalker, like you. I work for a coterie organization that I'm not comfortable divulging to you right now. But I get information. I find cities useful for that. What I told you about the genocide was true," he said.

She nodded; Gwen had confirmed that.

"So there are still people out there who want us dead. And the more people who know who we are, the more dangerous it is. Those ghosts were clearly after me."

The waitress arrived then with their six drinks. Reynard waved her away, saying they weren't ready to order yet.

"So let me get this straight," Zoë said, picking up her water glass. "You lied to me to scare me about ghosts, and then ghosts attack the train and end up hunting you, making them scarier than you had originally intended, so the ghosts made a truther out of a liar." She frowned. "Truth-teller. Something."

She took a sip of the water, then the coffee, then the gin. This could keep her going all night.

Reynard thought for a moment. "I guess you can look at it that way. Anyway, what I really want to do is talk to you and see if I can get you to join our team. You'll have the safety of my employers behind you, and we can use all the citytalkers we can get."

"Safety like keeping you from a train robbery?" Zoë asked, raising an eyebrow.

"Hey, I told you that I had protection in the vampire car, you just didn't believe me," he reminded her.

Water, coffee, gin. "So you work for vampires?"

"Among others, yes. The organization is made up of many coterie."

"So do I. Work for vampires and have some semblance of safety over me, although clearly it's not guaranteed. And I'm getting a little tired of people hanging out with me who can eat me. Why would joining your monster organization be different from my own?"

Reynard smiled, with the look of a gambler who had been saving his ace.

"We'd teach you what it means to be a citytalker, for one thing."

CHAPTER 13
Dining

Café Soulé ****

Those who glory in the past—namely gods and vampires—may prefer the Old World elegance of Antoine's, but a quick jog across the street to Café Soulé will show you one of the best-kept secrets in the city: actual bottled souls for ingestion.

The bartender is a zoëtist who controls most of the waitstaff, and makes incredible drinks with recipes she prefers not to share—but try the Captain Spaulding if you're fond of gin. The meals cater to death gods and demigods on Wednesday nights, with the head chef having a knack for gathering wayward souls and trapping them for ingestion.* ▪

---

*Public Works has investigated Café Soulé, but as its job is keeping the balance between living humans and coterie, it has allowed the restaurant to continue, however begrudgingly, as long as it does not take its souls from live humans.

CHAPTER TEN

Water, coffee, and gin.

Somewhere in the evening, Zoë and Reynard ordered a spinach dip. They ate it, Zoë having the solid feeling that no souls had perished for the creation of their dish.

"'M a very wide-awake drunk," Zoë said, blinking several times.

"You wanna see something awesome?" Reynard asked. He hadn't drunk as much as Zoë, but still seemed more relaxed than before.

"Always. I always want to see awesome. Why would you think otherwise? Who doesn't want to see awesome things? Losers. That's who. And zombies."

Reynard paid the bill and they left to join the ever-increasing crowd on the street. "You know they do ghost and vampire tours in the city, right?" he asked her as they staggered toward Jackson Square.

"I've heard of them," Zoë said. "I figured the visiting coterie wouldn't enjoy that kind of thing, find it offensive, or something."

"No, it's hysterical, let's go."

"What the hell, let's do it," she said.

Their conversation had veered away from the subject of Reynard's mysterious employers to swapping coterie stories. Zoë found herself actually having a fun time, making Reynard laugh as she told how the zombies had accused her of stealing brains out of the company fridge. Was she rethinking her decision to leave the coterie world entirely?

She was, however, still considering leaving Underground Publishing. But a tiny sober cell in her brain cautioned against committing to a new organization before finding out what exactly it did.

"So talk to it!" Zoë said, giggling.

"What?" Reynard asked.

"Talk to it! The city! Ask it what's going on! It won't talk to me, maybe it'll talk to you?"

"It doesn't quite work like that. You need to align yourself on a deep level before you can get clear communication. I haven't done this with New Orleans yet, so all I get is the occasional image. That's what you're getting, right?"

"Yeah. I thought I was doing it wrong. Hah! I'm awesome at this." She straightened a little bit.

"Right," he said, smiling at her.

They were a block from Jackson Square when they saw a group of tourists following a tall man down Decatur Street, listening to him talk about the French architecture. He had to speak loudly over the partying people, but he was heading for a quiet residential neighborhood.

The man was dressed in a long black coat with ruffles on the cuffs, and his face was long and thin and very pale. He spoke in solemn words to the group, which consisted of tourists in various states of inebriation. Some listened, some snapped photos, and some giggled and jostled each other.

"Uh-oh, frat boy alert," Zoë whispered, pointing to two beefy young men in pastel polo shirts with the collars up.

"Shh," Reynard said. "Listen."

A woman at the back of the group looked at them and sniffed. "You have to pay for the tour," she said.

"Oh! I can do that!" Zoë said brightly. She pulled her wallet out of her satchel and grabbed a couple of fifties. "Do you think that will cover it?"

The woman looked from the bundle of bills back to Zoë. "Yeah, I think that will do you just fine."

"Great!" When the tour began walking again, Zoë sneaked up to the front and pressed the money into the hands of the tall guy. "Hey, can we join the tour? We are a bit late."

His dour goth expression faded into surprise, and he accepted the bills and put them in his pocket. "Uh, sure." He fished a roll of stickers out of his pocket and handed her two. "These indicate you're with the tour."

"Awesome. Thanks!" Ignoring the stares of the rest of the group, she dropped back to the end of the line to join Reynard. "We're good."

She handed him his sticker. She put her own on the outside of her leather jacket and patted her chest to adhere it. She crumpled the paper backing and stuck it in her pocket. "Now let's learn about vampires."

After one block of hearing the man talk, Zoë was ready to leave.

"If I know vampires, and I do, they would find this offensive," she told Reynard, who watched her with an amused expression. "I mean, I think it's hysterical. But I have my readers to think about." She felt very grown-up for coming to this conclusion while she was drunk. "It's racist."

"Racist? These people are essentially walking around the city worshipping them," Reynard said. "How many vampires do you know, anyway?"

"Three," she admitted. "But one is the kind who'd get pissed at any little thing. Like a vampire tour."

"Look. This is a touristy thing to do. You're writing a book for tourists, right? Don't tell your vampire friends you paid to hear silly stories about them, that's all."

Zoë snorted loudly, and some heads turned. She covered her mouth and whispered, "They're not my friends. They'd love to see me die."

"Come on, just a few more blocks," Reynard said. "Then I'll walk you back to your hotel." They rejoined the tour, which had gotten about a block ahead of them.

The guide spoke in a whispery voice that still managed to carry to the back of the group. "Back in the eighties, those who practiced the goth religion pretty much took over this area of town, but we got it cleaned out. They practically worshiped Bram Stroker."

Zoë clapped her hand over her mouth to stifle the laughter. "Did he say Bram Stroker?" she asked in a stage whisper to Reynard.

He nodded. "Mr. Stroker, high priest of the Holy Order of Goth."

The guide continued. "And when people take pictures of that tree, sometimes the photo is developed with the image of the woman hanging from the topmost branch where she died—"

"Is that a three-legged dog?" someone interrupted.

The man grimaced and turned. A large yellow lab that was missing its left hind leg was walking on the opposite side of the road. Step-step-hop, step-step-hop, he went happily down the sidewalk. He trailed a leash behind him, and limped along with purpose, not doing typical dog things such as sniffing or urinating. It had been such a long time since Zoë had seen a non-neutered dog that his bouncing testicles looked obscene. She giggled.

"Yes, that's Hank," the guide said impatiently, waving a hand. "He's fine."

"It looks like he got away from someone," the woman in front of Zoë and Reynard said doubtfully. "He's got a leash on."

"Nah, he's always pulling that behind him. He belongs to the street. Everyone feeds him." The man's voice had lost its dreamy quality and had become nasal and annoyed. He cleared his throat. "Now, we'll go to noted vampire Comte de Saint Germain's—the first one, anyway. He played music here, hosted fantastic parties where he reportedly never ate a morsel of food, and then in the privacy of the night, was reported to have done dreadful things."

The dog stopped and turned its large head toward the group and watched them for a time, then turned back toward Jackson Square.

"I wonder if Opal knew him," Zoë said.

"Who?" asked Reynard, who was staring after the dog, his face pale in the streetlight.

"That Comte guy. She's the only vampire who doesn't scare me. Although she probably could," she amended, remembering how unthreatening she had thought Gwen had been. "I wonder how that dog lost his leg."

"That's no dog," Reynard whispered. "That's an inugami."

Zoë snorted with laughter. " 'That's no dog, that's a space station!' What the fuck are you talking about?"

The tour had continued without them, but Reynard hadn't noticed.

"Wake up, Zoë," Reynard hissed. "That is a serious thing. You don't fuck around with inugami."

She felt sullen. "Now I want sushi. And hey, I've had more than you. I can't sober up just like that." She frowned and considered him. "You weren't really drunk at all, were you? That's twice you've lied to me, bucko."

"Bucko" had sounded a lot more challenging in her head.

"So what's so scary about bouncing-testicle three-legged Rover? What is he going to do, chase us down and wave his testicles at us?"

Unexpectedly, Reynard laughed. "Your innocence is really charming, but if you don't lose it fast, you're going to die."

"I'm not innocent, I'm drunk. Again, you're not answering my questions," she said, putting her hands on her hips. "Tell me now, or I'm walking."

"In short, it's a vengeance dog demon. Very dangerous, very single-minded. Very little can distract it from its quarry."

"Dude said his name was Hank. Do vengeance demons commonly beg for scraps on the street? And why was it missing a leg?"

"The guide was likely lying to get the focus back on him. And if the demon is not whole, it has likely broken away from the master who commanded it. I have a really bad feeling about this," Reynard said. "The ghost bandits on the train, now a vengeance demon."

"Those ghosts were corporate team builders who died in cowboy outfits," Zoë protested.

"And yet the bullet was real, right? We're not safe here. Can you get back to your hotel all right? If you can't, then you need to find a ghost."

"A ghost? Why in the world..." Zoe turned, but Reynard was off in the opposite direction from Zoë's hotel—and in the opposite direction from the weird dog.

"So much for seeing me back to my hotel!" she shouted after him. "That's twice you've run off to save your own ass!"

Seriously, that guy. It had been a fun distraction, talking to a human, but even human coterie had their drama.

If he was so worried about people hunting citytalkers, why was he not doing more to inform her of the threat? Zoë chewed on her lip as she tried to navigate the streets home.

Either he was truly a self-obsessed asshole, or the threat was to him rather than to citytalkers as a whole. Either could be true, really, she decided. And why find a ghost? He had lied to her once about ghosts, why should she believe him now?

Crossing Bourbon Street was problematic, with women lifting their shirts, beads flying, and beer being drunk and spilled at similar rates. A crier in front of a strip club tried to entice her inside, but she felt the pull of hungry incubi inside. "No way," she said, and hurried across the street.

When the crowds had thinned a bit, Zoë did a search for "inugami" on her phone, with little hope, but she was surprised when she got several hits. They were created by Japanese families—zoëtists, Zoë assumed—and would avenge those families. She shuddered. She couldn't think of a more embarrassing death than being killed by a three-legged dog with bobbling testicles.

Her phone dinged; a text from Bertie asked if they were supposed to just go out and party or if they were going to have a meeting before they started researching. She groaned and picked up her speed. Maybe Freddie's magic B and B would have a miracle sobering-up-and-hangover-remedy.

Later, Zoë would muse that she was being punished for allowing herself to have fun and get drunk. She had let her guard down once, and now she was paying.

As she opened the door to Freddie's Ready B and B, Freddie Who's Always Ready met her with a phone in his hand.

"It surprises me that modern ladies these days don't have cell phones," Freddie said. "I got my first cell phone when they came out, I said, Freddie, you're gonna need this kind of technology. I knew it was important. It was about the size of a brick. My grandfather thought it was the devil, but I knew better. Did I tell you about him? He was a voodoo priest, and—"

"The phone, Freddie?" Zoë interrupted.

"Right. This is Public Works, for you. Get a cell phone, is my advice right there," he said.

"I have one, I just don't give my number out to everyone who asks for it," she said, but Freddie had retreated inside, clearly away from whatever drama followed Zoë.

She stepped inside the door and was distracted immediately by the sound of a Norse goddess's sobs.

She looked down and saw Eir crouched in the hallway, her back against the wall, her thick white arms covered in fur and blood from cradling the body of a dead cat.

"I couldn't save him," she said. "I tried everything, even the primitive things they taught me in medical school. Nothing worked."

"Hello? Hello? Zoë, are you there?" the phone demanded.

"Yeah, what is it?" Zoë said, confused.

"This is Christian from Public Works. Since you were kind enough to inform me of your presence here today, I wanted to let you know that there's a warrant out for a visiting vampire that matches the description of one of your writers. There's been a murder. They're sending someone over."

"Wait, what? How do you know about my team, you don't even know who is with me?" Zoë asked, looking around for Kevin.

"Ms. Norris." The voice had lost all sex appeal, perhaps he had eaten, or perhaps it was just that she couldn't see him. It was placating and slow, as if he were speaking to a child. Or a tired, drunk human. "Public Works sees a lot more than any coterie expects. I thought you would know that."

Zoë closed her eyes. Of course, Public Works had eyes and ears for misbehaving coterie, just like New York. *The cats.*

She swore to herself. "Hang on a second, we've got a little chaos here." She dropped her hand to her side and looked at the sobbing goddess and the dead cat.

Gwen knelt by Eir, stroking her head. Her black eyes focused on Zoë. "Bygul is dead. Kevin is missing. We have a problem."

Eir was inconsolable. The cat had wounds all over his body; it was clear he had fought hard before his death. The goddess cried too hard to answer any of Gwen's questions, so Gwen just returned to consoling her.

Zoë took a deep breath and put the phone back to her ear, stepping outside into the cool night that was minimally quieter than the hallway.

"So tell me what happened," she said into the phone, rubbing her face with her free hand, hoping some feeling would return with sobriety.

"We found the body of a human in a cemetery. We believe she was part of a tour and lagged behind. One of our agents says someone who looks like him was seen running from the cemetery, and the body was clearly exsanguinated."

"And you're sure it's him?"

"He dropped his business card," Christian said.

"Fucking idiot," she muttered. "But no one saw him attack anyone?"

"Not that we could find. But when the agent went into the cemetery to find the body, no one else was there."

"I thought the cemetery was a popular hangout? Coterie actually bunk there sometimes? Isn't that a little like finding a hotel completely empty?"

"You ask a lot of questions. It can be, but it's closed for renovation right now."

"During Carnival?" Zoë's tone was incredulous.

"The renovations went longer than expected," Christian said, an annoyed tone to his silky voice. "The facts are a Public Works agent saw your vampire, Kevin, fleeing the graveyard."

It was too much to take in. Eir's sobs had calmed down inside, but Zoë still had a dead cat demon and a missing writer to deal with.

"Fuck," she muttered.

"Normally I would say yes," Christian said. "But we do have a vampire to catch."

"Listen, you have to give me till sunrise," Zoë pleaded. "I want to try to find him on my own. You look for other leads."

Christian paused, and then laughed. "And what else should I do, boss? You want me to hold all your calls?"

Zoë took a deep breath. "I know this guy, OK? You said yourself it's circumstantial evidence. I know what happens when you guys find someone: there's no trial. Let me find him first and you look at other leads. I'm not local; I can't look for other leads. I know Kevin, I have his sire here, and would be able to find him better than you can. Just give me seven"—she checked the time on her cell phone and grimaced—"six hours. By then he will have gone underground and if he's not here, you can look at your usual vampire hiding places."

"There is no underground in New Orleans," he said, sounding smug. "We're already below sea level."

"It's an expression, you pompous ass," Zoë said, rubbing the back of her neck and trying to relax her muscles. "Look, if you want my help, you have to give me six hours."

"Done," he said abruptly. "Give me your cell number."

Zoë started to give him her number, and then backed up and

gave him the number to her coterie phone. "I'll have it on all night."

"Set it to vibrate," he said, low and soft, and hung up.

"Fucking incubus," she said, and went back inside.

She put her phone back into her pocket. Eir was allowing Gwen to gently clean the blood off her arms. Zoë knelt on the floor and touched Gwen on the shoulder. "What happened?"

"We left the restaurant, and Eir wanted to see Bygul again. Wanted to make amends, she said. I think it was her inebriation. We got to Jackson Square and a vengeance demon was there. It was too late for us to help," Gwen said softly. "It targeted Bygul, I don't know why."

Zoë finally felt sober, as if cold water had washed over her. "A vengeance demon? Was it an inugami?"

"How do you know about inugami?" Gwen asked, raising her face to stare at Zoë.

"Is that important? We can talk details later. Was it?"

"Yes. An inugami killed a divine cat of Freya's." Gwen shook her head. "I can't reach Eir right now, she's not sober yet. I'll try to find out later. What was the innkeeper saying about Kevin?"

Zoë grimaced and sat back on her heels, leaning against the wall. She closed her eyes briefly. "There's a dead woman, someone apparently witnessed Kevin doing it, the idiot dropped his business card. Or someone trying to frame him dropped it. Public Works are giving me till sunup to find him, else they go hunting."

"It's odd for you to stand up for Kevin," Gwen said.

Zoë opened her eyes. "I don't like the guy, but if he's innocent then he shouldn't be hunted like a dog."

Eir raised her swollen eyes. She gripped the cat's body as if she were trying to throttle it, but Zoë thought it might not do any good to point out that the cat was already dead. "I'm going back to Jackson Square. I'm going to find that inugami."

She rose to her feet with more grace than someone her size should have had, and walked to the door and abruptly exited.

"That was, uh, weird," Zoë said.

Gwen rose with similar speed. "I should go after her. This may not end well."

"I'll get Opal to help me, then," Zoë said, feeling tired and lost.

"Get Bertie to help. Dragons have skills humans don't," Gwen said. "And Zoë? This between us isn't over. We must talk later." She hurried after Eir.

"Oh, thanks for the understatement of the century," Zoë muttered.

The door shut behind Gwen. Freddie came out of the kitchen, holding his hand out for his phone, and Zoë handed it over, feeling guilty. She looked at the blood smeared on the floor and wall, and groaned. She'd leave a big tip for the maid the next morning.

Feet hit the stairs above her head, and she looked up.

When she saw Opal's face, she officially became scared of the last vampire she hadn't been scared of.

CHAPTER 5
The French Quarter

VAMPIRE AND GHOST TOURS

The vampire and ghost tours of Jackson Square are highly popular with tourists, but mainly human tourists. Tour guides lead their group on a walking tour and tell them of some of the more "haunted" places in town. The ironic thing is they almost never touch on the real haunted areas, or vampire homes, because the coterie involved have requested privacy and Public Works has accommodated them.

However, there are tours starting up FOR vampires and ghosts to see the city, and from them you will learn about the more famous resident coterie, the historical areas, and the true stories of the city. You will learn Marie Laveau's strange history and where she got her power, learn how much of Anne Rice's work is fiction and how much is historical documenting, and visit the graveyard that even the ghosts won't hang out in. ∎

CHAPTER ELEVEN

Most days Kevin's sire, Opal, was nearly his polar opposite: sweet and friendly and motherly. She had not been able to have children in life, so she loved her baby vampires with all her heart—a love that annoyed the hell out of Kevin, who did not hide his disdain at being mothered. Opal had shown interest in turning Zoë, but she had politely turned down the offer.

Opal, like Phil, didn't seem to have the stereotypical vampire personality of angst and torment that Kevin so fully embodied. Zoë couldn't imagine her hurting a fly. But as she descended the stairs, her fangs elongated and her eyes glowing red, Zoë took a step back to give her room.

"So you've heard what's going on?" Zoë asked.

"Something is wrong with my son, that's all I know," Opal said, an edge to her usually soft voice. "He has done something bad, and he is angry and frightened and possibly in danger."

Zoë nodded and told her the details. The vampire stood with her spine rigid and a frozen smile on her face. Zoë explained the evidence against Kevin and tried to ignore the tears leaking from Opal's eyes. She stared at Zoë with an intensity that made Zoë twitch.

Freddie Who's Always Ready was true to his name and had supplied Zoë with sandwiches—three of them—and Opal with a warm mug of blood. The kitchen of the B and B was not as homey as the house; it was more industrial, with white walls and steel appliances. Freddie confided in Zoë that he didn't want Opal going into a bloody rage in the dining room littered with antiques, so he put them in the kitchen to talk.

"So we need to find Kevin, and fast," Zoë concluded. "I figure if we find him before Public Works does we can find out what happened."

"I'll tell you what happened," Opal said with a tense, brittle tone. "He has left me. He wants to go sire another, he wants to be his own vampire. My baby has left me."

"I, uh, don't think he sired anyone. Public Works thinks he just killed her."

"That's because I've never told him exactly how to do it," Opal said. "That information is dangerous to give to a new vampire. Before you know it, they're off turning their spouses or their best friends or someone they want to fuck."

Zoë blanched at the word coming out of sweet Opal's mouth.

"You don't learn how to turn until you're at least ten years old, and then only if you're incredibly mature. I didn't think Kevin would be ready until he was at least fifty. Regardless, he's done with me." Opal collapsed into the kitchen chair as if someone had cut her strings, holding her head in her hands and weeping.

Blood sloshed out of her mug and onto her lap, and she made no move to wipe it up. Zoë grabbed a dish towel and put it over the spreading stain. She fought the urge to grab the vampire by the shoulders and remind her that this had absolutely nothing to do with Opal, that Kevin was probably an asshole before she turned him. But she knew Opal wouldn't listen. She tried a different tack.

"I think," she said, hating herself for putting on the kid gloves, "that if you are with me when I find him, we can find out what happened and maybe convince him to come back with us. He hates me, Opal, he won't listen to me. He will listen to you. He has to. He respects you."

"Dregs from a mumblecrust," Opal muttered.

Zoë was entirely flummoxed. "What?"

"That is what my generation calls bullshit. You know he doesn't love me. He respects me because that's what one does with a sire, but nothing else ties him to me. He couldn't leave me in New York, but he sees New Orleans as his way to get free of me, this job, and everything else."

"Whoa," Zoë said, holding up her hand. "You're not telling me he is quitting, are you?"

"That's exactly what I'm saying. He wants nothing to do with either of us."

Zoë closed her eyes, thinking of whether they could take up his slack with the remaining writers.

Oh sure, said that little sober part of her brain. *Dude murdered a woman, has threatened you, but you don't get up in arms till he threatens to quit? This job is seriously messing with your priorities.*

Opal stood abruptly. "Let's go. We're losing the night."

Zoë stepped back. "OK, do we want to bring Bertie along? Another person might—"

"No," Opal interrupted her just as Bertie walked into the kitchen.

"What's all the hubbub?" he asked, yawning. His brown hair was rumpled, and Zoë could have sworn he actually grew an inch or two as he stretched.

"Kevin's apparently gone on a killing rampage and Public Works knows it, and Eir and Gwen are hunting a vengeance dog demon for killing a cat," Zoë said, collapsing onto a kitchen chair. "Nothing new."

"Oh, OK," Bertie said. "Can you guys keep it down, then?"

Zoë groaned. "How can any of you get attached to other

coterie if you just blow it off when one of you dies? If they find him, they will kill him. Uh, again."

Opal's jaw was clenched. "They will *not*. Not unless they want this town to bleed."

The voice in Zoë's head was very small. *Bleed?*

Now is not the time, she thought. Not with an angry, determined vampire in front of her.

"Bertie," Zoë said, turning to the wyrm. "Can you help us find Kevin, or are you going back to bed?"

Bertie sighed and looked longingly at the kitchen door, then back at Zoë. "I don't know, Zoë. It's not in the job description."

She put her hands on her hips. "Dude, if you knew the shit I've had to do that hasn't been in the managing editor's job description, you'd go back to New York without another word. A coworker is in trouble. We could use someone with your experience. And"— she added, wondering if she could play on his vanity—"someone with your wisdom. You're one of the oldest here." This was a lie, of course. Bertie was two hundred years old, only a baby to his race, but Eir and Gwen had to be at least two thousand years old each, and she didn't know how old Opal was. But the point she was trying to make was that he was older and wiser than she.

He pursed his lips, but she could tell she had gotten to him. "You do know that if it was him, and he's not on his way out of town, we have to turn him in or we are accomplices?"

"I've seen a few police shows in my time," Zoë said, nodding.

"And if he has fed directly from a frightened person, he's likely to be in bloodlust. Vampires in bloodlust are not great negotiators," Bertie said.

Bloodlust? When Phil had fed from the deranged zoëtist attacking the city (after feeding on her milquetoast husband) he had managed to keep his cool, Zoë remembered. But perhaps he was a rare vampire.

178

"I didn't know that," she admitted. "But this is why we need you."

"Of course we need a wyrm," Opal said archly, rounding on Bertie. "Because who among us would be able to give advice about a vampire?"

"Can we not turn this into a pissing contest?" Zoë asked. "I need all the help I can get. And why the hell am I the only one apparently concerned about Kevin, who incidentally I loathe?"

Opal actually looked hurt at that, the stiffness leaving her spine and her dark eyes pleading with Zoë. "I am very concerned," she said softly. "He's my child. But you do understand we have to find him on my terms."

"Actually, I don't understand that at all. I thought we just needed to find him. But if you think we can find him on your terms, lead the way."

"I don't have a choice in this, do I?" Bertie asked, rolling up his sleeves. Zoë couldn't keep herself from trying to see if he had scales, but still the only thing that betrayed him as coterie was pupils that seemed more snakelike than human. He said he could shape-shift, but she had never seen it.

She shrugged. "You could have a choice. But if Public Works finds him, then that means you have more work to do tomorrow. If you want Kevin here to pull his weight on the book, you will need to help us. Are you in?"

Bertie's strange snake eyes stared into her own, and then he finally sighed and nodded. "He'll be at Bourbon Street Terror. Let's go."

"What?" Zoë asked. "How do you know that?"

"He'll be hungry. That's the weird thing about vampires—feeding makes them want to eat more. Making deals with blood banks is the best thing that's ever happened to them. Bloodlust doesn't peak as much."

Opal stood at the back door, arms crossed. "I wouldn't talk, Bertie. Your eating habits are foul."

Bertie stood up straighter. "I beg your pardon? I eat in private, and always clean up afterward."

Zoë realized she didn't know how, or what, the dragon ate, and got a bit uncomfortable.

"Let's argue as we walk, OK?" Zoë said, pulling her coat back on and heading out the door.

Sounds of celebration and parties drifted from the French Quarter. Laughter, music, horns, cheers, the sounds of New Orleans. An hour earlier Zoë had been enjoying that. Well, in a drunk haze while running away from her problems, but enjoying it nonetheless. Zoë rubbed her arms against the slight chill and hurried to follow Opal and Bertie back into the French Quarter.

It was still difficult to maneuver through the drunken revelries, but Zoë found that her own buzz had left, thanks to adrenaline and shock, and she made her way with purpose, following the baby dragon.

"So do *you* think Kevin will be at this bar?" Zoë asked Opal, who leaned forward as she walked.

Three young men on a balcony, holding plastic hurricane glasses and draped with beads, catcalled to them, asking to see their tits. Opal didn't even look up, but Bertie paused, faced the men, and lifted his shirt. His back was to Zoë, so she didn't see what he showed them, but the drunken men went silent, stepping back from the balcony. It looked as if one of them started to cry.

Opal dragged Zoë's attention back to her. "I don't know where he will be. He's never been the most compliant child," Opal said. Her fangs were out, and she bared them when she spoke.

"So there's no sort of bond between you two?" Zoë asked. She itched to take out her notepad to write this down, but she felt that would be bad form. "Like being able to find one another?"

Opal gave her a withering look as she shouldered her petite form past five people with white demon masks. One grumbled a warning and Zoë realized they weren't wearing masks.

"There is no bond. Not like that. He is compelled to obey me, but he's fought that since he was turned. I think perhaps now he's severed it completely. My heart is breaking."

She didn't sound as if her heart was breaking. Her voice was sharp and focused, without any of the mothering tone Zoë had heard before.

Zoë picked up her pace to keep up with the angry vampire, and noticed Bertie had fallen behind to raise his shirt again, again with the effect of quieting the revelers. She ran into Opal's back when the vampire abruptly stopped.

"Sorry," she muttered. "Why are we stopping?"

"Bertie said Kevin was on Bourbon Street. We are here. Which way?" She looked both ways, nostrils flaring.

Bertie joined them then, ambling up the street. He had several strands of purple and red beads around his neck.

"That bachelorette party actually appreciated what I have to give," he said as Zoë pointedly looked at his beads.

"Which way is the bar, Bertie?" Zoë said with forced calm.

"About two blocks. I'll show you."

Their progress was considerably slower now that Bertie was leading them, and Opal's hands clenched and unclenched as they walked.

"Do, uh, do you have a plan?" Zoë asked. "We need to find out where he was and everything. See if he has an alibi."

Bertie looked over his shoulder. "You don't have a plan yourself? You seem to never have a plan. Don't you think that's dangerous?"

"I have a plan," Opal said. "And, Zoë, I appreciate you giving him the benefit of the doubt, but do you really think he is innocent? He's a vampire who's been chafing at the bit of both his sire and his employer. I can sense he is out of control tonight. Of course he's guilty."

Zoë blanched. "Seriously? You're sure? But—then why are we doing this? Why not just call Public Works?" Her hand went into her coat pocket for her phone, but Opal clamped her hand onto Zoë's and squeezed. Zoë winced.

"Because if Public Works gets him, I won't be able to."

The vampire bar was disappointingly dull. Vampires had centuries to refine tastes, save up money, and build great things, and what did they have? A bar on Bourbon Street with the windows painted black and a big drop of blood in red over the black paint. This of course meant you could only see the symbol when up close, and it looked as if it had been painted by high school sophomores with the goal of decorating for the Halloween dance in a condemned house.

Perhaps that's what they were going for, Zoë thought.

They walked into the bar, Opal first. She hissed at the bouncer, a small black teenage boy who thumbed through a copy of *Rolling Stone* as he sat on his stool. The boy snapped his head up and hissed back at Opal, and even though Zoë knew they could both rip her throat out without a thought, it was clearly only a display of tail feathers.

The boy let Opal through, but stuck his hand out after she walked past. Zoë ran into his arm, and then Bertie plowed into her. Although the bouncer appeared young and slight, his body had the ropy steel muscle that Zoë identified with vampires.

"Vampires only," he said, with a heavy Southern accent. Then he looked thoughtful. "Unless you're lunch," he added.

"I'm with her," Zoë said. She really didn't want to lie and say that yes, she was lunch. She'd had bad experiences with that ruse before, and had nearly been dinner for an incubus.

Opal charged down the hall ahead of them, which was draped with bare lightbulbs and black cloth. The place was *tacky*. The hallway turned left and presumably opened up to a larger room, but Zoë couldn't see around the corner. The earnest crooning of ABBA karaoke floated down the hall.

"Is that 'Dancing Queen'?" Zoë asked, smiling.

"Yeah. And?" the boy said. He pushed her back out the door. "No humans. And no whatever he is." The boy jerked his head toward Bertie.

Bertie drew himself up. "I am a wyrm, young man, and over two hundred years old."

"Big deal," the boy said, examining his fingernails. "I've got two hundred fifty."

"Wow, who turned you so young?" Zoë couldn't help asking.

"That is none of your goddamned business," the boy said, frowning at her. "I don't ask about your parents, do I?"

Zoë was about to tell him to go ahead, she didn't know anything anyway, but Kevin interrupted her, barreling toward her down the hallway. He shoved the boy aside and pushed past Zoë with the force of a charging bull.

Zoë and Bertie shared an uncomfortable moment of being tangled together, and before they could right themselves, Opal went storming after Kevin and into the night.

Zoë and Bertie righted themselves and ran after the vampires, ignoring the outraged questions from the bouncer.

"Where?" Bertie asked. The street was full of revelers, but no vampires. There wasn't even a sign of their passing.

Zoë had never seen a vampire in full sprint before. She had seen Phil attack humans and zombies, and knew he was a surprisingly quick and brutal fighter. But she had never seen them run.

It was clear that Zoë and Bertie had no chance to catch up to them.

Please, if there's any way you can give me a hint as to which way the vampires went, I'd really appreciate it, she pleaded to the city silently, and felt a mental pull to the left. She could have been imagining it, like kids playing with a Ouija board, but she had nothing else to trust and Bertie wasn't helping.

Honestly she didn't know how she was supposed to prevent the vampires' fighting. She couldn't stop a truck from running down a hill; angry vampires didn't seem much different.

Zoë crossed the street as quickly as she could to get into the flow of the crowd, Bertie on her heels. She had to jerk him away from lifting his shirt again to screaming groups of men and women. "Later," she said through gritted teeth.

A thought struck her as she shouldered past a large, half-naked man. "Hey, vampires can't fly, can they?" she asked Bertie.

"The very old ones can," he said in an offhand manner. Zoë guessed it took some pretty impressive flying to impress a dragon.

"Kevin's nowhere near very old," Zoë said. "He's like five or something. I don't know how old Opal is."

"Kevin would be old enough to run, though," Bertie said. "We're not going to catch them. You know, your sense of team leadership is illusionary at best."

Zoë glared at him and turned down St. Philip Street on a hunch—or maybe guidance from the city. She didn't know. After a few blocks she heard a howl and a thump.

"The train yard," she said, and ran. Luckily she had seen it during her walk that day, and knew the most direct way there.

Again, it was painfully obvious that her body was a lumbering sack of organs and muscles and the others were fueled by magic or blood or something. Still, she was in shape, and she sprinted with Bertie grumbling behind her. Then Bertie was ahead of her. Still grumbling, but faster than she was.

"Sure, I'm a secret member of the almighty coterie, the hidden citytalker, powerful and sly. And I run like an ox."

Another thump. "What are they doing up there?" she shouted to Bertie, who was outdistancing her.

"Fighting!" he shouted back. "Do you have a plan how to deal with this?"

"Why does everyone want to know if I have a plan! Jesus!" She honestly didn't know what she could do. Threaten to fire them? Call Phil and put him on speakerphone? See if she could summon up one of those demon dogs to help her out?

The large warehouse buildings of the train yard sat at the edge of the Mississippi River, casting shadows on the gravel lot. Above them, a tangle of struggling limbs leaped into the sky.

"I seriously don't have a plan to deal with this," she whispered.

Opal flew Kevin higher and higher until they were a dark spot in the light-polluted night sky. "Oh man, she isn't going to—"

Opal dropped him. Kevin fell, arms and legs flailing, reaching terminal velocity quickly. It took only a few seconds for him to reach the warehouse roof, where he slammed with a great boom that even cut over the noise of the parties up the street. Then Opal drifted downward, arms out, palms up, like a slowly falling angel.

"Baby vampires can't fly," Bertie said softly when Zoë caught up with him. They stood under the gutter of the warehouse, the tin roof beginning about ten feet above them. He leaped lightly and suddenly was gone.

Panting, Zoë stared at the roof where she had lost sight of most of her writers. She stood there, dumbly, and watched Bertie wave at her over the edge.

"What's going on now?" Zoë asked.

Bertie leaned over the edge. He grinned at her. "Can't get up here, can you?"

Zoë looked around for a ladder to prove him wrong, and then made a face up at him. "No, smartass. What's happening?"

"This is why you're not a leader," he said conversationally as he leaned over and held his hand down.

"There's no way you can leverage me up there," Zoë said, but took his hand anyway. With a yank that nearly removed her arm at the socket, Bertie pulled her up to the roof.

"And you forget, I'm not human," he said.

"Yeah, yeah, you're so smart and old and strong. All hail the baby dragon. Is that enough thanks for you?" she said.

"It's getting there."

Despite his fall, Kevin was still alive. He and Opal struggled like Irish wrestlers, wrapped around each other, each trying to get the upper hand. Finally Opal lifted him as if he were a sack of flour and threw him—in the direction of Zoë and Bertie.

"Oh God," Zoë said, and ducked. Bertie slid out of the way immediately, but Kevin's foot caught Zoë in the back of the head and knocked her down, where she rolled toward the edge of the warehouse. Woozy from the hit, she tried to slow her progress, trying to gain purchase on the tin roof. Her feet slid over the edge, but she finally slowed enough to grab on to the edge to stop herself.

She panted for a moment, trying to get her wits about her, and only too late realized she didn't know where Kevin had landed. But by then he had already grabbed her leg and yanked her off the building.

CHAPTER 13
Dining

STRIP CLUBS

EXCERPT FROM THE
UPCOMING BOOK *TROILUS'S
EATS, NEW ORLEANS
RESTAURANT GUIDE*

Hers N' His: A Bourbon Street Speakeasy

There is a reason New Orleans is consistently rated one of the best places for incubi and succubi to eat, and that reason is Bourbon Street. Not only can the succubi feed by simply answering the call of "Show your tits!" but some of the more exclusive sex clubs cater to a wide variety of human tastes. While Hers N' His is a members-only club, visiting incubi and succubi can get a night of dining (or "work" as the humans would call it) by calling and asking for the Tree Man. (A woodland spirit, he's called that because of his massive size.)

As with most speakeasies, any prostitution in the back room is illegal and hidden and under a strict no-tell policy. Public Works knows of all the clubs in New Orleans, but turns the other way unless someone gets hurt. So, as with usual encounters, know when to stop. ∎

CHAPTER TWELVE

It sucked to be unconscious. Zoë had only a fuzzy knowledge of what was going on around her. Unmoving, she lay on top of Kevin, who wriggled beneath her. He gnawed at her leg, but didn't seem to have enough strength to actually break through her jeans, much less her skin. Then Opal lifted Zoë as if she were a rag doll and threw her, snarling.

Oh, sorry to get in your way, she thought.

She landed on gravel, hitting her head again, which was just insult to injury at this point. Bertie had leaped off the roof and watched impassively as Opal, weeping, slammed Kevin into the air, and then down on his back. She reached down and closed her hands around Kevin's throat.

That seemed like a stupid idea to Zoë, as the vampire had no air requirements. What was she going to do?

Opal's arms bulged as she squeezed, and Zoë winced as Opal ripped Kevin's throat out with her fingers. She kept swiping at it, spreading the blood and gore out on both sides, coating herself in it, then let out a heartfelt cry that would have moved Zoë to tears, if she hadn't been unconscious.

Which she was. Right?

Something behind her snarled.

Well, that's not good.

She got to her feet and took stock of her injuries: what felt like a broken left wrist, two large bumps on her head, one of which streamed blood into her face, and ripped clothing from skidding along the gravel. Which wasn't necessarily an injury, but they were her favorite jeans.

The endorphins and adrenaline rushing through her body kept the pain at bay, but she had no idea how she was standing, as it didn't feel as if she was actually driving her own body. Maybe it was all a dream?

I'm sorry, but you looked like you needed a hand, the shy voice said in her head, and Zoë would have jumped if she were actually conscious enough for her body to experience involuntary reactions.

Anna? The ghost? You're possessing me? How is that possible? I didn't let you in!

You're injured quite badly. That reduces your defenses. I can leave if you want, but you'll lose consciousness again.

No, I think being aware would be a good thing right about now. I'm still not in fighting shape. Not to mention I don't have a weapon. Why did I go out without a weapon? Oh yeah, had a vampire with me, thought she could help me. Those wacky vampires. Always ripping throats out. Don't suppose you brought a weapon?

No, I'm sorry, I can't touch things unless I'm in someone's body.

Yeah, I was kidding.

The growl again. Then something came around the corner of the warehouse. Step step hop. Step step hop.

Oh. It's that dog thing. An unagi? No, inugami. Right. Do you know what that is, Anna?

She wanted to pull her phone from her jacket pocket, but her hands wouldn't obey. She had expected reluctance from her left hand, with the wrist being broken and all, but the right one annoyed her.

So do you know how to deal with one of these things, when you're one-handed and injured?

I don't think I've ever seen a demon like this.

Japanese vengeance demon, apparently. He killed an important cat tonight. A friend of mine is looking for him.

The demon still had blood around its mouth, matting the yellow fur. Its feet and claws were also bloody, with cat fur caught between them.

I don't think he's done being vengeful. Maybe we should run, Zoë thought.

Zoë felt her body's control return to her, and she felt much heavier now. She took one step and fell down. Her ankle must have been sprained.

"So running is out. This is really going to hurt tomorrow," she said out loud, and momentarily was delighted to hear her own voice. But how was she going to let Eir and Gwen know the dog was here?

The dog leaped at her, silhouetted against the moon. Time seemed to slow, and Zoë had a bizarre flashback to the movie *Watership Down*, and wished she had a General Woundwort to distract it for her.

Battle cries sounded to her left, and Eir ran forward, ablaze with her divine Valkyrie glory. Behind her a dark cloud of sparrows followed, Gwen in battle mode, but they were too late. Zoë braced herself and raised her right hand to shield herself, but the dog's jaws opened and her hand went straight into its mouth.

She waited for more pain, but none came. Instead of hitting the back of the dog's throat, her hand went straight down its gullet. Before she had a moment to think it was impossible for this to happen, she was up to her shoulder in the dog. She nearly expected to see her hand come out the other side, but her fist instead found something, and Anna pushed her, her influence making Zoë's hand convulse and grab tight to something. The dog's eyes went wide and it whined. It thrashed once, not biting down, and went limp.

Zoë pulled her arm free. She was covered in black goo reminiscent of the snake demon that had swallowed her a month prior. In her hand she held something red and white, about a foot and a half long. It looked like a coral snake with a white dog's head, and it thrashed in her grip.

In revulsion she dropped it, and it dove into the ground, disappearing and leaving no trace behind it.

"What the hell just happened?" Zoë asked out loud, staring at her ichor-covered hand, which was beginning to itch. She wondered if she was developing an allergy. Dimly she registered Opal's weeping in the background.

"Editor, you have slain what I and Gwen were unable to, and you did it while grievously injured. Why did you hide what a warrior you are?" Eir asked, respect in her voice.

"I have no idea how I—what the hell was that snake thing?" Zoë was having trouble keeping her thoughts together, and she struggled to sit up. Her head began to throb, and she felt dizzy. She silently pleaded with Anna for support, and felt her equilibrium come back, although the pain remained.

"That was the essence of the demon," Gwen said. "You separated it from its body, effectively killing it."

"But that snake thing is still alive," Zoë protested.

"It's the spirit of vengeance. That can't be killed, any more than love or greed or altruism," Gwen said.

"I bet those are prettier demon essences than vengeance," Zoë said. "So we're OK now?"

"We're OK," Gwen said, nodding slowly.

"Except for Kevin," Eir added, pointing to the mourning Opal.

Zoë's body had begun to react to her injuries, and she decided to lie back in the gravel again. Her voice felt very far away as she struggled to make the words happen. "Maybe someone can give me a trip to the hospital?"

She closed her eyes, but didn't fall unconscious just yet.

Anna, what the hell happened back there?

The ghost was silent for a moment. *There are some things you need to know about citytalkers. And ghosts.*

Zoë woke slowly, as if she were peeling layers of gauze from her eyes. She was in Freddie's Ready B and B, and Gwen sat beside her bed. The clock said ten a.m. Eir dozed in the desk chair.

Zoë blinked, and then focused on the death goddess more closely. "Jesus, what *happened to you?*"

Gwen's immaculate hair was disheveled, her gown torn at the shoulder. She had a cut on her left cheek that leaked silvery fluid. She sat slumped, exhausted.

Gwen's voice was very low and tired. "Eir and I fought the inugami. Then Kevin and Opal fought. Then the inugami got away from us and found you. You killed it."

Zoë rubbed the back of her head, which was sticky with blood, but it was leftover blood. There was no pain, no bump. She flexed her wrist, which was wrapped in a bandage. It ached, but the break was pretty much healed. "I got knocked off the roof when Opal threw Kevin at me. And then I passed out. Then I came to and the demon was there, and a ghost. Then... *that* happened."

"I saw the ghost inside you, the girl from the train, yes?" Gwen asked.

"Right."

"Eir was able to heal the wounds you got during Opal's battle with Kevin, but not the burns from the demon."

Zoë glanced at the dozing goddess. "Is she all right? Are you?"

Gwen nodded slowly. "The creature is gone. Eir will need sleep; she used far too much of her strength yesterday, first at the hospital, and then for attempting to heal Bygul, then on you. Not to mention the night before with the bullet wound. We will recover. The real problem is, we don't know who sent the inugami, and why it attacked Bygul. Or how you killed it."

Zoë held her hands out in front of her and looked at her fingers. They wiggled when she told them to. They were dirty and bloody. She felt an intense desire for a bath. "Anna was with me, she helped bring me back after I got knocked out. But how did I—we—get rid of the demon?"

"Tell me what happened after you left the restaurant," Gwen said.

Zoë went through what she remembered of the evening, the story of Reynard, their conversation, and how he acted when he saw the inugami.

"He told me to find a ghost, right before he left!" she said, her eyes going wide. "He knew how to beat it! How did he know that?"

"The ghost has just arrived here," Gwen said, focusing at the closed door. "She looks as if she wishes to talk to you. I require sustenance, so I will leave you two."

Despite Zoë's exhaustion, she felt the chilly, uncomfortable air between her and Gwen. It wasn't time to reconcile, but she needed to say at least one thing.

"Thanks for saving my life, Gwen," she said.

"You did most of the work, we just got you back here," Gwen said, but she smiled slightly and left the room.

"OK, Anna, what the fuck?" Zoë asked into the room, and felt a shivery, awkward feeling as the girl entered her.

I'm glad you're all right.

"Apparently it's thanks to you," Zoë said out loud. "But what the hell *happened* back there?"

I think there's something you need to know about citytalkers. We weren't just tasked with communicating with cities. We were also assassins.

Zoë nodded, feeling the disconnect with reality that so often came with outrageous coterie revelations. Luckily, the phone rang, and she allowed herself to be distracted.

"That's my boss. I have to take this."

"All right. Tell me what happened from the beginning." Phil's voice was patient.

Zoë gritted her teeth and tried to retell the story more calmly, leaving out the rather important citytalker information. "Public Works thought Kevin killed a woman. We went looking for him. Then Opal went apeshit crazy and attacked him. She killed him. I got into the middle of it and hit my head and got knocked out."

"But Gwen says you saved them from a Japanese demon dog? A real inugami?"

"Yeah, that happened, too," she said, picking at the bedspread with her right hand. "I think I was possessed by—a ghost." She had almost said "another citytalker, who was apparently also an assassin." That would have been very bad.

"And how do you feel now?"

"Well, I'm tired. And my arm is burned from where Eir couldn't heal my demon injuries. But hiring a healing goddess was the right move."

"I just hope she can write," Phil said.

"Always the bottom line, huh, Phil?" Zoë asked.

Phil was silent for a moment. "All right. Tell Opal I want her to call me at sundown. I want a report from Eir as well, when she wakes up. As for you, it does sound like possession, and it sounds like a good thing, too. The bigger problem is who sent the inugami, and why. How have you managed to piss someone off after being in town less than twenty-four hours?"

"It's my magnetic personality, I guess," she said, leaning back in bed. She really wanted that shower.

"An odd thing is that ghosts don't possess people so often anymore," Phil said.

"Anymore?"

"Now that we have establishments settled for giving ghosts jobs, it gives them fewer reasons to seek corporeal form. So why did she target you?"

Zoë could feel him getting close to guessing her secret. "I guess I have a guardian angel," she said. "Anyway. So Opal is supposed to call you. So is Eir. Kevin's apparently dead. Sorry about that." She thought she should feel bad, but she just felt tired and annoyed.

"And you haven't lost Bertie, have you?" Phil's tone was wry. *Do vampires ever mourn?* Zoë wondered. She thought of Opal's tears last night, and then amended her thought to . . . *vampires they're not related to?*

"Not that I know of," she said. "He helped us find Kevin last night, but I haven't seen him today."

"Check on him. Try not to lose any other team members. Get Gwen to find out who set the dog demon on Jackson Square. And how's the book going?"

Zoë glared at the ceiling and gave it the middle finger. It made a poor proxy for the vampire. "About as good as the NYC book was going around this time two months ago."

"You'll get your feet under you. Try to stay alive. And if you can't manage that, get Opal to turn you. I'd prefer not to lose you entirely, although"—he paused, considering—"chaos does seem to follow you."

"Don't remind me," she said. "I'll call you when the next team member bites it." She ended the call, then texted Gwen to come into her room.

Gwen peeked her head in a moment later, eyebrows raised.

"I think I'm down for the day. All I want to do is sleep. Phil wants to hear from Opal and Eir, if you don't mind telling them."

"I can't imagine he is too happy with Opal."

Zoë thought for a moment. "He didn't seem too upset. I don't know if it's a vampire thing or if Kevin was just that disliked."

"Both," Gwen said.

"He's more concerned about the team being reduced. And what about you, you didn't answer me. Are you all right?" Zoë asked. "I've never seen you physically affected by anything. And you look . . . rough."

Gwen waved her hand, dismissing the concern. "I can be damaged by very strong metaphysical beings. But no one has ever injured me gravely. Once I feed I'll be fine."

"Gravely. Death goddess. I get it," Zoë said. Gwen didn't smile. "Work on that sense of humor, OK?"

"Noted," Gwen said. "I will inform the others of their duty to our boss."

"Can you ask Freddie for some Tylenol?" Zoë called after her, but Freddie was at the door, ready with Tylenol and a glass of water. Zoë managed to grin at him.

She wished she had packed some of the teas she had gotten from Granny Good Mae, but she had run out. Since she had gone several weeks without getting injured in a coterie encounter, she kept forgetting to find a new supplier.

With Freddie and Gwen gone, Zoë lay back in bed and swallowed the pills past the lumps in her throat. She took some deep breaths to calm her mind and deal with the incidents of the previous night.

"OK," she said to the ghost she hoped was still in the room. "Let's talk this out."

"Citytalker history, one-oh-one. Go!" Zoë said. The ghost waited patiently in Zoe's head, not trying to take over her limbs, just waiting.

Anna began. *Magical humans have always had as much, or more, natural power than the coterie. Zoëtists could create zombies and constructs, and the really powerful ones could even control some zombies. Weres straddled coterie lines, slave to the shapechange, human most of the month, animal the rest. And the citytalkers were the most efficient assassins ever trained, because if they were linked to a city, they could find anyone or anything hiding within. They also proved very difficult prey in urban environments.*

A group got together—and by 'group,' I mean coterie in every large city in the world—and decided to remove the human coterie.

It took decades before the humans realized that the attacks were more than random violence; they were being hunted. They tried to rally, but only the zoëtists were community-based and struck back. The citytalkers were solitary, communing mostly with their cities, and the weres tended to group together only for defense, not offense.

"So werewolves don't exist anymore?" Zoë interrupted.

Lycanthropes are only one of many, many weres. These humans could turn into wolves, or cats, or pigs, or any number of things. You'd be surprised at the things a human can turn into.

"And they're gone?" Zoë persisted.

As far as anyone knows. That's another story. I'm sure a handful exist; it's honestly very hard to eradicate a global species.

"The zoëtists clearly did OK."

Their ability to raise armies of mud, water, metal, or flesh was formidable. The weres were only powerful for a couple of days a month. They could force the change at other times, but it was difficult. They were easy prey during the rest of the month.

"OK, but what about this assassin stuff?" Zoë asked.

Citytalkers are hard to kill, and hard to track since they could tap into the cities they were with and know when something was hunting them. This made them immensely useful assassins. A high coterie organization began to employ them, and even say that if you didn't join it, you would be one of the hunted.

"Harsh," Zoë said.

So now we had citytalkers hunting each other, parents hiding their children, and the general genocide happening everywhere.

The zoëtists fought back as they always do, and managed to make a treaty with Public Works and its governing body for protection. But by the civil rights era, most of the human coterie, barring zoëtists, were gone.

"So citytalkers are still around, they're just hiding, or working for the Man?" Zoë asked.

As far as I know.

"So what about what happened to us? Out there with the dog demon thing?"

Possession by a ghost does something strange to human coterie. You will be able to see other ghosts, and your magic combined with my access to other planes means we could merge to create something to fight the demon on both levels, the physical and the metaphysical. It can only defend against one at a time.

A shy, proud tone crept into her voice now. *I was trained in demon assassination, and I knew what to do when it attacked.*

"Then I owe you a beer. Or twelve," Zoë said. "So can you tell me anything about this shadow organization?"

I don't know much about it, only that it's called the Grey Cabal, it's made of coterie, even zoëtists, and it employed citytalkers. It controls the ruling coterie in every city, as well as Public Works.

"Seriously? The watchers of the watchmen are what the watchmen hunt? Now we're getting into conspiracy theory territory."

...Something like that, yes.

"Who knows about this stuff?" The concept of Phil, or Morgen, having this information was too weird.

Very few people. Citytalkers did, once. Perhaps the head of state Public Works.

"So even Phil doesn't know. Weird. So wouldn't citytalkers and Public Works be redundant?

I didn't say the citytalkers were police instead of Public Works. They were a secret police for the Grey Cabal.

Zoë wondered if Arthur knew this. His boss was a fertility goddess, but Zoë had thought that was an anomaly. Now that she knew an incubus was in charge of New Orleans's Public Works, she wondered.

"If the coterie know citytalkers exist—I mean, fifty years ago wasn't that long ago, especially among immortals—why did no one figure out me or Granny Good Mae?"

People rarely see what they're not looking for. It's how coterie have hidden all these years.

"If the Grey Cabal is all-powerful, did they protect their own secret police from the genocide?" Zoë asked.

I assume they tried but not a lot survived. I just know the citytalkers, both the secret police and those of us just trained as assassins, suddenly began dying, and the Grey Cabal couldn't stop it. I don't know if they sanctioned it, or were behind it, or simply decided to let it happen because they had found better assassins than the citytalkers.

Zoë's head seemed to swim. "So the real purpose behind my abilities is to be a secret assassin. But if most of the coterie or the Grey Cabal find out about me, they'll kill me. Lovely. So what do I do now?"

Have you ever attuned yourself to a city?

CEMETERIES

New Orleans is famous for its cemeteries, and for good reason. The water table requires all burials to be above ground, so instead of fields with headstones, New Orleans citizens get marble crypts. Some of these crypts serve as residential areas for coterie, so tourists aren't welcome there. But the best place to rent a crypt for a pleasant, light-tight stay would be St. Louis Cemetery #1. Within walking distance of much of the nightlife of the city, this cemetery offers crypts that still frequently receive offerings from curious tourists or family members who are not aware that their relative has rented out the apartment to a tourist.

The real estate agency Kenneth Crewe and Great-Grandson oversees cemetery rentals, and is open 24-7, always staffed by someone ready to rent out a crypt. ▪

CHAPTER THIRTEEN

Zoë was getting out of the blessed shower when her cell rang. Arthur again. She had nearly forgotten about him.

"Hey, did you have any luck?" she asked, wrapping a towel around herself.

"None," he said, morosely. "I searched miles of swamp. Nearly got lost. I think I saw a gator."

"I'm sorry. I had a rough night. One of my writers killed a person. Then he died. Then I got possessed by a ghost and got attacked by a dog demon, then I killed it. Broke my wrist, got a concussion, it was a mess."

"Nice try on the one-upping, but I'm still the one who's going to be a zombie at the end of the day," Arthur said, his voice flat.

"I wasn't—"

"Forget it. I need some sleep, I'm going back there tonight after I do some information gathering," he said. "When I could get Ben to talk about his mentor, he said she was somewhere in the Barataria Swamps."

"That's pretty broad," Zoë said. "And didn't Ben say that Lucy had killed his mentor?"

"When has death ever stopped anyone? I figure I'm looking for a zombie or a vampire," he said. "Or something else."

"Then you'll need backup," she said.

"I'll call you if I need you. Zoë, you have a whole mess of monster drama that follows you, and I don't need that shit right now. I'm going to die and come back as a fucking zombie if I don't work this out. Nothing is more important to me right now." He hung up.

"But if nothing is more important then you should take all the help you can get!" she shouted, knowing he wasn't there.

She stared at the phone, hurt. But what hurt more was that he was probably right.

While Zoë had no trouble with her zombie coworkers—except for the one who had attacked her, but he was high on formaldehyde and she didn't hold that against him—Arthur had a different view of them, as monsters that needed policing. He didn't want to turn into what he feared, didn't want to suddenly be policed or hunted by his coworkers.

And to be honest, a zombie was not the most... sanitary of coterie. She didn't know if she could stay with him if that happened. Be there for him, sure. But a physical relationship?

He was pushing her away, he didn't want her there to see him fail, to see him change. That was the only explanation. That coupled with his death wish would pretty much shut her out of his life entirely.

She dressed and cleaned the blood and demon junk off her jacket, then put it on. She strapped a knife to her arm. Granny Good Mae had given it to her, and it remained dear, even though she had cut herself with it more than once. Anna had given her privacy—or at least Zoë had asked her to—and waited outside the bathroom door. She made her presence known when Zoë exited, and Zoë allowed her in.

So this merging-with-the-city thing. It helps you actually talk with the city, right? Could the city help me find the Doyenne?

If she's in the city, yes. If not, then no.

Let's go, then.

Zoë didn't see anyone as she left the B and B, not even Freddie Who's Always Ready.

The day was cloudy and cool, and an early-morning rain had washed the cat and human and vampire blood from the sidewalk in front of Freddie's Ready B and B. At least Zoë assumed her party had left such biological hazards behind them.

To merge with a city is more than talking to it, or being its friend, or even being as close as we are now, Anna instructed, and Zoë could hear the shyness leave her voice as she got down to business. She could almost see the girl's earnest dark face beaming at her.

You must give a part of yourself to the city. Willingly.

"A part of myself? Like a toe?" Zoë asked aloud.

Blood will do.

Zoë still had pink scars from her adventures in New York last December. A cut on her arm, one on her shoulder, and a self-inflicted deep gouge on her hip from when she had tried to use a knife while being swallowed by a snake demon. And yet still the idea of cutting herself and feeding her blood to the city was scary, somehow.

She firmly reminded herself that she had reached down a demon dog's throat the night before, and this was nothing compared to that.

The morning was calm and gray. Beads, trash, cups, and vomit had been swept from the streets already, and the city looked new and fresh, ready for tonight's partying.

We need to look for the heart of the city.

Zoë looked up and down the street, then started walking away from the B and B. "How do I find the heart? Is it Jackson Square? A jazz club? A strip club? A cemetery? Bourbon Street? A bead manufacturing plant? The Superdome?"

Take the knife; cut your hand. Your dominant hand.

She couldn't help but feel it was a supremely bad idea, but Zoë obediently slid her knife across the heel of her palm, wincing at the pain. The cut wasn't deep, but it bled, and that was what she needed. She held her hand above the cobblestone street and watched the blood drip down and seep into the dirt between the stones.

The sensory improvement was subtle, but it was there. She could feel the number of bodies in the buildings around her, who slept, who stirred, who played video games, who read the same sentence over and over again because of an argument with a spouse. She could sense the humans and coterie, and tell them apart.

"Wow," she said.

In front of her, she felt rather than saw a golden line on the sidewalk, a line that pulsed as if from a great heartbeat. She followed it down the sidewalk, her head down. She stepped over a homeless man, dropping a dollar in his lap.

The city became awake around her. She could sense waitstaff coming into work to open for the early lunch rush. The shop owners opening their doors. A trolley rumbling by two blocks away.

The walking became meditative to her, and she began thinking apart from the golden line.

Arthur is off in another hotel saying he doesn't need me. I somehow killed an ancient dog demon. Arthur doesn't want me. His drama and my drama don't click. I come from a long line of assassins. Some of the assassins were assassins for the assassins. And other guys, too.

The thought process hit her hard then, and the hairs on her neck prickled. She continued to walk, absorbed in thought, not paying much attention to where she was going, or to the golden thread in front of her, or to her cut hand, which dripped blood onto the ground as she walked. Anna was quiet in her head, letting her learn the way herself, but Zoë could still sense her.

The golden thread got brighter and brighter. Zoë was dimly aware of her phone buzzing in her pocket, but she ignored it, seeing nothing but the gold and hearing nothing but distant jazz music. She turned down a residential street with short houses and walled courtyards. Colorful shards of broken bottles were glued to the tops of the walls, layman's barbed wire. Or perhaps artists' barbed wire.

The gold thread led to one of the walled courtyards. She couldn't see into the yard, but she knew it was the right place.

"What am I supposed to do now?" she asked.

The wall was about ten feet high, redbrick, with green broken glass atop it. In the middle was a wooden door. Zoë hesitated for a moment, her hand over the handle. She was sure it would be locked, or that the owner was on the other side with a shotgun. Before she could touch it, though, it swung open.

Did the city do that? she wondered.

I did.

The voice was not Anna's, but one far older, a touch of the Southern Creole accent, a tone of amusement underneath the very presence of it.

Instead of hearing the words in her head, Zoë *felt* them. She stepped into the courtyard. It wasn't a backyard, in that it didn't have the back of a building as one of its four walls. It seemed to be completely enclosed with brick, with only the wooden door as a way out.

Anna stepped out of her and remained visible, nearly corporeal. Zoë jumped back in alarm. The girl twirled around, laughing.

"You can be seen here?" Zoë asked.

"I can almost touch things, even," Anna said. She sank to

her knees and ran her fingers through the grass, saying, "Thank you" over and over again.

Along the borders of the garden grew long purple flowers, sunflowers, and rose bushes. Ivy dripped from the wall, and in the far corner, in the morning shadows, a fountain bubbled secrets to itself.

"Did—did you know this was going to happen?" she asked Anna, loath to interrupt her, but having no idea what was going on.

"I hoped. I didn't know. I haven't visited a city heart since I died," Anna said. "I can't talk to her, or rather, I can't hear her, but you still can." She twisted so she sat on the ground, cross-legged, skirt over her knees.

"It's time for your next step," she said.

"Cutting myself and bleeding on the street wasn't enough? What does she need now, my appendix?" Zoë was frustrated and feeling a little left out with the city and the ghost citytalker knowing more than she did.

Not seen a talker in decades. Not one who'da speak to me.

"What about Reynard? He's still here, arrived yesterday, a little after me," Zoë asked.

I seen him, but he don't talk.

"That dude is too mysterious for his own good," Zoë said.

Or maybe he do speak, but I ain't been myself since before.

Zoë was starting to realize that "before" referred to Hurricane Katrina, and that perhaps the city was damaged even beyond the devastation that the human world was aware of.

"So what do I do now?" she asked.

"She brought you here to connect with us. You can get a stronger bond with her, and you'll be aware of everything going on in the city. It's intense at first, but you get used to it," Anna said.

"So what do I have to do?"

"Your goal," Anna said, "is to deepen your connection." She pointed to Zoë's hand. "Reopen your wound. Stick it into the dirt. You must sacrifice some of your life directly to her."

Zoë pulled out her knife and looked at it distastefully. "So . . . bleeding all over her all the way here wasn't enough?"

"Just a bit more," Anna said, smiling.

Zoë took a deep breath and cut into her hand again, wincing.

"And I can't even put this in my book, I bet," she grumbled.

Anna pointed to the flower bed, where a hole had been dug. At the bottom lay a small brown flower bulb. Daffodil, perhaps? "Put your hand in the hole."

"Putting your hand somewhere mysterious is never a good idea," Zoë said. "I learned that from Flash Gordon." But she did as Anna said, and let the blood run down into the hole, coating the flower bulb.

"So I just sit here and court an infection while . . ." Zoë trailed off as scenes assaulted her senses.

The first sensation was size. She, Zoë, was a cell in an organism that was vast, stretched miles. She could feel it, sense its borders, feel its roads and its people and its music and laughter and businesses and power and parties and secrets and crimes. The edges felt ragged and painful, as if a page had been torn from a book. It was hard to focus any one place; she could feel pain here, pleasure there. She couldn't feel one specific person or car or building, but she knew that life was happening inside a hospital, and in a poverty-stricken neighborhood. She could feel death happening in nursing homes, and bedrooms, and inside a Dumpster.

The second sensation was that the city herself was a human, a tall black woman, thin and old, with high cheekbones. Her thick hair was in cornrows, and she wore a simple blue dress.

So now I'm you and you're human?

The woman smiled. *Not exactly. I just wanted you to have someone to look at. I got some memories to show you.*

She took Zoë's hand—now Zoë realized she had hands!—and pointed.

The citytalkers had the power of omniscience once upon a time. They'd connect to a place and know it immediately. The really good ones could search the city in an instant from the inside, spot crimes, spot targets. They were silent assassins; no one could hide from them as long as they were in a metropolitan area.

Weren't there some who didn't want to kill? Zoë interrupted.

They was raised to be that way. They didn't know any other way. They were a secret society, with close families that held they secrets. You couldn't spot a citytalker, they wasn't like weres or zoëtists, who were damn powerful. Good citytalkers can talk with a city while having a whole separate conversation with a human.

So what happened after that? How did they find people to kill?

At that moment, images rose in front of Zoë's metaphysical state, men and women being slaughtered in hotel rooms and in sewers, slaughtered by coterie they hadn't seen coming. Weres died when they were in their human form, and only the zoëtists were able to fight back.

How did the talkers not see the coterie coming?

The woman looked very sad. *I don't know.*

Who got to choose the targets?

The same people who run Public Works, and the coterie council. The Grey Cabal.

Isn't that a conflict of interest?

The genocide shattered that Grey Cabal, which had many powerful zoëtists and weres as well as other coterie. Once the humans were gone, the Cabal died. Went silent. Most of the citytalkers was dead. There was chaos for years. Only now is it starting to die down. And the Cabal want what's theirs.

Who mourned assassins, anyway? Zoë wondered.

Zoë was dimly aware that she knelt in a garden with her hand buried in a hole over a flower bulb, but she could sense the whole city in front of her, could feel it, could smell it. If she focused in, she could taste the spices one cook threw into a pot of stew. She could see the shades of blue an artist chose for her painting. She could smell the Mississippi River.

How do more people and coterie not know about the Grey Cabal and the citytalker assassins?

Citytalkers guard their secrets. And the Grey Cabal isn't in a city, no one knows where it is. I've learned what I could from conversations and during assassinations. Some talkers will tell me more than others. But no one talked about where the Grey Cabal made its home.

The woman was silent then, and Zoë couldn't think of what else to ask, so she took the opportunity to feel the expanse of the city, and tried to home in on some of the people she knew. She found Christian the incubus feeding in the back room of Public Works, and she quickly retracted her consciousness. Gwen and Eir were in Gwen's room at the bed-and-breakfast, and Eir was ranting loudly while Gwen listened passively. Zoë could feel the tension in the air. She left before she invaded their privacy.

Opal was on the phone, and Zoë guessed she was talking to Phil. She stood stiffly, staring down at the empty desk in her room with the windows blackened.

Bertie was the most shocking. Zoë hadn't seen him in his natural form yet, and was surprised to see him stretched out on the floor, looking like a giant snake with silver scales. Thin, paper-like wings were folded against his back and his face was vaguely doglike.

He doesn't look like a baby... I wonder when he'll reach full size. He's going to be huge!

The wyrm snoozed on the floor, the gas fireplace in his room throwing gentle light that bounced off his silver scales.

Arthur...

She expanded her consciousness, not sure what she was looking for. She pictured him, thought about how he smelled, the sound of his voice. Something tugged at her, and she found a taxi caught in traffic from an accident on the highway out of the city. Arthur sat in the back, staring out the window, one hand massaging the zombie bite on his shoulder. He toyed with something in his hand, his talisman.

She wanted to call out to him, but she knew he wouldn't be able to hear her. The image of him faded as he left the city limits when traffic lightened.

Curiosity pulled her back to Public Works, not where Christian fed in his office, but the first floor with the Poison Ivy secretary, and then to a basement. It was small, barely six feet tall, and concrete-lined. A trap door and a ladder went from ground to basement floor, and inside the basement lay a number of coterie in a variety of chains.

Their prison, Zoë realized with shock. She had been under the impression that Public Works just killed whatever monsters it found, but most of the beings in the basement were elemental. A fire demon raged inside what looked like a block of ice. An earth elemental, looking like a man made from bark and vines, hung from the ceiling by chains, secured several feet away from the ground, his power source.

And in the corner was a huge tank with thick green glass. It was sealed on all sides like a fish tank with a lid, and the water inside surged and thrashed, a water sprite imprisoned.

She thought of Morgen, then wanted to leave immediately and talk to Christian. If he knew how to bind water elementals, then perhaps he knew how to free them.

She tore her awareness away, determined to learn what she could from the city.

Now what?

She wondered what had happened in Jackson Square the night before, so she shifted her focus there. It looked completely different in the daylight, with the shining statue and the cats all gone. But there was something odd about it—the whole square had a sense of dread to it, as if the square itself had witnessed something horrible, but people still walked around, music still played, and the fortune-tellers still set up. Closer to the train yard, Zoë could feel the spilled blood, the bit of the demon that had joined with the city. It was foul and corrupt, and the grass beside the gravel had already withered, as if sown with salt. There was no sign of Kevin, and Zoë wondered what Opal had done with his body.

The vampire dissolved when the sun rose, which killed the grass there, the city said.

Did you see what happened last night?

The woman looked sad and confused. *I saw the demons fight. I saw the vampires fight. Then there was a lot of blood. That's all.*

When Zoë returned to Jackson Square, the old limping man who had invited her to the party suddenly looked up from his tarot cards. It looked as if he looked right at her, and smiled a big, wide smile.

That party is tonight, she realized. *When am I going to sleep during this trip?*

She could always not go. It was pretty damn clear she had a lot on her plate. Then again, if a being was so strong that he could recognize her when she was part of the freaking city, that didn't sound like someone she wanted to commit a faux pas against.

She gave a mental sigh. Too much to think about. She let her mind return to the garden, where she became aware of her body, still kneeling. The sun looked odd; she realized she had spent several hours as part of the city.

So now what? she asked the woman.

We are part of one another. You can reach into me and feel me when you need to, and I can call you if I need to.

Why would you need someone like me?

New York City needed your old woman, didn't she?

Zoë was quiet at that. She hadn't wanted to think about Granny Good Mae, or the implications of what she had learned. She had learned so much when she had trained with the old citytalker, but not about the citytalkers' history, or why they were citytalkers, or her destiny, whatever that would be. She had thought Granny Good Mae was an assassin because of her history with the CIA, not because of being a citytalker.

I—I would like to go back now. I need to follow Arthur, make sure he's OK, talk to Public Works about water sprites.

You don't want to stay with me?

Zoë felt her spine go cold, even within the floaty metaphysical state. Her awareness was transported to an old country house, and she and the city sat in rocking chairs on the front porch. The sun set in the distance over the fields, and a pitcher of iced tea sweated into a doily on the table between them. Zoë felt like someone trying to make a gracious good-bye, but who couldn't find the words.

I can't. You know that. And besides, aren't we already connected?

The human form of the city shrugged her bony shoulders. *Stay a while. Keep an old woman company.*

Zoë could feel the solid manner of the city fraying at the edges. She remembered how fragile this being was. She put a soothing tone into her words. *And I'm not going anywhere. Not right now, anyway. I just need to get back to, uh, me, and talk to my friends. And possibly stop my friend from getting killed in the swamps. But I can't stay here forever. I'm sorry.*

The city was silent, and she looked down at her shoes, which were sensible brown loafers. *I understand.*

Good. So. How exactly do I get back?

The sun dipped below the horizon, the farmhouse getting dark. Zoë looked to her left, and the old woman wasn't there anymore. Panic bloomed in her chest.

Hello? How do I get home? Will you help me?

With the cruelty of a child who has yet to learn empathy, the city's voice drifted over her as the sun disappeared.

If you don't know, I'm not gonna tell you.

CHAPTER 3
City Infrastructure

POST-KATRINA NEW ORLEANS

It's no lie, and it's no secret: in 2005, Hurricane Katrina nearly shattered the city of New Orleans. Humans drowned, rogue saltwater sprites wreaked havoc in the floods, and the thin lines between class, race, and human and coterie were all smudged or erased.

It has been a long time coming out of that, with some of the people never recovering, others being too stubborn to let "a little storm" beat them, and a rebuilding effort of monumental proportions. Still, the city's various balances are fragile, the mood of the citizens is less trusting, and the borders, both real and magical, are frayed. It feels like a smaller city now, and perhaps it is. But the heart of the city, the one built on music and food and commerce, that one still beats, and never stopped.

Walk her streets and tell her it's OK. Tell her you're happy to be there. Tell her you love her. Time heals all, and the further it moves us away from the events of 2005, the happier we all are. ■

CHAPTER FOURTEEN

When Zoë was agitated, she would pace. Right now, as she had no body, she felt like whizzing around the city like an untied balloon that had been released. But she took a mental deep breath and first tried to picture the heart garden and float over and force herself back into her body, which still knelt by the flower bed.

She found it, and Anna still sat in the grass, enjoying tactile sensations of smelling and touching. She tried to get the ghost girl's attention, but Anna was oblivious.

So that was how ghosts felt. Great.

She approached her body and tentatively reached an arm out and tried to get inside as if it were a new suit. She passed right through herself.

All right, you need to fucking tell me how to get back into my body right now or I swear to God, or—no, I will swear to Gwen— *that you will regret it.*

The city was stern now, an angry aunt who wasn't your mom, but also wasn't afraid to discipline you. *There's nothing you can do to me that'll be worse than the war, or the floods, or Betsy, or Katrina. Your threats is empty. Besides, I don't know how to get you back into your body. I've never had one.*

Oh, that's BS, you've merged with citytalkers before!

And they had all been trained, and knew what to do.

Dammit, Anna, she thought. *Why did you leave this bit of info out?*

Zoë zoomed away from the garden and fled southeast, the direction Arthur had gone in his cab. She began to weaken and feel her connection to the city ebb, and she fought to keep going, but realized she probably didn't want to sever herself from the city just yet. What would happen if she did that? Would she die? Exist as a ghost?

With one fleeting look at the highways and swamps past the city limits, Zoë sped back north toward the river. The same weakening happened there, too, which she had expected. Swearing eloquently in her head, she returned to the courtyard.

How did that go? the city asked her. Zoë ignored her. She went up to Anna and waved her hands at her, trying to get her attention.

Hey! HEY! Anna! HEEEEYYYY ANNA! I thought you knew all the details about merging with the city, and all that shit? HELP ME. She jumped up and down, ran around Anna in a circle, and tried to grab her head, but passed right through her.

She appealed to the city, who had appeared again and looked very amused. *Can't you ask her to help me? If you can make her corporeal, then surely you can find a way for us to communicate!*

The city smiled sadly, and then disappeared.

Oh, you did not just do that. Come back here so I can glare at you.

She chewed her bottom lip, or what passed for it, anyway. *I can't stay here and babysit you forever! I will find a way to get back, and if you don't help me, I won't talk to you or visit again!*

No one ever turns down help from a city, came the disembodied voice. *Besides, we connected now. You can't escape me.*

Shit. I'm a favorite doll the little girl won't let go of. Her stomach, whether real or metaphorical at this point, felt made of lead, and queasy. She could feel sweat break out on her forehead and her palms.

The thought came to her mind unbidden then. What about other coterie? Humans likely wouldn't help her, but gods might. Zoëtists might. And—

Had she had a body, the realization would have floored her. Everything from the previous night to perhaps even the slaughter of the citytalkers. All she had to do to confirm this was find one person.

Zoë calmed herself and let her mind expand, feeling the people within the city without her own thoughts and judgments coloring her view. She felt the life in the city—humans, animals, fae, gods, and demons. She extended deeper and then could feel the undead—the zombies (there were a lot of them), the vampires, and—there. The ghosts.

The city had an awful lot of ghosts.

Zoë was looking for one person in particular, not a ghost. She thought about what she knew about him: very little, but he was cowardly, inventive, self-preserving, and on some weird mission for his employers.

His employers. Oh shit. Seriously? *Seriously?* How could she have been so dense? Reynard had to be an assassin working for the Grey Cabal, or someone else who knew what citytalkers could do. That was why he was testing her.

He was also being hunted, first by the ghosts, and then probably by that damn demon dog that Zoë had had to deal with for him.

I'm done cleaning up your mess, dude. She said this to no one in particular, but it felt good to solidify the resolve.

Zoë hovered above the Life Day festivities taking place in a hotel north of the French Quarter. She caught sight of the girl Beverly, with her zoëtist family. They were in some hotel conference room, listening patiently to a woman in a business suit who was raising a golem from collected Spanish moss, the action contrasting greatly with her attire. A Life Day demonstration, Zoë guessed. She looked around the room, decorated with plastic flowers and moss, with mud and newspaper golems serving punch and cookies to people.

These zoëtists know how to party.

An old man slumped in the corner, hands on his cane, his face sad and scraggly as if growing a beard just took too much energy these days. Zoë looked closer and saw that he was transparent. She approached him.

She waved at him. *Hey, uh, can you see me?*

His eyes rose slowly and met hers. *Course I can. What's wrong with you? Just die or sommat?*

No, I'm not a new ghost. Or I don't think I am, anyway. I'm more of a disembodied spirit, and I need help getting back to my body. Can you help?

The man frowned, his bushy brows furrowing. *What the hell are you talking about? No, I can't help you get back to your body. What do you think being a ghost is?*

Honestly I don't know, Zoë said. *I have only been one for a few hours. And I haven't known many ghosts.*

He shrugged. *It's not like we have conventions to hang out like these fool zoëtists. But I'm here because some young vampire wanted a grandpappy, only my heart gave out before she could turn me. I was a failed vampire, you might say. She hid my body under the foundation and then they built this hotel on top of me. So I just prowl the hotel, break a mirror or two, upset a vice president—they're much more fun to upset than the working-class folk. And people don't believe them any more than they do the Mexican maids.*

One year the marketing department tried to pass me off as a hotel ghost to bring in the tourists, and I took a year off just to spite 'em.

Despite her panic, Zoë was intrigued. *When did you die?*

Almost a hunnerd years ago. Nineteen twenty-nine.

At least you missed the Great Depression! Zoë said, feeling lame immediately after she said it. The old man glared at her, and worked his jaw. Zoë realized he was tapping his few teeth together. She stopped smiling. *Please, is there anything you can do to help me?*

Accept death. It ain't that bad when you get used to it. Come on by here and visit anytime. Jean-Babtiste Martin, he said, and stuck out his hand.

Zoë shook it, realizing it was the first thing she had touched since becoming a city specter. *Zoë Norris. Thank you, Jean-Babtiste, I will be sure to remember you when I'm out of this situation.*

He snorted. *Good luck with that.* He worked his jaw again, and Zoë felt a weird desire for chewing gum.

The business-suit woman was finishing with her lecture, and she was taking questions. Beverly had pulled a cell phone out of her pocket and was thumbing through Twitter. Zoë wasn't sure what to do, so waved at the girl a few times, but nothing happened. She tried to touch her but her hand went right through her. It was kind of revolting, honestly. The girl did flinch a little as if she had felt something cold touch her neck, but didn't look up from her phone.

Zoë leaned in close and tried to whisper in her ear, but she didn't respond.

She was well and truly alone.

CHAPTER 16
Festivals

LIFE DAY

A celebration of the zoëtist way, and the power the zoëtists can command, Life Day is a festival that used to move around the country but now has a permanent home in New Orleans as of 1957. The zoëtists behind it found that New Orleans was the most coterie-friendly city, and something about it made it unique. The power that flows through this city is different, and many master zoëtists chose to make their home here to train their students. Famous zoëtists such as Beracha Zimmermann, Kreindel Sitz, Naira, Richard Silverman, and the mysterious ancient woman the Doyenne all resided in New Orleans at some point, and all trained students here. In 1973 Zimmermann and Sitz set up a school for zoëtists in the French Quarter, but the Doyenne sent a golem to burn it down. They rebuilt with constant gargoyle guards, but their second building was destroyed in Katrina. Both zoëtists are long dead, but their students mourn the loss of their school.

The School of Life used to host Life Day, but now it's in the Andrew Jackson Hotel every January. The festival consists of lectures by masters, contests of creation, and parties staffed completely by golems. ■

CHAPTER FIFTEEN

Nothing. Nowhere. Zoë didn't so much leave the hotel as sink down into the floor, leaving the convention and forming a puddle of misery.

She sank deeper into the grass. She could sense the wet ground, the soil around her. She became intensely aware that very few coterie could come down here. Well, aside from any earth elemental or sprite or other ghost. But the others, the zombies and vampires who claimed to be intimate with the earth by virtue of the fact that many of them were buried, them she knew more than about this.

Not that there was a lot to know. It was dark, which should have been blindingly obvious. But it was also full of life, the network of root systems, the worms and beetles that burrowed, and close were the Gulf of Mexico and the Mississippi with their teeming life. *I could stay here forever. I have nowhere else to go.*

What did you do to me? Why am I suddenly so emo? she asked. The city made no reply. Zoë ached with loneliness. *I could just sleep here.*

She thought about her friends, Morgen and Gwen and Eir. Morgen, who had sacrificed herself to save Zoë and her friends from a fire demon. Morgen who would never let Zoë quit even when it looked as if everyone was against her. She wondered what the water sprite would say to her right now. "What the hell, Zoë? That's not how you become an earth sprite! And you wouldn't want to be one of them anyway. They have no sense of humor, and they usually watch really bad television."

Eir simply would have no patience with her. Go big or go home, that would be the Norse goddess's motto if she were American and from a steel town. Zoë didn't know what the Norse said to pump themselves up. Something like, "Devour the whole pig or eat greens forever after!"

Gwen. Would Gwen see her as an errant soul and devour Zoë on her day off?

Once she might have thought Gwen could help her. Gwen was a psychopomp, and she knew exactly what to do with spirits.

Why hadn't she gone to Gwen right off? Did she really mistrust her friend that much? Ever since she saw her friend eating souls, yeah, there was mistrust there.

She floated up, up, and into the sunlight. The cloud cover had finally blown away and left a beautiful blue sky.

How long had she sulked in the ground?

Something pulled at her, and she followed it like E.T. following a trail of candy.

Or like Hansel and Gretel.

Gwen sat on a park bench several blocks away in Louis Armstrong Park, watching a brass band and waiting patiently.

Hey, Gwen.

"I didn't know how long you were going to wallow. I thought I would watch the band while I waited." She smiled. "What did you get yourself into?"

Zoë told her much of the story, from merging with Anna to following the golden thread to become one with the city. *My first problem was just that I didn't know how to get back into my body. Then I tried to go back but couldn't, and the city just . . . abandoned me. I feel like I lost my virginity to a boy who did it on a dare. I've been intimate with the city but now what?*

Gwen nodded. "I don't know much about cities, but I do know about souls. You are not necessarily a ghost, but you're close enough. I could guide you back to where you are meant to be, but your body isn't on this plane. It never was."

I need to fly another airline, then. Where the hell is it?

"Oh, it's here, but not here," Gwen said. "You need an anchor, not a guide. You can do this yourself."

That's wonderful, Gwen. Remind me to give you your merit badge in obscure and unhelpful.

Gwen smiled at Zoë's annoyance. "Just calm down and listen. You said you followed a golden thread toward the city's heart. You didn't follow some sort of heart line, but where you needed to go. Now what you have to do is do that again. Think of where you need to go, and follow your thread there."

That actually makes some sort of sense, Zoë allowed. *It still doesn't tell me how to find my body, or how to get back into it.*

Gwen opened her mouth. Zoë held up her hand to stop her. *And for the love of, well, you, don't tell me to find the strength inside me. 'Cause it's not there. I checked. Sang the Whitney Houston song and everything. And I looked behind the milk, and under the couch, and in my pocket. I don't know what to do, and I don't know who to trust anymore! I don't even know if you would eat someone like me, an errant soul just bobbing around!*

Gwen smiled sadly. "Zoë, we were both inebriated last night, a position I don't often find myself in. The souls pass through us unharmed, they are not processed, or eradicated, or devoured. I understand your objection, but it's not nearly as bad as you thought it was. And even if it were, I would never do that to you. You're my friend.

"Go find your body, we can talk about the rest of this later. You have a connection to the city now, if you concentrate you can find anything here you want. You have to do this yourself, Zoë, but understand you are not alone."

Zoë nodded and sighed, realizing that she had no mouth, and didn't need to breathe, but going through the motions made her feel better. She tried to think about what she needed to do to connect with the city, despite wanting to do the exact opposite. She really didn't want to talk to the city again, but she needed it now. She spread out, finding the borders of the city's presence, at the coast, through the bayou, over the Mississippi and the lakes and the sound. She found she couldn't go into the swamps, or the Gulf. She felt her friends, and more. She felt the anguish and shame of Opal, and the regret and grief of Eir. The people she didn't know as well, she couldn't sense their emotions. She found Christian, who was inspecting a block of ice in his freezer, and seemed to be talking to it. This cemented one of Zoë's theories about water sprites, but she couldn't think about that.

Zoë drifted and thought about what she'd learned. She thought about citytalkers and zoëtists and the mysterious Doyenne. She thought about the voodoo practitioners, and Freddie Who's Always Ready's grandfather, the one who fought Muhammad Ali. She thought of the host of the party she had been invited to, and how she could explain that she had been kidnapped by a city and had to miss his party.

The golden thread reappeared, and Zoë followed it gratefully. It led her east.

She drifted along into a small shop in the Warehouse District of town. Civil War museums, art galleries, the Superdome, the convention center, these were all upper-crust business and tourist destinations, but one shop stood out horribly. And that's why the humans ignored it completely.

Zoë headed inside, taking note of the seven people who lived in the small apartment above the shop. The aisles were dark and the few windows were coated with grime. A handwritten sign on the door read MAREE'S SHOPPE—WELCOM.

Zoë browsed the shelves, feeling many of the items fairly pulse with energy. This was a voodoo shop, a real one, not one with cheap masks and New Orleans mugs to appeal to the tourists. This was where zoëtists shopped.

The top shelves held jars of herbs and bottles of viscous liquid, some black, some yellow. One rack that stood apart held swatches of fabric, velvet, it looked like, alongside rolls of ribbon, bottles of glitter, and embroidery kits.

The herbs had names like crossing powder, calamus root, catnip, and holy thistle.

Another aisle held small boxes of edible herbs, such as basil, lavender, cloves, and ginger. This aisle also had oils Zoë was more familiar with than the items on the other shelves, like peppermint, cinnamon, and vanilla.

A lazy Susan sat on the counter at the left of the door next to an old cash register. On it were trays of things like rose quartz, jasper, eggshells, silver coins, and pink coral.

On the floor by the counter were a barrel and a large glass jug. The barrel held dried alligators' and rabbits' feet, and the jug looked to hold live leeches.

"You just lookin' or are you gonna buy?" asked the man behind the counter.

Zoë didn't know what startled her more—the fact that she hadn't sensed him there, or that he appeared to see her.

"Can you see me?" she asked.

"A'course I can see you. What kind of priest do you take me for if I couldn't see the dead?" He chuckled. He spoke with an accent, and Zoë guessed him to be from Jamaica, or more likely Haiti. He was bald and had a steel spike through his nose. He looked to be at the indefinable age between forty and seventy that some well-preserved people manage to achieve.

He squinted at her. "Only you ain't dead, is you?"

She felt herself grin ruefully. "You're good. I, uh, am not sure how I'd buy anything of yours, and I left my money in my other pants. Meaning my pants, you know." He didn't smile. She cringed and went on, less flippantly, "So I am kind of stuck, I got put in a trance and can't merge back with my body."

"Hokay," he said. "Where your body now?"

"Somewhere in a walled garden, near the St. Louis Cemetery, I think," she said.

"Dat ain't too far," he said. "Imma make you a gris-gris bag, and you hang it on your body, and that'll anchor your soul right smart there, yeah?" He got moving toward the swatches of cloth, pulling a pair of dirty gardening gloves out of his pocket.

"You have done this before?" Zoë asked, floating along after him helplessly.

"Once or twice. Ain't hard if you know what you doin'. And I can't read or write good, but I knows my gris-gris." He reached out and grabbed one of the swatches of cloth. He eyed her. "You got a favorite color?"

"Blue," she answered absently as she watched his hands deftly thread a needle while wearing gloves, then grab a swatch of blue fabric and begin sewing three of the sides together. Within a minute he had a little bag. He took a white ribbon and attached it to the mouth of the bag.

He moved around the store, muttering to himself. "Now a girl's not gonna want da chicory, she want da rosemary." He dipped his gloved hand into herbs, took a pinch of each, and then sprinkled several drops of oil into the bag. He then went up to the counter and dropped in a few eggshells, a small piece of jade, and then a dried baby alligator foot.

He put his mouth close to the bag and whispered into it, then quickly tied it up tight and knotted it a couple of times.

"Dere. That gonna anchor you but good."

"What do I owe you?" Zoë asked, knowing he would have to take credit since she had no cash on her.

"Blood. Freely given, that is. I don't traffic in the other stuff."

"Other stuff... but I am kind of separated from my blood right now. And I don't think I even want to know why you want it," she said. "And besides, how am I going to take the bag?"

He tossed it to her, and reflexively she put her hand up and caught it. He grinned, his teeth white and perfect. "Tole you it wasn't my first time. You put that 'round your neck, go get back in your body, and then you'll be good. You don't let nobody else touch it, ever. You come back to me soon and we settle up, yeah?"

"Yeah," she said, feeling out of her element completely. "Totally. Thank you so much."

She drifted toward the door, and he called to her, "And don' worry, she do this to every talker. She think it funny."

Zoë turned around slowly. "How did you know... and why do you know that about her?"

"Ain't. My. First. Time." He said the words slowly. "'Sides, my family got both strains in it, priest and talker. Only the talkers is gone." He looked sad for a moment, but then perked up. "So you go get back, and you make sure you don' let anyone else know what you are. Dat's what my sister didn't do, and she gone now."

Zoë thought for a moment. "If you're a zoëtist, do you know the Doyenne? Do you know if she's alive?"

The clerk's eyes narrowed and he spat on the floor. "You clearly don' know, so I'm not gonna curse you for that, but you don't speak her name in my house."

"Oh, I'm sorry, I just need to find her," Zoë said. "I'm sorry I offended."

He snorted. "You need to find her. Everybody need to find her. Some even think she dead, and they still try to find her. No body, no grave. But she out there. Mark my words." He spat again. "Now go on before your body piss itself or something. And come back, but say that name no more."

She nodded, and fled.

CHAPTER 3
City Infrastructure

Pharmacy Museum

If you find yourself injured or ill in New Orleans, the New Orleans Pharmacy Museum is the best place to go. Ostensibly to preserve the history of pharmacology, it is staffed by dedicated and talented health-care professionals, and many of their tools and medicines are still quite potent. If you need aid when the museum is closed to humans, someone is always on call. Their medicines are top-of-the-line, and their leeches well trained. They are able to treat any injury, and most illnesses such as rot, mange, and plague. ■

CHAPTER SIXTEEN

Gwen waited by her body, chatting with Anna, who looked panicked. Zoë went straight to her body, holding her gris-gris bag gingerly, and tried to step back home.

Feeling slightly like an oozy peanut butter sandwich being squashed together, Zoë settled back into her body. It responded to her thoughts, and she toppled over in relief, pulling her bloody hand out of the hole with the flower bulb.

Her hand hurt. She had to pee. And the ground felt wonderful.

Zoë felt the grass with her uninjured hand, and rubbed her cheek along it. Then she allowed Gwen to pull her to a standing position, and she looked around the courtyard.

Anna stared at the ground. "I'm so sorry. I lost myself in the garden and didn't notice you couldn't get back. I can't even see spirits when I'm here. I let you down."

Zoë shook her head, fighting the anger trying to replace the relief she felt. "It wasn't your fault. From what I understand, the city does this sometimes. I don't know if it was a test or not, but I actually had to bargain with my blood to get back here. I got one of these things." She held up the bag with her injured hand. Her blood had seeped into the fabric. "I'm not even sure what it is, but it worked."

It's a gris-gris bag. A voodoo spell. The city's tone was sullen, like that of a child whose toy has been taken away.

"Excellent idea, getting a spell to bring you back home," Gwen said.

"Yeah, but do I have to keep it with me all the time now?" Zoë asked. "Is my spirit in danger of separating from my body if I don't have it?"

Gwen leaned over to inspect the bag. She sniffed it, then straightened. "No, it's already done that part of the spell. But it's a powerful protection spell, especially now that you've added your blood to it. I'd recommend carrying it anyway.

"It's time to go. We have a party to get to," Gwen added, looking pointedly at the setting sun.

Zoë walked toward the garden door, clutching the gris-gris bag. She wondered if she could ever put it down. Something to try later, in a safer place. The ribbon looked long enough to hang around her neck for the time being, so she did that.

"Well, at least you know how to connect with a city now," Anna said.

"You think I'm going to do that again?" Zoë asked, incredulous. "No offense, Anna, but being a ghost wasn't that great."

Anna frowned. "None taken."

Zoë stopped at the threshold of the garden. "Listen, you're welcome to hang out with me more during the trip. You've saved my life, it's the least I can do. I'm not mad at you, really. Just would have preferred not to spend my day on my knees with my hand stuck in the ground."

The ghost girl nodded, and when they stepped out of the garden, vanished.

Zoë sighed and looked at Gwen. "Thanks for that. I couldn't have done it without you."

Gwen nodded and smiled. "Anytime."

They left the heart and didn't look back.

*   *   *

I'm sorry I'm sorry I'm sorry I'm sorry

"Dammit," Zoë muttered, staring at her suitcase. The city had been a constant buzzing in her head, something she was having trouble tuning out.

"Gwen, I'm not prepared for a masque! I didn't pack for this! And I certainly haven't had time to shop!"

She had managed a shower, with Freddie Who's Always Ready arriving with bandages and alcohol at the moment she was dressed. He bandaged her hand expertly and told her of his grandfather the voodoo priest who would solve people's problems in town. And he told her again that when the police came to the door, he would meet them, and not say a word, and then they would leave and never come back.

And did she know that when he died, Freddie's granddaddy transferred his power to Freddie? He'd covered it all in his blog, where he told the story in poetry. Zoë listened to the story as well as she could, trying not to fall asleep. She had taken a twenty-minute nap, which only made her feel more tired.

Gwen had awakened her with an imperious command to get up and get moving, and said that one did not stand up someone as dignified as their illustrious unnamed host. Zoë had mumbled something about how he would understand since he had sensed her with the city, but Gwen ignored her and left her to get ready.

Zoë stood in her ratty Pearl Jam T-shirt and sweat pants and frowned at the sweaters, T-shirts, and jeans in her suitcase. Masquerading as a shlubby travel book editor didn't seem glamorous enough, even if she carried a copy of *The Shambling Guide to New York City* with her.

Gwen swept in without knocking and spun in the middle of

the room. She had changed her long flowing black robes to long flowing red ones. Her hem had white down sewn into it, making her look as if she were walking on a cloud. She had tied her black hair into multiple braids that made a labyrinth all over her head. Her face was covered by a black feathered mask.

Zoë stared at her, mouth open. "OK, I'm definitely not going now." She tried to crawl back inside the fort that was her curtained bed, but Gwen caught her heel.

"What are you talking about? Of course you are going!"

"Hell no I'm not. I look like a hobo next to you, and the last time I went out with a coterie friend and I looked like a hobo, I nearly got eaten by an incubus. Now admittedly that probably had more to do with me being at a sex club with an incubus than looking like a hobo, but you know, associations."

"You're worried that you will get eaten if you go in what you're wearing?" Gwen asked the question slowly, as if Zoë were stupid.

"Yes. No. It's just I am just a human, showing up with a goddess. And it's not even like you're just divinely glamorous. Even if you were human and dressed like that, I'd still look like a slob next to you. I didn't plan for a party, much less a coterie one. There will probably be *fairies* there, Gwen!"

"What do fairies have to do with it?" Gwen asked, crossing her arms.

"They're prettier than me!" Zoë heard the whine in her voice and closed her mouth abruptly. Flashbacks from prom were looming dangerously close.

"And they always will be. Why is tonight different? You travel with coterie. Interesting coterie things just seem to happen around you—no doubt because of your association with the city. How can you not expect a fancy coterie party invite?"

Zoë ran a hand through her wet hair, pulling roughly at tangles. "Never mind, the point is, whatever the reason, whatever the bad planning, I did not prepare for a fancy dress party with or without gods. I do not want to go looking like this. I will stay home. Take Eir instead."

"I am going," the Norse goddess stated, and strode into the room. She was dressed in ceremonial armor, all black leather and shiny silver, contrasting beautifully with her blonde hair, which had been brushed out long to hang below her waist in wavy yellow sheets. She carried with her a spear with a gleaming steel head, Nordic runes carved into the wood shaft. She also wore a mask, hers made of white feathers that matched the feathers that made up Gwen's hem. They made a very striking couple.

They made Zoë feel more like a hobo than ever.

"That's it," she said, and headed back to her bed, swept aside the curtains, and collapsed in a dramatic fashion. "I'm not going."

Gwen's voice was heavy. "This is getting tiresome, Zoë. Here. I will give you five minutes to feel sorry for yourself. Just five. When Eir and I come back in, your tears will be dry and you will be dressed for shopping. We will take you out, get you appropriate clothes, and go straight to the masque. I recommend you wear clothing you don't mind throwing away at the dress shop." Her glittery eyes judged Zoë's sweats. "Those will do."

The goddesses left the room, closing the door firmly behind them. Zoë felt tears prick her eyes, and wondered where Arthur was. She was just exhausted. She normally didn't cry about her clothes, or boys.

"God, this is pathetic. They're right. Sheesh. I need help." She rubbed both hands over her face and then poured a cup of water from the glass pitcher on the bedside table provided by Freddie Who's Always Ready.

She wondered idly if the vampires had blood in their pitchers. Probably. Freddie had told her a long story about how his grandfather always had a pitcher of water and a pitcher of bourbon in his bedroom, and he always knew the one he reached for was the right one.

Then she wondered how Opal was doing.

You could check on her yourself, look at her through my eyes.

Zoë ignored the city's words. She didn't like having a more intimate connection with the city, not when she couldn't trust the being.

"No thanks, I'm not using you to spy on my writers," she said, choosing to give Opal her momentary privacy and focusing back on her room.

In four minutes she had her hairbrush and pins stashed in her purse, makeup on, and a jacket over her old T-shirt. The gris-gris bag hung inside her shirt against her skin. She sat in her chair, purse in her lap, and waited for the goddesses.

Precisely five minutes after they'd left, they returned, and Gwen smiled to see Zoë ready to go.

"So where are we going?" Eir asked.

Zoë shut the door behind her. "Don't you guys know? You're the ones determined to get me all dolled up."

"Yes, and you are the one with the connection to the city. Find out the best place to shop." Zoë hated it when Eir sounded as if her suggestions were actually orders.

She wanted to protest, but she didn't have a lot of energy left. She closed her eyes and tapped into the life force of the city.

Is now when you come a-running back home?

This is not my home. I'm just looking to see where the fancy coterie shop, Zoë said.

I can help. I suppose I owe you.

Sure, helping me shop will completely make up for trapping me in a ghost state. We would be totally square.

The city was quiet at that, and Zoë focused on the shopping

districts, and found Rose's Fair on Magazine Street. It was a short distance from the innocuous warehouse in which the ball was to take place. Several of the customers looked to be coterie, and she even saw some vampires exiting a black-windowed limo in a back alley and entering the shop under a heavy awning.

"Found a place," she said, leading the goddesses out the door.

They passed by the doors of Opal and Bertie, but both were closed, and she heard a stifled sob coming from the vampire's room.

"Is she going to be all right?" Zoë asked.

"She had to kill her son," Gwen said. "That's not easy in any culture. She will likely have a blood debt to pay at home. We can ask Phil."

Zoë paused outside her door. "Should we check on her?"

Eir put her large hands on Zoë's shoulders and guided her toward the exit. "Editor, a human doesn't console a sobbing vampire. They enjoy comfort food as much as humans do."

"Point taken. I just hate leaving her like that."

"Bertie said he will look in on her. He can handle her, maybe take her to a club later to get some food," Gwen said.

"He's not the most sympathetic," Zoë protested, but let them steer her out of the inn.

"What happened last night? With the cats, I mean?" Zoë asked as they got onto the sidewalk and checked the address on the invite.

Eir became very still, even as she continued to walk.

"We still don't know why Bygul was targeted, but the cats see everything in the city, and Bygul was their leader. Kill the eyes, and no one can see," Gwen said, lifting her skirts as she stepped from the curb to cross the street. "He killed only Bygul, so we know it wasn't a random demon attack. After the attack, we don't know where the demon was, but clearly he wasn't done, as he found you. You know the rest.

"It was something amazing, frankly," Gwen said. "You and your ghost made a good team."

Zoë nodded. They were approaching the sounds of a parade, and she had to speak up to be heard. "Thank you for taking care of me, again," she said to Eir.

"It is who I am," she said gruffly. "I'm only sorry I couldn't heal your arm."

Her arm. She had forgotten about the burns—they were healed since her adventure with the city, so thoroughly that she hadn't even noticed. Her hand still stung from where she had cut it, though. She had refused Eir's offer to heal it; after a bullet wound and broken bones, she felt asking for what would amount to essentially a boo-boo kiss was like using Hercules to clean up Chihuahua shit.

"And I figured something else out, incidentally." She told them of her theory about ghosts helping the citytalkers kill humans during the purge. "Cities can't see people possessed by ghosts. So citytalkers can't either."

"It makes a certain bit of sense," Gwen said, forcing her voice loud as a brass band passed them. Zoë got hit in the face with a strand of gold beads, and she bent to pick them up. Eir caught her arm.

"You don't show up at this party with other beads on. You show up pure," she said. Zoë shrugged and left the beads on the ground.

The parade was taking its time, with dancing women carrying huge feathered fans, and grinning lanky men with horns. It was followed by a long line of people eager to follow the parade to a ball, and when it was past, Zoë shouldered her way through the crowd.

Rose's Fair was lightly occupied when they got there, with racks of sleek, glamorous black, white, and patterned dresses hanging on racks. Shoe shelves lined the left wall, and the clerk's counter was on the right. The woman behind the counter looked ready to close. She was fae, to judge from her super-high cheekbones and slightly glowing eyes. She greeted Gwen and Eir, ignoring Zoë.

Zoë opened her mouth to speak, but Gwen stepped in front of her. "This one needs a dress for the ball tonight."

The fae woman looked down at Zoë, one perfect eyebrow cocked. "You're taking that to his ball?" she asked.

"She was invited specially," Eir said, hands on her hips. "Do you want to be the one to tell the host that you wouldn't give her proper attire, or should we?"

The fae sniffed. "What host? There are many."

"The man whose name you should not say," Gwen said.

The fae dropped her eyes. "I'm sorry, I didn't realize you were invited by *him*. Please, we are closing in ten minutes but take as much time as you like."

"You'll close now and let our friend browse as she pleases," Gwen said, passing the woman a bright-blue hell note. With a nod, the woman drifted to the door and closed it and latched the deadbolt.

Gwen removed Zoë's coat for her and took an appraising look at her. "What do you think, Eir? She's short, so something with a short skirt to elongate the legs?"

Eir sniffed. "Unless you are fitting her for armor, I am not going to be helpful. I am against exposing skin, it is unsafe if knives come into play."

"You know what?" Zoë said. "I've had knives come into play unexpectedly several times in the past few months, so I'm going to go with Eir. The less skin showing, the better."

"You ladies have no sense of fun," Gwen said.

Zoë snorted. "You sound like Morgen." The thought sobered her. She thought the water sprite would have been the ideal shopping companion, with the right sense of fun and style to pick out the perfect thing.

The fae showed up. "If you are looking for a dress that has smart armor capability, may I show you something from our back rooms? That is where only our *sophisticated* shoppers visit. I recommend a dress made from Cinderella fabric."

Like Freddie's Ready B and B, the dress shop seemed to be larger on the inside, with rooms here and there that looked structurally impossible. They were separated by color: a sign indicated the red room was up a spiral staircase, and a closet beside the cash register held what looked like yellow pantsuits and canary-yellow go-go boots. The fae led them past this, as well as a hexagonal room filled with green taffeta—literally filled; Zoë could not see into the room past the lacy green stuff.

The clerk brought out a key ring and unlocked a blue door in the back, beside a storage closet that stood open, showing office supplies.

The blue room had white walls and blue clothing of every style. There were older styles like Victorian gowns, simple drop-waisted dresses, long, sleek sheaths, and a Little Black Dress, only in blue. The clerk led Zoë to a rack of blue evening dresses, long flowy gowns made from something that seemed close to gossamer, bordering on silk, puffy like taffeta, but nothing she could clearly identify. Not that she was likely to understand the intricacies of fashion, she realized, but she liked to think she could have identified silk if her life depended on it, and this wasn't silk.

The clerk handed her a simple strapless gown that would hug her curves and then spread out like a waterfall to pool around her feet. With the proper shoes she might just not trip and kill herself—or worse, embarrass herself in front of the New Orleans coterie.

"That's perfect," Gwen said over her shoulder.

"I should try it on first," Zoë said.

The fae woman's eyes sparkled as she led Zoë to the dressing room. "These dresses are fairy-made, they're designed to form to your curves. A true one-size-fits-all garment. It will fit you."

In the dressing room, Zoë had a brief moment of panic when the dress, lacking a zipper or any other sort of closure, stretched out like a snake and wrapped around her of its own accord. Cinderella smart fabric, she remembered.

Now that it was around her, the dress revealed itself to have small gems along the neckline and the hem, as if she'd been dipped into sapphires at both ends.

"You will need these shoes," the clerk said, and slid under the door a pair of glittery ice-blue pumps with two-inch heels.

"One size fits all again?" Zoë asked through the dressing room door.

"Indeed," the fae said.

When she put the shoes on, the dress hem adjusted itself and just barely brushed the ground.

"Handy," Zoë said, looking at her feet. She straightened, then accepted the final accessories shoved inside the dressing room: white gloves that went up to her elbows and a white mask that covered the right side of her face.

The dress did fit perfectly. Zoë suffered through Gwen pinning her hair up, revealing her neck and the scars on her arms and shoulder. The clerk ran back into the blue room and returned with a wrap of similar fabric and presented it. Zoë put it on and was pleased the wrap covered most of the scars.

Zoë tried to pay for the clothes, but the fairy had decided they were Somebodies and said she would appreciate nothing more than a nice word said about her clothes to other Somebodies, if one of those Somebodies was to compliment Zoë on her ensemble.

The fae woman looked her up and down, then frowned. The one thing that was unglamorous about Zoë now was her necklaces, her talisman on a chain and her bloody gris-gris bag. The clerk reached thin fingers up to pluck the necklaces off.

Zoë's hand went up automatically to keep her from meddling with them. The clerk held her hands up and said, "No threat here, ma'am. I am merely wondering if you would like to wear the talisman where it would not be so out of place. Like as a bracelet, perhaps? And the bag, it can go around your ankle if you prefer."

The talisman was the signal to coterie that she was an ally, and that Someone Somewhere would be quite put out if she were to become someone's meal. Not everyone respected the talisman, but she would rather have it than not.

She nodded at the clerk and fumbled with the chain, her gloves proving ineffective at removing it. Gwen stepped forward and deftly unclasped it for her, and attached it around her left wrist. The gris-gris bag was easier to manipulate, and she tied it around her left ankle.

"Will you be requiring any jewelry?" the clerk asked.

"The minimal look is fitting," declared Eir, startling them all. "The editor needs nothing more. Can we go?"

"I didn't know you had an opinion, Eir," Zoë said, smiling at her. The goddess huffed and looked away.

Zoë insisted on tipping the fairy for her attentions and help (and to smooth over any ruffled feathers, literal or metaphorical. She didn't like thinking coterie held grudges against her) and they stepped into the night.

Gwen suggested hiring a carriage to the party, which would keep their finery from liquor or vomit or worse.

Zoë wondered if there would be mice and pumpkins and godmothers involved, but they just hired a normal carriage.

FINERY

While many coterie—especially those with human roots—enjoy shopping at human-focused stores, some prefer to shop at stores more suited to their needs. Enter Rose's Fair, a store where you can get finery that is fitting for Carnival or just a night out on the town. If the coterie world had a patent system, store owner Lilac Thorn, a fae of the plant kingdom, would make a killing with his Cinderella fabric. A dress that does what you need it to, only it won't come off until midnight. The story is that he can enchant fabric to do your bidding forever, but the cost is so high that no one but the oldest vampire who has invested wisely can afford it. Hence the Cinderella fabric, clothes that suit your needs for a set time. ◼

CHAPTER SEVENTEEN

The horse, a definitely unmagical brown gelding, plodded along toward the warehouse. The driver looked uncertain that he was in the right place, but Eir took no heed of his warnings that they were in a bad part of town, tipped him, and helped Gwen and Zoë out of the open carriage. Zoë didn't like to be helped down, but she had to admit the dress somewhat demanded it.

The warehouse at the address was in an empty parking lot, well away from the Bourbon Street revelries. A broken streetlight guttered and popped as they walked under it.

Zoë looked at the empty parking lot and then back at Eir and Gwen. "I see no signs of civilization. Is this the right place?"

Eir looked at Gwen. "You said she would have powers. Why does she not know the answer to this?"

"Right, 'just fucking Google it,' I know," Zoë said. She closed her eyes and reached into the life force of the city. The city herself was busy focusing on something else, and didn't acknowledge her, which was fine with Zoë. She could sense a great deal of life coming from the warehouse—even if not from living humans, the life force was strong. Inside the warehouse were dozens of people, coterie included.

She opened her eyes. "Yeah, this is the place. And give me a break, Eir. I'm not really used to having this ability. It's going to take some getting used to. Anyway, I don't really trust the city right now."

I heard that.

Then deny it, she retorted.

The city was silent, and the women walked to the door. Zoë leaned into Gwen and hissed, "Why did you tell her?"

"She knew you were a citytalker because she overheard us on the train," Gwen said. "Remember, she was inebriated but still aware. She will keep your secret."

"Why do people keep telling me that?" Zoë said to no one in particular.

The door was metal and dented, with gray paint chipping off to show dull steel underneath. Eir raised her hand to knock but the door opened. A zombie stood there, impeccable in black tie and tails, with a top hat. Eir nodded to him and handed over her invitation, careful not to touch him.

The zombie focused on Zoë. "Ms. Norris," he drawled, his slow Louisiana accent made even slower by his natural zombie state. "He will be so tickled to see you. Welcome." His cloudy eyes shifted to Gwen and Eir. "The goddesses Gwen and Eir, he bids you welcome as well."

They followed him into a dirty office area with a gray metal desk that stood askew in the middle of the room. A torn piece of cardboard sat on the desk with the words COAT CHEK scrawled on it in red marker. Tiny gremlins were folding coats into impossibly small parcels and stacking them in the desk drawers. The far end of the room held a door with a torn poster depicting the top half of a toned man standing next to half a motorcycle.

"Are we ever going to know who 'he' is?" Zoë whispered to Gwen as she removed her wrap.

"I told you, no one says his name. It's bad luck," Gwen whispered back.

"Is it a good idea to come to a party of a bad-luck god?" Zoë handed her wrap over to the waiting gremlins working the coat check. She rubbed the scars on her arm self-consciously, but the gremlins distracted her by taking her wrap, spreading it out on the desk, and efficiently folding it by running along the seam to join the corners together. Then one of them handed her a piece of paper with the number 41 written on it. She smiled, tucked the paper into her purse, and tipped the gremlin a hell note.

"He's not a bad-luck god," Gwen hissed, "and I'll advise you not to refer to him as such again. He is not evil, but people fear what he represents, and so they don't say his name. At this point, it's just common practice. If you must call him something, call him 'The One Who Kills and Is Thanked for It.'"

"Can't I call him 'The' for short?" Zoë paused, watching Gwen's face for any sign of the goddess's odd attempts at humor. When she didn't smile, Zoë nodded and said, "OK, then, I'll be using the name 'he' from now on. Thanks."

Gwen smiled. Eir walked around Zoë pointedly and offered her arm to Gwen. Feeling distinctly like a third wheel, Zoë followed the two goddesses through the door with the torn poster, and they were transported.

"I'm living a goddamned *Doctor Who* episode," Zoë muttered as she walked into the huge ballroom. Again, much larger than the warehouse had looked from the outside, it also wasn't the tin box Zoë had expected.

She could have sworn that the warehouse hadn't had windows. She could also have sworn that the evening had been cloudy, with no moon visible. Still, tall windows showed a crystal-clear, starry night. The windows were framed by rich brown curtains the color of old blood. What the color didn't add to the look, the high-quality fabric made up for: it was a rich, textured fabric that nearly begged to be stroked. Huge chandeliers dotted with moving orbs of light gave the room an unearthly glow. The floor was made from wooden planks, cherry, it looked like, and had been polished to a glossy shine. Masked coterie swirled and danced around while suited coterie carried trays of wine, blood, and hors d'oeuvres. (Zoë made a mental note to avoid the trays, in spite of the fact that she hadn't eaten all day.) Heavy cloth streamers draped the walls in a scalloped pattern, with glittering jewels hanging from their ends. At the far end of the ballroom, a tuxedoed zombie staffed a bar, her dead eyes focusing on each patron with determination. She looked to be serving all sorts of drinks, for both human and coterie, with a speed Zoë had never seen a zombie exhibit.

Their host sat at a table near the bar, his hands on his cane. He talked to his companion, a fat vampire with a sickeningly pale face and an eye patch. The host wore purple tails and a top hat, but this was clearly a worn and well-loved suit that looked to have hosted many balls with him. It was threadbare and one of the lapels had visible white stitches where it had been ripped at one point. His cane was made from black wood and had an ivory handle in the shape of a snake. When Zoë and her friends entered the room, he swiveled his head around immediately and focused on them. He stood and tipped his hat to the vampire and left him looking disgruntled. The host limped toward them, grinning widely.

"Ms. Norris, I didn't think you would make it," he said, opening his arms to them.

"I wouldn't miss it," Zoë said. "I've never been to a masque before, much less an exclusive one, much much less one with such a charming host."

He cackled. "You flatter an old man, Ms. Norris. Now who have you brought with you? You I know." He pointed the end of his stick at Gwen, who smiled and embraced him. Zoë frankly stared at the sudden show of physical affection. She hadn't seen Gwen embrace even Eir.

"Does she do this with all old friends?" she whispered to Eir.

"She has never met him before this trip, not in person. They just work in the same circles. When that happens, you get to know people by reputation after a few hundred years."

"It's a god thing, right, I get it," Zoë said.

The god released Gwen and looked at Eir. "Now, you I don't know, but I think we have some things in common as well."

Eir inclined her head, holding her spear upright in front of her. "Indeed. It is an honor to meet The One Who Kills and Is Thanked for It at last."

"You as well, Lady Eir." He bowed back at her. Zoë noticed they kept a polite distance. "Divine ladies, please enjoy yourself to the fullest extent that I can provide. And Ms. Norris, will you accompany me to the bar? I find myself thirsty."

He held out his arm, and Zoë, after a brief, panicked look at Gwen, who nodded to her, took it. He led her along the perimeter of the room, with the masked dancers moving along the floor to the sound of slow jazz played by a zombie band at the other corner. He didn't speak, and Zoë took stock of the whole room. The dancers were all coterie, mostly fae and vampire, but a demon with tentacles coming out of her face was dancing with a fire sprite in the corner, an interesting mirror dance that allowed them not to touch each other. Which, since she looked like a water demon, and he was clearly made of pure blue fire, was the wisest way to go.

A couple of zombies hung out near the band, drinking thick white drinks from martini glasses, tapping their feet slowly.

"Your invitation was a surprise, but I'm still not sure why you gave me such an honor, though," she said to her host, who limped beside her, cane in one hand and her arm in the other.

Had he been limping on the other leg before? She couldn't remember.

"You're very interesting, Ms. Norris. You have a...dangerous glow about you." He spoke as if he chose his words carefully.

Zoë looked down at herself self-consciously. "Dangerous glow? Like I'm pregnant with a killer robot?"

He stopped and looked her up and down, frowning. "No, I don't think so. I mean you shine unlike most humans. Especially after your little adventure yesterday."

Zoë snorted. "I'm sure I didn't see you yesterday. I was dealing with some staffing problems."

His fingers tightened on her arm, not quite painfully, but in an insistent and annoyed way. "I see a lot more than you think, Ms. Norris. Do not lie to me. I know what you are, and I know where you were and what you accomplished yesterday, not to mention what you accomplished today. Understand this is my adopted city, and I will protect her."

Granny Good Mae had never taught her how to fight a god. Zoë forced herself to relax, and smiled. "I understand, sir, but please understand my position. I am only now learning about my heritage, but one thing I am learning is that secrecy and self-preservation seem to be the priority these days. My kind seems to have been hunted almost to extinction. I don't advertise what I am any more than coterie tell humans what they are." She looked around the room at the masked dancers. "Well, in most places besides New Orleans, anyway."

Her joke amused the god, and he chuckled and released his iron grip. "I forget that sometimes the hunters are hunted. I have so long viewed your kind as the ones to fear, not the ones who hide. Times change. We all have changed."

"We have?" Zoë asked. They reached the bar, and the old god stepped to the front of the line. Everyone in line stepped aside in deference.

The zombie bartender waited for him, her back straight and

her suit immaculate, despite the fact that her right ear was only half-attached, which gave her an odd doglike look, drooping forward.

"Give me something from the old days, Greta," he said. "I'm feeling nostalgic." The zombie nodded once and turned to the bottles behind her. Instead of the usual liquor and beer and wine, the bar featured bottles of water—both salt and fresh—what looked like jars of salt, thick bottles of blood, clear plastic bladders of colored gases, and multiple bottles Zoë didn't recognize.

Greta opened the refrigerator; it had a glass door showing brains and other organs, on obvious display for the patrons to choose. A blender was beside the fridge, and Zoë realized what the zombies had been drinking. Her stomach tried to clench, but she firmly told it that she'd been involved with this world for too long to get squicky about it now.

Greta pulled a small circular plastic container off the bottom shelf of the fridge and passed it to the host. It was a Petri dish with a web of bacteria inside. Zoë felt simultaneously more curious about who this god was, and certain that she didn't want to know. He accepted the dish with a nod and looked at Zoë.

"Oh, right, something in the plain old red wine variety, if you have it. If not, then just water. Plain water, that is," she amended, remembering that some coterie ordered water from different lakes, oceans, and time periods as their intoxicating drinks.

The zombie pushed a glass of red wine over to her across the bar, and she smiled. "Thanks." She rooted in her purse for a hell note, but her host put his hand on her. "The bar is free, my dear."

"Can I tip her at least?"

"Be my guest," he said, removing his hand. She put a hell note on the bar, and the zombie accepted it without changing her facial features.

Zoë still wasn't used to zombies and their lack of body language, but she managed to remind herself that the cues were not the same as with humans.

They retreated to the table she had seen him at earlier. The fat vampire was gone, his seat vacant. They sat down and watched the dancers, Zoë sipping her wine, the host dipping his finger into the Petri dish and swirling it around absently.

The band changed to a faster number, and the coterie who preferred slow dances left the floor for the more energetic dancers—Zoë was interested to see that a lot more demons took the floor at this point, including the blue fire sprite and his tentacled date.

Her wine was surprisingly good. It was a dry Shiraz, an excellent vintage, if she wasn't mistaken. She had figured the coterie would choose crappy wine for the stray humans who were invited.

She took a deep breath and met her host's amused eyes. "So you know who and what I am, I understand to not ask who you are, but the question still stands of what you want with me."

"Who says I want anything? I think you're interesting, and I'm delighted to be able to host one of the last of your kind at my party. Although the social worth of it is somewhat lessened by my being the only one to know that secret." Zoë frowned, and he patted her hand. "Don't worry, dear. I will keep the secret. In fact, you were told to bring a gift. That secret will suffice."

Before Zoë could feel the crushing embarrassment of not having brought a gift to the old god, someone spoke behind her. "The One Who Kills and Is Thanked for It," said a familiar voice speaking in a very formal tone. Zoë gasped and turned around.

Her host raised his head and looked at the newcomer as well. "Ah, Mr. Anthony. I was expecting you. Please join us."

Arthur stood there looking none too pleased to see Zoë.

*　　　*　　　*

Zoë tried desperately not to fidget at the table as Arthur, dressed in a very sharp white tuxedo and a simple domino mask, carried a cane in one hand and a wooden box in the shape of a cube in his other. He gave her a curt nod as he sat down with them, and otherwise did not look at her.

"You have been quite persistent in requesting this meeting. I admire that," their host said. He licked his finger with a white tongue and closed his Petri dish.

"I didn't expect to get invited to the party, honestly. Thanks for that." Arthur looked around, a frown creasing his face. His eyes still didn't land on Zoë's.

"I was kind of hoping for something a little more intimate," he finished. "My topic is rather"—he pursed his lips—"uncomfortable and personal."

"Oh, I know all about your little problem, Mr. Anthony. There's not a lot that happens here that I don't know about, including what goes on in the swamps. Most of what goes on in the swamps, anyway. Did you find the Doyenne?"

Arthur's jaw clenched. "I couldn't find her."

"That's a pity, but few can find her. That is because she doesn't want to be found. You were silly not to accept Ms. Norris's help." He indicated Zoë, politely.

"I wanted to fight that battle myself," Arthur said, looking at the table. "I didn't want her hurt."

"Noble, and ridiculous. Also, are you speaking metaphorically or literally?"

"Pick one."

The host laughed. "Frankly, Mr. Anthony, I would love to help you. You're more special than you know, and the world is a better place with you in it. However, your affliction is not something I can fix. You're already half dead, you see, and bringing folks back from that threshold isn't my purview. I can help you in the other direction if you like, but you don't want that." He paused and smiled slyly at Arthur. "Despite what you may think. Also you don't necessarily need help finishing the job the zombie started."

Arthur's long, scarred fingers fiddled with the box he had brought. "And how can you tell that?"

"I know everyone who longs for release. You don't. You long for a cure, and you're fighting every step of the way. You need the Doyenne, but the price she demands will be high. And that's if you can find her. Are you prepared to pay her price?" He settled back in his seat, hands wrapped around his cane.

Now Arthur glanced at Zoë, then back at their host. "I normally would say yes. But I've dealt with enough coterie to know that if you're smart, you don't make blind promises, no matter how much you want something. I'm prepared to hear what she needs from me as payment for whatever herbs or magic she does, but I can't promise I'll give it."

"You're wiser than I thought, then," their host said. He held out his hand, and Arthur looked at it, mutely. The host raised his eyebrows. "Your offering?"

"Oh, yeah, right," Arthur mumbled, and put the box into his waiting hand.

Zoë watched the exchange with interest, wondering what was in it. The host opened the box and pulled out a little specimen cup that looked to be half filled with blood.

Do you consider a cup of blood half empty or half full? Or do you just go into why is my sort-of-maybe-probably-not-boyfriend passing around his blood to ancient gods whose names we're not allowed to say?

The city's voice was stern. *Ain't you figured it out yet? He's a god of disease, you damn fool. Giving him diseased blood is considered an offering.*

Zoë pursed her lips. *I liked you better when you couldn't speak directly to me.*

"Is that your blood?" Zoë asked.

"Yeah," he said. "That and an anticoagulant, anyway. Couldn't have it clot before I got here."

"Weird. It's apparently currency at a little shop north of here. Lot of people want blood, I guess." Her tone was light, but Arthur didn't relax.

"Fascinating," the host said, shaking the cup a bit to mix the blood back together. "You truly are caught between living and death. While it's not my usual offering, it's unique, and I appreciate it. I'll give you this, then. When you find the Doyenne, you do not tell her I asked about her. To find her, you must look in the dark areas, the areas you wouldn't normally look. It's possible your death goddess friend can find her with her unique abilities. I would ask her, but she owes me nothing. She may do it if you ask her. Tell her that you and the Doyenne have something in common. The Doyenne will offer you the herbs when you find her, but the price will be too high for you. You may choose to die instead, or find a way to pay it and then live with your choices. Even though I know what you will choose, what makes humans glorious is their free will. And their lovely diseases, but mostly the free will. You go to her. Hear your options. Make your choice. If you choose to become a zombie and stay in New Orleans, I have a place in my court for someone like you."

Arthur stood up from the table, his eyes wide. "No, I'm not going to choose to be a zombie. I'll die first, or pay whatever price she wants."

Some nearby coterie looked over to them with curiosity, and

Zoë was pretty sure a zombie who looked like an old Southern gentleman looked shocked and offended at Arthur's comment.

The host did not respond to Arthur's rudeness. "As I said, you have a choice. I'm not telling you what you have to choose. I just know what you will choose. Oh yes," he added as if just remembering. "And Zoë must go, too. She is rather important here."

A cool, thin hand touched Zoë's bare shoulder, and she jumped. Gwen stood behind her, smiling. "I thought I heard someone mention me. Also, your life expectancy just dropped drastically. What's going on?"

CHAPTER 16
Festivals

JAZZ FEST

The coterie don't like to admit it, but jazz was created entirely by humans. However, several of the jazz greats were then turned to be vampires or zombies, but they prefer their privacy. That said, if you go to Jazz Fest, you can likely find them on the coterie stages, late at night.

Since the creation of jazz and the forming of New Orleans's second biggest party, certain coterie have taken a shine to it, and make yearly visits. At previous Jazz Fests, performing coterie have included Kokopelli, the god of fertility, agriculture, and music, and every year since 2000, Euterpe of the Greek Muses has made an appearance. (There was a notable concert in 2006 where she brought all eight of her sisters for an epic performance.)

All coterie concerts begin after dark, and some are invite-only. Several innkeepers in town have the connections for tickets. ▪

CHAPTER EIGHTEEN

The zombie band took a break, bringing on an air sprite DJ, who clearly hadn't moved beyond the late 1980s in his musical education. The song was "Penny Lover" by Lionel Richie.

The host had demanded Zoë and Arthur dance once before Arthur stormed out. His stiff arms held Zoë awkwardly as if they had never touched before, never been intimate. With the music and the swaying dancing, Zoë realized the only thing different between this and her first middle school dance was the fact that she could have a big glass of wine when she was done with this travesty.

Arthur reminded her of Matthew Wise, the object of twelve-year-old Zoë's affections. He wouldn't meet her eyes, his steps were stumbling, and his hands on her waist were sweaty. He kept glancing back at their host, who watched them with a grin on his face.

"Is there anything you want to talk about before you go on your suicide mission?" she asked finally.

He glanced at her eyes and then back down at their feet. "Dammit, Zoë, I'm sorry. This is so big, I can't control it. I can't endanger anyone else."

Zoë narrowed her eyes. "You need people to rely on. And by 'you' I mean everyone. No one can deal with something like this alone."

He shook his head. "The problem is, people like us shouldn't date each other. We both need someone like Orson."

He was referring to Ben's husband, a man who knew about the existence of coterie, but had no association with them, and frankly hated Ben's association with them. Zoë had suspected Ben's MIA status was due entirely to Orson's wanting him to be unreachable during their vacation.

Arthur's eyes met hers, and they held nothing but despair and certainty. He opened his mouth to speak, but she spoke first. "You've already quit, haven't you? Not only us, but quit fighting. You're just wanting to go out on your terms." She swallowed; her throat felt constricted.

He nodded at last. "I feel like I'm at the end, and despite what the old man said, I don't see any choices."

Zoë's voice was flat, devoid of emotion. "This is the part where you're supposed to say now that you're close to death, you can see everything clearly and you need me more than ever."

He looked away. "It's not a movie."

"This is why rom-coms are depressing," she said. "All right, fine. Do what you want. We're done here. But I'm not letting you go to the swamp alone. You'll stumble around and get eaten by a gator or something."

"I don't want you hurt," he began.

She raised a finger, shushing him. "No, you don't want me distracting you. If today is your last day as a human, having me with you for that last day is worse than being alone, apparently. But I don't have to respect your wishes anymore. You're not my boyfriend, you're just a dude with a death wish."

He let her go. "I have to go tonight, my time is running out."

She was glad for the mask that hid half her face. She wished it could hide the whole thing. "Take Gwen, she's better with this stuff than I am. I haven't had much sleep lately, and I'm not thinking clearly." She rubbed the nonexistent bump on the back of her head.

She turned from him and left the dance floor, Lionel Richie still crooning over the speakers. She snatched her wineglass from the table where the host still sat. "Thank you for the invite, sir, and the conversation. It was a true pleasure, and please forgive my rudeness. I have to go now."

He nodded once as if he had expected this. "Don't forget your weapons as you go to the swamp tonight, Ms. Norris. And if you find what I'm looking for, let me know."

"I'm not going to any fucking swamp," she snapped. "And I still don't know what you're looking for." Walking to the bar, she drained her wineglass, and cut in front of three vampires and a horned demon. She put a hell note on the counter and pointed to one of the bottles of Shiraz behind the counter. "I'll take the bottle," she said.

The zombie's eyes flicked up behind Zoë, and she realized the bartender was checking with the host. She unconsciously slipped into the city for a wider look at the room, and saw him give a nod. Arthur was exiting the dance floor, heading for Gwen, who stood along the wall in deep conversation with Eir.

She snapped back to herself, shocked that the transition had been so easy. The bottle was in front of her, and the vampires and demon glared at her.

"I just broke up with a dude who's going to die tomorrow. Cut me some slack," she said to them. One of the vampires, a short Latina woman, looked sympathetic, but the others waited impatiently for her to stop blocking the line.

Something tugged at her attention, and she skirted the room with her bottle, sidestepping demons and vampires, and nearly stepping on what looked to be a leprechaun. She left the ballroom and stepped through the door to the little office area. Now that she was in a safer, quieter area, she expanded her awareness again. Christian the incubus had arrived alongside Reynard the citytalker. They were talking with the host. Reynard looked strange through the city's eyes, almost transparent as if he were a ghost as well. He would shift in and out of Zoë's awareness, but Christian and the host didn't respond to this.

Zoë stuck her head back into the ballroom—Reynard looked solid and normal as he shook the host's hand. So it was true. Ghosts and citytalkers together were not only deadly to demons, but harder for the city to notice.

He had probably found a ghost to help keep him safe from demons. Smart. Zoë probably should have made some kind of deal with Anna to stick closer to her.

Zoë ducked into the office again and slid down the wall, her bottle clutched in her hands. She tried to look as much like a depressed drunk as she could to keep people from wondering why she didn't respond if they called to her, and then expanded her awareness again and eavesdropped on the table.

The host knew she was there immediately. He smiled and looked right at her vantage point, but returned his gaze to Christian.

"I didn't know the Grey Cabal was sending an ambassador. I also didn't realize it was sending a human," the host was saying. "Still, it's delightful to meet you. How can I aid the Grey Cabal?"

Silence. Reynard looked to be talking, but Zoë couldn't hear more than some kind of odd static. She really wished she knew why a ghost/human combination was invisible to the cities, but at least she understood why the citytalkers had been so easy to hunt—all the assassins had to do was have a ghost riding with them. So it was true, he was working with the Grey Cabal.

Were citytalkers assassinating again? Zoë felt cold, and very much an outsider. Already something had tried to kill her, but she was fairly sure that the one person who truly hated her, the zoëtist Lucy, was dead.

Well, there was Kevin, but he was dead, too.

"I am aiding Mr. Reynard by providing census numbers of the city, but he needs information on where to find the more independent coterie living in the bayou," Christian said.

They paused again, presumably while Reynard spoke. Then the host took a cocktail napkin and drew a quick map. "She was last reported living in her houseboat on this river. She likes to move around. Doesn't like to be found for some reason." His voice dripped with amusement. "I would go myself, but of course, circumstances..." He trailed off.

"Thank you," Christian said, and bowed his head to the host.

"Y'all going tonight?" the host asked nonchalantly.

Silence again.

Before she could hear a response, Zoë was dimly aware of fingers on her shoulders, shaking her. She returned her awareness to find Eir holding her in midair by her shoulders and shaking her like a rag doll. The bottle of wine slipped from her fingers and spilled on the floor, splashing Eir's boots.

"God, what, I'm back, let me go!" Zoë shouted, struggling.

Eir set her down, and Zoë frowned sadly at the spilled wine. "There goes my evening."

Gwen retrieved the bottle, still half full, and handed it to Zoë. "We wanted to see if you were all right. Arthur has asked us to accompany him to the swamps tonight, but he said you weren't coming. Are you spending the evening with a bottle instead of your friends?"

Zoë put the bottle down on the desk, where the gremlins pounced on it, using teamwork to tip it over and taking turns guzzling the wine. It ran down their chins and over the desk.

"I was kidding about the bottle, but yeah, Arthur made no secret that he doesn't want me, and he's probably going to die out there. Screw him anyway. Still, he needs help, and if you can give it, give it. I don't want him to turn into a zombie just because my feelings got hurt."

Zoë rubbed her arms, the ache still new. Maybe he was right. They didn't belong together, and she would get in the way.

Gwen nodded once. She gave Zoë a wry smile. "Maybe tomorrow we can get started on the book?"

Zoë groaned. "The book, I almost forgot. Is anyone taking notes about this ball?"

"I will do it," Eir said. "Gwen and I will leave for the swamps in an hour. First we party."

The idea of the stoic goddess partying was enough to push a smile back on Zoë's face.

CHAPTER 21
Plantations

Arcadia

All New Orleans plantations are now tourist attractions for humans—all but one, that is. Arcadia is still a living, breathing, working plantation.

In its ugly past it had a ruthless master, Harold King, who was famous for using his wealth to buy more slaves than he needed, and having them fight for the "honor" of working the fields. One night, a visiting vampire from Morocco took pity on a slave—Jenny—and turned her, then set her loose on the plantation. Jenny was a zoëtist of growing power, and her mixture of vampirism and zoëtism was a sight to behold as she killed her master and trapped his soul within the plantation itself. She freed her fellow slaves and turned several of them, and they took over Arcadia. For some time, the evil that dwelled in the land turned the crops sour, but even evil gets tired, Jenny learned, and after some decades the fields began to be fertile again.

Jenny died her second death when some zoëtists hunted her down, screaming that she had blasphemed against her culture by accepting a vampire's embrace. Many of the original slaves still live in Arcadia, but no other vampire at the plantation has retained their gifts. However, they still say they can feel Master King in the soil beneath their feet, and they refuse to sell the plantation for two reasons: they don't wish to risk anyone else owning the haunted place, and they want to continue the punishment of the most evil man they knew. ▪

CHAPTER NINETEEN

Don't go.

Zoë glared out the window of her taxi (driven by a human), hoping the city could see her annoyance.

Go where? I'm going back to the B and B.

The taxi was taking her back to Freddie's Ready B and B, and she was trying to decide what to do with the rest of her evening. She could sleep. Or maybe she and Opal could split a bottle of wine and commiserate. Girl bonding.

Oh right. Opal was a vampire. Was a human friend too much to ask for?

The city sounded frantic. *No, don't go to the swamps with those friends of yours. I can't watch you there.*

Zoë remembered to answer in her head, despite her impulse to yell at the voice. *I'm not going to the swamps, and frankly, I don't need you looking after me. I don't trust you, remember?*

You're considering going. You are. I can feel it.

Zoë thought for a moment. *I wasn't till you said something. But you're right, I don't like the idea of that assassin dude heading out there the same time as Arthur. Even though Reynard is a complete coward.*

Don't! You won't be able to contact me, or view the dangers around you. You are only safe in the city.

Zoë thought of all the times in the past thirty-six hours she had not been safe in the city. She could think of at least once each week since she'd discovered the coterie's existence that she had not been safe.

She didn't answer, and the city remained silent. Zoë leaned her head back and closed her eyes, trying to decide what to take with her. First change out of the dress. Then get weapons, definitely. Flashlight, cell phone. And what was she going to do? Follow Arthur? Reynard? Stop...something?

She wanted to find out what Reynard was up to, definitely. And she was rather nervous about Arthur going out there on his own to look for a possibly undead zoëtist. He could likely handle himself, it was his job, after all, but he would be clouded by desperation and despair. It could affect his judgment.

The taxi pulled to a stop outside the B and B. "Can you take me to the bayou?" Zoë asked.

The cabbie, a large man in a white tank top, twisted around. Zoë tried not to look at his back hair. "That's a broad question. The bayou ain't like a store you go to. It's kind of big, yeah?"

"Yeah, right. Never mind." She paid her fare and slouched up the front steps to the door. How was she going to get to the Doyenne's place if the zoëtist master was constantly on the move, and even the host couldn't find her?

She walked into the B and B and found Opal's bedroom door open, and Bertie lying on her floor. Opal's face was red from tears, but she looked calm as she sat on her bed in a white blouse and jeans and heels. Bertie, in human form now, lounged on her floor and Zoë got a weird sense of déjà vu, from memories of visiting college buddies as they hung out in a dorm room.

Zoë knocked on the door and poked her head in. "Hey, how are you holding up?"

Opal shrugged. "Bertie is helping. I talked to Phil. He's not going to fire me."

"I would hope not. I need you. And coterie laws are a bit different than human rules, right?"

Opal shrugged, a more tired response than an "I don't know."

Bertie answered for her. "A bit. Anyway, what are you doing back? I thought you were going to be at the ball all night."

Now it was Zoë's turn to shrug noncommittally. "Something came up that requires, well, all of our attentions."

Bertie snapped to his feet, faster than Zoë had ever seen him move. "What can we do? I'm ready to be part of your adventures." He reached out and snatched Opal's wrist, pulling her to her feet. She whined a protest but stood listlessly next to him.

Zoë looked at him suspiciously. "You seem way too eager, which is pretty much the opposite from last night. What gives?"

Bertie grinned. "Last night was more fun than I've had in a while. You may not have plans, but being with you is exciting. Besides, Opal needs something to give her some pep."

"OK, well, we're looking for a zoëtist who may or may not be dead," Zoë said. "She apparently is somewhere in the swamps. She's supposed to be dead but that hasn't stopped just about everyone I know from trying to find her tonight."

"Great, the bayou is my assignment," Bertie said. "And between us we can find one human, right, *cher*?" He elbowed Opal. She raised an eyebrow. He shrugged. "I like how they talk here. Sue me. So why are we doing this, boss?"

She had no desire to discuss the situation concerning Arthur. But Opal looked completely miserable and could probably use some distraction. Zoë laid out the situation in brief, essentially that they were looking for the Doyenne and had to find her tonight.

"I'm going to go get changed. Be ready in ten," she said.

She got out her phone and texted Gwen.

DO YOU KNOW IF THE HOST SENT ANYONE ELSE TO FIND THE DOYENNE TONIGHT?

Gwen was swift with her reply.

NOT THAT I KNOW OF. WHY?

Zoë thought for a moment, and started to text—**I'M HEAD-ING TO THE**—but the phone powered down.

"Shit. I've never charged it," she said, staring at the phone. She stuck her head out of the room. "Guys, does anyone have Gwen's number in your phone?"

Bertie and Opal answered in the negative, and Zoë groaned. What an awesome leader, not even making sure they all had each other's numbers.

She plugged her phone into the wall and watched it. A red light began to blink sluggishly, and she tried to turn it on, but it refused. "Dammit, how long does it take these phones to charge, anyway?"

"If you drain the battery all the way, it needs to get to fifteen percent before it will even turn on again," Bertie called from his room. "Didn't Phil tell you not to let it run out all the way?"

"Phil doesn't tell me stuff like there was a whole genocide against a part of the human race, why would he tell me about how to work a cell phone?" she muttered as she left the phone on the desk to charge. She forced her mind back to the pressing topic.

She had no idea what the host was angling for, sending a bunch of people into the swamp. Whose side was he on? What was Reynard up to? She did know what Arthur was up to, and that was enough reason to go after them.

She closed her door and tried to reach for the zipper of the dress, then remembered it had formed itself around her. Cinder-ella fabric. It was "smart."

It was also not coming off.

Zoë groaned. It probably wouldn't come off until midnight. She looked at herself in the mirror. "Am I really going into the swamp dressed like a fairy princess?" She probably had just insulted fairies, but who cared; she didn't employ any, right?

If Morgen had heard her say that, she would have called Zoë a bigot. Damn, but she missed that water sprite.

Zoë bent down and slipped her shoes off, glad she could at least put on her Chuck Taylor high-tops. When she stood, she noticed the dress subtly rearrange itself to fit her loss of a few inches. Then she looked in the mirror and jumped.

Anna, the ghost, was standing behind her.

She whirled, but saw nothing in the air behind her. She peeked back at the mirror and saw the ghost girl pleading with her eyes, and Zoë guessed what she wanted.

"All right, come on in."

The ghost stepped into her and they merged. In the mirror, Zoë could see the girl's face on top of her own. It was very strange.

"So how much have you witnessed tonight?" Zoë asked.

I've been watching you since you got to the ball. I'm sorry about your boyfriend.

As she spoke, Anna moved Zoë's hands over the dress and tweaked here and pushed there, and even though she couldn't remove it, she coaxed the dress into something a bit shorter, something that covered the shoulders and protected a bit more. Zoë nearly forgot to listen, she was so entranced by the girl's casual modification of the magical clothing.

"So am I right that the citytalkers were killed by assassins working with ghosts?" Zoë asked.

Some of them, certainly. That kind of information is pretty tightly guarded, but yeah, it makes sense. I knew we could kill demons if we merged, but didn't realize we were invisible to cities. Those who did know, and knew how to hide from the citytalking assassins, were probably taken by surprise. For some of us, it was a quiet war, or one that we thought was happening to others. Besides, being an assassin is a dangerous job. Many just thought that their friends and loved ones were dying on the job.

"I guess cities wouldn't know to look for something they couldn't see," Zoë said.

I suppose not.

"OK...so why are you here now? I hope we don't have more demon dogs?" Zoë said.

I thought you might need help with the swamp.

Zoë nodded. "I can use all the help I can get. Especially if there are more demons out there. I'm not sure if I want you inside me the whole time, if that's OK. It's a little disorienting."

I will only possess when you ask me to.

"Thank you. I'm not sure how I could repay you."

I've no need for payment. Being with you has been more exciting than my last fifty years.

Zoë stumbled as she regained control of her body unexpectedly.

She glanced in the mirror again and saw Anna by the bed. "So even if you're not in me, you'll be nearby?" she asked. The ghost nodded.

"Human, wyrm, vampire, and ghost. Going to save a Public Works dude from I don't know what. Why am I not surprised my trip has ended up like this?" she asked herself in the mirror. Either the city or the ghost could have answered her, but neither did.

Zoë packed her satchel with her notebook and pen, both phones (the coterie phone had barely fifteen percent charge left), her knife, a stake (hidden from Opal), and a really old compact of foundation she had found in her suitcase. The makeup was crumbly, but the mirror was just fine.

She texted Gwen that she was going to the swamp and added that a citytalking assassin was also headed there. Gwen didn't reply.

Bertie raised his eyebrow when Zoë came out of her room. "You always go tromping through swamps in an evening gown?"

"It's Cinderella fabric or something. I can't take it off till after midnight. Who thought this was a good idea?"

Bertie smiled at her and she made a face. Opal exited her room dressed in a black turtleneck and black jeans. She still wore black heels.

"You look like a poet," Zoë said.

Opal looked her up and down. "If you'd rather I not go, I'd be delighted to go out looking for a bite. Besides, I'm in mourning. And I can't even begin to wonder what the hell *you* are wearing."

"Cinderella—Oh, never mind. Yes, I'm wearing a ball gown in the swamps. You're a poet. Bertie, who are you playing at tonight?"

Bertie shrugged. "Human?"

"You have no vision," Zoë said.

Freddie Who's Always Ready met them at the door with canteens of water and a first-aid kit. "Never know what will happen in the swamps," he said. "I once met Muhammad Ali out there, and we boxed in the parking lot of a swamp tour clubhouse. He said I was the best he'd ever seen. Wished we'd had a first-aid kit then, the poor bastard's lip was swole up good."

Zoë nodded at him, trying to extract them from another story. "That's awesome, Freddie. Thanks."

"Also I tried to call you a cab. The bad news is, no one will go out there at night. More money made in the city, they said. Did I ever tell you about the time I drove a cab?"

"No, but how did you know where we were going?" Zoë asked.

He grinned at her, the gold tooth catching the light. "I'm always ready," he said. "One of my guests needs something, I'm ready to help. Within reason, that is. So let me tell you about the time I had President Obama in my cab. 'Course, he wasn't president at that time, he was just an ordinary Joe."

"That sounds like a great story to hear over some coffee, so will you save it for when we get back?"

Freddie nodded, smiling. He looked used to putting aside his stories for later.

On the sidewalk Zoë frowned and started looking on her phone for where the closest car rental was. Bertie looked over her shoulder, smiling. "No plan, huh?" he asked.

"Can't you go back to being silently superior, please?" Zoë said, exasperated. "You know exactly how we can get to the swamps, but you won't tell me because I'm a lowly human who can't get to the answer myself."

She was starting to shout. She took a deep breath. "Fine, then. I'll make a decision. Turn into your natural shape and fly us there."

His eyes widened. "What?"

"You heard me. I said, in a handful of words, that I know what you look like when you're not human. I know you're big enough to carry both Opal and me. And I'm pulling rank, reminding you that even though I'm a human, even though I'm only in my thirties, and even though you could eat me with one bite, I'm still your fucking boss." She forced her voice back to its normal volume. "Unless you have a better idea."

His face darkened to the point that Zoë was afraid he was going to scream at her, or storm off, or eat her. But he continued to change color until his skin reached a slate gray.

He stooped over until his hands hit the sidewalk, and, in full view of everyone, he began to change.

"What, here? Is this a good idea?" Zoë asked, looking around.

"Our friend had too much to drink," Opal said to a passing couple, who looked with pity at Bertie on his hands and knees on the sidewalk.

"Stand in front of him. Look like we're building a float for a parade," Opal suggested, so Zoë and Opal shielded Bertie from the onlookers, and Zoë started telling Opal to check the airflow and make sure the chicken wire was hidden.

"Chicken wire." Opal's voice was flat and confused.

"Parade floats have chicken wire," Zoë said pointedly.

"Right," Opal said, starting to pat the changing Bertie as if she were setting up a float.

Bertie ended up even larger than Zoë had seen him in his room—he must have still been keeping himself under some sort of constraint. He grew to at least twice the length of a horse, with a long, slithery body, and his wings were bright red when they sprouted.

He turned his head to them and hissed.

Zoë smacked his shoulder above a well-muscled leg that ended in four long claws. "Hey, quiet, you. You wanted me to make a plan; I did."

"He wants us to get on him," Opal said mildly.

"Oh." She rubbed Bertie's shoulder. "Sorry, Bertie. I guess it's good Opal can understand you, right?"

His sinuous neck dipped low, and Zoë and Opal stepped on, climbing up to his broader shoulders. Zoë struggled a bit with her dress.

Zoë put Opal in front of her to make sure that the vampire could communicate with Bertie. It didn't hurt that Zoë's neck would be far out of Opal's biting reach.

"What are we supposed to hold on to?" Zoë asked, but Bertie launched himself into the air.

"Oh shit," she said, her breath catching in her throat as Bertie gained altitude easily. She grabbed on to Opal's waist, but her dress shifted and one side looped itself around the wyrm's neck like a safety belt, and she was anchored solidly to Bertie as he gained altitude.

"You OK, Opal?" Zoë yelled past the noise of the wind. Opal sat quietly, not having the problems Zoë seemed to have when it came to holding on. "So, ridden a lot of dragons in your time?"

Opal still didn't answer, and Zoë made a face at her back and tried to enjoy the scenery, but by then Bertie had climbed too high. The city beneath them was a sprawl of colors and sound, and Zoë actually had her first feeling of appreciation for the city and what it had been through in the past decade.

Zoë felt Bertie rumble underneath her, and Opal turned to look over her shoulder. "He needs to know where to go." Her face was utterly dead, as if she were describing a really boring meteorologist.

"Right!" Zoë said, and rooted around in her satchel, which lay against her hip. "Head southeast, Bertie! I'm not sure where we're going, but we can find things from the air, right? At least we can maybe spot Gwen and Eir."

They flew on through the night. As they edged closer to the city limits, Zoë could hear a plaintive call to turn back, that the city was sorry.

Riding a dragon. Yeah, not all it was cracked up to be. For one thing, every time Bertie dipped in elevation, Zoë was left behind momentarily in midair until the seat belt dress caught her and brought her down with him. Opal seemed fine holding on with her legs. For another thing, it got pretty damn cold at the higher elevations. Zoë had asked Bertie to fly lower and slower, and he had replied that it was fine for people to see him on the ground and think he was a Carnival float, but even the drunkest frat boy probably wouldn't make the same leap if they were spotted in the air. At least, that's what Opal said he said. Zoë was getting cold and cranky and anything the stoic vampire told her seemed suspect.

Not to mention that time on a dragon with a vampire who wasn't very chatty left Zoë alone with her thoughts. She had been dumped. Or she had dumped him, mainly because he wanted it. And now she was off to help the guy who had dumped her.

But they hadn't been in love, and while hurt, she didn't feel completely lost and brokenhearted. And besides, the world was bigger than her and her hurt feelings. Arthur's concerns were real, and he could easily die and become zombified if he couldn't find the Doyenne and get her to help him.

Although it was moot at this point, she still wondered whether she would have stayed with him if he became a zombie. The zombies she knew were rotting things with gaping wounds attesting to their violent deaths. But Arthur's shoulder wound was healed, with only the lurking virus inside the proof that his life could go away anytime if he didn't treat it.

Would he rot? Would he stink? What would sex be like? She didn't really want to picture it.

They'd only been going out for a month, but they had shared a number of life-or-death situations, and that has the tendency to form a bond. But now he was not her boyfriend anymore, and once they were done finding this zoëtist, they would be done with each other.

Except that they were neighbors. *Damn.* She wasn't going to move. She liked her place.

"Hey, Opal," she said into Opal's ear, surprising even herself. The vampire turned her head, listening. "Tell me about Kevin, why you turned him into a vampire."

It wasn't a request, and considering what the vampire had just gone through, Zoë knew Opal had every right to bite her head off—metaphorically, she hoped. But still, the thought of losing someone to coterie lifestyles had her thinking.

Opal surprised her. "We were in the same book club," she said. "And—"

"Hold up, a *book club*?" Zoë interrupted.

"We are both great readers," Opal said coldly. "I found one that met at night to discuss Russian literature. I had known Dostoyevsky, so I was interested to see what people were getting out of his work these days. Kevin loved Russian authors, and we ended up getting along fabulously. I hadn't turned anyone in years and was lonely."

"Were you two ever romantic?"

Opal made a face, her first expression since Kevin died. "Heavens no. He had a wife, and I was looking for a child, not a lover. I turned him after the book club was done, you know, to keep the conversation going."

"You turned him to keep talking about books?" Zoë was incredulous.

"Dostoyevsky wrote some very long books," Opal replied patiently. "It can take over a lifetime to study all of them thoroughly."

"And he had a *wife*?" Zoë said. "You took him away from her?"

"Zoë, if we only looked to turn people with no loved ones, we'd only be turning crotchety old people in the nursing homes whose families are dead and they've alienated everyone except for the people paid to care for them. Or sociopaths. Leaving loved ones behind is part of being a vampire." Opal paused. "It's something we all go through when we're turned. It's part of the pain of being reborn. Kevin was very angry with me for some time. But for everyone, the first few decades can be sad, especially if you're seeing kids grow up or spouses remarry. And then even after you get over it, watching your family die is another blow. Kevin was still in the early moody period. But he was coming out of it, I thought. We were starting to be happy."

"Do you regret it? If you could go back to last night and change what you did, would you?" Zoë asked.

Opal was quiet for a long time. Zoë wondered if she'd angered her or upset her or something to that effect. "I'm sorry," Zoë said. "I've just been thinking about what I could have done to keep Arthur from getting bitten that day, but I don't think I could have done anything differently."

"I could have joined him," she said softly, so that Zoë had to strain to hear. "We all understand the reasoning behind the balance, behind working with humanity instead of hunting them to extinction, but that doesn't mean we don't feel the lure of the blood. Kevin was becoming a beast, and I could have joined him. And in the time between our leaving humanity behind and our eventual final death at the hands of Public Works, it would have been *glorious*."

"But you didn't," Zoë said. She was slightly sickened by the longing in Opal's voice to just give up control and go murdering people for food.

Opal turned to face front again. "No, I didn't."

With the conversation over, Zoë was alone again with her thoughts. The view below them was nearly all black now, with the few houseboats casting lights on the water.

But ahead, some blue and green lights were dancing in the darkness, almost too dim to see. Their eyes were accustomed to the dark now, and they caught them. "I think that's it," Zoë

called, pointing. It was confirmed when a flock of sparrows—
Gwen's heralds that went with her everywhere—joined them
briefly in the sky before diving down again to join the goddess.

Bertie, probably to be a jerk, dove after them, and Zoë held
on with a death grip and tried not to scream as she was pulled
after him.

"You can't kill me, we have a book due!" she shouted as she
hung on. Bertie rumbled and vibrated, and Zoë realized he was
laughing.

His wings flattened out and beat twice, stopping their ascent.
Zoë smashed forward into Opal's back, splitting her lip.

"Goddammit, Bertie, I'm renting a car next time," she grumbled, putting a hand to her lip.

Opal rubbed her shoulder. "You have a hard head," she said.

"Yeah, it's to protect my brain so zombies don't eat it." Her
dress loosened its hold on Bertie, and she slid off his back and
rubbed her butt. "Riding a dragon is definitely more romantic
in books."

"You asked for it," Bertie said calmly, startling her. She turned
and saw him in his human form again. His human form and
nothing else.

"So you left your clothes behind at the B and B, huh?" Zoë
asked, her eyes firmly fixed on his face.

He shrugged. "Where else would they go?"

"Maybe one of us could have carried a pair of pants for you if
we had known we needed to," Zoë said, exasperated. She turned
her back on him to look at Opal, who looked amused, but her
eyes were riveted to Zoë's bleeding lip. "Now where are we?"

Opal looked around. The waning moon shone on the trees
that dripped with Spanish moss, silhouetting them against the
sky. They were on a dirt road littered with potholes and grass,
and ahead of them a fallen log lay across the road.

She pointed down the road past the log. "The place where we saw the lights is about fifty yards that way."

Zoë took out her flashlight and turned it on. The dark trees seemed even darker with the pitiful beam of light challenging them, but at least they would see if they were about to fall into the swamp.

"Do you have a plan?" Bertie asked. "Most people don't like visitors late at night, and if she lives out here, I'd bet she doesn't like them any other time, either."

"And a vampire and a naked dragon aren't exactly the welcome wagon," Zoë said.

"Not to mention a rumpled princess," Bertie said.

"Did you see where Gwen and the others are?" Zoë asked.

"I lost them when the sparrows left us," he said.

"Be quiet a second, I want to hear if anyone else is around." Zoë shut her eyes and found herself automatically trying to expand her awareness, as she had in New Orleans. The sensation of being only inside her body, with its defined borders of bone and skin, was horribly restricting.

She wasn't in a city, of course she couldn't use the city's power to eavesdrop or scout ahead. She felt very alone, despite how much the city annoyed her.

Using only her ears—*how primitive!*—she tried to see if she could sense any other person in the swamps. She could hear breathing from Bertie behind her. Animals rustling in the distance. But nothing that sounded like humanoid feet.

She smiled bitterly. It wasn't as if she were a nature-loving tracking guru. She was drawn to cities for a reason, and rarely ventured out of them unless it was to travel to another one.

"Can you two hear anything?" she finally asked, whispering so that if there were people listening, they couldn't hear her.

Opal shook her head. "This is a pointless trip, Zoë. We're

going to go to a house and the owner won't answer the door because she's smart. Other people will show up and you will have some sort of heart-to-heart with that man from Public Works, and it will be very sweet, right before he turns into a zombie. Then we will go back to New Orleans, probably walking because you will say something to piss Bertie off and he will leave us here, and I will just hope I can find a place to go before sunrise."

Bertie stepped up. "You may want to keep it down, ladies."

Zoë opened her mouth and then closed it, outrage boiling over. "Look," she said, raising her voice. "I didn't ask you to kill your child, you did that on your own. I know you're mourning but don't let it bleed all over us."

Bertie put his hand on Zoë's shoulder. "We don't know what's in these woods, can you please—"

"If he hadn't been working for a human, someone who knows nothing of our kind, he wouldn't have needed killing!" Opal shouted. "It was you and your precious books that got him killed, not me."

"Really," Bertie said. "I really think this would be better discussed in calmer voices."

Zoë shook off Bertie's hand and stepped closer to Opal, forgetting entirely that Opal could rip her in half. "That is complete bullshit and you know it. You're just trying to lay the blame on me to soothe your ego, because you know if you had made a stronger bond with him, he'd be alive now!"

If Opal had a retort, Zoë didn't hear it. Something hit her from the left, something fast and hard, and she flew off the road and landed hard against a log.

CHAPTER 20
Swamps

SWAMP TOURS

Most coterie who venture into the swamps are doing so in order to experience the lawless frontier, but some just want to see the beauty and learn more about the swamp. There is one coterie-only tour company, the Cypress's Knees, that specializes in taking coterie around the swamps, giving water-loving coterie a literal taste, and introducing people to some of the local tree nymphs.

You will want to look out for the creature known only as the Sway, an ancient (meat-eating) nymph who prefers to stay out of the public eye, but whose advanced age has made her huge and treelike. Many coterie wish to see her, even though they know that if they anger her, she could easily capsize the boat and devour the coterie tourists (and she has done so, more than once).

If you're lucky, you might be able to see the great roc, which nests in the swamp in the spring. Other creatures can include feral inugami, the elusive phoenix, and raccoon spirits. But if you think you're going to see something like an ivory-billed woodpecker, that's impossible. ∎

CHAPTER TWENTY

Had Opal really hit Zoë? She couldn't remember. Phil would kill the vampire if she had, though.

Something pricked her arm.

Had someone picked her up? Where was she?

Someone brushed the hair from her forehead, tenderly. Then a piece of tape was pressed over her mouth. When Zoë finally opened her eyes, the presence was gone.

She was in a small room, lying on a cot. A lantern hung from the ceiling, lighting two individuals on other cots. They were an old man and an old woman, shriveled, looking at least ninety years old. Their mouths had the caved-in look that hinted that no teeth were inside. They wore stained white boxers and T-shirts that looked as tired and worn out as they did.

The wall next to the door was lined with shelves holding huge jars of herbs, flowers, and salts. None were labeled, but Zoë recognized many of the herbs and powders from the voodoo shop she'd visited as a ghost.

She couldn't have gone far from the road; the humidity in the room was the same as in the swamp, and the small windows near the top of the room were propped open. The chilly humidity made the sour smell of unwashed bodies and illness nearly unbearable.

She struggled to pull the tape off her mouth, but discovered leather cuffs at her wrists and a leather strap around her chest, keeping her securely on the cot. She winced as the movement upset the needle in her arm, shooting a pain up to her shoulder. Her neck went cold with alarm when she realized the needle was diverting her blood through a tube and draining it into a glass jar. Clearly the IV wasn't to give her anything beneficial.

She looked away from the needle and tried to think past her pounding head. So she had been kidnapped away from Opal and Bertie. She wasn't sure if the two would have lifted a finger to save her, but she had to assume they were either incapacitated, captured and held somewhere else, or in on whatever weird kidnapping was going on.

Instinct made her want to scream out for help, but the tape was firmly keeping her mouth shut.

She looked around the tiny room to get a bearing. The people on the other two cots were sleeping—this she discovered after watching them closely for signs of life. They were not restrained. The thin windows looked to be made of cheap yellow plastic, but were too high and too small to crawl out of. The walls were covered with torn brown wallpaper over drywall, and the carpet was horribly stained and worn, and Zoë had no idea what color it had once been.

The door had no hinges, and had a small concave area to put your hand in to slide it aside to open.

She was in a trailer.

A boat motor rumbled outside, and the room dipped and swayed a bit. A modified trailer that's also a houseboat, she amended. Houseboat. Someone was looking for a houseboat, she remembered.

The IV was worrying her. She had no idea how long she had been out, only that it was still nighttime. The glass jar was much bigger than one liter, and it was about halfway full. The needle was taped in place, and no amount of wiggling was going to dislodge it. The straps, while loose, were still firmly keeping her down on the cot.

She looked down at her dress, now filthy. But the fabric was still shiny and blue and firmly around her. It was before midnight, then. Not much time had passed since they had gotten to the swamp. She thought as hard as she could to communicate the way she did with New Orleans.

Hey. Dress.

She felt ridiculous, but if her Cinderella fabric had saved her on Bertie's back, it might be able to help her here. *Can you work me out of these restraints? I just need the left wrist, I can do the rest.*

The hem of the dress twitched, and the bow around her waist untied itself and snaked over to the restraint. She didn't remember a bow at her waist, but the dress apparently had use for it. She couldn't believe it had worked. She wanted to laugh with relief but tried to keep the muffled noise low. The dress fumbled with the restraint, then just wrapped itself around the leather that was pierced by the buckle. It had nearly lifted it off the prong when a bell dinged somewhere outside the room.

The sash from the dress dropped, and the whole dress wilted around her. Its color faded from blue to dirty white, and the gems hanging from it turned to gravel.

Oh no. She twitched under her leather. Midnight. Apparently the fabric lost all its magic at midnight. What the hell was the point of a dress that dies at midnight?

Her roommates didn't stir at all during this, and she began to worry about them. Were they in comas? Why weren't they in hospitals getting life support instead of out here in the swamp, apparently getting their life drained?

Her struggles had increased her heartbeat, unfortunately, which increased the flow of blood from her arm. She began to get light-headed, so she relaxed back to calm herself. She'd fainted once while giving blood, and knew it only meant low blood pressure, and not impending death. At least, she thought, not yet.

She wondered what Bertie would say. Probably mock her for not having a plan. She had a plan, dammit, it was to use her magical dress to get out of these restraints. It wasn't her fault her dress became impotent at midnight.

While she took deep breaths to slow her heart, she heard rustling outside, footsteps.

"Is this the place you saw from above?" It was Arthur's voice.

"It has to be." Gwen. "Knock on the door, it is your battle."

"Did you see where Zoë and the others went?" Arthur.

"No, I lost them. They were heading in the same direction, so they probably are in the woods somewhere. Unless she was just flying Bertie for a look over the Gulf."

Eir spoke up. "That is probably what she did. I understand humans need a distraction after ending relationships."

"Lay off," Arthur said. "Can we focus on what we need?"

The house shook a bit under Arthur's knock. Someone stirred outside Zoë's door.

She was in the Doyenne's house. This was the woman who had trained Ben, who had trained the terrifying woman who tried to destroy New York. The woman who had the secret to halting the zombie virus. Why was Zoë trapped in the back?

Blood. Freely given, that is. I don't traffic in the other stuff. That's what the zoëtist in the shop had said he wanted from her. Her blood had power. It made a certain bit of sense: she was coterie, her blood had to be different from a regular human's blood.

That zoëtist had wanted blood freely given. This, tying her down and taking the blood, was presumably the "other stuff."

Zoë started to get a very sick feeling about how the zoëtists imbued their herbs with their life magic.

Or maybe that was just the blood loss.

"We can search for Zoë and the others after we leave here," Gwen said.

"We could leave the man, if you like," Eir said.

"I'm right here, you know," Arthur said.

"No, we need to keep him safe. We promised Zoë," Gwen said, continuing as if Arthur wasn't there.

Eir snorted. "You promised. I did no such thing."

"Then go. If you know where to start looking."

Pause. "I will text her again," Eir said.

Although it made Zoë feel like a complete idiot, she began to grunt in a pitiful attempt to scream. "Mmmph! Mmmmmrrrrr!"

Sure. It could sound like "Gwen" and "Arthur" if they were listening. Sure.

She realized it would be a better idea if she listened to discover what they were talking about. She had missed some of the conversation while she was grunting at them.

The door had opened. "You must want something real bad," came a croaking voice, "to visit the Doyenne this late. Who sent you?"

"Ma'am. My name is Arthur Anthony. Your former student, Ben Rosenberg, is my doctor," Arthur said. "He supplies the herbs I need to avoid, uh, turning. Zombie. He left town and I had an accident where I ran out of my supply."

Croaking laughter interrupted him. "Accident? Do you leave everything that keeps you alive up to the accident gods?"

"It doesn't matter how I lost the herbs," Arthur said, sounding annoyed. "What matters is I am out. And I need more. And I can't reach Ben. You're the only person I know that can supply them. We weren't even sure if you were alive. We needed a psychopomp to find you."

"You don't know me," she said slowly. "If you did, you wouldn't have come, bringing death goddesses and life goddesses to my home."

"Are you saying you won't help him?" This was Gwen.

"What you want with him? If he die, then you get to eat. Or that big woman could cure him."

"I am a god of healing," Eir said. "But this is zoëtist territory."

"And that's none of your business either," Arthur said. "It shouldn't matter how I lost my herbs, or why these ladies are with me. I have payment. Are you going to help me?"

There was a long silence and Zoë wondered if they were doing a standoff or some sort of silent communication.

"You already paid," the Doyenne said finally.

"I have?" Arthur asked. "You mean you'll give them to me?"

"Yah. You pay lots. You pay that you don't tell no one about where you found me. You tell, I will know, and maybe those herbs won't work so good no more." She chuckled. "Yeah, you pay. Whether you like or not. Stay. I get what you need."

The door slid open and the Doyenne slipped into Zoë's back room and closed the door behind her. She was tall and stooped, with heavily wrinkled skin. She might have been of African descent but her skin was now faded and gray. She paid no attention to Zoë, who struggled and "mmmph"ed angrily at her. She took a small empty pouch off the shelf and then opened three jars of herbs. A handful of one, a pinch of both the second and third. It looked a lot like the gris-gris bag the zoëtist had made for Zoë.

The Doyenne finished with a sprinkling from the jar of salts. Then she came to Zoë.

"He pay, he just don' know how much. You draining nice

here, girlie. You come along at just the right time. I thought you'd be that fox boy, I been huntin' him for some time, but you'll do nice-like. My kids over there are just about done."

She plucked the tube from the jar, dribbling Zoë's blood on the floor before she held the tube above the herb packet. She let it soak into the herbs and then smiled.

Realization sank in and Zoë's eyes went wide. The Doyenne smiled now, showing graying, rotted teeth. "You know now, ah? Life is the only thing that can hold off death, but not just any life. Human coterie life. Citytalkers were the best, they only powerful in cities. Sometimes I use weres. I used my students if they was bad." She pointed to the woman. "But lately my supply ran low. I been draining these kids for nigh on forty years. They got almost nothing left."

Zoë began furiously "mmmph"ing again, struggling and no longer feeling the sting of the needle in her arm. The Doyenne reached out with her hand and smoothed the hair out of Zoë's eyes.

"Don' fret, you bleed more if you fret. And I need you for a good long while."

She cackled again as she left the room. Zoë listened with dawning horror as Arthur gushed thanks to the woman, and the goddesses gave her polite farewells.

Then they left.

The Doyenne was draining Zoë's very essence. She felt as if she were in a Jim Henson movie, a puppet that existed only as sustenance for others. So the other two were talkers? Or zoëtists? The room didn't look secure enough to hold an angry werewolf, even a geriatric one.

Her head swam. She longed for the cookies that the Red

Cross gave out during blood drives. She had eaten nothing all day, which was not helping things. Was she still bleeding? She had to think she was; the needle was still in her arm and she hadn't seen the Doyenne put a clamp on the tube.

Her friends' voices faded into the woods, and were gone.

She felt herself instinctively searching for the city's presence again, if not for advice then at least for companionship. But again there was nothing.

Anna. Where was the ghost? She looked around for a reflective surface to see if she was there, but the only slightly reflective surface was the jar of blood, and it showed nothing but the floor.

Anna? Anna! She tried to call out with her mind. The ghost could only hear her in her head. Had she lost interest? Or been detained?

She flopped back on the cot, exhausted now, and starting to feel light-headed again. Tears pricked at her eyes as she stared at the ceiling.

Zoë really was truly alone.

CHAPTER 20
Swamps

The swamps that lie between the city and the Gulf of Mexico are largely lawless. The infrastructure is still undergoing a rebuilding effort within the borders of New Orleans, which has allowed the swamps to become a lawless land, much like the American Southwest used to be for humans.

Some of the water sprites who caused so much chaos during Hurricane Katrina remained after being kicked out of the city. Zoëtists who operate outside of the scope of Public Works have been known to stay there, including a master zoëtist who was reported dead twenty years ago, though some swear she still lives.

It's not the best place for vampires, as it's not a population center, and zombies may find the oppressive humidity unfavorable if they have dermatology issues. But the swamps are teeming with life and are a lovely place for water-loving coterie, or plant lovers.

There are few official hotels if you're looking for a place to stay that involves someone taking care of you (we all like someone to wash our linens from time to time, after all, and everyone likes room service), but if you are a vampire or someone else who prefers human or coterie contact and service, the Other Shoe is an elaborate hotel carved into a giant cypress tree. The trunk is hollow and contains a ladder to the surprisingly luxurious rooms in the branches of the tree. For coterie who need a more accessible entrance, the concierge is a tree nymph who controls the Spanish moss that hangs from the tree. The tree itself can grab its guests and bring them to the branches.*

* This of course also comes in handy for coterie who choose not to pay the rather pricey bill.

The hotel has accommodating places for different coterie to sleep, but where it stands out is the catering. It could be its stable of bewitched gators that go hunting every night, it could be its contacts within the city, or it could be the humans on the staff who allow for (chaperoned) feedings for vampires. Regardless, it is known for its remote location and romanticism—it is a popular honeymooning spot—and for being one of the best out-of-the-way places to eat in Louisiana. ∎

CHAPTER TWENTY-ONE

Zoë.

Anna! Holy shit, man, where have you been?

Zoë had been trying to find constellations out the window to keep herself awake when the ghost found her. She still had the tape on her face, which was starting to itch, but at least the Doyenne had come in and removed the needle at last. She had said nothing else, despite Zoë's silent demanding. The Doyenne hadn't bandaged her arm, so the blood still oozed out of the puncture and had coated her inner elbow.

Now there were more voices coming from outside, but Zoë didn't pay attention to them.

I couldn't keep up with the dragon! The ghost girl wailed in Zoë's head.

Can't you guys just teleport, kind of?

Not somewhere we haven't been. So I had to follow, and then find you. I almost couldn't do it, but there are a lot of people in the woods tonight, so I figured out where this place was.

I'm glad you're here. Do you know where my friends are? The dragon and the vampire?

The dragon is caught in a trap. The vampire is hiding.

Hiding. Zoë was incredulous. *From what?*

Zoëtists as strong as the Doyenne can control the undead. She probably felt safe with the dragon, but he's gone now. She doesn't know how to get out of the swamp, and she's afraid to come help you.

Lovely. Can you get me free?

I don't think so. I can't touch anything, and you're restrained.

Can you go tell Gwen where I am?

Yes, but that will take some time. I have another idea.

The ghost left her. Zoë looked around but couldn't tell what Anna was up to.

To distract herself, she focused on the new voices. One of them was Reynard.

"...And we have on good authority that you are practicing a forbidden branch of zoëtism," he said. "Not to mention I believe I can prove you released an inugami on the streets of New Orleans, where it attacked humans."

"I knowed you was gonna find me some day. I hoped I'd find you first. But tell me, with vampires killin' people and zombies eating people and citytalkers goin' around assassinating everyone they find, why *my* magic the forbidden one? My magic, it save lives."

Reynard was calm. "Some lives, yes. But you steal from others to do it. Every other zoëtist creates life, while you take it."

"You steal from me. You kill my dog."

"Your 'dog' attacked my associate and murdered an ancient ally of the goddess Freya. Now, I can turn you over to Public Works. Or perhaps He Who Kills and Is Thanked for It will wish to know your whereabouts. Or we could just take care of things here." Zoë didn't like the tone of his voice.

He's here to assassinate the Doyenne. Zoë let this sink in and didn't know which of them was worse.

"How you find me?" the Doyenne asked. "I been hidden from He Who Kill for a long time now."

"I followed a psychopomp," Reynard said.

"I make life. I *make* it. I just gave life-savin' herbs to a young colored man. He gonna be a zombie without."

"And where did you get the life force? Was it given freely?" Reynard asked.

"It was, once the citytalker was held down!" The Doyenne laughed at her own joke. Outside, branches cracked and trees creaked and fell. Something moaned. The Doyenne was ready to fight.

If anyone could stand against an assassin, it would be the woman who had trained Ben and Lucy.

This wasn't going to be pretty.

Reynard began shouting instructions to someone, and the Doyenne cried out. A louder crack came, then heavy footfalls. Zoë pictured a giant tree golem preparing to rip Reynard apart.

The woman on the cot on the other end of the room twitched and sat up. Zoë jumped. Or tried to, being that she was tied to the bed.

"Zoë," the voice was cracked from exhaustion and disuse, but the Irish lilt was there. "This woman has allowed me to use her body, I've promised her freedom if she helps free you. She's greatly weakened, though." Anna held up the old woman's hands, which were swollen and twisted from arthritis.

This woman wasn't going to be unbuckling anything anytime soon.

"She's a citytalker, but she has zoëtist blood. She's from a mixed family. She has rudimentary experience in golem raising, and she says if I can keep her body going, she can focus on helping you."

Zoë nodded fervently.

There was a huge crash and the houseboat rocked alarmingly. A male voice cried out, and Zoë heard a sickening crunch.

A wet sound came from under her bed, and she looked down as best she could. A little golem was climbing out of the bottle, made entirely of Zoë's blood. It left behind most of the blood;

it apparently took only a cup or so of blood to create a little humanoid.

You're kidding me.

Zoë swallowed in revulsion when her own bodily fluid climbed up the dirty sheet that she lay upon, leaving little bloody footprints in its wake. It stopped on her chest to wave at her, and she was grateful for the shadows that made it look like a little person made of wet clay instead of her own blood.

The blood golem trotted down her arm and started wrestling with the strap on her left wrist. Once her hand was free, she pulled the tape off her mouth and then freed the rest of her limbs. She sat up.

"Fuck, it's so good to breathe," she gasped. "Thank you." The little golem in her lap did something that looked oddly like a salute, and then lost all form, splashing down on her dress.

"I could have done without that part, but beggars and choosers and all that," she muttered. She threw her legs over the side of the cot and grabbed her leather jacket from the end of the bed. She checked her pockets for her phone, but both had been removed. Too much to hope for.

She stood up. "Anna, are you going to stay with the woman?" Zoë asked. "Is she OK? She looks really weak."

The woman nodded. "She has asked me to go help you, and come get her after the excitement is over."

Zoë nodded. The woman lay carefully back down, and then the ghost was with Zoë again.

"Thank you. We'll be back soon," she promised.

She took a step and the world swam.

She had forgotten how much blood she had lost. Black flowers bloomed in her vision for a moment, and she felt Anna help her stand until her blood pressure got to where it needed to be.

"I owe you, big time," Zoë said. "Now can you help me get out of here? Any idea what's beyond the next door?"

Just a living room, and a front door. Bedroom on the other side of this wall. The thing is, the only way out is the front door, and that's somewhat blocked by a very angry master zoëtist who isn't really human anymore, and a very angry citytalker who's clearly been trained by whatever old talkers remain.

"But there's no city out here to talk to. How does he have power?" Zoë asked.

He is a trained killer. The citytalking ability makes it easier for him, but he doesn't need the city *to kill.*

Of course. Just as Granny Good Mae had trained Zoë to defend herself against coterie without specifically asking New York City for help. Only Reynard seemed to have been working on that skill a lot longer than Zoë.

"What are they doing now?" Zoë asked.

Anna left her briefly, and Zoë held on to the doorjamb to keep upright.

The ghost returned. *The Doyenne has killed one of the citytalker's companions and has raised him as a zombie. They are not fighting now, just a zoëtist and her golems and one small citytalker. I think she's trying to intimidate him.*

Zoë felt impatience rising in her chest, and knew it for her own, not Anna's. "There's only one way out and I have to go through that way. Unless you have a way of knocking down this wall," she said.

Anna was silent, so Zoë continued with her rudimentary plan.

She slid the door open and peeked into the living room.

The smell hit her first. It was closest to rotten potatoes, the foulest thing Zoë had ever smelled—and this was even after working with zombies and being devoured (briefly) by a snake

295

demon in the New York sewers. She could feel her nose hairs trying to curl up and escape.

The location of the smell was obvious: a table lay under a window, and on it was an eviscerated possum. A bucket under the table held shiny entrails, and blood spotted the pad underneath the animal. Taxidermied animals were everywhere in the room: an elk stood in the corner, a hawk hung from the ceiling so low Zoë had to duck underneath it. It was not a living room per se, in that it didn't look like much living was done there. The place was filthy, with dirt and blood smeared on the wall. The window had been boarded up with plywood as if the Doyenne expected a hurricane. Lanterns hung from the ceiling, guttering pale yellow light into the room.

Zoë thought she saw something move in the corner of her eye, but when she turned she just saw a low table made from the body of an alligator. On the chipped glass tabletop was a statue covered in a black cloth. She glanced around and gingerly reached out and picked up a corner of the cloth and pulled. The cloth was heavier than it should have been, but she got it off.

It was an ebony statue of a dancing man dressed in snail shells, holding a cane. She had seen that before, but her woozy head didn't let her place it. Around his neck hung a black bag, much like the one around Zoë's ankle. Zoë closed her hand around it and pulled it off the statue.

The bag around her leg began to warm, heating up until it was almost unbearable. She fumbled for the bag and pulled it away from her skin. She dropped it on the floor and stared at it. If it had the power to protect her, she really didn't want to leave it behind. But it was far too hot to hold right now. She picked it up by its string and left both bags at the foot of the statue, adding them to her mental list of things to come back and deal with After It Was All Over.

After she dropped the bags, she looked at the statue a bit more closely. From the face, it was pretty obviously the party host, He Who Kills or whatever his name was. Was the Doyenne a worshipper of a disease god? That did not bode well. Why was she hiding?

Underneath the statue, she caught sight of something smeared on the nose of the gator that served as the table's base. She peered closer and saw a Hebrew character written there.

Outside, the Doyenne screamed one word in a language Zoë didn't know, and the living room came to life.

The hawk that Zoë had nearly hit her head on began flapping and struggling against the wire that held it, zooming in a circle close to Zoë's head. She ducked, and at the same time tried to sidle away from the gator, which had begun to thrash around to free itself from the table's weight.

The elk and another possum came to life, but weren't restrained in any way, so they both leaped toward the open door to their mistress's call.

Luckily the animals took no notice of her; the door was their only goal. Still, the adrenaline rush she was having did nothing but weaken her in her bloodless state. The gator's tail hit her as it threw off the glass tabletop, and she stumbled to her knees. The hawk broke free then, and zoomed around the room once more before exiting.

Zoë froze in fear as the gator trundled past her, but like the other animals it kept going, leaving the trailer.

Zoë struggled to her feet and chanced a glance at the table where the eviscerated possum lay. If the empty, opened animal was about to get up and wander out the door, Zoë would be done with this whole bullshit and just go ahead and go mad right here. Zombie possum golems were the absolute limit on her weird-shit-o-meter. Luckily it stayed where it had been pinned in place.

I need a weapon, Zoë thought once the animals had left the room. She looked around the dark living room for anything that looked pointy.

Most of the weaponlike objects were small surgical tools that the Doyenne had been using to work on the possum. Zoë ran into the kitchen, which was a nightmare of dirty dishes, and, oddly, a microwave and an electric kettle that were plugged into a generator. A hole had been knocked into the wall next to the generator, presumably to release exhaust.

The counter where the microwave and kettle sat was pristine, standing out from the rest of the trailer as if it had been attended to by a maid who had then just given up and left. Behind the kettle, in a shadow, was a knife block.

"Now you're talking," Zoë said, grabbing the chef's knife in one hand. A machete hung on the wall and she grabbed that with her left hand.

As she ran for the door, something in her mind started screaming at her. Whose side was she on? Was she thinking of supporting the monster who drained people for their essence like a mosquito—but helped people like Arthur stay human? Or was Zoë embracing her heritage and supporting the assassin, whose profession she was pretty sure was evil? Hours of playing Dungeons & Dragons with her friends in college had told her that.

She could just leave, and let nature take its course, as it were. She was free, she had a ghost buddy who could go find a friend to rescue her.

But she had promised to help that woman who helped free her.

She opened the front door, still unsure of her allegiance, but knowing she couldn't sit inside and be passive.

Zoë stepped out of the front door and into chaos.

At first it just looked like a bunch of human-types and a bunch of golems in a bar fight—everyone fighting everyone else, no one paying attention to friend or foe. She watched while a vampire dressed all in black lunged for a man wearing sweat pants and a hooded sweatshirt, then a golem struck out at a demon, and the hawk dive-bombed everyone.

A vampire? It was Opal, fighting alongside the Doyenne, trying to take Reynard down. Either Opal was secretly evil, or what Anna had said was true and the Doyenne had taken control of her.

The sweat pants man—now identified as Reynard—deftly avoided the lunge by jumping on the back of a golem and riding it like a bronco. The mud golem's arms were too thick to reach its back, and it flailed around trying to reach its rider.

The hawk went for Reynard's eyes, and he flung up his arms to shield himself. The hawk raked along his forearms, drawing blood.

Every time one of the sides struck a blow, Zoë winced, still not sure which one she was behind. She was no assassin. But she couldn't let Arthur just waste away to zombiedom. But she couldn't endorse the draining of anyone. And now she was back to not being an assassin.

Figures appeared at the tree line, and in the light of the houseboat's floodlights, Zoë could see Arthur, Eir, and Gwen. Arthur took in the undead incubus/zombie wearing the Public Works coveralls, and the strange man who bled and fought golems, and Zoë watching it from the doorway.

Blood flowed down to Reynard's elbows and began to drip off, onto the golem. It immediately began growing, swelling, and actually glowing in the dark woods.

Citytalker blood really was pretty potent for zoëtists. The golem paused in its struggles and then turned and focused on the Doyenne, who muttered a curse. She hobbled away from the demon who fought on Reynard's side, who reached for her even as the elk attacked it with its horns time and again, drawing sluggish black blood from its marbled, naked back.

Zoë chewed on her lip as she watched Reynard drive his new toy, the huge mud golem, onward toward the Doyenne. "Anna, do citytalkers and zoëtists ever fight over golems?"

No. She sounded shocked. *That would be rude.*

"Oh, please. Our blood has power, another thing no one bothered to tell me. Can we use it to control golems?"

Maybe. But it's pretty obscene, Anna admitted.

Zoë ran inside the trailer. Her companions were still dozing on their cots, and she wondered how fast an ambulance could make it out here for them. But she would think about that later.

She grabbed the bottle of her remaining blood and ran back outside.

It was perhaps not the most efficient idea, but the first thing that came for her was the hawk, and that was her first target. As it swooped in, Zoë poured some of her blood on her hand, and, swallowing her revulsion, threw it at the hawk.

The blood splattered on the feathers and into the open mouth. It veered away from her, flapping awkwardly, and then landed hard on the ground. It shook its head, and then took wing again, landing on Zoë's leather-clad shoulder.

"That was awesome," Zoë said.

Arthur, Gwen, and Eir watched the battle with open mouths. She waved at them, but had to focus on the gator, which had noticed her and judged her as a threat. It ran at her. "They really are fast on land," she said as she quickly filled her hand with blood again. She flung it at the gator, whose open mouth was nearly on her when it stopped, took a moment, and then stood at her side.

"Don't kill anyone," she told them. "But neutralize this fight."

They took off on her command. She sneaked into the trees so

the Doyenne wouldn't notice her, and wiped her bloody hands on the trees that hadn't been raised as golems yet. Just to be safe.

The tide of the fight was turning. Despite having his own golem and a still-quite-powerful demon on his side, Reynard struggled in the arms of a tree golem. It walked him slowly toward the river and threw him in. It then turned and ripped the Hebrew character off the mud golem, and the mud man dissolved.

Reynard surfaced, coughing and sputtering, and started to swim to shore. But the tree waded in after him and came down with a mighty branch hand. It landed on his head and pushed him under.

The elk had successfully stabbed Reynard's companion demon enough with its horns, and the demon lay panting in the dirt. Opal stood in front of the Doyenne, shielding her from any attackers.

The tree golem held Reynard under, easily handling the thrashing and struggling. His reaching hand came up and started brushing at the tape on the tree trunk that bore the Hebrew letter that gave it life, but another hand grabbed its wrist, stopping it.

Arthur had come to help the Doyenne.

Instinct hit Zoë, and she ran toward the golem and splashed half the glass jar onto its bark and leaves. In a moment it froze, then grabbed Reynard in one great hand, and Arthur in the other.

"Keep them safe," Zoë whispered. She turned to face her kidnapper.

Now that Zoë wasn't being drained of life force while being tied to a cot, she didn't think the Doyenne looked so intimidating. The zoëtist was so intent on killing her assassin that she had yet to notice Zoë, and instead was shouting instructions at the tree golem, which ignored her.

The gator golem hit her at the knees, and she fell, grunting. She commanded it to take down the tree, but it returned to Zoë's side.

Opal was still a problem. Vampires were fast and strong. She rushed forward, hands reaching out to get Zoë. Her fingertips brushed Zoë, but instead of grabbing, she just barreled into her and they both fell over. Opal was still, and Zoë struggled to get out from under her.

A spear sprouted from Opal's back, and Eir stood twenty feet away, intent on Zoë.

"Shit," Zoë said, voice shaking.

Gwen appeared beside her. "Tell me what is going on. Quickly."

"Doyenne captured me," Zoë said, panting. "She's draining human coterie and that's how she makes her life magic, how she is so powerful to keep the zombie curse away. Reynard is here from the Grey Cabal to assassinate her. I don't know who to support so I'm trying to stop them all."

"Right. I will tell Eir," Gwen said, and disappeared again. Zoë wanted to examine Opal, but she had bigger things to worry about.

Bodies were rising out of the river, waterlogged zombies with dead eyes and swollen, grotesque bodies.

"Oh dear God. Will my blood help against zombies?" Zoë asked Anna.

I'm not thinking so.

"Well great," Zoë said. She wanted to gag at the sight of the bloated bodies, but there was no time for vomiting.

The Doyenne had continued to create golems while the zombies struggled out of their watery graves, but Zoë could at least handle those. The Doyenne seemed to realize she was giving Zoë an army, because every time a mud or stick golem approached

Zoë, she would shower it with blood and send it after the zombies. A mud golem couldn't do much to hurt zombies, but it could keep them away from Zoë.

"This has to end now," Zoë muttered, and shouted for the hawk to dive-bomb the Doyenne.

The woman threw up her hands to shield her eyes, all the while shouting commands to more and more zombies and golems, and didn't notice Zoë running toward her, knife raised.

Zoë's nerve failed her at the last second. As Arthur screamed at her to stop, Zoë flipped the knife to hold the hilt, blade up, and slammed the Doyenne in the back of the head, knocking her out.

She went down hard, and with her the fighting golems collapsed. The zombies stopped in the river, looking around, confused. Then they turned and trudged back under the water.

The tree golem dropped Reynard and Arthur, who both fell into the river, and the other golems went inert as well.

"So it's over?" Zoë asked.

"Oh yes. At long last," said a voice behind her. She whirled around, knife ready for defense.

It was the god whose name they weren't supposed to say.

Reynard ran, again. As everyone tried to sort out what had happened, he had taken the opportunity to disappear into the forest. Zoë wasn't surprised.

Arthur sat and stared into the river, while Eir removed her spear from Opal's back.

"Is she dead?" Zoë asked, looking nervously at the vampire.

"Yes, she's a vampire. But I only knocked her out," Eir said, wiping the blood off the spear with a handkerchief. "The spear is steel, it certainly doesn't feel good, but vampires are tougher than that." She focused on Zoë. "You have lost a lot of blood, how are you still standing?"

"I've got some help," she said, silently thanking Anna. "Why did you guys come back?"

"We were heading out of the woods when we saw Bertie counting gold coins. Dragons can be distracted by gold on the ground, and whoever attacked you dropped a lot of gold. Gwen got the coins away from him with no bloodshed, since she doesn't have blood, and he told us what happened to you and Opal.

"We came back to find you, but found you attacking the Doyenne while she tried to drown her assassin. We didn't know what was going on, but Gwen told me to protect you. Then the assassin ran away."

Zoë looked over at the Doyenne, being ministered to by He Who Kills and Is Thanked for It. "Did—did I kill her?"

"She cannot be killed, not by a human," said He Who Kills and Is Thanked for It. He had shed his tuxedo and wore a coat that rattled with snail shells, and leaned heavily on his stick. Zoë could smell the rot coming from his injured left foot and tried not to wince. His limp had never seemed that bad before, but now that he looked more like the statue inside, which presumably was how he normally looked, his foot was clearly necrotic and foul.

"Why not?" Zoë asked.

"Because she is not fully human. Years ago, her apprentice attacked her and left her for dead, but the Doyenne had twisted the magic of life so much she found a way to prolong her life using the life force of others. Then she began selling the herbs to others. She was a worshipper of mine until she perverted the magic, and she hid from my sight. Tonight I figured one of you would lead me to her."

"The statue," Zoë said, understanding. "Was taking off the cloth all it took?"

He smiled. "That, and you had to remove her spell, which you did by touching her gris-gris bag. You're lucky you had one of your own, otherwise it may have burned your life from you."

He knelt with difficulty over the body.

Gwen was nodding. "I understand now. I could sense a little life in her, but she is between life and death. Kind of what I sense in Arthur," she added.

The god rolled the Doyenne over, and she opened her eyes at his touch. They had trouble focusing, but she saw him. "Lord," she murmured.

"I am here to give you a gift, Doyenne," he said, and took his fingers and closed her eyes for her.

"Thank you," she said. And didn't move again.

"It's over," Arthur said. He was not referring to the battle.

APPENDIX III
Worship

While the city is primarily Catholic, many residents and visitors practice voodoo, and some even try to mix the two.

This, understandably, annoys the local deities.

If you find yourself at a loss, or needing to pray or find a place of worship, nearly any church will take you in, so long as you do not shout the name of your god too loudly.

However, considering so many deities make their home in New Orleans, even the retired ones, sometimes praying on the street corner, on Bourbon Street, in Jackson Square, or in the Superdome will get you faster results.

And remember, sometimes all you need is a good rest and a good meal. Things will look better when you wake up. ▪

CHAPTER TWENTY-TWO

The god gathered some of the herbs inside the Doyenne's house and brewed everyone some tea. Zoë took the lanterns outside and sat while Bertie (after a cursory apology to Zoë for letting her get taken, which she accepted) gathered up the bodies and the golems. Eir tended to the humans in the trailer.

The beautiful incubus Christian had been early to fall in the battle. In death he looked like an average white man with dirty-blond hair, with the addition of a gaping wound in his chest. He lay next to the Doyenne, who seemed much older and smaller in death. Reynard's demon ally hadn't made it, bleeding out after the elk's repeated attacks.

"I think I know why Ben didn't want us to meet her," Zoë said, looking at the corpses. "I wonder if he knew everything about the herbs. I can't see him endorsing this kind of operation."

"We can find out when we get home," Gwen said. "Phil will be quite interested in the events, I'm sure."

Zoë winced. She did not want to be debriefed by her boss. "We're going to have to work hard to get the goddamn book done. Especially since we've lost Kevin."

"Such useful medicine came from such horror," Eir said after visiting the back room. "The man in the back room is beyond my help. I was able to restore some health to the woman, but she is close to death regardless. This is your domain, I'm afraid," she said, looking at both the disease god and the death goddess. They both nodded and went to the back room together.

Neither Opal nor Arthur would look at Zoë, although she suspected they had different reasons for their silence. Zoë busied herself with the tea—thank goodness the supernatural beings could confirm that it was simply chamomile grown in the Doyenne's garden, downstream from where the golem had tried to kill Reynard.

"It's over," Arthur said again, breaking the silence.

"I know," Zoë said. "I'm sorry. You understand she couldn't be allowed to continue doing what she did? That Public Works was trying to shut her down? And there are a lot of herbs in there to keep you going for some time, anyway..." She trailed off. Arthur was shaking his head.

"It's inevitable now. Why fight it anymore? I'll just let it happen; tomorrow I'll turn. There's no hope now. I can't believe you had a hand in killing her," he said, his voice tense.

Her rage countered his own. "You want to live on the life force of other people? You want to live off *my* life force? She was taking it while you were talking to her, the herbs you bought were already soaked in my blood. If you took them right now, I would be directly responsible for the next few weeks of your life. I could have died back there, no extra days, no purchased months. She was draining me dry, I could barely walk at the end. And you're calling me selfish?"

He buried his face in his hands. "I know," he said, his anguished voice muffled. "I was just so ready to die when I got bit, and then when life continued, and it was good, I suddenly wanted it. I don't want to die."

Opal looked up from where she had been staring into the lantern's flame, her face a mask as she slowly healed.

"There's another option," she said softly.

Zoë shook her head. "No, that's no better than being a zombie. I mean, no offense, but he doesn't want to be an undead anything. This is a guy who likes being human."

Arthur looked at the vampire. "I think that would be all right," he said. "If you'll have me."

"Seriously?" Zoë asked.

He nodded. "I'm going one way or another. Vampires don't rot and they don't lose their shit if they don't eat. At least, not as bad as zombies. If I have to choose, I choose vampire."

"And I need a companion," Opal said.

"I'm not agreeing to anything intimate here," Arthur said, holding up his hands. "I just got out of a relationship."

Zoë smiled sadly. "I can hear you, you know. Anyway, she doesn't want to have sex with you, she wants a baby vampire to call her own. She'll show you what it is to be one. She'll take care of you. She's good at it."

Opal looked at Zoë and actually smiled. "Besides, I owe Zoë. If I can help her friend, then I'm happy."

Arthur got up. "So, uh, when do we do this?"

"Whenever you like. Before the sun comes up. Before you turn into a zombie, naturally."

"Now. Before I change my mind," he said, holding out his hand to help her up. She accepted, and turned to walk into the forest.

"Now? Just like that?" Zoë asked.

Arthur nodded. "We knew it was coming. Something was coming. I need to go." He put his arms around her, his shirt still wet from the river. "I'm sorry for the drama. Sorry for hurting you." He kissed her softly on the forehead.

"I'm sorry, too. Don't eat me when you turn, OK?" She smiled, even though the request was real.

He grinned at her. "You take all the fun out of everything."

"I'm actually not kidding," she said.

He sobered. "I know."

And he walked after Opal.

"And he dead now," said He Who Kills and Is Thanked for It, coming out of the house. "Doyenne has been draining them for years. Possibly decades, considering the scarcity of citytalkers. She must have been happier than a pig in slop when she found out you and that other talker was in town, Zoë."

"How did she—Oh, the inugami. Right," Zoë said.

He nodded. "She had spies all over the city. Her dogs, her golems. She knew you were in town, and she knew the other citytalker was coming for her. Good work with the golems, by the way. Quick thinking."

"So first I talk to cities, then I am descended from assassins, and now my blood is the elixir of life? No wonder we got hunted to extinction," she grumbled.

The god hobbled out to where she was sitting on the ground. "I am turning this place into a shrine, once I cleanse it with fire. But before I do that, I want to bless you, child. You fight for the earth, and for my people."

Zoë frowned in confusion. "Who are your people?"

He laughed. "All people are my people." He stuck out his hand and pressed his thumb on her forehead, and she felt a warm rush come over her. "That will come in handy, to be sure."

The god turned his back and raised his staff, calling for everyone in the house to vacate.

Gwen and Eir came hurrying out, leading behind them the old woman who had helped Zoë.

"Is she going to be OK?" Zoë asked.

"Shh," Eir said, watching the god. "This is a sacred moment."

He Who Kills and Is Thanked for It called out over the swamp, beckoning. Fire answered, coming from the sky to bathe them all in fierce heat. They all retreated to a safe distance as the heat became unbearable for all but the god.

It burned for a good five minutes, white hot, and then as quickly as it had lit up, it was gone, as was the god. The only thing left was the charred bank of the water, where a smoking black statue of the god was overturned.

Gwen went and picked it up, not affected by the heat that the statue clearly was radiating, and righted it on the bank. "This is a blessed space now," she said. "You have witnessed something glorious."

"I'm starving," Zoë said suddenly.

Ten minutes later Opal and Arthur returned, Opal looking very pleased, Arthur looking dazed.

"Is—is it done?" Zoë asked.

Arthur nodded.

"Sometime you'll have to tell me how it's done. Do you feel different?" she asked.

Arthur blinked a couple of times. "I'm tired," he said.

"We'll go get your things from your hotel and you can come to the bed-and-breakfast to stay in Kevin's old room," Opal said happily. "Freddie will have a meal for you, and then I can teach you how to hunt without getting caught by those awful Public Works people. This will be such fun," Opal said sweetly.

"You know I'm Public Works, right?" he asked.

"That's what will make it fun!" Opal said.

Arthur looked at Zoë, panic flaring in his newly red eyes.

Zoë tried hard not to laugh.

Later that night, in Freddie's kitchen, they ate their respective meals and had a long talk to officially end their relationship. They agreed that both their lives were too complicated at this point. Arthur had to focus on his new life, or undeath, or whatever. Zoë had a book to manage. They'd stay in touch, but now, mutually, it was agreed to be over.

"I wonder if we'll be safer, or in more danger, this way," Zoe said after they'd hugged for the last time.

"Guess we'll find out," he said.

Phil was furious.

"You lost a member of your team, you killed the most powerful zoëtist in the world, and you kept from me that you were a citytalker? What else are you hiding, Zoë? By all the gods around me, I trusted you!"

Zoë held the phone away from her ear. Anna had left her after the group had returned to the B and B, and after her talk with Arthur she had slept for twelve hours. She felt much better after sleep and a shower, and was looking forward to an iron-heavy breakfast, but she'd had to call the boss first.

Phil was reacting the way she had feared. She had confessed she was a citytalker when she had called, afraid that too many people around her knew the secret, and that his finding out was inevitable.

"I work with people who would eat me, Phil. I needed whatever ace I had," she said. "And it was self-defense! She was going to kill me slowly over the next few decades."

"But if you had told me this when you found out, I could have protected you, have let you know your heritage without you having to go through all of this!"

"Wait, you're mad because you're concerned about me? Not because I lied?"

He sputtered, and she realized his fangs had elongated because of his anger. "Of course I am! Just think of what you could have avoided! Have you heard from this Reynard person since the battle?"

"Not at all."

"He will be in touch, I guarantee it. He's not going to let a powerful rogue citytalker loose in the world. He will recruit you for this mysterious shadow organization," he said. "And I'm going to have to look into that more closely. I knew about the purge and about citytalkers, but I thought they kept to themselves."

"Great."

There was silence. Finally Phil said, in a calmer voice, "So do I need to send another writer to you, or are you all right?"

"I've got someone who may work out," Zoë said, thinking about Anna. "I'll let you know."

"And you think Opal can keep it together?"

Zoë snorted. "Are you kidding me? She's practically glowing with excitement now that she gets to have another 'baby.' I had to stop her from taking Arthur shopping last night."

"So your boyfriend is a vampire now?" Phil sounded amused.

"Yeah. And he's not my boyfriend, not anymore."

"Can't date a vampire?" he asked, a funny tone in his voice.

"Actually, he pretty much dumped me. Says we're both dealing with too much shit to support the other one." She didn't say that she honestly didn't know if she would have stayed with a vampire or not. She'd burn that bridge when she came to it.

"All right. Keep me posted for the rest of the time, is that too much to ask? I want to know even if a coterie looks at you funny while you're down there."

"Sure. We're taking the ghost train home the Sunday after Mardi Gras. I can probably hold it together till then. And when I get home, Phil?"

"Yeah?"

"I want to know everything you know about citytalkers. And we can find out Grey Cabal stuff together. The city told me all sorts of shit, including about the assassins, the murder of the citytalkers, and stuff. But I want to know what you know. No more secrets about the humans' past."

"Fine. I'll see what I can dig up on the Cabal. But we'll discuss that when you get home," Phil said.

"I can wait. Thanks," she said.

"And for the sake of all the gods, Zoë, be careful, please."

She smiled. "But boss, I'm always careful!"

CHAPTER 4
Travel Essentials

DANGERS

Since Katrina, New Orleans Public Works has been a tightly run operation, with a solid coterie liaison, so you won't find a lot of prejudice there; they will still bust you if you go overboard on feeding from a local or a tourist, but everyday coterie should be fine. Some of the local vampires have taken residence in Louis Armstrong Park and are not friendly to tourists. Visit during the daytime, or simply steer clear of the park if you're worried about your safety.

The only unwelcome coterie in town is the water sprite. Water gods are not forbidden, but you may find prejudice in Uptown.

As for sexuality, anything goes in New Orleans, but the asexual budding fae will possibly face teasing here and there. ■

CHAPTER TWENTY-THREE

Zoë had worried about losing more blood to repay her debt to the voodoo shop, but it turned out the owner was so happy about the return of his missing sister, the old citytalker from the Doyenne's houseboat, he called it square.

Her gris-gris bag was gone, all its power burned away to protect Zoë from the release of the Doyenne's concealment spell. She turned down his offer for a new bag, saying she'd let them know if she needed anything in the future.

Zoë also visited Public Works again to report Christian's death to the Poison Ivy receptionist, and after allowing the woman to cry on her for a while (all the while batting away curious vines trying to entwine their mistress to comfort her), Zoë asked what the woman knew about imprisoning water sprites. Namely, could they be frozen?

"Of course they can," Poison Ivy said, sniffling. "That's how we held most of the sprites we caught after Katrina."

"How do you thaw them? Can they be hurt by the process?"

"I don't know. We've never thawed one before," Ivy said, thinking.

"Good enough, thanks," Zoë said, and left, deep in thought.

The rest of the trip was relatively uneventful. They gathered their information, they took notes, met for meals to discuss chapters, and continued research. They attended another ball hosted by He Who Kills and Is Thanked for It, and Zoë even danced with the host.

Arthur spent much of his time with Opal, and Zoë would talk to him nightly about what he had learned. He enjoyed testing his new abilities, but his first feeding on a human was traumatic for him, even though it was a mugger who had just rolled a young tourist.

"Just think. You were like Batman. Hey, maybe Batman is a vampire," Zoë suggested, which made him laugh.

The time was over all too quickly, and the Sunday after Mardi Gras, with the city moaning in Zoë's head as if she had the biggest hangover ever, Zoë boarded the ghost train.

Lastly, both Arthur and Anna resigned from their jobs. For different reasons.

Arthur got to sit in first class with Opal, using Kevin's ticket. He looked resigned, used to Opal's maternal attention, even if he may not have liked it. Right after Zoë had settled into her seat, her phone dinged with a text.

I AM GOING TO REGRET THIS, AREN'T I?

She smiled. IT'S BETTER THAN THE ALTERNATIVE, RIGHT?

The response was immediate. THAT REMAINS TO BE SEEN.

YOU WILL GET USED TO IT. AT LEAST YOU'RE IN FIRST-CLASS. ALSO, COACH SUCKS.

Ten minutes before the train was set to leave, someone sat in front of Zoë, across the table from her. Reynard's wounds from the battle were still fresh, but he moved with an easy grace.

Zoë looked back calmly at this man she wasn't sure she should have saved.

"Why did you run? You won, the Doyenne died," she asked, finally. "You did your job. Or someone did, anyway."

"It's not wise to be around too many gods," he said. "They can figure us out faster than most people. Besides, as you said, my job was done."

Zoë raised an eyebrow. "You run away a lot. It seems I might be better at your job than you are."

"Would you like to do my job?" He smiled that cocky smile.

"Not really," Zoë said. "Assassination is not really my thing."

Reynard examined his fingers. "I prefer to be considered a cleaner. I get rid of messes."

Zoë leaned back in her seat, trying to her hide her anxiety. "So how long until I'm a mess, Reynard? A rogue citytalker with no allegiance? When will you come clean me up?"

"You could avoid it entirely. Come with me for training, learn about the cities, learn about the coterie. Your skills are raw, but strong. You need a mentor."

Zoë shook her head slowly. "I'm not sure I want to be an assassin. Or a maid. Cleaner. Whatever."

Reynard nodded once and slid a business card across the table. "Have a good trip home, Zoë. I'll see you around," he said. Then he exited the train.

The card was blank except for an address in tiny, cramped, precise writing. It was an address in England, but that's all Zoë knew.

The location of the Grey Cabal? Is this the recruiting Phil mentioned would come?

Probably. They don't want to lose a power like yours. The city sounded soft and sad. She'd been relatively quiet since morning, when Zoë had firmly informed her that she was leaving.

Zoë stashed the card in her pocket and looked out the window at the city in the night.

I'm sorry I tried to kidnap you. I just like you so much.

"I understand," she whispered.

The other talker did say he'll keep me company until he has to leave for London.

Zoë sat up straight and felt the train's engines come to life. "Really?"

Sure, and he said some really interesting things about the Grey Cabal! We joined last night, and he told me that they were recruiting, and that he had a promising... As the bullet train gained speed, it shot out of the city limits, and the voice in her head stopped.

"Shit. She couldn't have told me that stuff earlier?" Zoë muttered as she fished the card out of her pocket again. While researching the book, she had ignored the occasional pleas from the city to forgive her, and discovered she could access the power of the city without engaging her in conversation while she was doing her research. She had decided to forgive the city before she left, and realized she probably should have done so earlier.

She punched the address into her phone, and found a small village west of London. The Grey Cabal couldn't be in a city, she remembered.

"He will recruit you or hunt you," Phil had said.

He had also said they needed to find out more about the Grey Cabal.

"Looks like I'm going to England. I wonder if I can get Phil to take the Shambling Guides international."

New Orleans for the Sober, the Solitary, the Humble, and the Quiet

[No content provided.]

ACKNOWLEDGMENTS

Thanks to the people at the Stonecoast MFA program who helped workshop this book: Joseph Carro, Cecilia Dockins, Katrina Ellyson, Rachel Halpern, Sean Robinson, Emily Swartz, and especially David Anthony Durham, Elizabeth Hand, and James Patrick Kelly. Others at Stonecoast without whom I'd be a poorer writer include Nancy Holder and Tony Pisculli. I would like to thank the members of the Magic Spreadsheet community, and the spreadsheet itself. Also the chefs and servers at Café Soulé, who gave Ursula Vernon and me a hysterical, memorable evening in New Orleans.

The ever-vigilant group of Orbit folks, editors Devi Pillai, Susan Barnes, and Jenni Hill, work tirelessly to make me sound awful smart, and my agent Heather Schroder is there to have my back at all times. My husband Jim and daughter Fiona Van Verth keep me loved and sane, and family members Bill Smith and Niki Lamotte form a support system I couldn't do without.

extras

extras

about the author

Mur Lafferty is a writer, podcast producer, gamer, geek, and martial artist. Her books include *Playing For Keeps*, *Nanover: Hacked!*, *Marco and the Red Granny*, and the Afterlife Series. Her podcasts are many. Currently she's the editor of *Escape Pod* magazine, the host of *I Should Be Writing*, and the host of the *Angry Robot Books* poscasts.

Find out more about Mur Lafferty and other Orbit authors by registering for the free monthly newsletter at www.orbitbooks.net.

if you enjoyed
GHOST TRAIN TO
NEW ORLEANS

look out for

FULL BLOODED

Jessica McClain: Book 1

by

Amanda Carlson

1

I drew in a ragged breath and tried hard to surface from one hell of a nightmare. "*Jesus*," I moaned. Sweat slid down my face. My head was fuzzy. Was I dreaming? If I was, this dream hurt like a bitch.

Wait, dreams aren't supposed to hurt.

Without warning my body seized again. Pain scorched through my veins like a bad sunburn, igniting every cell in its path. I clenched my teeth, trying hard to block the rush.

Then, as quickly as it struck, the pain disappeared.

The sudden loss of sensation jolted my brain awake and my eyes snapped open in the dark. This wasn't a damn dream. I took a quick internal inventory of all my body parts. Everything tingled, but thankfully my limbs could move freely again. The weak green halo of my digital clock read 2:07 a.m. I'd only been asleep for a few hours. I rolled onto my side and swiped my sticky hair off my face. When my fingers came in contact with my skin, I gasped and snapped them away like a child who'd just touched a hot stove.

Holy shit, I'm on fire.

That couldn't be right.

Don't panic, Jess. Think logically.

I pressed the back of my hand against my forehead to get a better read on how badly I was burning up. Hot coals would've felt cooler than my skin.

I must be really sick.

Sickness was a rare event in my life, but it did happen. I wasn't prone to illness, but I wasn't immune to it either. My twin brother never got sick, but if the virus was strong enough I was susceptible.

I sat up, allowing my mind to linger for a brief moment on a very different explanation of my symptoms. *That scenario would be impossible. Get a grip. You're a twenty-six-year-old female. It's never going to happen. It's probably just the flu. There's no need to—*

Without so much as a breath of warning, another spasm of pain hit clear and bright. My body jerked backward as the force of it plowed through me, sending my head slamming into the bedframe, snapping the wooden slats like matchsticks. My back bowed and my arms lashed out, knocking my bedside table and everything on it to the ground. The explosion of my lamp as it struck the floor was lost beneath my bona fide girl scream. "*Shiiiit!*"

Another tremor hit, erupting its vile ash into my psyche like a volcano. But this time instead of being lost in the pale haze of sleep, I was wide awake. I *had* to fight this.

I wasn't sick.

I was *changing*.

Jesus Christ! You've spent your whole life thinking about this very moment and you try to convince yourself you have the flu? What's the matter with you? If you want to live, you have to get to the dose before it's too late!

The pain buried me, my arms and legs locked beside me. I was unable to move as the continuous force of spasms hit me one after another. The memory of my father's voice rang clearly in my mind. I'd been foolish and too stubborn for my own good and now I was paying the price. "*Jessica, don't argue with me. This is a necessary precaution. You must keep this by you at all times.*" The new leather case, containing a primed syringe of an exclusively engineered cocktail of drugs, would be entrusted to me for safekeeping. The contents of which were supposed to render me unconscious if need be. "*You may never need it, but as you well know, this is one of the stipulations of your living alone.*"

I'm so sorry, Dad.

This wasn't supposed to happen. My genetic markers weren't coded for this. This was an impossibility. In a world of impossibilities.

I'd been so stupid.

My body continued to twist in on itself, my muscles moving and shifting in tandem. I was locked in a dance I had no chance of freeing myself from. The pain rushed up, finally reaching a crushing crescendo. As it hit its last note, my mind shattered apart under its impact.

Everything went blissfully black.

Too soon, pinpoints of light danced behind my eyelids. I eased them open. The pain was gone. Only a low throbbing current remained. It took me a moment to realize I was on all fours on the floor beside my bed, my knees and palms bloodied from the shards of my broken lamp. My small bedside table was scattered in pieces around me. It looked like a small hurricane had ripped apart my bedroom. I had no time to waste.

The dose is your only chance now. Go!

The bathroom door was five feet from me. I propelled myself forward, tugging myself on shaky arms, dragging my body behind me. *Come on, we can do this. It's right there.* I'd only made it a few thin paces when the pain struck again, hard and fast. I collapsed on my side, the muscles under my skin roiling in earnest. *Jesuschrist!* The pain was straight out of a fairy tale, wicked and unrelenting.

I moaned, convulsing as the agony washed over me, crying out in my head, searching for the only possible thing that could help me now. My brother was my only chance. *Tyler, it's happening! Ty, Ty . . . please! Tyler, can you hear me? Tyyy . . .*

Another cloud of darkness tugged at the edges of my consciousness and I welcomed it. Anything to make all this horror disappear. Right before it claimed me, at that thin line between real and unreal, something very faint brushed against my senses. A tingle of recognition prickled me. But that wasn't right. That wasn't my brother's voice.

Dad?

Nothing but empty air filled my mind. I chastised myself. *You're just hoping for a miracle now.* Females weren't meant to change. I'd heard that line my entire life. How could they change when they weren't supposed to *exist*? I was a mistake, I'd always been a mistake, and there was nothing my father could do to help me now.

Pain rushed up, exploding my mind. Its fury breaking me apart once again.

Jessica, Jessica, can you hear me? We're on our way. Stay with us. Just a few more minutes! Jessica ... Hang in there, honey. Jess!

I can't, Dad. I just can't.

Blood.

Fear shot through me like a cold spear. I lifted my nose and scented the air. Coolness ran along my back, forcing my hair to rise, prickling my skin. I shivered. My labored breaths echoed too loudly in my sensitive ears. I peered into the darkness, inhaling deeply again.

Blood.

A rumble of sounds bubbled up from beneath me and I inched back into the corner and whined. The thrumming from my chest surrounded me, enveloping me in my own fear.

Out.

I leapt forward. My claws slid out in front of me, sending me tumbling as I scrabbled for purchase on the smooth surface. I picked myself up, plunging down a dark tunnel into a bigger space. All around me things shattered and exploded, scaring me.

I vaulted onto something big, my claws slicing through it easily. I sailed off, landing inches from the sliver of light.

Out.

My ears pricked. I lowered my nose to the ground, inhaling as the sounds hit me. Images shifted in my brain. *Humans, fear, noise ... harm.* A low mewing sound came from the back of my throat. A loud noise rattled above my head. I jumped back, swiveling away, searching.

Then I saw it.

Out.

I leapt toward the moonlight, striking the barrier hard. It gave way instantly, shattering. I extended myself, power coursed through my body. The ground rushed up quickly, my front paws crashing onto something solid, my jaws snapping together fiercely with the force of the impact. The thing beneath me collapsed with a loud, grating noise. Without hesitation I hit the ground.

Run.

I surged across hard surfaces, finding a narrow stretch of woods. I followed it until the few trees yielded to more land. I ran and ran. I ran until the smells no longer confused me, until the noises stopped their assault on my sensitive ears.

Hide.

I veered toward a deep thicket of trees. Once inside their safe enclave, I dove into the undergrowth. The scent pleased me as I wiggled beneath the low branches, concealing myself completely. Once I was settled, I stilled, perking my ears. I opened my mouth, drawing the damp air over my tongue, sampling it, my nostrils flared. The scents of the area came quickly, my brain categorizing them efficiently. The strong acidic stench of fresh leavings hung in the air.

Prey.

I cocked my head and listened. The faint sounds of rustling and grunting were almost undetectable. My ears twitched with interest. My stomach gave a long, low growl.

Eat.

I sampled the air again, testing it for the confusing smells, the smells I didn't like. I laid my head down and whimpered, the hunger gnawing at my insides, cramping me.

Eat, eat, eat.

I couldn't ignore it, the hunger consumed me, making me hurt. I crept slowly from my shelter beneath the trees to the clearing where the tall grass began. I lifted my head above the gently waving stalks and inhaled. They were near. I trotted through the darkness, soundless and strong. I slid into their enclosure, under the rough wooden obstacle with ease. I edged farther into the darkness of the big den, my paws brushing against the old, stale grass, disturbing nothing more.

Prey.

The wind shifted across my back. They scented me for the first time. Bleating their outrage, they stamped their hooves, angry at the intrusion. I slipped under another weak barrier, my body lithe and agile as I edged along the splintered wood. I spotted my prey.

Eat.

I lunged, my jaws shifting, my canines finding its neck, sinking in deeply. Sweet blood flowed into my mouth. My hunger blazed like an insatiable fire, and my eyes rolled back in my head in ecstasy. The animal tipped over, dying instantly as it landed in the dirty hay. I set upon it, tearing fiercely at its flesh, grabbing long hunks of meat and swallowing them whole.

"Goddamn wolves!"

My head jerked up at the noise, my eyes flickering with recognition.

Human.

"I'll teach you to come in here and mess around in my barn, you mangy piece of shit!"

Sound exploded and pain registered as I flew backward, crashing into the side of the enclosure. I tried to get up, but my claws slipped and skidded in the slippery mess. *Blood.* I readjusted, gaining traction, and launched myself in the air. The pungent smell of fear hit me, making my insides quiver with need.

Kill.

A deep growl erupted from inside my throat, my fangs lashing. My paws hit their target, bringing us both down with a crash.

Mine.

I tore into flesh, blood pooled on my tongue. "Please ... don't ..."

No!

I stopped.

No!

I backed away. "Bob, you all right out there?" Danger.

Out.

I loped forward, limping along in the shadows. I spotted a small opening, jumped, and landed with a painful hiss. My back leg buckled beneath me, but I had to keep moving.

Run.

I ran, scooting under the barrier. A scream of alarm rent the air behind me. I ran and ran until I saw only darkness.

Rest.

I crawled beneath a thick canopy of leaves, my body curling in on itself. I licked my wound. There was too much damage. I closed my eyes. Instantly images flashed through my mind one by one.

Man, boy ... woman.

I focused on her. I *needed* her. *Jessica.*

I called her back to me. She came willingly.

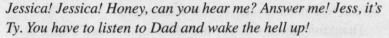

Jessica! Jessica! Honey, can you hear me? Answer me! Jess, it's Ty. You have to listen to Dad and wake the hell up!

My brain felt foggy, like a thick layer of moss coated it from the inside.

Jessica, you answer me right now! Jessica. Jessica!

"Dad?"

I squinted into the sunlight filtering through a canopy of branches a few feet above my head. I was human again. I had no idea how that had happened, but I was relieved. I tried to move, but pain snapped me back to reality the instant my leg twitched.

With the pain came everything else.

The change, the escape, the poor farmer. I shuddered as the memories hit me like a flickering film reel, a snippet of my life one sordid frame at a time. I'd been there, I'd seen it, but I hadn't been in control for any of it—except at the very end. I hoped like hell the farmer was still alive. Saying *no* had taken so much effort, I couldn't remember anything at all after that. I had no idea where I was.

From everything I knew about wolves, not being in control was an extremely bad sign. If I couldn't subdue my wolf—couldn't master my Dominion over the new beast inside me—I wouldn't be allowed to live.

Holy shit, I'm a wolf.

I lifted my head and glanced down the length of my very exposed, very naked body. I focused on my injury and watched as my skin slowly knit back together. *Incredible*. I'd seen it happen before on others, but until now I'd never been in the super healing category myself. Young male wolves gained their abilities after their first shift. My body must still be adjusting, because my hip was still one big mash of ugly muscle. Dried blood stained my entire right side, and the heart of the gunshot wound resembled a plate of raw hamburger.

Thankfully there was no bone showing. If there'd been bone, there would've been bile. Now that I was awake and moving, the pain had increased.

I closed my eyes and laid my head back on the ground. My encounter last night better not have been a normal night out for a new werewolf. If it was, I was so screwed.

Jessica!

My head shot up so fast it slammed into a pointy twig. *Ow.* "Dad?" So it hadn't been my imagination after all. I knew the Alpha could communicate with his wolves internally, but hearing his voice was new to me. I concentrated on listening. Nothing. I projected a tentative thought outward like I used to do with my brother.

Dad?

Oh my God, Jessica! Are you all right? Answer me!

Yes! I can hear you! I'm fine, er ... at least I think I am. I'm in pain, and I can't really move very well, but I'm alive. My hip looks like it went through a meat grinder, but it's mending itself slowly.

Stay where you are. We'll be right there. I lost your scent for a time, but we're back on your trail now.

Okay. I'm under some thick brush, but I have no idea where. I can't get out because of my leg.

Snort. *You're not healed yet?*

Tyler?

Who else would it be?

Hearing my brother's voice in my head released a flood of emotion. I hadn't realized how much I'd missed it until right this second. *It's safe to say I wasn't expecting you back in my brain. We haven't been able to do this since we were kids, but it's good to hear you now.*

Tyler's thoughts shifted then, becoming heavier, like a low, thick whisper tugging along the folds of my mind. *Jess, I heard you calling me last night. You know, when it first happened. It sounded awful, like you were dying or something. I'm so sorry I didn't make it there in time. I tried. I was too late.*

It's okay, Tyler. We haven't been able to communicate like this in so long, I really wasn't expecting it to work. It was a last-ditch effort on my part to take my mind off the brutal, scary, painful transition process. Don't worry about it. There wasn't anything you could've done anyway. It happened mind-bogglingly fast. Almost too fast to process. My heart caught for a second remembering it.

I heard, or maybe felt, a stumble and a grunted oath. *You'll get used to it*, Tyler said. *The change gets easier after you do it a few more times. Hold on, I think we're almost to you. We lost your scent back at the barn. Jesus, you ripped that place apart. There was blood everywhere.*

An ugly replay started in my mind before I could shut it down. *I hope the farmer survived.* I shifted my body slightly and winced as a bolt of pain shot up my spine. My injuries would've killed a regular human. I was clearly going to survive, but it still hurt like hell.

My dad's anxiety settled in sharp tones in my mind. *We're*

close, Jessica. By the time we picked up your scent on the other side of the barn, we had to wait for the human police and ambulance to leave. It shouldn't be long now. Stay right where you are and don't move. Your scent grows stronger every moment.

Yeah, you smell like a girl. It's weird.

Maybe that's because I am one. Or have you forgotten because you haven't seen me in so long?

Nope, I haven't forgotten, but you don't smell like a regular wolf, Tyler said. *Wolves smell, I don't know, kind of rustic and earthy. You smell too female, almost like perfume. It sort of makes me gag.* I could feel him give a small cough in the center of my mind, which was totally bizarre.

Then I should be easy for you to find.

Snort.

We'll be right there, my dad assured me. *Don't worry. We've got a car not too far from here waiting to take you back to the Compound.*

All this effort to communicate was taking its toll, and my head began to ache in earnest. The pain in my hip flared and a whooshing noise started in my ears. *I'm feeling a little woozy all of a sudden . . .*

Hang on—

2

I woke to white walls and the smell of disinfectant, latex, and coffee. The room resembled a typical hospital room, clean, bright, and sterile, except this one catered exclusively to werewolves. It was underground because wolves weren't known for their calm cool natures, and dirt was damn hard to claw your way out of if you went crazy.

No one else shared the space with me, which made things easier. Newborn wolves meant chaos, and less chaos was preferable, since last night I'd managed to achieve the impossible. I'd become the only living female full-blooded wolf on the entire planet. My new identity was going to rock the supernatural status quo, and the sooner I could prepare for the fallout—which was inevitable—the better. Hauling my ass out of this hospital bed was a good place to start. "Hellooo," I called. "Is anybody there?"

While I waited for a response, I flexed my leg and tested for pain. A small twinge lingered high on my thigh, but otherwise it felt normal. I couldn't actually see the wound, since the top of my leg was wrapped with enough gauze to stuff a throw pillow. Recalling the mincemeat it'd been, I was more than happy to go without a visual. I had no idea if I would scar from the ordeal or not. I had a lot to learn about my new body.

A conversation started on the floor above me. My father's low baritone stood out. I cocked my head, half expecting to hear a bionic beep as I homed in on the conversation. It was amazing how clear it was, like they were in the same room with me. I tested my vision on a tiny container across the room. I could read the fine print on the label, no problem.

Footfalls hit the steps and my father, Callum McClain, the Pack Alpha of the U.S. Northern Territories, stepped into view. "Well, it's about damn time." I flashed him a big grin. It'd been a while since I'd seen him and I'd missed him. Since I'd left the Compound seven years ago, we'd only seen each other a hand-ful of times. We'd been extremely cautious about our meetings, because being spotted together would've set off alarms in the supernatural community. Any gossip could have compromised my alias, abruptly ending the independent life I'd worked so hard to create for myself.

"Jessica, you scared the hell out of me." My father strode to my bedside. With a full head of dark hair and no wrinkles in sight, he didn't appear a day over thirty-five.

"I scared the hell out of myself." I chuckled. "Shifting into a wolf hadn't been on the evening's agenda. Plus I kind of thought I was dying, so that put a serious damper on the whole thing. My limbs felt like they were being sawed apart by a dull blade."

"The first time is always rough," my father said. "Especially if I'm not there to guide the transition. It's much better if you don't fight the process and stay calm. The tranq would've elim-inated the pain. Why didn't you use it?" My father slid a chair over and pulled it next to the bed and sat. "That was our agreed-upon failsafe if you ever started to shift. You were to inject yourself, knock yourself out, and we would find you. No damage to you in the process. You could've died jumping out of your apartment and it's lucky the gunshot didn't sever your spinal cord. I put my trust into you, into our agreement. I expected you to follow it to the letter."

"I'm sorry." I plucked at the bedsheets like an errant child. "I tried to reach the dose, but I didn't make it. I have no one to blame but myself. I transferred the case from my bedside stand to the bathroom cabinet a few years ago. I thought it was close enough, but honestly, I never thought I'd need it. It's been over ten years since I hit puberty and we'd always been told I wasn't genetically coded to shift." I paused for a second. "I'm sorry. I thought you were being overprotective as usual."

"Dear Jessica!" Dr. Jace entered the room, his familiar white hair fanning around his face like a fragile halo, his expression full of open amusement and wonder. "You gave us quite a fright! You're a miracle, young lady, truly a miracle." He shuffled to my bedside, grabbed on to my hand, and patted it affectionately. "Who would've thought it possible? A true female among us. Amazing! Truly amazing!"

"Doc Jace." I tilted my cheek toward him so he could give it a quick peck. "It's great to see you again. It's been too long. You're looking well." This man was the closest thing to a grandfather I'd ever known. He was an Essential human in our Pack, like his father and grandfather before him—meaning he knew our secrets, worked for us, but was not supernatural himself. Essentials were a necessity in every supernatural Sect, since the human race had no idea we existed. They were doctors, teachers, lawyers; individuals recruited to play a special role within the Sect. Doc Jace was a brilliant doctor, an extreme asset to our Pack. "I'm so glad you're here"—I flashed him a grin—"because you're just the man to answer a burning question."

"Of course," he said. "I will always do my best to answer your questions, Jessica."

"How did I survive? I thought I wasn't coded for wolf, that it would be impossible for me to make a full transition, and if my body chemistry did change late after puberty I'd likely die from the ordeal. But I'm alive."

Doc absently stroked his short beard. "Males carry their wolf markers on their second Y chromosome, very uncommon indeed, but they are there, coded very clearly. You have never had any such indicators and no second chromosome. My best guess is your body must carry the gene, the one that marks you as a wolf, elsewhere, perhaps in a noncoded region. But as you can guess, I will be doing exhaustive research on that very topic." He patted my hand. "Exciting work it is." Puzzling over our genes was his life's work. "Having you make a successful transformation as a female is revolutionary. We are blazing a new trail with this research. It will be marvelous indeed."

I already knew it was revolutionary, because females didn't exist in our race. My birth had sparked a frenzy of discontent, which was enhanced to a breaking point by a certain unsubstantiated but extremely well-circulated myth proclaiming I was pure evil, a menace placed on earth for the sole purpose of bringing down the race of wolves. Once the Pack found out about my new status as a full-blooded wolf, there was going to be a huge uproar, and everything I'd built for myself would slide straight down the drain. Without going into all that with the Doctor, I asked instead, "What time is it? How long have I been out?"

"It's seven o'clock in the morning," Doc answered. "You've

been asleep for nearly eighteen hours, which is not uncommon for a wolf recuperating from a traumatic injury. I'm guessing you're ready for some coffee and some breakfast? You must be famished. Shifting utilizes an incredible amount of energy, and newborn wolves are more hungry by nature."

"Yes, coffee and food sound heavenly." My stomach growled on cue. "I'm actually starving." Dr. Jace left and I turned back to my father. "I've been asleep for eighteen hours? Are you telling me it's Monday morning already?"

"Yes, it's Monday." My father leaned forward in his chair. "But don't worry about missing work. I've already been in contact with Nicolas. He's already on his way. You've actually been asleep with a little extra help from the Doc. He wanted to be perfectly sure you would heal completely with no complications, and I wholeheartedly agreed with him. Injuries like yours take time to mend, especially for a newborn. I'm just thankful you came back to us in one piece. That was a hell of a ride you took us on."

I was relieved to hear my business partner and best friend, Nick Michaels, was on his way. It would be good to have another ally here, since I had no idea how this was going to play out. "The whole transition was insane, but I don't really remember how it went down." I corrected myself. "No, that's not exactly what I mean. I do have a clear memory of the pain, but for some reason I can't remember the actual turning very well."

My father sat back. "It's not uncommon to disengage with your wolf during your first turning. Your change was an unexpected, traumatic event. As we discussed, fighting the process can make it excruciating. Your wolf likely took over while your human side remained in a shocklike state. It happens. It's not ideal, but it happens."